Last Light Falling

The Ten

Book III

By

J. E. PLEMONS

Published by Blarney Stone Publishing
7860 183A Toll Road
Suite 21305
Leander, TX 78641

BLARNEY STONE PUBLISHING

ISBN: 978-1-7356623-3-6

This book is printed on acid-free paper.

Printed in the United States of America

Library of Congress Cataloging-in-Publications Data Plemons, J.E.
The Ten / J.E. Plemons. — 1st ed.
p. cm. — (Last Light Falling series; bk 3)

Summary: In the third installment of the *Last Light Falling* series, tragedy strikes again and it may be too late to survive. America is left behind to wither, but what's brewing overseas proves to be much worse. Arena's heroic efforts to rescue her twin brother Gabe in a Cairo prison may come at a cost, but she refuses to give up as she fights to lead her group to Jerusalem where it's safe. While the rest of the world unites, Israel stands alone in a fight to survive a political battle among ten nations that are forced to fall under the reigns of the Russian tyrant, Gorshkov. This relentless push to continue the new world order forward may bring Israel to its knees, but Arena's fight to move on could staunch its momentum.

I. Title.
[Fic] — dc22
First edition, March 2017

Dedication

This book is dedicated to the one who brought me into this world and helped me grow into the man I am today. Thank you, Mom, for your love, kindness, and understanding. Without you, this couldn't be possible.

"Hardship often prepares an ordinary person
for an extraordinary destiny."

— *C.S. Lewis*

Part I

Adrift

CHAPTER 1

It's been two long, arduous weeks since we left Trinity Bay and into the open waters aboard these rusty cargo vessels. American soil is well behind us and we will never return. The land of the free is now just another nation under the rule of Russian politics and relentless fervor.

President Kriel, the mastermind behind America's tragic turn from supremacy, gave Russia and its political allies an open window to govern over the United States and its global prowess. Kriel damaged a once powerful nation to the submission of other nations and left its people in dire straits. I only made things worse when I killed him. Because of his absence, negotiations with China trade deals have stalled, giving America economic hardships that may never recover.

The world is in ruin, and the only thing keeping me from falling into the perpetual darkness is the burden of a covenant I shall die with.

We may have slowed Russia's attempt to take full control of our nation now, but it has left us searching for hope and safety in another. We are now destined for Jerusalem, Israel—the last place for hope and perhaps the only place Russia has not touched. We will seek refuge in Jerusalem and take a stand against the rest of the world.

The taste of salt water stings my lips as the bow of the boat bobs up and down in the water. The sun grows low in the sky, casting orange-yellow shadows across the lapping waves that seem to go on forever. I've never felt so alone.

The ship plows through the waves and the horizon dims. My stomach churns. I still haven't adapted to the lively sea. I haven't puked this much in my entire life. I inhale deeply, trying to calm the slight tremor in my body. Tears burn my eyes, threatening to fall, but I don't let them. This laborious and daunting pilgrimage has caused more pain and death than I could have ever imagined. I must do what I can to thwart the evil that resides in every corner of this world even if it kills me. This is my mission, and I will stop at nothing to finish it.

Though my fate to endure the heavy burden of God's wrath upon the world has not changed, it has certainly shifted off course. My twin brother, Gabe, who has shared the same pain of this destined journey, is gone, locked away on some Russian slave ship bound for Cairo. For the first time since we were born, I'm disconnected from him unable to share the comfort I desperately need right now.

Though Jerusalem is our destination, my only hope on this journey is to rescue Gabe. He is the sole purpose I departed America. I will selfishly cling to that, despite whatever hope lies within the people on this ship.

I lean against the side of the bow and watch the dark waters churn below.

"Everything okay," Niki says, coming up behind me.

I turn to her and smile. "Not sure what I'm doing anymore."

"I don't think any of us really do."

Since reuniting with our friends, nothing has been the same. Niki, my twenty-year-old foster sister, has fallen in love with Harold, a man I greatly misjudged. I owe Harold my deepest gratitude for helping Gabe and I escape the night Uncle Finnegan was shot.

"Do you think Gabe is really alive?" I solemnly ask.

"Do you?"

"It's strange, but sometimes I can feel him standing next to me."

"Then that's all that matters." Niki hugs me and kisses me on the forehead. "Hang in there, sis. I need to go check my rounds."

We've traveled a weary and lonely journey, from dark place to dark place, through lively forests and open lands, but the innocent people who have died along the way will not be in vain.

General Iakov, America's tyrannical Russian liaison, failed to fulfill what Russia and China were creating: a new world order under one government. Bullying citizens into submission was his downfall and it forced me to initiate a nationwide revolution to stop the war-mongering scoundrel. But even after I killed him, things have worsened. America may have created its own decline, but Russia has propelled it into further chaos. Something sinister is surely brewing, but whatever is out there waiting for us means nothing to me without Gabe by my side. He's been taken from me along with thousands of others who were forced aboard in shackles.

"I'll find you, Gabe," I whisper into the wind.

A few feet ahead, Henry is sitting on the deck with his legs dangling over the side. The only person in our fellowship who seems to stay an emotional distance from me is Henry, but I'll need him the most if I'm to find my brother alive. If it weren't for Henry and Uncle Finnegan, I wouldn't have the needed skills to survive this unwanted journey. Henry's a warrior, a steadfast and devoted friend amid a world of callous men, and he is ready to fight by my side.

As I turn to walk away, Henry shouts, "Arena! Come join me."

I saunter over and sit next to Henry, dangling my legs over the side. I lean my forehead on the railing and watch the small swells crash into the side of the boat.

"Everything going okay?" I ask.

"As good as it gets, I suppose. And you?"

"I feel like I'm about to puke again."

"Nice to see you out of your element. It'll make a better warrior out of you." He smiles.

I take a deep breath to keep my stomach from arguing with the food inside. "I don't suppose puking on my enemy would be considered progress?"

Henry chuckles and pats my back out of charity. "It's the unexpected we learn from that makes us better prepared."

If there's truth in his wisdom, then I secede. I'm too nauseous to embrace his wise words right now. I stand, gripping the railing for support, and look away from the water. "I'll take that under consideration. I think I may throw up again, so I'll be going. Enjoy your peaceful evening."

I return to the foot of the bow and watch the sea vanish into darkness. If there truly is light at the end of the tunnel, I don't know if I'll be alive to see it. This is my world now.

CHAPTER 2

The rusted shipyard just outside the San Jacinto Memorial Park proved to be more than a deterrent to our Russian adversaries. The harboring fleet of abandoned steel gave the Southern Resistance a little more hope to hold onto, which had been deteriorating.

The Southern Resistance was America's last hope for survival. After the Northern Resistance collided with new government policies, they began to dwindle in numbers. Those numbers vanished with the insurgence of the Russian military invasion.

Many of the rebels who were left migrated south to Texas where the Southern Resistance was born. They grew in large numbers and fought back against Gennadi Gorshkov, Russia's head of state and militant leader who will stop at nothing to see a new world order.

Many men among the twenty-five thousand refugees camped along the park grounds managed to give life back into a few of the abandoned cargo ships near the docks. These men, gifted with skills to labor over goliath machinery, have been greatly unappreciated. Without them, we would have been undyingly grounded, scraping to survive an onslaught of soldiers who were dangerously closing in from the north. We managed to escape just in time with the help of Jacob, an eighteen-year-old man who I thought had been taken from me a year prior.

Jacob, the boy I love, is alive, and the shock of seeing his face again had nearly made me numb. I'd been informed he was shot for resisting arrest during the government's relocation raids. I just assumed he was dead. We all did. My life has been full of unexpected surprises, but none like this. He did more than just survive. He created an insurgence, leading the Southern Resistance. It was more than just a rebellious group defending its keep—it was a refuge of hope that Jacob had shaped. While many people agreed with Jacob's decision to endure the daunting task of crossing the Atlantic, thousands have departed the group, refusing to risk their lives through the treacherous sea.

Those who decided to stay and ride out the strenuous trip may be rethinking their decision. It has been far from pleasant and just short of a living hell. These cargo ships were not meant to house passengers on its decks, much less a few thousand people fighting from sliding off the sides to the swaying waves.

I gaze out across the darkened waters for the other vessels, but they have vanished into the night. A mighty roar blasts from the ship's horn as it does every hour. A red-and-white light blinks in the distance signaling the position of another ship. It's one of ours.

The five vessels in our fleet each occupy about two thousand passengers. The men who maintain these cargo ships were lucky enough to crane about a hundred empty containers onto four of the ships to help stabilize the people from carelessly wandering off the edge. But the metal pods—twenty-foot steel containers—are mostly used to keep everyone covered from the unpredictable weather, which has proven to be just that. The men guiding these ships have grown up in the shipyards or have at one time shuttled cargo across the volatile oceans. They know exactly what to expect, unlike many of us who have never seen the ocean, much less displaced in the middle of it.

Captain Shelling guides our ship. He's a portly fellow, old and gray, and keeps to himself. His gnarled face resembles a crumpled blanket, but I suspect it's from the long days out on the seas, laboring over the ship deck as a young lad. He's a man of few words and coheres to his quarters like a hermit. I may have said hello to him twice since being on board. He's reclusive, but he knows these waters better than anyone.

I swiftly lean over and wretch over the side of the ship . . . again. For two weeks, the grueling sea has managed to torment more than my unsettling stomach. These waters seem to run endlessly in every direction without any land in sight.

While the waters calmly dip into silence, the movement of the water rocks me back and forth, but it's as if my body is not physically here. I can only imagine the hell Gabe has endured. A tear trickles down my cheek as I fight to remember the look on his face when he was taken—those big brown eyes, his messy hair. I imagine his wrists and ankles rubbed raw from being chained. I shiver at the thought of him tucked into uncomfortably tight quarters where the only place to rest in is in his own urine.

I struggle to stand upward and throw up on the deck. I've never experienced sea sickness before. I don't know how sailors do it. Something evil must be in the air because I'm hallucinating. I swear a colony of bats just flew past. My head swirls and pounds into a migraine. I clench my teeth and press my fingertips into my temples to ease the pain. If I have to endure one more day on this floating iron vessel, I fear I will lose more than my lunch. All I have left is my sanity and even that has been tempted to fail from time to time.

A few malevolent clouds to the right begin to shadow the little sunlight that's peeking from behind the unceasingly dark skies. I glance over to the quarterdeck where Jacob is standing next to Captain Shelling and looking down upon me. My heart hitches and I quickly look away. His soft blue eyes burn into my thoughts. His shaggy hair is gone, leaving a clean-shaven man to emerge.

In the short time we spent together before I was thrust into all of this chaos, there was a special place in my heart for him and it hasn't faded once. Even after all hell broke loose during the government's relocation experiment, not once did Jacob leave my thoughts. I know it's ridiculous to believe in love at first sight, but I knew he was the one. Can any girl really say they've fallen in love with a boy within two weeks? Probably never, but I like to believe I did, and that's all that matters.

Jacob curiously watches over me from the captain's deck, gazing down every so often. My heart warms over, but I don't know why I feel so secluded from his gaze. His death haunted me for so long, and I'm struggling to come to grips with this unexpected reality that he's alive. At least that's what I keep telling myself. I should be overcome with joy that I can once again be held in his arms, but it's not that simple now that Nadia is part of the picture. I know it's unfair of me to be angry about something I can't control, but I fear nothing will ever be the same.

Almost a month ago, when I saw Jacob at the San Jacinto Memorial Park, I was pierced with an indescribable elation. Jacob was alive, standing before me, a year after I had been told that he'd been shot by federal officers.

In that long, elated moment, tears retreated from Jacob's eyes and he pulled me into a strong embrace. It was all I had left in me not to just lay down and waste away. His existence is my strength, but all of that has changed because of Nadia, the girl who pulled me from my horse and saved me after I had escaped from a Russian camp with Matthew. It's been two months since that day, and I have yet to extend any gratitude to Nadia. I'm sixteen going on seventeen and I'm none the wiser — just a stupid, jealous girl.

The look in Jacob's eyes when he stares at Nadia causes my chest to tighten. I've caught them embrace a few times, but have never witnessed them kiss. I can only assume they have. Their intimacy is better kept behind closed doors for my sake. I had my opportunities to approach Jacob about my feelings, but it just seems too late at this point. My passive aggressive behavior has created no more than just a friendship now.

They have a closeness I only wish I shared with Jacob. I never knew that love could be so strong until it's been stripped away. I realize it's unfair to be bitter when I see Nadia and Jacob together, but my feelings for Jacob have not strayed nor do I intend to let them. The short, affectionate relationship I had with Matthew wasn't any different than the intimate one Nadia and Jacob share now. I guess I'm just being a jealous brat.

Jacob's death left me broken, but it was Matthew who filled my lonely heart. I admired his selfless loyalty to rescue everyone from the tents before the Russian soldiers came barreling across the fields, but it also got him shot. My decision to detach from the fellowship to rescue him left our group in jeopardy, and it was all in vain. Matthew died in my arms. If it wasn't for my obstinate adoration toward Matthew, I wouldn't have been separated from my friends, and Gabe wouldn't have been captured during his selflessly heroic attempt to come looking for me.

Nadia descends the stairs from the upper deck; I peer up to the captain's quarters and watch Jacob's eyes follow her. Nadia is quite stunning and is every bit as beautiful as I wish I can be. Her long, silky raven hair shimmers softly against the moonlight, while her ice-blue cat-like eyes glimmer. Her petite, thin frame would make anyone envious. I may not be as skinny as she is, but my athletic build suits me just fine.

The past few days have been extremely irritating. A cold sense of hostility comes from Nadia anytime I'm near Jacob while he stands there smiling. I've known Jacob long enough to recognize the confused innocence in his eyes, and I'm still convinced he has intimate feelings for me.

So why do I feel so incredibly empty inside? Even with Jacob here, I almost feel more alone now than I did when I thought he was dead. I'm beginning to think I may have made a terrible mistake wanting to come aboard this ship. If not for Niki and Juliana convincing me otherwise, I would have been just as happy on one of the other ships. *Oh, hell, who am I kidding?* I would have been miserable, but not as miserable as Juliana. She's an emotional mess without Gabe, her one true love. She's become distant and is dangerously drifting from a hope that Gabe may still be alive.

While a cluster of storm clouds steadily grow darker to the west, an unsettling fright disperses throughout the crew. Chattering voices run amuck, the murmuring getting lost in the wind. I wander past the maze of steel containers, some with their doors hinged open. The men, with worrisome faces, huddle wearily against one another inside the metal walls, bracing for another storm.

Many of the containers are tightly lined with cloth that forms a regimented row of suitable bedding. It makes the metal dwellings feel less claustrophobic. It also keeps shifting bodies from sliding into the walls during those sleepless nights when the sea decides to be cross. It's not very comfortable, but it's bearable. On the ship's deck, there are one hundred containers nestled tightly against one another in four rows. Each row of twenty-five is split into five container sections. This allows everyone to move between the pods to communicate with ease.

I prefer to wander the deck to keep from going stir crazy, but many people prefer to lie down inside the containers and not know that we are surrounded by water. The fear of our survival throughout this endless voyage has proven to be detrimental. Many gave up hope the second they boarded the ship, but a new fear has approached with the shifting storm clouds, and its poisonous infection is spreading like a cancer. A storm is brewing.

An eerie silence comes in with the salty breeze, as the crisp wind brushes against my neck. Father Joseph stands near the middle of the ship, watching the sky. He's much more than just a priest; he's been my guiding light, transfixed with my every step ever since we left the den in search for the Southern Resistance. Though he has wavered with uncertainty over some of the decisions I've made, Father Joseph's faith in me is bound to something deeper than I can comprehend, and in that aspect, I owe him my life. Even when my sanity was teetering on the brink destruction, Father Joseph has been by my side.

Father Joseph's brow buries under the small wrinkle across his forehead. He stands tall, stoic, and wise underneath the brown and ashen stubble on his face. I sidle up beside him. "Something upsets the sea," he says as he looks beyond the black horizon.

"No more upsetting than usual," I say, hoping to distract his disquieting stare.

Father Joseph turns to me and smiles. "Well, you seem quite different today, Arena."

"How so?"

"I don't see that scowl you've been wearing the last two weeks. I was beginning to think that wrinkle above your brow was permanently drawn there."

"It's good to know your sense of humor is still intact," I say with a smile. I look toward the captain's deck and search for Jacob, but he isn't there.

"You know, life has a way of changing us," Father Joseph says, "but you don't have to let it change who you are."

I sigh and turn toward Father Joseph. "What do you mean?"

"Are you really that stubborn that you would rather sleep in misery?"

"Excuse me?" I huff.

"Far be it from me to be play the casual spectator here, but don't think for one minute that we all haven't noticed how you feel about Jacob," he says.

Heat rises to my cheeks and I feel a sudden urge to curl up into a ball and hide. "You know, you really need to be more subtle," I say weakly. His expression changes to a jovial smile, which is quite different from his cantankerous grin, and I find myself suddenly on the defensive. "Besides, I've made my choice," I stammer.

"Have you?"

"It doesn't really matter now. Nadia belongs to him." I look down for a moment, wishing for a way to squirm out of this conversation.

"And you really believe Jacob just suddenly stopped having feelings for you?" Father Joseph continues, "If you're not going to tell him, how is he to ever know?"

I'm lost . . . again. Lost in the middle of the ocean. Lost in my feelings. "He already knows how I feel about him," I whisper.

"Perhaps, but it's always nice to hear it."

"I better go make sure everyone is secure," I quickly say to diffuse this uncomfortable conversation. "There's a storm coming."

With my head down, I briskly walk through the rows of containers. Most of the doors are open to give those still hunkered inside some humid but fresh air to breathe. Row after row, I see sunken faces shivering with a fright. Besides the looming storm, something else ails this group beyond my insight.

I head toward the front deck quarters and grab the ship's manifest that's hanging securely on a wall inside the crew deck entrance. Kale, Nadia's older brother, descends from the deck above.

"There you are," he says.

"Yep, here I am," I echo.

"Been looking for you."

"And why's that?"

"Just wanted to make sure you're doing okay."

I'm pretty sure Kale has never wondered if I was doing okay. Our relationship has been quaint and respectful, but nothing beyond that.

"Is this coming from you or elsewhere?" I ask.

"Honestly? A few of us have been a little worried about you. You've seemed a bit distant lately."

"I have my reasons."

"Would one of those be Jacob?" He dare asks.

"That's no one's business." I sneer.

"Fair enough, but for what it's worth, no one asked me to come look for you. You've been a good friend, Arena. I look after you like a sister. You're family to me."

My heart warms and I smile. Kale has been tentative about every decision I've made since we left San Jacinto. He resented my idea of leaving America, but he reserves himself from saying so. I think now he believes it was the right choice. Kale and I share a stubborn personality, but we have remained friends nonetheless. Aside from our differences, we have managed to avoid any conflict with one another. I respect his resilience to move on.

I move closer and wrap my arms around Kale. "I can always count on you to put a smile on my face," I say blushing. He returns the hug and quickly vanishes.

To be quite honest, if it weren't for Nadia, Kale might not be on this ship right now. Kale was insistent on staying in San Jacinto, but Nadia had other ideas like me. She knew we wouldn't have been able sustain there so she lent her voice along with mine and helped persuade Kale and Jacob to retreat to a safer place of refuge. Of course my reasons were far more selfish. I just wanted to find and rescue Gabe. But in the end, Kale proudly stood by Nadia's side and concurred. It was time to leave America.

I take the ship's manifest and pass one of the open containers. Juliana walks past with Niki. As expected, they too are checking in on the passengers. Besides her usual generosity and caring nature, it's therapeutic for Juliana to keep busy. The people on board have welcomed her with open arms for needed comfort, which has lifted some of the pain from her heart and occupied her mind away from Gabe's absence.

I briefly stop and secretively watch from the corner. Juliana looks the same as she did on the first day of school when we met—chocolate curly hair and caramel skin. Her brown eyes, wide and alert, slope above her cute pixie nose. The only difference is the pain etched in her eyes and mouth.

Hands extend from within the containers and reach out to Juliana like a child to a mother. Juliana has unknowingly created a gesture of gratitude among these refugees. I'm reminded of how much she means to Gabe and her true role in this dying world.

Because of the potential predicament we may be facing with this unpredictable weather, I hand the manifest of passengers to Niki and Juliana. We three have been designated safety officers of the children under the captain's orders.

Niki makes notes of all the children on board and Juliana arranges to have them ready if we're asked to flee into the two small compartments below the ship's deck. There are two hatches with two surprisingly roomy spaces in the inner hull. The buttoned-down quarters may save lives if the weather gets bad enough.

Very few of the children have close relatives on board, and most are without families who have either died from the first attacks or have been stripped from them during the invasion. A year ago, the American government issued a relocation policy that caused a rebellious uprising. People were forced to relocate because of their financial status, and those who refused were either detained or killed. When the government failed to contain and control its citizens who rebelled, Russia stepped in and made sure the fire was put out. Russian soldiers invaded nearly every territory and wiped clean the growing revolt, leaving children homeless and without parents. They have a new home on this ship, and I will keep them safe at all costs.

According to Captain Shelling, the storms in this part of the ocean have been known to be some of the most violent, and most certainly unforgiving. Like a worried mother, my thoughts turn to Allison and Luke. I bid farewell to Niki and Juliana, then head toward my container. I pass the first two aisles toward the middle of the first row where my container door is wide open.

I peer into the darkened container and find Allison and Luke asleep on a pile of ruffled blankets with their heads resting on makeshift pillows made from bags of rice. I lean against the wall and stare at their cute, tiny heads resting peacefully.

Unexpectedly, our group has grown during these dark times, but they have also withered. A few months ago, eleven-year-old Allison was suffering from the grips of starvation and grief. Her mother died of terminal cancer, leaving Allison all alone, and I've made a vow to care for her as long as I can. And then there's Luke, a six-year-old mute boy whom Matthew saved from a hopeless camp. It's likely that Russian soldiers slaughtered most of the two hundred people in that camp, but Luke's safety somehow soothes my grief.

Now he and Allison lie sound asleep. I can't remember the last time they've slept this much. In fact, they've never slept more than six hours without tugging on my shirt asking for some food.

Hanging above their bed is the wooden clock I found abandoned on this rusted ship. I snagged it before anyone else. The time shown behind its marred glass face may be incorrect, but it ticks nonetheless. I smile at the children, then it dawns on me: the children have been asleep for over thirteen hours.

"Allison," I call out, rushing over. She doesn't budge. "Allison!" I say a bit louder. There's still no movement. Anxiety consumes me.

It's too dark outside to shed any light on their sleepy faces in this shadowy box. I search around for my flashlight until I find the end peeking out from beneath my bedding. I quickly turn on the light.

My heart sinks into oblivion. Luke and Allison's lips are tinted blue against their pale faces as they lie there in a dead slumber.

CHAPTER 3

My knees buckle as the numbing pain of my heart overshadows my will to stand. In a desperate panic, I shake Allison's body.

"God, no, no . . ." I cry as I jiggle Allison's shoulder and stroke her face. Suddenly, a moan of discontent exits her mouth.

"Just a few more minutes," she groans, and a sudden whoosh of relief churns throughout my body. I quickly turn to Luke; his eyes are half-open and he slightly shifts his body.

"What the hell is going on?" I whisper. Puzzled, I lick my finger and gently wipe a small corner of the blue stain from her mouth while she insistently grumbles with displeasure. The blue stain on my finger bears a familiar sweet scent. I quickly taste it, but I can't figure out what it is.

When I turn around to Luke, my shoe grazes against something hard that rolls across the metal flooring. . I shine the light and find a glass jar nestled against the wall under the bed. I crouched down, pick up the mysterious jar, and chuckle

I place the jar next to Luke's bed, then leave the container feeling a bit calmer. If only I had seen the nearly empty jar of blueberry preserves earlier, I wouldn't have allowed my internal demons to suggest such grim thoughts. The only thing that could possibly rustle my feathers is the fact that their gluttonous food-gorging sugar-crash will soon escalate into whiny, disagreeable bellyaches. If they didn't like the sea before, they sure aren't going to be very pleased with it now; they're about to learn how persuasive these ocean waves can be. I guess I can't blame them for sleeping so much. They've been restless the past few nights. Couple that with a jar of sugar and it will surely put anyone in a coma.

That jar of jam didn't come from any of the rations we brought on board, so the only other place they could have snatched it from is in the galley's large walk-in refrigerator, which is normally locked. I guess those hungry little monsters found a way. Even if they did take it, I can't possibly be mad at them. I'm just glad they're alive.

As I turn the corner, I bump into Nadia.

Nadia gasps. "Excuse me, I didn't—"

"No, it's okay, my apologies," I say.

"I was just looking for . . . someone."

"Well, I hope you find him . . . her, or whoever you are looking for." I stand there awkwardly.

"Have you seen Jacob?" she dares ask me.

"No, sorry, I . . ." I hesitate to tell her the truth, but my tongue is tied. I shift my eyes up toward the quarterdeck and catch a glimpse of him walking by. "I haven't seen him all day. I was just checking up on the kids," I rush out.

"Sure, okay," she stutters. Her brow furrows slightly.

"Well, I better get back. There's a storm heading our way, and I really don't feel like fishing people out of the water." I try to avoid as much eye contact as possible as I slither past her.

"Hey, Arena," she calmly ushers, and I turn around reluctantly. I really don't want to continue this conversation, but the tone in her voice begs me to listen nonetheless. My eyes lock on hers.

"Look, I know we haven't exactly been best friends, but I think it's time for us to set aside any differences we may have," Nadia offers.

"I have no ill feelings toward you, if that's what you mean," I respond quickly.

"And I have none toward you."

"Then what do you want from me?" I say in a hastier tone than I intended.

Nadia places her hand on her hip. "Look, I'm not going to pretend that it doesn't bother me that you and Jacob had a relationship long ago, but you have to understand what's happened in the last few months—"

"I'm quite sure I understand! I've been through a living hell, and I don't need your condescending remarks to justify it so—"

"Arena, I'm not your enemy."

"No, you're not," I say, feeling demoralized. I realize I'm just another jealous, whiny girl in a world with much bigger problems, but I just can't seem to get past this interchangeable conflict. "But you're not the person I want to sit down and have tea with either."

"Look, I'm not here to debate my relationship with Jacob. I just want you to know that we're on the same side, and I'm willing to fight for you."

I feel absolutely dejected and suddenly disconnected from my true self. I can't believe I've let myself become so intertwined in this childish conflict, but I can't stop thinking about Jacob. What am I supposed to do? I turn away from Nadia for a moment and suppress any anger from exploding, but it's useless. I love Jacob and she has him. I'm an emotional wreck, and I can't leave this issue hidden any longer.

"You're right," I snap. "We are on the same side, but where does that leave Jacob in all of this?" I take a step forward, feeling defiant. "Do you think I can just suddenly let go as if none of this happened? I've been dwelling in sorrow for far too long, and I don't have the strength to let it linger on any further."

Nadia's eyes grow wide. "Arena, wait—"

"You want to settle differences, then fine, have it your way, because my love for Jacob hasn't ceased for one second. There hasn't been a day that I don't think about him, and now that he's alive and on the same ship, I can't even get close to him because of you."

"Arena—"

"I would appreciate it if you would at least extend me the courtesy of my grief. Jacob is all I know and now he's slipped away from me."

"Arena, he loves you!" Nadia shouts.

My eyes brim with tears. I'm in complete shock. My mouth opens, but my tongue refuses to speak. Then a hardened guilt emerges as I search Nadia's face. I can almost see the pain hiding deep behind her eyes. I am the foolish one. Nadia should be receiving the grace and compassion she deserves.

"That's right, he loves you," she whispers. "I'm not going to lie to you: my affection for Jacob has not gone unnoticed, but I don't think I've done a damn thing wrong. He doesn't feel the same way toward me anymore, and I'm struggling to believe if he ever did."

"I didn't mean to—"

"Nothing has been the same since he looked upon your face," Nadia says. "You may feel forgotten, but I assure you, I'm the one in shadow around him. Even when you were gone from him, you are all he talked about. I love Jacob, but when the truth overshadows your feelings, that love you hold onto is just a mirage and nothing more."

Nadia gingerly steps forward. With her lips clenched, she peers deep into my eyes. Whatever she's harboring, it's about to be unleashed.

"I'm not here to argue over petty differences. I just wanted to shed some light on the truth, that's all. I think we both at least deserve that," she says.

"I don't understand," I say, baffled by her enigmatic approach.

"No, you don't. Because the truth is . . ." She pauses for a moment. Her eyes fill with tears, but she stifles them back. "Jacob loved you more when he thought you were dead than he could ever love me alive."

Nadia walks away in silence while I just stand there dumbfounded, stricken with mixed emotions of joy and sorrow. I feel completely and utterly lost.

CHAPTER 4

As Nadia scurries away, I feel horrible. Jacob loves me, and I should have never questioned that. It's evident that Nadia is in need of more comfort than me. I feel happy, yet sad. Why couldn't Jacob have just told me from the beginning? I desperately want to see him, but my heart's adrift. Nadia's pain saddens me. I quickly follow her, hoping to bridge any unwanted gaps between us, but I come to a sudden halt at the quarterdeck.

An ominous shadow emerges from the clouds. Thunder bellows and lightning flashes in the distance. As the sky is briefly lit, I catch a glimpse of the demon that has been haunting me. It's the same crow that has been following me from the beginning of this journey. I clench my fists. Every time this bird shows up, something bad happens.

My insides grow cold. I brace myself near the deck railing as the ship begins to rock from side to side. The engines have stopped, and the ocean waves slam into the sides of the vessel.

The wind blows a fowl stench into the air and with it brings the very breath of which evil itself exhales. I struggle to pull myself over to the side of the ship. Then an unyielding shriek showers down a piercing sting. I cover my ears from the squawking pain, shouting at the top of my lungs, but nothing can be heard over the roar of the ocean. I look up, frightened, and my body seizes from fear. The demon bird is perched on the deck above, staring down at me. Its soiled ebony wings flutter with disdain. My personal hell has returned.

The sky is abruptly illuminated from the brief flashes of lightning, but this time a more distressing image causes my spine to stiffen. In the distance, something is protruding from the depths of the dark waters. "No," I utter. It's a Russian submarine.

Suddenly, a horn blows a pulsating warning, and red lights signal a distressing flash from the bow to the back of the ship. People scurry down the metal staircase from the two decks right above me. Jacob is shouting from the deck quarters and looks to be in a dire panic. Another man shouts. Then a woman screams from one of the containers just as a gunshot is fired. The scream quickly ceases, and now people are scampering the main deck with extreme alarm. Two rafts filled with soldiers motor across the waves from the sub.

I race across the backside of the quarterdeck just as Jacob comes rushing down the backside stairs. "Jacob!" I shout. He quickly turns in my direction.

"Arena!" He pulls me into a quick embrace.

"They're coming for us," I say, distressed.

Jacob nods his head. "The Russians made contact with us ten minutes ago. We've been ordered to stop. The captain has locked himself in his quarters. Arena, I don't know what to do."

I'm suddenly disoriented by our compromised position and troubled by what may occur when Russian soldiers begin to board our ship. All I can think about is getting everyone back into their containers, but in my mind, we are already dead.

Just then, Juliana and Niki sprint around the corner in a panic. Their eyes are wide with fear, and I'm reminded of the children. "The children, where are they?" I ask.

Juliana grabs my hand. "We didn't take any chances with the storm coming, so we began leading them down below the hatches, but—"

"But what?" I ask frantically.

Juliana's worried face turns grim. "We're missing two," she finally answers.

"Allison . . . Luke?" I solemnly ask.

"We couldn't find them," Niki pants.

I turn to Jacob. "Jacob, grab the other men and get these people back in their containers." I cock my gun.

"Arena," he says, grabbing my arm, "it's not safe. Go down in the bottom deck and hide. I'll find them."

"You have enough to worry about."

"I'm not going to lose you again!" Jacob shouts.

I clench my fists. "I will not leave Allison and Luke out there alone. Now go!"

I rush back toward my container with a small sense of hope that the children are still there. I quickly scan the area, making sure they aren't hiding under the covers, but there's nothing but a pile of tattered blankets that are still warm from their body heat.

I grab the rest of my weapons except for my bow, which is resting on a couple of screws attached to the wall. I double-check my magazines before loading them into my guns. I jump at the sound of shots being fired. The Russians are here. I poke my head outside. People are screaming and running in every direction. Some are fleeing back into their dwellings, but many are scattering the ship's deck in utter chaos. Suddenly, the ship's lights blacken.

I race past a couple of rows searching for Allison and Luke. With the pandemonium and firefight between the crew and Russian soldiers, I find myself stretched thin with a sense of calm. But I will soon be in utter hysteria if I don't find the children.

Cautiously, I peek around the side of the container I'm nestled against and feel a sense of rage wash through me. A few Russian soldiers, donning black wetsuits, climb over the bow of the ship's railing. Even with all the commotion, they stealthily approach the ship with caution. People are taking cover in the containers until only a few are scurrying the deck.

Another spray of gunfire, and the commotion all but ends. A woman falls dead beside me with a shot to the head. I crouch down behind a container and shiver. Allison and Luke are somewhere still out there. My only hope is that they are huddled together under some blankets in one of the hundred containers on board.

I quickly glance around the corner, waiting for an opportunity to scamper to the next row without being seen. The aisle is clear, so I make a rapid dash to the other side, but not without a dangerous consequence. My position is now more vulnerable. I'm trapped to one side of the ship, and the only way out of this spot is to turn down one of the main aisles, but it appears to be occupied by a couple of soldiers coming my way. I hold my gun tightly against my chest and patiently wait so I can get the cleanest shot.

After accessing the situation, I realize that my only option is to fire my way out of this. Suddenly, another gunshot goes off, and I'm temporarily reprieved from this unwanted altercation. The two soldiers rush down the aisle away from me.

I quickly take advantage of the empty aisle and move quickly past the next section of containers. I continue my search for Allison and Luke. I hug the sides of the rigid metal walls and look in every direction of this cargo maze.

Shouting grows louder toward the bow of the ship and a few more gunshots are fired. My body clenches in terror, knowing that one of those shots may have been for Jacob. I rush over to the container cattycornered to my right to get a better look, but I'm immediately greeted by a soldier who passes by the other end. Startled, I fire three times into his chest. He falls dead as a bullet exits his chamber. My shoulder stings, and red-hot pain lances down my arm. I fall back into the container and catch a glimpse of Allison hunkering on the ground one row behind me. She's shaking.

Adrenaline pumping, I ignore the pain in my arm and race toward her, but a soldier is barreling around the main aisle, and I dive over to the next row opposite of Allison. My arms throbs from the grazing bullet and my shirt is soaked with blood.

Luke is nestled beside Allison and I sigh in relief. Several soldiers are searching through the front row of containers. Allison slowly unburies her face from her arms revealing a stream of tears running down her cheek. On the other side, a soldier walks by with his head turned, heedless of our location. I raise my arms, ignoring the pain in my shoulder, and shoot him in the back of the head.

Allison's face grows pale. Luke wraps his arms around her shaking body. She looks at me, then begins to get up, but I quickly gesture for her to sit tight. I glance once more around the corner to make sure it's clear before I race over to them.

Without any regard of our defenseless position, I take a brief moment to embrace them both. Like burrowing rabbits in a storm, they shiver in my arms.

"Shhh, don't you worry, my love, I'll get you out of this," I whisper, trying to calm them down. A sense of urgency grows as the gunfire toward the bow echoes with unsettling punishment. How many lie dead on the deck, and is Jacob one of them?

I quickly get up, grab Luke's hand, and place it firmly in Allison's. "No matter what happens, you don't let go of her hand, you hear me?" I say firmly. Surprisingly, Luke doesn't seem as frightened.

I turn to Allison. "When I say 'go,' you and Luke run as fast as you can to our container, understand?" They both nod.

Near the front of the ship, gunfire has now escalated into a furious firefight. Someone runs past, and it takes a moment for me to realize it's Nadia.

"Nadia!" I shout.

Nadia turns around. "Arena, what are you doing out here?" she says.

"Quickly, take the children back to my quarters."

Allison grabs Nadia's hand while Luke hangs on tightly to Allison. Suddenly, a roar of fuming thunder breaks the skies wide open as a torrent of rain pours down with violent conviction, assaulting the ship like a shower of bullets.

"Hide in my container and cover them up with blankets," I order.

"But what about . . ."

Two soldiers power around the corner with their guns raised. I shove Nadia out of the way, shielding the children, and empty six rounds from my chamber. The two men fall onto the deck.

"We must go!" I shout, nudging Nadia forward. I follow closely behind them as we race down the right aisle toward the quarterdeck.

Rushing past container after container, I notice that all the doors are shut. We finally reach the back row against the quarterdeck where my container is one of the few that still remain open. As the rain pounds endlessly and the dark clouds drown out any peeking light, we hurry inside were we are able to hide in dark shadow.

The children are crying and hovering beneath the shroud of blankets. Nadia grabs the back of my arm. "What are we going to do now?" she asks.

The sight of the frightened children numbs me. I have no other option but to unleash the hatred I've consumed. Even if Jacob is still out there somewhere, I will not let my heart compromise these children.

"We wait." I pull my hooded cloak around my cold, shivering body and draw my dagger close to my chest.

It's so dark in this container. I can't see my hand in front of my face, which is the only reason we haven't been noticed already. The only semblance of light illuminating from the stormy sky is the sporadic streaks of lightning. With every cracking burst of flashing radiance, I'm able to see soldiers rushing pass containers.

Then I see him.

Jacob's hands are bound behind his back with a long piece of rope that is tied to the railing. A soldier stands over him, holding him at gunpoint.

My stomach tightens, and I don't know if my soul is prepared to suffer through another tragedy. I waver over Jacob's inevitable ending predicament and watch as the children shake beneath the blankets. I'm simply unable to protect everyone. My hands slide against the corrugated metal wall until my elbow brushes against the limb of my bow hanging on the wall.

A new spark of hope emerges as I grab my bow and search for my quiver of arrows on the floor. Another streak of lightning glows bright white, and in that split second, I see Jacob kneeling with his head down in defeat. After an insufferable effort to locate my quiver, I finally find it while brushing my hands in the corner. Each flash of lightning reveals another unsightly image of Jacob at his end.

I struggle to pull an arrow from the quiver as Jacob lies facedown on the ground and the soldier is drawing his gun to Jacob's head. *Steady, steady . . . Arena,* I tell myself, and retrieve the arrow and string it. Squinting my eye, I hold up the bow, pull back the string, and aim into the darkness until an illuminating flash suddenly lights the bow of the ship.

Now . . . I release the arrow and fall to my knees, waiting for the next strike of lightning to either calm me or unpen my anger.

After a minute of churning angst, the sky is lit. Two men lie next to each other motionless: one with an arrow pierced deep into his neck and the other my heart stings for. Jacob's body is limp and unmoving. Blood pools under him. My heart shrivels. *It can't be.*

The world around me grows pale. I bury any kindness that dwells within me and give in to the hate. I step out into the open, ready and willing to kill. Darkness hovers over the bow, but I refuse to turn from it, hoping for a different outcome. Denial perhaps. The sky flashes once again, but Jacob is gone. *He's alive.* I must find him.

Clogging boots stomp against the wet deck to my left. An armed soldier is approaching me. I quickly retreat back into the shadow, gripping my dagger, waiting patiently as the man slowly crosses into the entryway. I hold steady with the tip of my blade pointed forward.

There's a bright flash of lightning, and the soldier's eyes widen at the sight of me standing in the shadows. As he raises his gun, I lunge forward, thrusting my knife into his neck. He lets out a groan and drops swiftly to the ground, pulling me down with him. The acrid scent of blood permeates the air, and I twist and gouge until he is no longer a threat. A pool of blood spills out onto the deck.

I peel back into the container and blindly search against the wall until I find my pack resting in the corner. I dig deep into the bag and pull out the small wooden box that Gabe gave to me for our sixteenth birthday over a month ago. It seems like an eternity since I last saw him as I muse over his gracious but dangerous gift.

I carefully open the box and grab one of the two thermo-explosive tips custom-made for my arrow shafts. Each tip is housed in a titanium shell with a small switch near the bottom to arm the explosives. I carefully attach the tip to one of the arrow spines, making sure that it isn't armed until I'm ready to use it. I know the extreme precaution may be overkill, but I'm not willing to underestimate what awaits us out in the waters.

"Arena, whatever you are about to do, I strongly advise against it," Nadia urges.

"Stay here and guard the children, and no matter what happens, do not let them out of your sight." I grab the rest of my weapons bundled near the entryway, then creep out from behind the shadowy container and brace myself for anything.

I pull the dead soldier's gun from his shoulder strap and carefully hand it to Nadia. "What are you doing?" she asks.

"What I was set out to do."

"Wait, I'm coming with you," she asserts.

"No!" I shout. While I admire her bravery, her striking resilience will safely lead this group if I die. "You must guard them with your life," I softly add.

Nadia can only serve to protect these children now and safeguard the rest of the crew. I will not allow these people to suffer anymore. I will die aboard this ship if I have to, but I will be damned if these children are to be tormented.

CHAPTER 5

The pelting rain has subdued just enough to leave my position slightly vulnerable, but not without the annoyance of the slow, persistent drizzle still hindering my vision. It's time to kill as many soldiers as I can.

I race past the left side of the containers and slip down next to the outer railing of the ship. Two black shadows skim by to my right. The sky is putting on a light show, revealing a few soldiers scattering around the deck by the container rows. I cautiously make my way across the next row with my guns drawn. I brace myself against the metal wall waiting to move forward, but a flash of lightning reveals a half-dozen soldiers breaking into the containers two rows over. I step out and face them.

In an instant, guns fire. A bullet grazes my leg and I fall. I wince in pain, grabbing my lower thigh as the sting of the wound burns my flesh. The friction from the bullet has singed my skin.

I push myself up and hug the backside of the adjacent container. With my body and feet planted securely to the metal wall, I carefully peek around the corner, but the row is empty and clear. With my gun drawn, I creep around the corner to the next row, ready to unleash my rage with the pull of a trigger.

"Drop the gun!" a Russian voice shouts behind me.

I slowly lower my hands, unwilling to drop my guns, but then they fall from my grasp in a moment of hopelessness.

"Down on your knees," he continues.

I kneel down on the soiled deck. As the sound of the gun cocks back, I close my eyes. Painful memories resting beneath the folds of my subconscious race through my mind. Thoughts of Gabe suddenly deepen. Will I ever see him again? I hold my breath, wait, and hope for a miracle.

In an explosive and intense instant, a shot is fired, but I'm still shivering on my knees waiting for the pain. I struggle to open my eyes, afraid that I may face something worse than death. The rainwater runs red next to me. Suddenly, I hear a deep thud behind me and the soldier's rifle slides in front of me. I turn around. Battered and beaten, Jacob hovers over the dead soldier, pointing a gun.

In disbelief, I quickly stand, favoring my wounded leg, and smile with pure joy. Jacob's face is swollen and bloodied. I bury myself in his arms, relishing in his warm touch.

"I thought you were dead . . . again," I weep.

"So did I. But you can thank Harold."

"What?"

"He killed two soldiers who were about to attack me and then dragged me inside one of the opened containers. He saved me, Arena."

"Where is he now?"

"I don't know. He went looking for Niki."

Before I can get lost in his blue eyes, two soldiers jump out from behind Jacob with guns firing. "Jacob!" I scream, then pull him aside and draw both guns, firing into the moving shadows. Jacob grabs my arm and pulls me to the side of the container where I load another full magazine.

Jacob can barely hold himself against the container wall; I pull him up before he collapses to the ground. "Stay with me, Jacob," I say as his eyes roll back.

"I'm fine, just a little sore," he whispers. "We need to get back to the bridge. It's not safe out here."

"They won't stop. We need to do something."

"Arena, you can't, not like this. There are too many of them. If we resist now, all they have to do is blow us out of the water."

"They don't want us dead just yet."

"What makes you think that?"

"They would have killed us already." I grab my bow and carefully draw the thermo-explosive arrow from my quiver.

"What are you doing, Arena? We need to find shelter, and fast."

"I'm doing exactly what I set out to do." I hold the arrow gently against the string. This is the only way out of this mess.

"Please . . . Arena," Jacob says. He stares into my eyes, pleading. His cold hand squeezes mine. "I need you."

"If I don't take out that submarine, you won't have me," I say. Jacob nods in agreement.

The violent swells from the stormy ocean churn harder against the freighter. I brace myself onto Jacob. The ship crashes into an angry wave and dips hard to the right. I stumble to the hard deck and pull Jacob down with me. The bow and arrow slip from my grasp. I try to pull myself up, but The wild sea tosses the ship into the valley of the swell A container slides near the edge as do I.

"Jacob!"

I slip across the slick deck and grab the rusty railing hinged to the edge. The ship tilts to the right as my legs dangle over the side. My bow lies just out of my reach in front of me next to the thermo arrow. Jacob carefully slides closer to me and grabs my bow.

"Hold on to this!" He instructs.

I keep one hand on the railing and stretch out the other toward the bow. Water sprays the deck and moves the arrow closer to the edge. I can't lose it. My grasp slips as I reach for the thermo arrow instead.

Arena, what are you doing? Grab onto the bow!"

"We need that arrow."

I stretch my fingertips onto the fletching, but the arrow slides further from me and balances halfway off the ship.

"Arena, forget about it!"

The ocean swell shifts the ship upright momentarily. I swing my body over, stretch out my hand, and catch the arrow before it plunges into the water. I clinch the arrow between my teeth and grab the end of the bow.

"Pull, Jacob, pull!" I look into his eyes with fierce determination. "You have to pull! My hand is slipping." The string of the bow cuts into my skin as blood trickles down my arm.

"I'm trying, but my foot is caught in-between the deck plating."

Russian voices shout from the ocean. I turn and watch the submarine shifting dangerously closer to our ship.

"Pull Jacob pull!"

He unhinges his boot and pulls me over the side. A soldier quickly pops from the sub hatch and fires toward us.

Bullets spray the side wall of the ship, knocking me backward on top of Jacob. He is too weak to move, so I carefully help him to his feet. He leans his body on mine as I safely direct him inside one of the containers. Hopefully this will shield him from the explosion I'm about to unleash.

With the arrow firmly tucked between the bowstring, I turn down to the end of the last container and slam into an oncoming soldier so hard I fall backward. My bow and arrow flies from my grasp. Without hesitation, I draw my gun, but the soldier quickly kicks it from my grasp. He points his gun at me and smiles.

Click, click, click.

He pulls the trigger, but the magazine is empty. His eyes grow wide. I eject the hidden blade from my boot and sweep it across his neck. Standing there like a mime in distress, his eyes glaze over and his neck gushes red before he drops to the deck.

Voices shout and a slew of bullets graze the ship railing. I carefully pick up the arrow and bow and rush behind the last container near the side of the ship. Shadows move across the waters as more troops are deployed from the submarine.

I set the switch on the arrow's thermo head and stretch back the wet string. Without a moment of pause, I step onto the open deck and release the explosive tip into the belly of that iron turtle. My fingers sting from the recoil of the string. I retreat behind the container and anxiously wait while the heavy arrow soars through the rainy storm.

It feels like an eternity before a sudden wall of heat lights the sky orange. The magnitude of the thermo tip flushes anything around it into a ball of fire and forces a wave of energy into the side of our ship. My body is flung across the deck, and I smash my head. Everything turns into a black abyss.

CHAPTER 6

An eerie silence moans painfully in my ears. I'm lost in a black endless space swimming inside my head. No memories, thoughts, or pain awaken me from this trauma. The only agony I feel is my life suspended indefinitely, or as it may seem. I have no meaningful recollection of what has transpired. If this is where people go after they die, I want no part of it.

I feel trapped in a lonely, shadowy nightmare when a whisper creeps from out of the calm, cold dark. It grows louder and louder until the muttering fills my head. Imprisoned by my own thoughts, I cannot tear away from the maddening voice. Its cry bellows, mocking and raping my ears with a verse that's all too familiar. It's from a poem I wrote when I was ten years old—a very dark year in my life after my parents were killed in a car accident.

When a crow is flapping with its beak a-rapping beneath my bedroom floor;
My head now tapping, haunting my napping, my eyes can see no more.

I want to scream, but my lips will not open. My mouth halts to speak, but my thoughts painfully linger in place of it, shouting inside my head to stop. The voice grows even louder, tormenting every bit of my existence.

When a crow is flapping with its beak a-rapping beneath my bedroom floor;

My head now tapping, haunting my napping, my eyes can see no more.

Though my mouth is still void of uttering a syllable, I attempt to scream anyhow, pleading for this damn voice to cease. "*Stop! Stop! Stop!*" When I think all is lost from this impenetrable torment, the most unusual thing occurs.

The dark shadow fades away and opens up to the sunlight peeking through my bedroom window. I sit up in my bed, slightly startled, wondering what kind of nightmare I have awoken to. My room looks the same as I left it — the bed sheets are still warm, the dust-covered curtains expose the glowing sunlight, and my clothes are still scattered on the floor. It's just as I left it the morning I woke up on my fifteenth birthday, except from a different nightmare. Surely I'm dreaming. This can't be real.

I look over by the mirror and notice my mother's locket is still lying on the wooden music box. I nervously rub my hand over my neck, stunned that the locket is not thee. I haven't taken it off since that morning and now it's sitting on my dresser. I slap myself to assure this is just another dream, but the sting on my cheek reveals otherwise.

I rush over to the dresser and gaze into the mirror in utter shock. My hair is long and flowing as it was on the first day of school, not cut short and choppy when I butchered it in the den. The tiny scar on my left cheek has vanished. The dagger that created it is no longer worn at my side. My hands aren't even calloused from the handle of my swords. Tears fill my eyes. I don't know how to feel, but I shudder to think this is just another cruel and punishing joke. Not until my bedroom door creeks open do my tears change from confliction to shocking elation.

"Honey, are you okay?" Myra, the foster mom who cared for Gabe and me the past four years, is standing at the door. She looks the same as I remember her on my fifteenth birthday—dark brown hair, shimmery red lips, and her arched brows. Whether this is real or not, I'm not about to let this moment fade away like the others. I rush over and wrap my arms tightly around Myra. She embraces me with a familiar warmth, and it's not until I open my eyes and search her face with my hands that I know she is truly real and not a figment of my imagination.

"It's really you, isn't it," I choke out.

"What's got into you, Arena? Why so many tears?"

"I'm just so glad to see you again."

"Again?" Myra furrows her brow. "I just saw you last night."

"It's just nice to wake up to a familiar face, that's all. I'm just so happy right now."

"You should be," she says with a smile. "Turning fifteen is momentous event in a young girl's life."

I'm confused and happy at the same time. If I have been under some dark, nightmarish, hypnotic slumber, then I surely never want to sleep again. I look into Myra's eyes until I finally convince myself that this has all been a dream—Father Joseph, that black menacing crow, the Russian soldiers, and every bit of death that surrounded me. Even Jacob may have been a needed security hiding deep beneath my subconscious, though I wish it weren't so. But the one person who is on my mind . . .

"Gabe? Where's Gabe?" I frantically ask.

"I think he's in the bathroom. Why, is your brother in trouble?"

"No . . . I just need to see him," I say with a small hint of uncertainty. I race out into the hall, but I force myself to move slowly toward the bathroom where light emits from the bottom of the door.

"Arena, what's got you all in a fuss?" Myra asks, concerned.

"Nothing . . . I'll explain later." I carefully place my hand on the doorknob and sigh disquietly before I turn it.

"Make sure you wash up before you come down. I've got breakfast waiting for you, Gabe, and your sister," Myra says as she walks past me. *Sister*? She must mean Niki.

"Tell Niki I can't wait to see her," I say, barely able to hide my excitement.

"Niki?" Myra asks. "Who's Niki? You mean Grace, of course."

The blood warming my glowing face suddenly departs and flushes me pale with an unsettling sting. Grace was Niki's younger sister who died tragically of a gunshot wound in the parking lot several years before I met their mother, Myra. A shiver runs through my body. My lips tremble at the thought of being fooled again. I shut my eyes while unwanted tears rain down my face.

"What is it, my love?" Myra walks over to comfort me. I hesitate to speak, afraid I may leave Grace's memory in disarray. For a moment, the truth fails to slip from my lips, but I know I must resolve my conflicting subconscious if I'm to move on from this plaguing nightmare. Myra gently places her hand on my shoulder, and while it feels as genuine as it would if she was alive, I know this is all a lie.

"You're not real," I quietly weep under my breath.

Myra kisses me on the head to further this tormenting dream. "Are my kisses not real?"

I just sob and shake while she comforts me. I've become disinterested in the bane of these memories that I have no choice but to end it now.

"You're not real," I say with conviction. Myra backs away, but I cannot look upon her face, for guilt is pushing me into a dark place.

"I'm here, aren't I?" Myra says.

"You're not real!" I scream, trying to wash away this illusion.

"Arena, I'm your mother. I'm here for you—"

"Go away! Just leave, now!" I scream in a raging fit. I lose control of every emotion and cry uncontrollably as she talks over my shouting. I have to cover my ears to draw out the cluttering lies spewing from her lips. When I open my eyes, I look up and cringe in horror. Myra's face is battered and covered in gouging scars. Her arms, cut beyond recognition, profusely bleed as she stretches them out to me.

I rip open the bathroom door to escape this hellish scene only to be painfully pulled into another. General Iakov is standing in the bathroom. If there is one image I could discard from the folds of my brain, it's his grisly face. He's the only man who could torment me more dead than when he was alive, and if there's one thing I'm forced to remember from his unsightly expression, it's the day I slit his throat at the training facility where I fought my way to end this war. Unfortunately, his murder has done nothing but proliferate this world further into chaos.

Iakov's hideous, haggard face is highlighted by an amber light that glows from the cracked ceiling. Gabe's body slumps to the side as Iakov's bloody knife rests beneath my brother's slit throat.

Though I know it's not real, I still try to battle my fear away from this terrifying image, but I can't pull myself away from Gabe's ashen face long enough to notice that the room has suddenly changed into a darkened prison. The dim light shining from above slowly fades, but not before I get a glimpse of Gabe's eyes opening as he whispers my name, "Arena."

The world before me turns black before I wake up sweating and clinging to the bed sheets in a panic. I frantically fight the covers halfway off the dingy bed before I realize I'm in a small room that looks like the lower deck quarters of the ship.

Nadia is sitting next to me caressing my left arm. "Arena, it's me, you're okay. You've just had a nightmare."

I pant with exhaustion as the back of my head throbs. "Shh, it'll be okay, just lie back down," Nadia continues.

"How long have I been out?" I murmur.

"A few hours now."

I feel like I've been secluded from the world. Nadia gently brushes my hair back with her fingers, trying to sooth the worry painted on my face. I'm grateful for her generosity and comfort. For whatever little disdain I may have had toward her in the beginning, it has completely fled. She deserves more than just my respect; I will gladly give my life for hers. I have selfishly allowed this internal conflict between us to dictate an unwarranted behavior, and it's not who I am.

I lay my head against the soft pillow while she strokes my hair and places a cold, wet cloth on my forehead. The cool rag soothes my sticky, sweaty skin from the stale air. I lie here unaware of the world around me until I suddenly realize the events that led me to this unusually comforting moment with Nadia. I bolt upright. "Where is Jacob? Did he survive the explosion that nearly got me killed?"

My questions pour out in a rush, but Nadia holds up her hand to silence me. "He's fine, Arena."

"Where—"

"He's on the bridge. He carried you in here and laid by your side. He asked me to look after you until he got back from the bridge."

"And the submarine?"

"It's gone, but that's the least of our worries now," she says as the lights above begin to flicker on and off. I'm not feeling comfortable anymore with her disquieting expression and the troubling tone in her voice.

"What's going on?" I ask.

"We don't know exactly how it happened, but the ship's electronics went completely out. We lost communication with the other ships, and everything on board is dead, except for the lights and some minor equipment. But that's only due to the small back-up generators, and they can barely keep up. Until the engine room is restored, we're floating blind out here."

I feel a sense of responsibility for this calamity. I may have inadvertently set us off course with blowing up the submarine, but I had no choice. We can either be floating blind or floating dead. I'll gladly accept any repercussions if we make it out of here alive. It's quite apparent now that the perilous storm has made this adverse situation even more dangerous.

The calm Nadia has displayed toward me is starting to fade and it's making me worry. Her eyes glaze over and the corners of her mouth twitch. My head begins to throb again, but I have no intentions of lying back down; I'm too nervous to be stuck in these tight quarters knowing we are aimlessly adrift. I attempt to pull myself out of the bed, but the soreness around my neck and lower back forces me to halt.

"Arena, where are you going? You need to rest," Nadia snaps.

"I want to see Jacob."

"Arena, wait."

I struggle to stand, but my feet wobble and I become exceedingly dizzy as I stumble to the floor. My vision blurs while my head spins, and darkness consumes me . . .

Trapped again in a dark world behind a black canvas of empty thoughts. The only thing different from this nightmare is the audible chatter in the background. It's a familiar voice, but I'm too inundated by the pounding pain inside my head to fully recognize who it is.

The writhing sting in my head slowly dissolves. I peer open my eyes to see Nadia and Jacob standing by the door speaking in hushed whispers. Nadia embraces Jacob, then leaves the room.

When Jacob meets my eyes, I quickly fall victim to self-loathing and disappointment. While I'm sure I missed the better part of their intimate exchange, which may or may not have been but just a friendly gesture, I allow my feelings to vent with jealousy anyway. Jacob walks over to sit by me.

Jacob gently holds my hand and rubs the back of my arm. As much as I want to enjoy this rare moment with him, I can't seem to block out the mysterious relationship he shares with Nadia any more than I can stand to see mine suffer without him. If I don't say anything now, I fear I will let this enigmatic bond between us perpetuate into something much worse. I have enough to deal with to let some petty love quarrel obsessively hijack what strength I have left in me.

"Do you still love her?" I ask, barely getting the words out. His silence is a disappointing surprise.

"I thought you were dead, Arena," he softly says. His blue eyes are glassy. "I wanted to believe you were still alive . . . I did. But everything just seemed . . ." He looks away from me.

"Seemed what?" I ask, provoking him to finish.

He stares at the floor. "After I was shot, I thought I would never see you again. What was I supposed to do? I didn't know how to feel anymore. Everything felt so numb."

I feel deeply wounded by his recalling memories that it never really dawned on me to ask how he survived. I was so overwhelmed by his presence that I didn't care to know or had the desire to ask. "What happened that night?"

"When the officers fled, I was lying there unconscious for God knows how long until I woke up on a pile of bloody blankets in some basement. My neighbor saw me after I was shot in the street and thought I was dead until he realized I was still breathing. He managed to drag me into his basement during the mayhem and patched me up. I was lucky that the bullet went clean through me. I stayed there a week to heal before I went searching for you. That's when I went to your house and found it empty."

"Jacob, I'm so sorry." Tears trickle down my cheeks. "I would have come for you, but your landlord told us you were dead. You're not the only one who felt completely numb."

"I guess it doesn't matter now. We shouldn't be beating ourselves up for knowing what we didn't know. Considering the circumstances, and the hell that we've both been through, it's understandable that we've changed."

I feel overwhelmed with sadness. "Changed? Jacob, I'm still the same person you bumped into on the first day of school, the same girl who held your hand in the hallway, and the same girl who kissed you on the porch swing. That same love she shared with you then hasn't gone astray now."

"I don't blame you for being mad."

"I'm not mad at you, Jacob. I'm just confused, that's all. You've sent mixed signals and I don't know—"

"I'm sorry for muddling things up between us. I just didn't know how to react to all this. Nadia has been a comfort to me you know. She ha—"

"Jacob," I quickly say, "I understand."

"Which part? The part where I screwed up everything between us? Or the part where I was going to tell you that the girl I fell in love with on the first day of school has not once left my heart."

I eagerly sit up and wistfully gaze upon his softened face.

"I never stopped loving you then, Arena, and I have no intention of stopping now."

A warm sensation fills my heart, and my cheeks burn from embarrassment and confusion. "And Nadia?" I ask, wondering how she fits into the equation.

"Nadia is my friend, but she knows that my heart belongs to you," he says softly. "I give you my heart if you'll still have me," he says.

I smile and squeeze his hand. "I'm yours."

"I just want you to know—"

I brush my fingers across his lips, lean in close, and plant my lips on his. My body tingles as we kiss. I wrap my arms around his neck and run my fingers through his hair, then pull him closer. I lean back on the bed, pulling him toward me, as I throb with a passion I have not felt before. There we lie through the night, our bodies entangled, engaged in an intimacy I have only dreamed of. I hold onto today as I embrace the only person I want to spend the rest of my short life with in a dark, brooding world I'm trying to forget.

CHAPTER 7

"Gabe?" I whisper. "Are you here?"

Jacob rustles beside me, and I suddenly remember where I am. I slide closer to Jacob, feeling the warmth of his body, and feeling safe for the moment. Jacob has given me a small piece of comfort that has temporarily shadowed the memory of my brother, but a stinging pain on the back of my neck where my birthmark rests causes me to sit up. Maybe Gabe feels it too, as we share the same cross-shaped marking. I believe twins have an extraordinary connection with each other, and this shared attribute may be the link between us.

An image of Juliana covered in blood flashes through my mind and I cling to the bed sheets. Whether this is a prophetic glimpse or just my feelings deceiving me, I fear I'm being haunted again by an evil that attempts to possess my thoughts.

Feelings of guilt overpower me. "Gabe," I whisper again, calling out to him. My brother—my rock—is gone, and the aching hollow hole he's left can't be filled. Through a small moment of gracious content, I run my fingers through Jacob's hair and gaze upon his peaceful face while he sleeps.

A musky, stale breeze slithers across my face and lifts beneath my hair. Suddenly, the door to the quarters swings open. I grab Jacob's arm as he begrudgingly wakes up slightly disoriented. A beaming flash of bright white shines from the doorway.

Kale is standing there holding a flashlight.

"I don't mean to disturb you two, but you better come quickly," he says.

"What is it?" I ask uneasily.

"You need to see this for yourself," Kale says.

I start to climb out of bed, but Jacob restricts me from leaving. "Arena, you really need to stay here and rest," he says.

"I'm not going to let you leave without me."

"I'm not trying to, Arena. I just want you to be safe, that's all."

"I appreciate your concern, but I'm okay."

Jacob sighs. "I'm not going to win this, am I?" He surrenders with a smile.

"Nope," I answer.

While the fear in Kale's eyes doesn't feel comforting, it's his trembling hands that beg for concern. It's clearly obvious that nothing good can come from what we are about to see.

Though it's early morning, the waters around us reflect a shadowy darkness from the brewing clouds still lingering, and the only light is caused by a drifting vessel that's ablaze. Most of the passengers wander out from their containers and stare at the disturbing image in horror.

"It's one of ours," I whisper to Jacob.

One of our ships that had been further ahead of us has been brutally attacked by the Russians. The fueling fire atop the deck quarters and near the engine section blazes uncontrollably from the burning diesel fuel flowing within the belly of the ship. A few bodies, charred from the fire, lie scattered below the deck quarters, but the horror only begins there. Just past the quarterdeck and near the bow of the ship are several children lying facedown in their own blood—lifeless innocence butchered by a hate that only evil can conceive. Erected toward the tip of the bow, mangled with twisted steel, stands the ship's radio beacon that is painted red from what I can only assume came from the spilled blood of the two men and women who hang from it.

As we float closer to the horrific sight, I can hardly contain the anguish I feel. The man and woman not only hang there, but their bodies have been skinned, leaving their bloody tissue and muscle-covered skeletons dangling for the seagulls to feed on. It's not bad enough that they were executed, but to go through such suffering and unfathomable torture is beyond disturbing. It's revolting and sickening, and I feel somewhat responsible for it. I know they made their own choice to leave the bay, but I was the one who encouraged them to do so.

"My God," Jacob gasps as he holds me close.

One of five ships in our fleet is no more, and the telling signs of the abhorrent death left on board breeds a fiery hate I fear I won't be able to control from this point forward.

"Where are the other ships?" I ask.

"They must have been displaced during the storm," Kale answers.

"No distress call?"

"We haven't been able to regain any communication since the storm."

A chorus of weeping ensues from the crowd, but it will soon turn to fear before this ghastly sight leaves us. *Have I led us all to die?* All of a sudden, a burst of tiny chatter in the back of the crowd grows louder, and I squeeze Jacob's hand.

"The children!" I exclaim. "They can't see this."

I dash over to Nadia and Niki on the quarterdeck. "You need to get the children off the deck now! They need not look upon this wretchedness."

"Arena, you okay?" Niki asks with concern in her flat voice.

"I don't know anymore." I turn back toward Jacob and catch a glimpse of two children walking toward the edge of the railing. I race through the crowd and notice Luke's curly red hair flash by and get lost in the crowd. I don't see Allison with him.

A burst of thundering clouds clap with an aggressive vengeance, and the wind suddenly changes from the north. People remain, watching the fiery ship spew clouds of black plumb as it slowly drifts closer to us.

I angrily part the sea of people until I reach Jacob.

"Arena, what's wrong?"

"Luke's out here. I saw him."

"We'll find him."

"We need to clear this deck now!"

"Arena, calm down, he's not going anywhere."

"That's what concerns me. His eyes are not meant for this."

Jacob pushes through the crowd until everyone has gone, leaving the only two people left to witness the horror I'm afraid will haunt them forever. Standing close to the railing and shaking with unspeakable fright is Luke barely tall enough to see the dreadful sight before him. Next to him is Allison with her fingers clasped around Luke's wrist.

I rush toward them and turn their heads away. The fear painted on Luke's face is disheartening. His bottom lip bends downward while his eyes are filled with tears. Allison is pale and I fear she will never be able to overcome this horror. The world we live in now will show us no favor if some discipline is not in order.

"I trusted in you to have better judgment than this, Allison," I scold.

"I didn't know, Arena, honest I didn't," she mumbles.

"Go back to the container and stay," I say firmly. Her eyes, filled with tears, reveals a guilt I'm not used to seeing from her, but it's the disappointment in my voice that makes me crumble a little inside. I feel I may have damaged our relationship somewhat with my reproach, but I know deep inside it's necessary. The grimmest days will soon be upon us, and I want to make damn sure that nothing will detract Allison from surviving for as long as she can.

Jacob gently touches my arm. "Arena, I'm sure she meant no harm—"

"I know what I'm doing!"

"I'm sorry, I didn't—"

"No, I'm sorry, it's not you, Jacob. I . . . just need some time alone, okay?" I lean into his chest for comfort. Jacob has been nothing but honest and genuine with me, and he doesn't deserve to bear my frustrated temper. I just hope I haven't complicated things between us with my outburst.

"I'll take Luke back to your container and watch over him," Jacob says, then kisses me on the forehead.

While everyone is tightly secured in their metal dwellings, I stand alone on the deck, struggling to fight through my emotional discrepancies. I don't know if I've helped or hindered my relationship with Allison, but if this is what it feels like to parent a child, I'm not sure I have what it takes. I feel like anything I do now with her will be under a microscope if I don't make amends soon.

Just as the thoughts inside my head tumble about, so does the ship as it unkindly rocks back and forth into another storm. The waves repeatedly crash against the rusty hull. I look over the railing and see a future that is as cloudy as the black waters violently churning below. Fear has cast my spirit into a hollow aberration, but I'm no longer afraid to die, not now or ever. I'm just afraid to feel empty inside with nothing to live for. If I die today, will I have done what has been asked of me or change what will happen to these people?

Suddenly, the waters below stop swaying and the brewing storm ahead takes pause. In this rare moment of peace in this violent sea, I make amends to my Father. While the wrath of the storm has been chastened momentarily, I free myself temporarily from the burdens that will soon follow. My Father has promised me more than I can remember, and if it's comfort I ask for then it's comfort I should come to expect.

The light breeze blowing from the north changes course and pushes hard with a vengeance from the west. I can't seem to find my way through this misery, and I don't know if I'm worthy enough to carry on. Have I truly been chosen to help lead these people from eternal death, or has my faith finally slipped from my grasp? I feel lost and abandoned, but when the water calms and the dark clouds swoon back into shadow, I find that we are all lost adrift in a raging tempest bellowing before us.

CHAPTER 8

My body shivers as I cuddle next to Allison as we wait for the storm to pass. Luke, who is passed out and wrapped in a shroud of blankets, is nestled closely on the other side of Allison. The anxiety of waiting out this grueling storm keeps me from sleeping, but it doesn't stop me from tending to Allison. I love her like my own daughter.

I prop myself up against the wall. Jacob sits patiently in the corner watching over us as our ship drifts aimlessly through the violent waters. Fear aside, I calmly wait inside this darkened hull with the sound of pelting rain showering down a noisy tune against the metal ceiling. After an hour of being trapped inside these walls, my anxiety takes over. But it's not the storm that unsettles my nerves; it's being closed inside a container I fear I can't escape from.

I impatiently shift from position to position until the peak of the storm gradually wanes, but I can't stand it anymore. When the rain slows, I walk to the end of the container and swing open the door. In a small peaceful moment, I breathe in the stale air before retreating back against the wall. As the clouds slowly shift eastward and the thunder quietly roars in the distance, I shift closer toward Jacob.

While the rain trickles from the dark skies, I sit back and stare deeply into his eyes. I muse over our newly restored affection for each other as he flashes me his glowing smile. My love is endlessly bound to him now until I can breathe no more. With a calm in my heart's stir and my eyes abating, I can finally drift off into a deep seclusion.

*   *   *

"Arena, wake up, wake up," a persistent soft voice whispers.

I unwillingly crack open my eyes to see Allison hovering over me. Luke is sitting on my legs, picking his nose, with a big grin painted on his face. Though I'm too tired to move, I'm delighted to see them smile. I catch a glimpse of blue sky from the corner of the container door.

"Hey, Luke, honey. You know, if you continue to wrestle with those nose goblins, your finger is eventually going to fall off," I say with a snicker. Slightly alarmed and somehow convinced, Luke heeds my playful advice and quickly pulls his finger from his nose. I give him one last stern but jovial glance before his smile flattens, and he examines his finger under false pretense. His worried face presses me to tell him the truth, but I just can't seem to stop laughing inside at my attempt to keep him from his daily gold-digging.

Allison stares at me with pursed lips, almost as if she's struggling to keep something hidden from me.

"Are you okay?" I ask, concerned.

"Are you still mad at me?" she gingerly asks. If I didn't know any better, I'd think she was giving me a guilt trip, but I can see the sincerity drawn on her pallid face and the honesty impending in her voice. "I'm so sorry I disappointed you. It will never happen again, I promise," she continues, and her eyes fill with tears.

"Oh, honey, I'm not mad at you," I answer, shamefully pierced with a guilt I suddenly can't purge. "I love you and I'm here to protect you. You know that, right?" I feel terrible that I let our exchange on the deck shamefully linger without resolve. "I'm sorry that I yelled at you, but I need you to understand that I'm not always going to be around, and I can only hope that I've helped you understand how to survive. You're going to be in charge someday, and I'm going to make damn sure you're prepared."

"I understand, I just . . ." She looks away sheepishly. "I sometimes miss those days when it was just you, me, and . . . Gabe."

The sound of his name brings on a wave of sadness. "I know what you mean."

"I understand what you're trying to do, Arena, but I'm not afraid to die," Allison says. "I just worry that I'm a disappointment to you. I've done things in the past I wish I hadn't, but I can't take it back now. Mama's gone, and you are all I have left."

A heavy weight rests on my shoulders as I'm expected to fill the void of Allison's mother. "You will never be a disappointment." My eyes refuse to stay dry.

Allison leaps into my arms and weeps, "I just miss Mama so much."

"I know." I clear my throat and fight back tears. Luke inches closer and nestles beside me.

Allison wraps her arms around my waist and I notice the bracelet I gave her dangling from her wrist. It's the same bracelet Niki gave me, the same bracelet Niki had given to her sister Grace before she died. It was a symbol of sisterhood, a special bond between siblings. When it was passed on to me, it became a token which often granted me a peace I could never understand. As it glimmers on Allison's wrist, I know it was rightfully passed on to the person who was meant to wear it.

Just then, Nadia walks into the container looking rather anxious. "What is it?" I quickly ask.

She pauses for a moment, looking thoughtfully absorbed over the small exchange I'm having with Allison and Luke before she smiles and says, "Land."

CHAPTER 9

"We've made it," Jacob says as he gently wraps his arms around me.

I'm delighted to no end to finally set this stomach-churning water aside, but I know deep down that whatever is beyond this passage won't be any more kind.

Whether or not it's from a desperate moment of release or deserving jubilation, the ship's horn blasts with certainty as we see water meet a mountainous terrain ahead. Most people on board have left their metal dwellings and gravitated toward the bow of the ship, cheering with joy.

Captain Shelling, Father Joseph, and Henry nudge Jacob and me to briskly move to the deck quarters for a private meeting. I'm as easily discouraged as I am delighted whenever Father Joseph summons for my presence, but the solemn expression in the captain's eyes proves there's something more troubling afoot.

When we reach the bridge, the silence is telling and makes the already somber moment that more unsettling. Captain Shelling called for this meeting, yet he doesn't say a word. He just mulls over charted maps as if he's waiting for something to strike him with importance. After a generous pause of silence, I gaze over to Father Joseph with confusion and decide to break this ridiculous pre-conversational etiquette.

"Okay, fine, I'll say it. What the hell is going on that would keep us from enjoying some good fortune?" I insist.

"That's a good question that equally deserves a good answer," says a voice coming up the steps. It's Ananiah Shemer, Israel's militant leader, Uncle Finnegan's respected friend and our ally in this inevitable war. The world has turned its back against independently governed nations from the likes of Gorshkov, who unceasingly strives to rule a one-world nation. Countries have fallen desperately to their knees under Russia's relentless commitment to cure a broken economy, but Israel will have no part in this political bullying. They will fight to preserve democracy at all costs, and I will proudly fight with them.

Ananiah is the one person I can't afford to lose favor with on this journey. Besides our connection with my uncle Finnegan, our mutual respect for each other keeps this darkness from swallowing us. What binds us now shouldn't be broken if we are to survive this, because he may be our only hope if we are to reach the Israeli border unharmed.

Ananiah, a tall well-built man bred for fighting, stands in the middle of the room, resigned. His dark beard covers any slight expression emerging from the creases on his face. He removes the Kippah from his dark hair, peppered with gray, and smiles. "Sorry to keep everyone waiting," he says.

"Ananiah," I address as a courteous pleasantry.

"Arena, you're looking well. How are you feeling?"

"Restless."

"I wouldn't have expected otherwise."

"You want to tell me what's going on, because I can't imagine you called us here to sing songs," I say.

"Arena," Henry interrupts in a patronizing tone.

"No, it's okay, Henry, that's fair enough. Everyone deserves the truth," Ananiah says. "We've made it to the Moroccan border."

"Well, that's great news, right?" Father Joseph says.

Ananiah strains to smile. "The fact is, I don't know how the hell we made it here, but we did. Without any working navigational instruments to correctly chart this voyage is beyond my comprehension."

"So where do we go from here?" Jacob asks.

Captain Shelling clears his throat and points to a map. "The closest conclusion I can make from these charts is that we're about ten miles south of the Strait of Gibraltar, the gate to our destination. We must pass through there to get to Israel.

"That's where the Russian ships would have taken route to Cairo with your brother," says Ananiah.

"And what of our other ships? Where might have they drifted?" I ask.

"It's hard to say. If they did make it, they would have had to travel the coast line north to the strait's passing," Ananiah says.

"Assuming they survived the storm," Henry adds.

"So what's the cause of concern here that we should meet like this privately? Is there something you're not telling us?" I ask.

Ananiah shifts his eyes away from me. He's not usually this passive about important information. If he's bringing us bad new then he just needs to rip it off like a Band-Aid.

"It's no surprise to anyone the hell we've been through," Ananiah says. "Honestly, this has been more than what I had expected. But the truth is, the hostility we've received on this voyage is just beginning."

"What do you mean? What lies beyond the strait?" I ask.

"The main maritime routes for European and Arab trade. Most of it has been under heavy scrutiny to regulate the trade routes. Some say Russia, others believe it's controlled by China. Either way, we still have to pass through these waters, and I don't expect anything less threatening than what we've already faced. We'll have to dock in Alexandria and find passage through the deserts to get to Cairo and Israel."

"So are you saying that we should just dock our ship in Morocco and forget about Alexandria all together?" Father Joseph asks.

"It's an option." Ananiah shrugs.

"I won't leave my brother to rot in a Cairo prison," I demand.

"I'm not suggesting you should, but let's look at this for the sake of everyone, not just Gabe. We could be putting thousands of our people at risk."

"And if we do dock here, how in the hell do you suppose we'll last without supplies, trekking through this rocky region?" Henry's face grows concerned, as does Jacob's.

"I don't expect to. Alexandria is much too far away from here for us to survive on foot. We'll have to make this land our home until other options become available. At least we'll be away from immediate danger."

"So forget Alexandria, my brother, and Israel? This is your option?" I scoff.

"It's not mine, but it is one. You need to understand that the strait may be patrolled by Russian warships or another one of those damn subs. Not even you can overcome that," Ananiah says.

I pace the room. "So how will I know if my brother is alive?"

"If we fall into Russian hands, you never will. We risk everyone's lives, including yours. Are you willing to die for that?" Ananiah says.

I slammed my fist down on the table. "If we stay beached in the middle of nowhere, he will die. I'm not willing to live with that."

"There must be another alternative," says Jacob.

"The uncertainty of what lies between the strait's entrance and Alexandria's port could prove to be fatal, which is far worse than what these people have already endured," answers Ananiah.

"And even if we do reach the port of Alexandria, there's no guarantee that we'll be greeted without enmity," Captain Shelling adds.

I mull over the less-than-desirable conversation before I turn to Father Joseph hoping for some wise or at least comforting advice. "So where do your thoughts lie in this?" I ask him.

"Ananiah is right. It's a risk, I must confess, but this entire journey has been nothing less than that," he answers. "What does your heart tell you?"

I sigh, feeling frustrated. "Gabe is my brother. His life depends on me."

"So do those on board," Father Joseph says.

I feel a responsibility to these people to uphold, but I'm no more prepared to do so than I was prior to this voyage. I question whether I made the right choice to leave American soil behind in the first place. "How much farther must we travel before we reach Alexandria?" I solemnly ask.

"About two thousand nautical miles," Captain Shelling says.

My glare of disappointment is noted, but it's nowhere near the contempt I may receive when I tell the others. I don't know how much more I can take being trapped on these balmy waters. "Can we not push this floating piece of iron any faster?"

"We've thrust forward with these engines hard enough. No more than fifteen knots can this beast handle, and that's pushing her a bit more than I feel comfortable with," the captain admits.

"How long?"

"I'm afraid you're looking at another six days from port, lass, if there is one left."

Ananiah fixes his stony glare on mine. "I can't guarantee the safety of these people if we decide to dock," he says. "It's been too long since I left the port to know what's changed."

Not long ago, before we left the San Jacinto Memorial Park, Ananiah promised us safe passage from Alexandria to the Israeli border, which seems to be the only true safe haven in this world, but there's nothing that can be guaranteed now. His assurance now lacks the confidence I trusted in him before.

"And what of your promise of passage to safety?" I ask him.

"My assurance to keep you safe has not wandered, but even I know its limitations," Ananiah responds.

"So this was all for nothing?"

"Your nation has been under severe scrutiny from the rest of the world. I will do what I can to secure you in mine, but I can't know that our position will be compromised."

I sigh in frustration. Ananiah is right. I may be at the pinnacle of my confidence, but even I'm not that stupid.

"So what are we to do?" asks Jacob.

"If my instincts serve my better judgment, then we should let our leader decide," Father Joseph says. Everyone looks around the room and nods their heads.

"I concur," Ananiah states.

Suddenly, all eyes are planted on me, waiting for a response that I'm not averse to answer. "What, you want me to decide for everyone knowing what they've already been through?"

"I know you shouldn't be burdened with a choice like this, but this is a decision only God can reveal to you. And no matter what you decide, we will proudly stand by you," Father Joseph promises.

Though too much stands between my brother and me, there's not enough failure in my heart that will detract my courage to get him back. We don't know if the ports have been taken over by Russian rule, or if the waters ahead prove to be threatening, but my feelings are destined to move forward nonetheless. It's a risk, but I must follow my faith.

"It's not my intention to lead us to further death no more than I will allow these people to suffer any longer on these waters," I say.

"So we ground this ship at first shore?" asks the captain.

"But my faith has not failed me either, and I will not let my brother rot in a prison," I continue. I can feel an unsettling stir from these men and a sigh of woe grumbling beneath their breaths. "We will pass on through the strait to Alexandria and endure the sea a little longer. There we can settle a few days before we plan our trek to Cairo."

"And what about the rest of the people aboard this ship?" Ananiah asks.

"I don't suspect I will receive any favor for my decision, but my choice in this matter stands firm. There's no need to share with the others what we may or may not face. Whatever hope they have left, it should be embraced."

"I expect we should let them know as soon as possible," advises Father Joseph.

"Thank you, Father," I say. "Thank you for trusting in me."

Father Joseph looks at me with weary eyes like my father used to do whenever I would ask for forgiveness. "I will not let my guard down for you," he says, embracing me warmly. His stony smile is kept under restraint, but the sincerity of his fatherly love for me hasn't fallen.

"So be it then. May God be with us all," Ananiah addresses.

With a seriousness now painted on their faces, the men slowly exit the bridge deck and descend the tight spiraled steps below. I casually pull Jacob back. When the men are out of sight, I pull Jacob toward me and plant a kiss on his lips. His body relaxes as he softly hugs his lips around mine.

There's not a moment I will waste to hold Jacob, even if it's for a few seconds. My days on this earth are numbered, and I can't fathom not knowing the sensation of being in love again. I believe it's one of the few things we should take advantage of if we are to keep our good sense pure in this world.

I stop for a moment to catch my breath, hoping to sustain this euphoric feeling. I open my eyes to see Jacob staring at me with shimmering eyes and a playful smile.

"What was that for?" he asks.

"Does there always have to be a reason to kiss?"

"I suppose I should say no if I'm to receive another."

"Now you're learning," I say with a smile.

CHAPTER 10

Whether it's just good fortune or not, our passage through the Strait of Gibraltar has gone unharmed and has unsuspectedly left this group of passengers with some hope. But I'm not sure that I've garnered any favor that makes this small moment of peace sustainable. Though it's clear to many on board that my alliance and good faith has been somewhat polluted, I carry on with an agenda nonetheless.

I've been ridiculed at times for convincing these people to leave America for a better place to live. The nation had been taken over by the Russian government under extreme hostility. How can these people believe that things would have been better if they had stayed?

Jacob may have led the Southern Resistance, but it is I who started this revolution from the beginning. A nation-wide rebellion had risen and I did everything I could to keep these people from being enslaved. These same people who embraced and honored me in their camp reside with harsh judgment now. Very few understand my choices while others bicker among themselves of my *undoing* and the uncertainties that lie ahead. Until we reach a safe haven, I'm afraid I'll be a source of continuous resentment.

Where there's bitterness, there's often conflict, and with a struggle to resolve differences comes something more dangerous than just petty umbrage: genuine hatred. I fear it will overshadow this withering fellowship with deadly consequences.

For the last few days, I've left Allison and Luke under the care of Juliana for reasons I'm almost ashamed to admit. I've spent most of my time with Jacob, holding on to a desperation that this may somehow be the last peaceful moments we may ever share together.

Though the calm Mediterranean Sea has secured a swift reprieve the past few days, it soon evaporates as tensions brew the closer we reach the port of Alexandria. The winds suddenly change as the clouds darken above us. An unsettling eastern breeze, spawned from a devil's night howls cool and lonely with a familiar stench. As a blanket of fog slowly rolls in, the sight of the port almost disappears, but I don't have to see what lies beyond the mist to know that it's the smell of death.

As if on cue, the metal decking below my feet vibrates with the pulse of a bee's wings. People emerge from their containers with curiosity. The roar of the ship's engines, churning in reverse beneath the black waters, slows our advance to the docks. When the rolling engines finally stop, silence dominates our arrival as our ship drifts with an eerie crawl into the abandoned shipyard.

With my guns drawn, I stand cautiously at the bow of the ship with Jacob by my side and wait for the unexpected. But as always in this unpredictable world, the unexpected has become the expected. Because everyone just assumed we would be met by severe opposition, we are instead greeted with no more hostility than that of sewer rats scurrying along the docks. There's nothing left here but a hollow discovery.

We enter deeper into the port where the shroud of dusty mist lifts from our ship and rises behind us. The small light emitting from the red of the moon sends a shiver down my spine. Upon a clearing ahead where our ship is to dock, an unforgiving image is revealed. It's one of our cargo ships that survived the voyage only to later suffer an unwelcoming of hostile militia. The ship stands abandoned by the docks, and several of its slaughtered passengers are lying on the deck to rot.

My heart quickly sinks. While the clouds cast shadows over the port, the large cityscape that lies just beyond the docks cast another mystery. Every building tall and small stands quietly in the dark like a silhouette of jagged shapes. Not one light piercing through any of the thousands of windows shine down on the town. What has caused a widespread blackout could only come from inhospitable adversaries drawing closer to control the region we are attempting to cross through. While this passage may be a death sentence, there's no other way around it now. We must press on, but with a cautious spring in our step.

The ship finally takes rest against the steel-girdled dock. Everyone stands around, murmuring with uncertainty. I take Jacob's hand and lead him to my container where Allison and Luke lie bundled up beneath a pile of blankets. Juliana and Nadia stand guard outside.

"Where's Niki?" I ask.

"She's with the children in the hull," Harold chimes in. Harold saved Jacob's life when our ship was under attack. He sacrificed his own life to save another during a relentless firefight near the bow of the ship, but it was more than just a sacrifice — it was the truest form of love. He was willing to leave behind Niki, his one true love, to save another from the grips of a cruel death. I have the utmost gratitude for his bravery, and we have developed a mutual trust.

"How are we going to do this?" Nadia wearily asks.

"Arena, we need to get these people off the ship as soon as possible," Ananiah interrupts as he approaches.

"I agree, but we don't know what's out there lurking in the dark."

"And we don't know what's going to come lurking on here either when those clouds begin to break," Father Joseph joins in.

"You saw what happened to the other ships. I'm responsible for these people now, and I wish no more suffering on anyone if I can help it," I argue.

"We'll be no more safer on here than we will be out there," Ananiah says.

"They're right, you know. It's a risk we may have to take. Like you said, from here on out, everything we do is a risk no matter what," affirms Jacob.

"Okay," I say with unsettling ambiguity, "but I want a scouting party at least a hundred yards in front of us. I'm not taking any chances. We have no means of communication, so you're going to have to use your better judgment."

"How?" asks Harold.

"Well, if you hear gunfire, I'm pretty damn sure you don't want to be standing around. I'll take point. Jacob and Ananiah will come with me, and the rest of you will fall back with the others." Father Joseph looks concerned. "Don't worry about me, Father. You're going to have enough to deal with."

"How do you figure?"

"You'll have to try to wrangle two thousand people from straying. That would be enough to keep me on edge," I say, and he smiles. "If anything should happen to me —"

"I trust you," Father Joseph interrupts. Whether it's just for his personal comfort or for my own, he keeps me briefly withdrawn from the grim reality that I might die out there. I'm not willing to accept defeat, but even I know my boundaries.

"I'll come with you," says Harold.

"No, you stay back." I pause for a brief moment. "Niki needs you."

"But I —"

"No!" I bark, and Harold flinches. "That's an order," I say more softly. The surprise on his face gradually dissolves and he nods in agreement. This private moment between

Harold and I assures me of two things: I know he will give his life for mine if the time should ever come, and I should never be surprised by his bravery ever again.

While the others leave to prepare the group's massive exit, Nadia waits waiting for me to say something, but all I can muster is a strained smile. I reach out and offer her my hand of friendship.

"What do you need from me?" she asks kindly.

"Though I'd rather have you by my side, I really need for you to help Juliana and Niki with the children."

"I understand," she simply answers.

"And especially stay close to Allison and Luke. I trust you, and I know you will guard them with your life." Her face brightens before she walks away. I'm forever grateful that she rescued me after Matthew's death.

I'm not sure what fortunes should come to us to leave this ship, but I'm just crazy enough not to care anymore. Only death itself will keep me from reaching my brother in Cairo. I look gravely down the darkened streets and realize just how slim our chances have become. I grab Jacob's hand and lean my head into his shoulder.

"You ready for this?" he asks softly.

"I wish not to wake up anymore and wonder."

I stay still for a moment as I hold on to the security of Jacob beside me and watch the crowd of people on board rustle with their belongings. Ananiah hovers over the railing, searching through the binoculars toward the city. I'm not sure what kind of expectations I have of him from this point on, but I suspect I should dig a little deeper to find out.

"Jacob," I say casually, "go grab Kale and three other men, and make sure they're armed."

"Is that enough?"

"For now."

I'm suddenly intrigued by the mystery surrounding Ananiah. With Jacob's absence to gather the other men, I strategically leave myself alone with Ananiah to collect the truth behind his promise to lead us through this unsightly region unharmed.

"So what's your plan?" I curiously prod.

He holds steady as his eyes undress our perimeter with bewilderment. "I just don't get it. Why would the entire city be covered in darkness?"

"Curfew?"

"Unlikely."

"I'm assuming you still have a plan though," I say.

Ananiah turns to be. "Alexandria has always been a point of interest to the Israeli government. Though Egypt's political ties with Russia has been somewhat of a deterrent lately, it's always been a region of mutual respect within the walls of diplomacy for its neighboring cities. Israel may be the target of rebellion, but political affairs aside, she still has a few unsuspected alliances outside her border."

"Well, I hope your coalitions extend further than Cairo, because I'm not getting a warm, fuzzy feeling here."

"Alexandria has never posed a threat to our agenda, but I'm feeling less eager to suspect something has changed."

"Why?"

"Over the course of the last five years, we've stationed many militia here to protect the city in exchange for safe passage and trade, but with recent turmoil brewing from an international pact with the Russian and Chinese governments, our means for survival may have diminished."

"Well, I'm not giving up here, and we certainly can't go back now."

"I have no means too, but this changes everything." Ananiah sighs.

"Surely, they haven't all left."

"I'm not too worried that my men have gone into hiding."

"Then what do you fear?"

"What's out in that darkness that made them flee."

A chill trickles down my spine. "So what are we to tell the others?"

"Nothing," he snaps.

"You mean lie?"

"I mean to tell them what they need to hear." Ananiah looks and me fiercely.

I agree with him to some extent. I know the truth can sometimes be better served in silence, but I am responsible for these people's lives, which changes the game.

"If you tell them anymore than that, this group is sure to break," he continues.

"I understand, I just—"

Ananiah's eyes soften. "I'm not trying to break trust here, Arena. Believe me, it's the last thing you need from me, but there needs to be a semblance of hope if you truly intend to keep this fellowship alive."

Right then Jacob, Kale, and three large men from the engine room walk over, fully armed, bringing our brief but undisclosed conversation to an end. I recognize one of the men as Scarface, an appropriate nickname for a man who bears a gouging scar that stretches from one side of his cheek across to the lower part of his jawline. He seems to accept the name as a badge of honor.

Kale introduces the other two men: Caspar and Francisco. Caspar is an arrogant, little British shit; his uncouth behavior and lack of gallantly courting skills did very little to woo me when we first met. The only thing memorable in that short-filled exchange was my knee meeting his nuts, and by his scowling eyes, it's the only thing he remembers as well. But I'm not looking for gentlemen to protect our perimeter, I want soldiers.

Francisco is a well-cut man who looks like he's seen military action in his days, but I'm not too sure he's ready to relive any of it.

Jacob's eyes briefly move over mine with an insecurity hidden in them. "Everything okay here?" Jacob asks, looking at me rather unsure.

"Fine, just trying to forge a plan," I say with my eyes piercing Ananiah's. I'm sure it's painfully obvious that nothing is okay by the expression on my face, but I'm disinclined to disclose anything to Jacob in front of the others.

Jacob holds my arm. "What's going on . . . and the truth this time," he whispers.

"Your inquiring tone is not with her but with me," Ananiah answers.

"Okay, so spill it," Jacob scoffs.

"The Israeli government has been keeping secret tabs on Egypt's political movement for quite some time now, but more importantly it has given the nation a reason to renew a coalition. And that coalition can only exists if there is a mutual deterrent."

"Russia?" Kale suggests.

"With the global economic collapse under severe duress, Russia and China have made it clear who is in control now. Although China refuses to claim second to the global helm, it knows Russia is the stronghold to keep the nations under an economic decree. Even America has relinquished its power to China's rule."

"So how does that help us here?" asks Jacob.

"Sometimes sleeping with the enemy is all you have. A top-secret Israeli militia has been stationed here for the past three years as a warranted means of protection for the Egyptian government," Ananiah continues.

"How do you know this?" asks Scarface.

"Because I'm the one who initiated this negotiation with our enemy. I'm not exactly fond of the idea of siding with Egypt, but it was necessary. Being Israeli's militant leader doesn't define my loyalty in this war, but sometimes there are undesirable decisions attached with it, and I was forced to make one."

"A trusted ally on enemy soil?" Kale sneers.

"Loyalty is what you make it without knowing the outcome. Before all of this chaos, Egypt served as a vital point in major trade for the Israeli government, notwithstanding from the harsh opposition of neighboring territories of course, but still a place growing with a mutual agenda and a supporting alliance."

"And now?" Kale asks.

"That alliance has come under siege."

"If you know you can't beat someone, you do the only thing logical to survive," I add.

"What's that?" Caspar asks in a slightly mocking tone. I glare at him.

"Join them," answers Jacob.

"Hell, maybe that's not a bad idea for us," Caspar says, chuckling.

I expect fear to draw these men back to our group, but that is a crippling response to this fellowship I just won't allow. I angrily draw my knife toward his nuts. Caspar's eyes grow wide as he cowardly shuffles behind Kale.

"I risked my life for these people while my brother rots in a prison. I'm not going to see it be exploited because you would rather cower behind the enemy," I sneer.

"Arena, stop it!" Kale shouts.

"Arena, don't, he meant no harm," Jacob calmly adds. I quickly put my knife away.

Caspar's eyes bulge and he trembles a few paces back. "Jesus, I'm sorry. You know, you might want to keep a chain on her," he says to Jacob. If not for Jacob and Ananiah holding me back, I would have reunited my knee with his crotch. "And this is who we want leading us?" Caspar nervously spews.

"Fine, you want me to leave?" I snap.

"I want to survive."

"Then I suggest you shut your damn trap."

"Look, I'm just a little uneasy about the whole thing, okay? I'm not suggesting we surrender." He takes on a softer tone, and for a quick moment I almost feel bad to have frightened him.

"Good, because I don't expect us to surrender," I say defiantly. The fear on his face is expected, but it will pale in comparison to anyone else on this ship when they discover the true danger that lies ahead. We don't need any more fear to infiltrate this group than it already has.

"Arena is right—this isn't a time to back down now. There's a small chance my men are still here," says Ananiah.

"And if they aren't?" Kale asks.

Ananiah sighs. "You want the brutally honest version?" he asks, and we all nod. "We will not survive this journey."

"You're telling me we're going to die here?" Kale exclaims.

"Shh . . . let's keep this quiet and civil," Ananiah says.

"So what's your plan then?" asks Jacob.

"If my men did flee, then yes, it's certainly a cause for concern, but seeing that there is nothing here but a darkened city, I suspect we'll find someone out there who knows."

Caspar boldly steps forward. "And that's your plan? To walk blindly in these empty streets for an answer? Hell, we'd be safer in the middle of the ocean."

"You'd be dead," I angrily assert.

"And we're just going to walk right in there uninvited?"

I look at him with a peculiar bode of confidence and simply say, "Yeah."

"Oh, okay, since you put it that way." Caspar rolls his eyes.

"Can we assume Egypt is still on our side?" asks Kale.

"For years the belly of this nation has secretly stood by Israel's response to Russia's global insurgence, but now I'm afraid Egypt serves as one of the Ten," Ananiah responds.

"One of the Ten?" I ask.

"Before your president was pouring out his cruelty, America was creating something much deadlier than just class wars. Two years ago, when the United States was forced to remove its global-power status to the likes of Russian adversaries and excessive Chinese levies, President Kriel vowed to settle his economic differences with the rest of the world. With the help of America's political allies and negotiating prowess, he and Russian leadership set up a global conference, which later became known as 'the Ten.' During that expanse, ten nations came together for a private summit held in Switzerland to discuss an international peace treaty, but it became more than that. A one-world government was introduced and it captured everyone by surprise. It was an election of power over commerce, and Gennadi Gorshkov, Russia's leader, had no intentions of leaving that summit without the support he needed."

Listening to Ananiah explain Gorshkov's cruel intentions sends a rare tingle up my spine.

"Those who removed their state to conform withdrew their trust and became expendable. Any radical party outside the Ten restricting their loyalty to this regime, being largely clandestine, will remain in fear until they are dead," Ananiah states.

"I'm assuming Israel wasn't a representative party at that assembly," Scarface says.

"No, but Egypt was. That's why we sent an allied delegate instead to get this information. You see, the only ruse in this political war is to determine whom to trust. And since Israel is the impeding factor to Russia's abrasive ideals, then no one is trustworthy."

"So why not negotiate then? I mean, if your nation is truly a visible target in this war, wouldn't it be logical to take the path of least resistance?" Francisco asks.

"Israel isn't in the business to reciprocate with nations under animosity. Russia is the one out for blood in this movement and it has taken a league of nations in secrecy to fight against it. I assure you, Israel will not fall to it. She would assume to be dead rather than be a slave under the rule of a one-world government."

"And what of this Ten? Assuming we do reach Jerusalem, what kind of hostility is expected now?" I ask.

"Ten delegates interceded into this pact, but only seven nations came together in agreement to form this new order, though I suspect that the three nations that remain — Egypt, the Republic of Germany, and what's left of the United States — will eventually grow loyal to Russia's offer. Either way, war is inevitable. Israel has always and will always be under severe hostility from the rest of the world. The Ten will not make any difference now."

"So if these nations are being threatened to unite for some world economic diplomacy, what kind of international relationship could Russia be trying to build without creating some kind global upheaval?" Kale asks.

"Gorshkov stands between a nation to reign and a worldwide genocide, but it's not a relationship he's trying to build."

"Then what is it?" Scarface asks.

There's a slight pause and the air feels heavy, as I answer for Ananiah. "An army."

CHAPTER 11

While night falls, the ship is quickly evacuated, leaving the abandoned vessel completely empty except for a few haunting memories. Though the port is enveloped in darkness, our group presses forward like a wandering caravan on the savanna. Jacob, Ananiah, and I scout up ahead while Scarface, Caspar, and Francisco carefully watch our perimeter. The closer we reach the city, the further from hope I become. If it's not the smell of raw sewage that discourages our trek, it's certainly the smell of rotting flesh that will staunch it.

Walking along the miles of empty streets outside the main interior of the city is dispiriting. Unfinished structures grace the black sky before us. Up ahead, there are cars abandoned on sidewalks, some toppled on top of one another, peppering the main road where rows of white-stoned buildings smolder in the night sky.

About two blocks ahead just around an intersecting street corner, the back end of a red double-decker bus, tipped on its side, sticks out from behind an apartment building. I'm not too concerned by the wrecked position of the vehicle as much as I'm troubled by what caused its unfortunate mishap. With Jacob and Ananiah close by my side, I carefully inch closer to the other side of the bus. When I reach the midsection, my heart sinks.

Protruding halfway out from one of the broken windows lies a bloated corpse. It's a woman, maybe in her thirties. I creep closer. Her bloody macerated arms stretch forward for help as if she tried to crawl up and out to safety.

Her pupils are still like a doll's eyes, but I swear that black soulless stare moves over me when I move past. I quickly turn my head away and gasp.

"Is this what you expected?" asks Jacob disdainfully.

"I don't know what to expect anymore," Ananiah replies gloomily.

"I'm sorry," Jacob softly apologizes. His complete disregard of Ananiah's feelings is a bit surprising, but I know his bitter distaste is only out of frustration..

I turn around to avoid the horrific scene, but I can't pull my eyes from the battered woman dangling from the broken window. Ananiah's grumbling sigh rings with anger. Jacob leans against the bus and curses.. He lends his hand as a hammer and pounds the roof out of frustration.

Suddenly, the woman's body shifts from the hammering vibration and slips down, but her shoulders are lodged between the broken glass. Everyone is silent for a moment until a shuffling noise inside the bus bangs against the roof.

I race over and place my ear to the bus, terrified that some poor soul may still be trapped inside. I run toward the front of the bus, jump, and grab the fender well to pull myself up.

"Arena, what the hell are you doing?" Jacob asks.

"There's someone in there." The bus must have flipped entirely over because the painted logo on this side is scraped beyond recognition. It's too dark to see inside the smoky cracked windowpanes.

"Throw me your flashlight," I say to Jacob.

"Careful, Arena, that glass is not stable," Ananiah cautions.

I carefully step across the metal riveted frame trying to avoid the large windows. There is a sudden rustle within the bus that keeps me still for a moment, but I still can't see anything below.

Gingerly, I walk across the glass windowpanes toward the woman. She immediately slips down further with her head turning toward me and I jump with fright. I'm almost convinced she's still alive, but I know it's just her dead body shifting. The only thing keeping her from slipping through the window back into the bus is her lodged shoulder tangled with a leather purse strap still attached.

The sound of a thud bangs against the roof of the bus, but this time I can make out a shadowy image swinging just below me. I shine the flashlight down, but the glare of the glass distorts the image even more. I walk a little closer to the woman, nearly on top of her now, and I place the flashlight directly on the glass. The inside immediately lights up and I scream.

A dead infant dangles from the other end of the woman's strangling purse strap and sways back and forth, banging into the top of the roof. Its ashen face sends disturbing shivers throughout my body.

"What do you see?" asks Ananiah.

I'm too numb to answer. The grisly image has burned into my retinas.

"Arena, what is it?" Jacob calls softly.

Suddenly, the glass where I'm sitting begins to crack. "Don't come up here," I shout.

"Arena, come down now!"

I carefully slide over to the metal siding of the bus, but the unstable windowpane is pushing inward leaving me stranded. Without warning, the jagged glass to the right of the woman breaks off and she falls down into the bus.

I carefully maneuver to the adjacent window. The brittle glass begins to crack. "Oh shit!"

"Arena, don't move, I'm coming." Jacob leaps up over the wheel well and onto the side of the bus, but the windowpane below me falls in. I manage to hang on to the metal framing as my legs dangle helplessly.

"Jacob! I'm slipping."

Suddenly, there's a growling duet below me. I peer over my shoulder just enough to notice two wild, angry dogs waiting to take a bite out of my legs. I struggle to swing my legs out of the way while the ravening canines are leaping angrily with their jaws stretched wide and chomping.

"Jacob!" I scream. One of the dogs leaps high and scrapes the side of my thigh with its gnarled claws while the other sinks its teeth deep into the tip of my boot. I can't hang on much longer with the weight of this dog pulling me down.

Jacob stretches his hand toward mine, but the side of the bus where Jacob is standing suddenly caves in. He falls hard onto the glass. My body shift dangerously closer to the dogs while Jacob struggles to reach me with his hand. The gap between us is too much. With all my strength, I pull my right shoulder up to grab him, but the integrity of the bus's structure pulls us farther apart. For every inch Jacob moves so does the bus frame. If I let go and jump down now, I risk breaking a leg and or being mauled. My arms are exhausted. Jacob stretches his hand out one more time, but it's useless. The side of this bus isn't going to hold much longer as the thin metal sheet crinkles and gives in.

While I'm fending off one rabid dog with one leg, the other is being violently shaken back and forth like a chew toy. Just then, I notice the remote to my boot ejecting blade peeking out from my jacket sleeve. While holding on to the metal deck, I painfully scoot my arm over the broken glass and press the button. The blade hidden in my boot springs forward and gouges the inside of the dog's throat. His teeth immediately retract from my boot and he drops dead.

The other dog's persistent fight leaves me breathless as I swing to avoid his sharp teeth sinking into my thigh. But with less weight pulling me down now, I'm able to swing my boot over and pierce him in the chest. He falls into the side of the bus below, but nothing immediately fatal, as I can hear the wounded mutt whimper beneath one of the seats.

With very little strength left in me, I have just enough to stretch out for Jacob's hand. A few rivets dislodge from the metal siding and bend inward. Jacob quickly pulls me over from the unstable edge and holds onto me tightly. We lie next to each other exhausted while just a few feet away the midsection of the bus suddenly collapses.

"Are you guys okay up there?" asks Ananiah.

"Now you ask," I pant.

"You seem like you have everything under control."

"Oh really. What part of 'oh shit' did you misinterpret, or is that not a universal expression for trouble where you're from?"

"Valid point."

If it weren't for Jacob, I'm not sure how much more of this I can handle. It seems like a lost cause to continue, but I know there is something more to my journey than just suffering or I would have been dead a long time ago. While I know these people need my help, it's the thought of my brother still alive that will keep me from quitting.

Suddenly, the whisking glide of boots scraping the cobbled street startles me. With a quick air of caution, I grab my gun. Just around the corner emerges Caspar and Francisco from the shadowy crook of the apartment building. I release my gun with a sigh.

With Jacob's help, I carefully climb down from the side of the bus and wrap my arm with a piece of cloth. The glass has cut jagged lines up and down my forearm.

"What happened here?" Caspar shudders.

"Don't look so shocked. It's what you expected, right?" I solemnly answer.

"Where's Scarface?" Jacob asks.

"He's behind us waiting for a signal," Caspar says while never taking his eyes off my bleeding arm.

"So how you going to keep this from the others?" Francisco asks.

"We can't, not anymore. I guess this is the reality they should come to expect."

"Just like that then? Well, at least I admire your honesty," he retorts dismissively. If it weren't for Francisco's usually quiet and reserved nature, I would take offense to his flippant remark. I understand his dissatisfaction to my response, and I feel a sincere tone in his voice for these people.

"I'm sorry if that's not what you're looking for, but I'm not here to babysit them." I grab one of my guns and lock in a fresh magazine. "I'm here to protect them."

I gravely hope there's more to this journey, but I'm afraid this city is left with less hope than what was on our ship. These people may deserve better, but this is our only passage now.

While the others fall back waiting for our signal, Jacob, Ananiah, and I scout up ahead just a few clicks where a less than desirable path leads to the open streets downtown. I hope to find an empty building for these people to take rest in. We all could use a good night's sleep.

The paved streets are littered with broken bodies none of which are recognizable. While many lie slaughtered, a smoldering brick façade that's barely standing erect is decorated with others. Their charred remains blend effortlessly into the shadowy banks against the wall. Even if any had a face to look upon, I don't know if I could identify a man or woman who many have belonged to our fellowship. I'd like to believe those people fled safely from the other ship, but my heart suspects otherwise.

The narrow street ahead is as empty as it is depressing, but to our left the space from one sidewalk to the other is plentiful. The buildings rise tall here, stacked upon one another, without hardly any room to breathe in-between.

The white stones used to grace these esthetically displeasing structures must be the only color available because one building bleeds into the other. But one stands out distinctively. Not far down the street near a blockade of wrecked vehicles, a regal building stands clean among the rest of the rubble. Its highlighted crowning roof perches stately just above the grand towering rotunda below. It's clearly the centerpiece of this tragic city, possibly an edifice for governing politics. It resembles the capitol building in America.

This is as good a place to settle as any for the evening, at least until we can get our bearings straight. I'm not opposed to moving on, but this is the only building that looks inviting. I gesture for Caspar to signal the others when out of nowhere a shadowy image races down the street.

"Wait!" I stop Caspar.

"What is it?" Jacob asks.

"Over there. Did you see that?"

"See what?" Ananiah scans the area and looks frightened.

"There someone out there." I grab my gun and stand as quiet as a mouse perusing each building. My eyes wildly shift to each side of the street to find a shadow among the shadows, but it seems almost impossible. Caspar and Francisco flank to the left while Jacob and Ananiah conceal themselves behind an abandoned car a few feet away.

I cautiously move to my right, kneel down, and screen myself behind a small palm on the corner of the sidewalk. It's too dark to really see anything, and the amount of litter and obstructions peppering the street make it more difficult to track movement. Like waiting out an opossum, I fix myself in a comfortable position and search over the last spot where the shadow vanished. I cast my eyes near the side of the capitol building and patiently wait until I catch a small glimpse of movement carefully inching behind a truck tossed on its side.

I gesture for Jacob and Ananiah to stay put while my eyes are still carefully planted on the person behind the truck. I know this stalemate is unlikely to continue, but it doesn't help when you have a bumbling idiot like Caspar to ruin this standoff. He moves from behind the building on the other side of the sidewalk and leaves himself conveniently exposed. I signal for him to stop, but he's too stupid to understand. The person settled behind the truck nervously shifts behind the hood, quickly crouches down, and draws his gun. Finally, Francisco grabs Caspar's shoulder and pulls him back out of the open.

Not much is going to change if we stay like this, and I'm getting hungry. There's only one way to see this come to some kind of closure unharmed. I'm going to have to flank this guy and catch him from behind off guard. Jacob has a worried look on his face, and I'm not sure what I'm about to tell him is going to ease it any either.

I motion for Jacob to move to the left, causing a slight distraction. The stranger shifts toward Jacob as expected, and I swiftly flank to the right of the building in front of me. With a sly skip in my step, I cautiously nimble around the backside of the crumbling façades until I reach the last alley that extends to the capitol building.

Around the corner, a toppled truck casts a long, narrow shadow, and a man donned in military clothing crouches down behind its crinkled hood. His gun drawn forward aims at Jacob. The man seems to be all alone. I take a few deep breaths before attempting to lure the man from his hostile position when he suddenly fires a few rounds.

With tender haste, I sidle around the corner, being careful to stay pinned in the shadows. I'm almost right on top of him, and baring no stupid, impending mistakes on my part, this will all end. I'm so close to the man, I can smell his sweat. Suddenly, Jacob pops out from behind a wrecked car and runs behind another directly in front of us. The man hastily pushes another magazine into his gun and aims for Jacob's head, which is completely exposed. Without hesitation, I jam the cold steel of my gun to the back of the man's head.

"Pull that trigger and you're going to permanently be a part of this truck."

The man slowly releases the trigger and lowers his weapon to the ground.

"Get up!" I shout through gritted teeth.

The man carefully rises to his feet and turns his head to me. "You got the wrong person—"

"Turn around!"

"Do they always send a woman to do a man's job?" he sneers.

"Mister, I'm only going to warn you once for your own good. I haven't had a shower in days, I'm hungry, so don't fuck with me today."

While at gunpoint, I walk the man out from behind the truck and into the open where the others are waiting in the street with their guns raised. The closer we get, the stranger Ananiah looks as he gazes mysteriously at the man.

The man's pace sharply slows, then in elation he spews, "Ananiah?"

Ananiah's eyes widen before a smile accompanies his jubilation. "Sadiq?"

CHAPTER 12

With surprising awareness drawn on Ananiah's face, I lower my gun away from the man's back. The odd presence of Ananiah recognizing this fellow by the name of Sadiq leads to me to believe their exchange is of a mutual acquaintance, but I'm not sure Jacob truly trusts the situation just yet, as he still has his gun planted on him.

"Jacob, please." Ananiah gestures for Jacob to withdraw his gun.

Sadiq approaches Ananiah cautiously, but he doesn't make any friendly attempt to make the already uncomfortable situation any easier. He slowly walks out of the shadow and just a few paces before Ananiah.

Just when I think this unsettling moment couldn't get any worse, Sadiq suddenly stops and quickly reaches inside his jacket. The sudden action triggers an untrusting instinct, which presses both Jacob and I to re-draw our guns. Sadiq, wide-eyed, turns to Jacob and raises his left hand as a small gesture of submission. With his right hand tucked into his jacket, he slowly pulls out a pin and hands it to Ananiah, but not until the two embrace does the mysterious exchange give us all a reassurance that the two are friends.

"Good to have you back, General," Sadiq says with a smile.

"General?" I question Sadiq harshly. I still have some resentment that this man could have shot us at any time.

"Yes, and I'm still in charge." Ananiah attaches the pin, with markings that are decorated for a general in the Israeli military, to the top right of his jacket.

"Well, I guess that doesn't bode well for your ranking, I taunt. His smile suddenly recedes, but the calm in his voice doesn't.

"You respect your superior," Sadiq retorts.

"Respect? And this is how you address yours? By welcoming him with hostile force?"

"I would have realized soon enough—"

"Would you?"

"Look, I don't know who the hell you think you are, but I'm captain of the Israeli specials unit and whether you like or not, I'm in command here."

"Well, Captain, I was beginning to wonder—you know, with my gun stuck in your back in all—because like you said, *they had to send in a woman to do a man's job.*" A snicker from Ananiah sends Sadiq's brows furrowing with further embarrassment.

"Ha, woman? I see a child begging for attention," Sadiq scoffs.

"Which must make it all that more embarrassing for you then."

Sadiq points at me. "Who the hell is this bitch?"

"Watch your tongue," Jacob snaps.

I swing my scorpion dagger just beneath Sadiq's neck. "If you attempt to seek any kind of approval from me, you might want to think before you speak." I know this arrangement Ananiah has organized for us includes a body of protection, but I'm not willing to take orders from this ego-seeking douchebag just so he can break me down in front of everyone to prove his masculinity.

"Arena, that's enough!" Ananiah commands. I'm not exactly in a trusting mood, nor will I keep my anger still. "Arena, stand down your blade," Ananiah says more calmly. I withdraw my knife, but not without staring Sadiq down.

"Arena?" Sadiq asks with disbelief. His tone shifts. "Surely you're joking."

"What were you expecting?" asks Ananiah.

"Besides a little less sass, a soldier with experience."

"She captured you," Ananiah retorts. The slight discomfiture displayed on Sadiq's face is priceless, but I can see now that this man is of no harm; he's just in need of some humbling banter.

"Yeah, well, what can I say, God must have a sense of humor. Besides, what is she without a gun?" Sadiq jokes. Slightly annoyed by his comment, I hastily draw my sword, and he quickly raises his hands, yielding.

"Apparently a madwoman with a sword," he says nervously. I had no intention of doing anything but cast a bit of fear, and I've succeeded.

Ananiah, Caspar, and Francisco suddenly take a step back next to Jacob. Their faces are painted with unexpected shock.

"You should probably show a little more respect toward women."

"My apologies." Sadiq winks.

I stand there hesitant to withdraw the katana. If I didn't know any better, I'd say he's smitten with me, and by the unkind stare Jacob is giving him right now I'm not the only one wondering the same thing.

"You can put the sword down now, honey. I'm not your enemy," Sadiq says.

"Oh, sorry, it's a habit."

"Interesting habit."

"You have no idea," Ananiah adds.

Sadiq slowly lends his hand toward me, signaling for a truce. "So, are we good?"

I grasp his sweaty hand. "For now, sure, but don't get too comfortable."

"Don't worry, I never do."

We abide by a handshake with a mutual understanding of the terms from this small exchange, but I'm still not certain I want him leading this group. I know our personalities may clash on the surface, but somehow deep inside they are not that far away from being the same.

"Okay, now that we've all been acquainted with one another, can we get the hell out of here?" Sadiq says.

"Something wrong?" Ananiah asks.

"Not unless you want to be greeted by stringers."

"Stringers?" I ask.

"I'll tell you later. Right now we need to find refuge. How many more of you are there?"

"We have about two thousand in our party," says Ananiah.

The look on Sadiq's face is unsettling. "We need to move quickly," he urges.

"You have a place in mind?" I ask.

"Just beyond the bank tower to our right, there's an abandoned hotel we've been camping in the last few days. The top floors have been burned and she isn't much to look at, but it will suffice. It's one of the few places left that has been kept secured. It'll be a little cramped, but we haven't any other options at the moment. Stringers are unpredictable in this area of the city."

"I'll take point. You and Ananiah stay close behind while the rest of you bring the others down the main street. We'll cross over the adjacent streets when it's safe," I say.

"So, you're in charge now?" Sadiq questions.

"I think I'm more than capable."

"Well, I'm sure you are, but I think I know this place a little better than you. I'll take lead."

"Whatever makes you feel better."

"I can see that you and I are going to have a splendid time together."

"Yeah, I kind of have that effect on men."

"Really?"

"Yeah, but they usually end up dead."

Sadiq looks at me like I'm crazy while Jacob quickly brushes next to him. "I'll take point with Arena," Jacob says.

"It's no problem," Sadiq offers.

"Well, I have a problem with it," Jacob snaps.

This is a side of Jacob I haven't seen before. I believe this is the first time I've witnessed jealousy from him. He peers back at Sadiq with disdain before kissing me on the cheek. I'm not sure how to respond to that, but I'm flattered nonetheless.

While our tired and hungry caravan follows a safe distance back from us, I'm reluctant to even speak a word to Sadiq with Jacob walking closely by my side. I'm enamored by his gallant chivalry, but I need him to trust me. I stay silent and restrain my tit-for-tat banter with Sadiq. It's not worth causing petty conflict with the man I love.

I can feel Sadiq's eyes planted on the back of my head, watching my every move as if I'm being tested. He is, after all, the captain of his platoon. There's nothing worse than being critiqued by someone just as self-assured as you, although I'm not feeling so confident right now. The eerie silence dominating these streets is as unsettling as these mysterious *stringers* I'm not too sure I want to know about. It's so quiet, all I can hear are Sadiq's mimicking footsteps behind mine.

My sleep pattern has been out of synch for some while now. I can't tell if it's early dawn or if evening is waning into the night. All I know is the hint of deep blue peeking through the billows is much more inviting than the hazy mist that engulfs this city port.

"It's just up ahead and to the right next to the crane." Sadiq points out our residing refuge. If he's referring to the neglected structure that represents a pile of rubble, I'm not sure that we might be safer just sleeping outside. The building looks like it's about to collapse any second.

The closer we approach, the more I really don't want to go inside. The Hilton sign that once stood proudly above the entry dangles helplessly on one end while the other rests halfway into the lobby roof. Most of the top floors have either been demolished or burned beyond recognition. The only thing that may be worth noting about this hellhole is that it's heavily guarded. Several men with sniper rifles sit atop the awning, while others pepper the grounds securing the perimeter. I feel slightly better, but this place is still a dump, and I just can't keep my tongue from eloquently articulating my thoughts on it.

"What a piece of shit," I simply express.

"Trust me, it's not as bad on the inside," Sadiq insists.

"I guess that all depends on your definition of 'bad.'"

The barbed-wire barricades in front of the entry don't exactly imply a spring invitation, but at least it's a refreshing change of scenery from the claustrophobic containers on the ship. It's difficult to see what lies inside the lobby windows, but I'm not going to expect anything different from the outside. Its fascia, riddled with gouging holes, isn't much to look at, but it will have to do for now before we move on.

Father Joseph and Henry slowly lead the others to the hotel entrance, but not without the distaste of its structure. Incessant grumblings mutter throughout the crowd of disheveled faces.

Two of Sadiq's men quickly remove the barricaded wire from the front doors as the crowd of people restlessly wait to go in. I'm unconvinced that we will all fit in this battered hotel as I watch each person file in to find rest. Weary face after weary face passes by and not a smile among them looks upon me—out of resentment, I suppose, or regret that I have led them here. Not until halfway through the massive exodus am I greeted with two precocious grins wandering in the middle of the pack: Luke and Allison.

Accompanied by Nadia, they struggle to move themselves from the group. It seems to be becoming less organized now, as I have to part through the belligerent crowd and grab Allison's hand. Luke clings to her as Nadia pushes her way through and out of the way. Allison holds onto my waist, trying to avoid a sudden rush of impatience forming within the assembly outside.

There's pushing and shoving now, when just to my right a tall slender man shouts slurs to another. An argument ensues followed by two childish imbeciles rolling on the ground fighting each another.

Jacob and Sadiq rush over to break up the fight, but the crowd is much too large to control. They are both pushed back while the two men continue to combat each other's egos. The level of testosterone in this group flows too effortlessly for me to be silent. I wouldn't normally waste a bullet on this ridiculous display of immaturity, but I've had enough of this crap. I draw my gun in the air and fire without warning.

There's a sudden hush over the crowd. If it's respect they lost for me, they've found it because they quickly withdraw from the scene. They pose like statues, waiting for the likelihood that I should fire my gun again. The only thing stirring among their immediate silence now is the two men who continue to tussle on the ground. I put my gun away and pull my dagger from its sheath. Angrily, I step toward the two men.

Ananiah stops in front of me. "Arena, don't do anything you'll regret," he advises.

"I've already done enough to regret and not enough to care anymore."

"This is her flock. Let her tend to it as she will," Father Joseph says, stepping in. Not a year ago, I would have thought it crazy to hear those words flow from his mouth, but now I don't expect anything different from him. I realize how much Father Joseph has sacrificed for me. We have a divine connection that no one can understand.

Ananiah slowly backs off as I push forward to the men still grappling. As they roll over, I kick one of the men in the chest while I hold the other by the back of his hair. He screams, thrashing his arms. I carefully tuck my dagger beneath his grisly neck; the touch of my blade against his flesh causes his childlike arms to stop flailing. Wide-eyed and quickly startled, the other man slowly slides over a bit, gingerly holding his sore sternum.

"Now, I'm only going to say this once, so I suggest you pay attention." The man I'm holding nervously nods. "You're going to get up, forget about whatever differences you may have had for each other, and get back in line with the rest who are patiently waiting to go inside."

"Go ahead and cut the son of a bitch. This was his doing," the other man shouts. He obviously doesn't heed to advice very well. Maybe he needs a 9mm to persuade him.

I chuckle. "I suppose it wouldn't bother you if I cut this man's throat," I say, shaking the man in my grasp.

"Why should it?" He pulls a large knife from a sheath tucked into his pants. The crowd gasps. I quickly draw my gun and aim it at his head.

"The same reason it shouldn't bother you when I pull this trigger," I say casually.

Fear flashes in his eyes, but just for a split second. "You don't have the guts," he dare incites.

Now I'm pissed that he would provoke someone with a gun pointed at him. I sheath my dagger, then approach the man with the end of the barrel pointing at the side of his head.

"Try me," I say. The man's confidence quickly abates as he drops the knife. Beads of sweat run down his forehead. He pauses briefly before returning to his cocky crowing. "You won't do a goddamn thing. I've pulled my share around here and this is what I get."

"What, feeling unappreciated? Now you know how I feel."

"Squeeze that trigger and you'll live with more regret then you want," he says.

"I simply do not care anymore." I cock back the hammer.

"Arena, don't do this," Ananiah chimes in. I've allowed my internal demons to resurface without warning.

"We all make mistakes, even you," the man argues.

"I can live with mine. Are you willing to die for yours?"

"Arena, let it go," Jacob softly reasons as he walks toward me.

The stubborn man nervously laughs. "That's the problem. She can never let things go. That's how we ended up here, so why should we listen to her?"

"You're alive because of her. You should be so grateful," Father Joseph answers.

"You call this grateful?" He points to the gun I'm jamming into the side of his head.

"Say anything else but an apology and it's going to get messy real quick," I say in a rush. My blood is boiling.

"I made a mistake—"

"I've killed men for less." I jam the end of the barrel harder into his skin.

"Arena, honey, just put the gun down, okay?" Jacob urges.

I press the gun into his head harder and he squeals in pain. My hands are shaking. My insides are screaming and fighting the temptation to rid this cancerous man from our group, but I know this is wrong no matter how I see it. What have I done to create such animosity?

"Arena, please, I know you don't want to go down this road. This isn't the person you are," Jacob coos.

Images of Myra and Gabe and Uncle Finnegan, and anyone I've ever loved . . . just gone. My vision blurs and my throat tightens. Too much pain and loss, and how many nights have I cried myself to sleep? How many mornings have I woken up to feel so lost and alone, and even the sun's heat can't warm the chill in my bones. And how the rage sets it. At first, it was a tiny nugget, a seedling, which then grew and expanded, and now I feel so lost in my own anger that I've forgotten the person I used to be. All I want is to see blood spill from this man. I press my finger on the trigger, pleading with myself to stop, and I let out a scream so guttural it sounds otherworldly, and then the tiny cold hands of a child on mine, and I let go of the trigger . . .

Luke is standing next to me. He carefully pulls the gun away from the man's head. I stand here in front of a wavering crowd that sees a young girl less in control than she thought she was, and only from a child's heart does she realize what she has truly become — a killer.

CHAPTER 13

Both men, scuffed clothes and abraded faces, rise from the ground, and warily walk back into the crowd. The look of distrust painted on these people's faces is as disappointing as my actions, but there's nothing I can do now to change it. I've dug my own grave with this group the minute we set sail on the ocean. To them, I must be plagued with misery and defeat, but I'm here to protect and shelter them. The very thought of my brother rotting in some cage makes it difficult for me to believe I'm capable of either. I feel their eyes shamefully staring.

Luke takes my hand and drags me away from the crowd. Allison and Nadia comfort me, but deep inside I'm crying. Allison wraps her arms around my waist, while Nadia reaches for my shoulder, but I'm too stricken from my own guilt to look upon her. Instead, I disgracefully stare transfixed at my gun, still firmly tucked in my hand.

"I wouldn't have done anything different," Nadia softly offers..

"I don't know who I am anymore." I disgustingly toss the gun on the ground, as I want no part of this feeling attached to me. I pry Allison's arms from my waist and walk away feeling despondently numb. I just want to crawl into a hole and be alone.

Father Joseph watches my every step while Sadiq and Ananiah struggle to say anything to me when I pass. Jacob's the only person brave enough to approach me, but even he can't make me feel any better right now. If anything, I'm too embarrassed and ashamed to see him.

"This isn't a time to walk away now," he quietly advises. I know he means no harm, but I disincline to relish his advice.

"Then you lead these people, because I'm obviously unable," I say.

"You did what you had to do regardless of what people might think. You've done more for these people than they are willing to accept. That's not your worry."

I walk away from him, not wanting to hear what he has to say.

"Arena!" he snaps sharply, grabbing my arm. I retract harshly from his grasp. "I love you much more than your stubbornness allows me to, but I'm not going to stand here and see you waste like this. I've worked too hard not to lose you like this."

I kick the dirt with my boot. "I haven't left. I'm just angry."

"You have a right to be angry—hell, we all do—but don't let some petty dispute cause you to flee. I know you, Arena, and hate does not dwell deep inside your heart. God knows where you stand. He didn't choose you without a purpose just to see you keep your sins unseen. Not even our darkest secrets can be hidden from Him."

"I just . . ." I turn from his gaze, unsure of myself.

"Just what?"

"I need to find myself again."

"Well, if Arena is hiding in there, tell her I want her back." He smiles in jest. Jacob's persistence is my strength, and I crack a rare smile. I sigh and embrace him. The fact is, the more I try to find myself, the more I'm lost.

"We need you," he says desperately. I unbury my face from his chest and look into his eyes.

"And you?"

"I need you," Jacob clarifies.

*   *   *

The wind blows cool from the port side, and after an hour of waiting outside the hotel doors with Jacob, I watch patiently as Kale ushers the remainder of the group inside. It's a tight fit, but everyone manages to find some place to rest, at least until things settle down long enough to forge a permanent plan.

Kale returns outside and grabs his pack. His eyes meet mine briefly before I turn away and peer back through the window. Without warning, he wraps his arm around my shoulder, catching me by surprise.

"Don't worry, we're going to get through this together," he says, reassuring me that I'm doing the right thing. I stand there, wondering if he truly trusts me now. Maybe it was just a kind gesture. Or perhaps a small token of forgiveness for his resentment toward me. Either way, we've found a safe place, even if it's temporary.

It's going to be quite an adventure to find a place to sleep for the few of us who are still outside. As we head inside, I explore the bottom floor for a comfortable place to rest, but there's no more than a few inches to spare between clumps of nestled bodies. With the size of this place, surely there's more room than this crowded floor suggests.

I carefully make my way to the back past the elevators and down a long narrow hall where people are crouched against the walls. At the end of the hall and to the left are several double doors that extend on either side as far down as a city block. *Why hasn't anyone come down here?* I try opening the doors, but they are locked. And there's my answer.

I try prying the lock with my dagger, but it's no use. If I want to relieve most of the congestion in the lobby and halls then I'm forced to waste a bullet. I fire between the doors, not once but twice, until the bolt weakens. I kick in the remainder of the damaged lock, and behold, the doors swing open to a dark empty space. I shine my flashlight inside to find an empty ballroom with more room to accommodate all of us and then some.

Suddenly, there's a stir around the corner, and a crowd of troubled faces stare down the hall. Sadiq, Jacob, and two other men come racing between the crowd.

"What happened, you okay?" Sadiq asks, alarmed.

"I'm fine, just making accommodations," I calmly answer. Sadiq walks over and peers inside.

"Forgot about these meeting rooms. Never thought we'd have to use them. How about some light?"

"Light? You're telling me this place has electricity?"

"We have a generator, but we normally keep all the lights off. With Russian soldiers that still may be lingering and unwanted stringers running around, lights are a luxury that would otherwise create unwanted attention."

"These stringers you keep talking about, who the hell are they?" I ask.

Sadiq's eyes grow dark. "Let's get these people settled first and we'll talk privately," he whispers.

I don't wish to discuss anything until I find sleeping quarters for Allison and Luke. Just behind the front marbled desk are two doors, one of which leads to a smaller interior room lined with cubbyholes and copy machines. The other opens to a ten-by-twelve space occupying a large desk with a computer made of glass and a small cot-like bed behind it. In the corners sit two chairs big enough to lean back in and fall comfortably asleep.

Allison and Luke wearily walk into the office. Nadia tucks Luke into one of the soft chairs with a piece of worn linen found folded behind the door. Allison has no trouble plopping onto the other chair and falls fast asleep.

I watch protectively over the two for a moment before I'm resigned to leave them to rest while Nadia and I join the others for some much needed answers.

There's a small gathering sitting on a couple of couches in the middle of the large lobby entrance. Among them are my closest friends — Father Joseph, Henry, Juliana, Niki,

Harold, Kale, and Jacob. Next to Father Joseph stands Sadiq and Ananiah. When we join the assembly, we are met with somber faces. Their gloom grows from hunger and exhaustion, and there is very little I can do to provide for them. We are no longer in the woods among beasts to eat. I'm at the mercy of a mysterious city shadowed in darkness and despair.

"I'm sure you all have plenty of questions that deserve answers, but let's get one thing clear: This conversation goes no further from your mouths than here, understand?" Sadiq says. Everyone nods in agreement.

"Three months ago, the city was taken by Russian operatives, most of whom were sent in to control the region's major resources—a small outfit, nothing to waste worry on. We first thought that Egypt may have struck a deal with Russia, temporarily barging for economical support, but we soon discovered this small relationship wasn't a bargaining tool. It was a far cry from the largely passive acquiescence we've come to expect from the Egyptian government. They're not exactly a trustworthy alliance. And that's when all hell broke loose."

Sadiq paces back and forth as he continues. "More and more soldiers were being deployed in the city, but not like the others. No, these men came with a hostile purpose. Local government was annihilated, curfews were enforced, and every piece of history this city had offered is but a distant memory. Whatever efforts went into exploring and preserving the antiquities of Alexandria no longer rest in its museums. This wasn't just an invasion to cause conflict and fear. This was a means to control and nothing else, and when the Russians managed to secure the port and divert all foreign trade, it had become evident that the world was becoming smaller while Russia was growing bigger."

"What happened to my men?" Ananiah angrily questions.

Sadiq sighs heavily. "After the first wave of soldiers came, we set up checkpoints to the four corners of the city. Most of the soldiers were planted near the seaport, but when a few civilians decided to reject their unwelcoming guests . . . well, hostility always intercedes to conformity. Russian forces gave no warning and killed anyone outside in the streets. It was a bloodbath. Soon they overtook the entire city, but it did nothing more but temper a laborious people, and they fought back."

Sadiq stares through the glass lobby doors motionless, as if he's recalling that troubled memory. "And we fought back."

"But you survived," I say, trying to break his troubling gaze. He turns to me with anger in his eyes.

"I had five hundred men under my command. Four hundred and seventy sacrificed their lives for a lost cause," Sadiq blasts.

"There is nothing lost in a man who trusts in God. I lost more people close to me than I want to remember and I lost a nation that started this war. Even now I'm afraid that I've lost my desire to want to live in this world, but this is our world now — love it, hate it, it's where we stand and who we stand with that makes it tolerable. None of this was your doing. My sympathies are with you, but it won't give you anything you can't get back —"

"And you?"

"I've accepted it, but it doesn't mean I have to like it. Tragedy aside, life continues, and you're a part of why we are here."

"You see those empty streets out there?" he asks crossly. "That's why you are here. There's nothing left, Arena. Where else are you going to run?"

"Is that what you think, I'm running?"

"Look, I don't know how the hell you made it here alive, but I know I had nothing to do with it. That's in God's hands."

"So where did they all go?" a sad voice interrupts. Buried beneath a blanket on the corner of the couch is Juliana. She lifts her head. Her eyes are sloped with dark patches from sleepless nights. "Where did all the people go to leave this city in ruin?"

Sadiq is quiet for a moment, then he says, "Most were slaughtered, and the rest who remained surrendered. They were thrown on buses, trailers, or whatever was available, and were driven away to Cairo for slave trade."

The sudden mention of Cairo hangs heavy on Juliana's face. Her glassy eyes stare coldly out the window before a tear slides down her cheek. I struggle with whether I should tell Sadiq about my brother being held prisoner in Cairo.

"How safe is it here?" Ananiah asks calmly.

Sadiq pauses again. He looks upon each of us with concern. "Safe enough, I suppose, but our supplies are limited now with this many people. We have electricity when we absolutely need it, but I can't guarantee how long our generators will last. Gas is scarce. We'll have to track some more down in the northern part of the city come first light, but even that's not safe anymore."

"Safe from what?" I ask.

"Amid the possibility of soldiers still lingering, it's the stringers we try to stay clear from."

I've had enough of this secrecy, this alluring mystery behind these *stringers*. "Stringer? Explain."

Whatever lifeless expression is painted on Sadiq's face morphs into a disturbing misery. "Madmen . . . savages, whatever you want to call them, they're possessed with a madness we cannot explain. We thought it might have been another virus like the 2035 flu strain, but there were no signs of death—just a sick savagery among them. Men, women, even some of the children we've come across have been stricken with it."

The deadly 2035 virus that killed nearly half the world's population is rumored to have started in West Africa from rotting animals, but the flu-like toxin was later dismissed after political advocates traced the lone source back to the International Center for Disease Control (ICDC), a restricted organization regulated by the Russian and Egyptian government.

The ICDC sited that the virus sample, which was being held under extreme safety measures, was found in West Africa. They assured the world that it was being researched for an antibody to ward off bacterial infections, but when word got out, no other samples of the virus strain had been collected or found in any of the rumored West African nations.

"What do you mean? Stricken with what?" Father Joseph asks.

"They killed ten of my men—skinned them, quartered them, and strung them up like a dangling deer. The only thing more disturbing than seeing my men cut up is the thought of these primal savages dinning on them later. Now, I don't know what possessed these people to turn like this, and I really don't give a shit. They are a danger to us, and I will kill them if they threaten our group."

"Where do these people roam?" asks Jacob.

"People? If that's what you want to call them. They walk where they may, but if you don't find them in the streets, scurrying around like rats scrounging for food, they're usually hiding in the northwest part of town. We figure that's where the remainder of the survivors held up after the Russians got here. They mainly come out at night, but you'll know where they have been."

"How?" I ask.

"On the account that they like to string up their prey from windows—ears, fingers, limbs, whatever garners fear. It's like their calling card. You call them people, but I call them stringers. I don't know exactly how they became what they are, but they're dangerous nonetheless."

"Sounds like to me these people were tortured, probably brainwashed," adds Juliana solemnly.

"Yes, but whatever they were before, they are my enemy now, and I will do what I have to do to stay alive," Sadiq states firmly.

"But they were people like you and me before—"

"They're possessed, I tell you," Sadiq snaps. "They don't know who they are anymore, and when they kill you, they're not going to care either. If there was a conscious hiding in them before, it's buried too deep to change them now. It's a cruel reality, but we're living in a new world among hell now."

The very image of these people surviving on one another is beyond disturbing. What hell has cast such behavior? I feel nauseous just thinking about it. Humanity is sinking deeper into madness I fear. Man has exchanged his hope for savagery now. What a sad state of affairs we've come to. "Look, stringers and Russian adversaries aside, there's something else that has been bothering me ever since we got here. If everyone is gone, why are you still here? Why haven't you left?" I prod.

Sadiq lowers his head. "A hope that somebody would come."

"Hope? I think we've established that doesn't exist here."

"Do you not understand what's happened?" he says, frantic.

"I understand that you've been grieving from the loss of your men, but what I don't understand is why you would stay in this city cast in shadow." Sadiq looks at me bewildered, then turns Ananiah even more puzzled.

"When we arrived, the city was black, not a light to be seen. We thought maybe Alexandria had been cut off the grid by the Russian government," Ananiah explains.

"My God, you really don't know, do you?" Sadiq says.

"Know what?" Ananiah asks.

"We did it, we actually did it."

"Did what?" I ask, troubled.

"Project X9 was launched two months ago," Sadiq says excitedly.

"Jesus, how many?" Ananiah worriedly asks.

"All of them. The last two were launched nearly seven days ago."

"Will somebody please tell me what the hell you are talking about!" Niki shouts.

Sadiq smiles and wrings his hands together. "American technology put to the test. They created it; we perfected it. Seventy-five E6 missiles packing fifty kilotons with geo-magnetic storm-like effects—a beautiful solar glow above the earth's atmosphere; a nuclear explosion without the explosion."

We all stand there like uninformed children waiting for a simplified answer.

"High and low-burst nuclear EMP weaponry," Sadiq clarifies. "If all the nations are against us, then we at least had to level the playing field. We didn't know how success-ful it would be after the first launch. It wasn't until two days later around the time after the first eclipse that the damage was done. EMP disruptions were suffered abroad, knocking out major power grids. We knew we had to act fast before the Russians and Chinese countered. We launched sec-ondary high-burst explosions disabling any orbiting defense satellites. That's when the decision was made to cover the rest of the world in darkness."

"Why?" I ask.

"It was our only hope to secure our nation's survival. We have no allies anymore. This is our last stand."

"And the total impact of these launches?"

"Enough to disrupt the world for a few years."

"Jesus Christ," I utter.

"Welcome to the Middle Ages Part Two."

Stomach churning, I feel a sudden relinquishing of my nerves. This changes everything I had hoped to find here, grim or not, but I'm not going to let it change my plans. Unexpected, yes, but finding my brother has and still is my sole agenda of this voyage. I'm not ready to recompense my life without knowing if he may still be alive, and I know Juliana wouldn't want that either.

The discovery of our situation, while troubling, won't tear me away from plodding forward. My mind is elsewhere, broken, but bent on finding resolve rather than worrying about the mundane eases of life before our world was turned into shadow. Without electricity now, it's fire we shall depend on and the rare appearance of the sun. Though I'm among friends, I feel secluded and alone. I can only sense that my brother feels the same, which makes it that much harder for me to want to linger around this godforsaken place any longer.

The chatter calms while a lit candle on the table next to me flickers. The front door opens and a young man, decked in military gear, shuffles languidly inside. His face is pale and his eyes droop from what I can only assume is from sleepless nights.

"Sir, the perimeter is clear. Preparing to shut down the front and lock the doors."

"Go ahead and commence," Sadiq orders. By his tone of command, this must be a regularity to the young man.

"I think it's best we all just get some rest for the night before we make any hasty decisions we're not willing to converge on just yet," Sadiq requests peacefully.

"Sounds reasonable," Ananiah agrees.

I feel alone, but I'm suddenly determined to tell Sadiq the truth behind this long journey. "I'm not staying here," I say.

"What are you talking about?" asks Sadiq.

"I mean what I say. I didn't come here to be closed up against my will and wonder how we're going to survive tomorrow."

"Arena," Father Joseph calmly addresses.

Sadiq slowly wanders closer, now irritated. "What did you expect?"

"Honestly? Not a damn thing. Look, I'm grateful for your service and your protection. I just know that I can't stay here, and they know it too." I point to the others.

"Whatever it is you're harboring, I suggest you follow your friends and sleep it off until the morning."

"I can't sleep anymore."

"Well, I suggest you try, because no one leaves here tonight."

Rational thoughts absolved, I briefly retreat from the conversation, as I have now become less motivated by it and more irritated by Sadiq's subtle threat. I slowly clutch the handle of my knife. "And is that your decision?" I tease.

Jacob quickly stages his body between us and gently places his hand on my shoulder. "Arena, we can discuss this in the morning, okay?" he submits. While I understand Jacob's attempt to diffuse the disagreement, my frustration grows. I pull my knife and raise it. Jacob's eyes grow wide.

"Where are you gonna go?" Sadiq asks nonchalantly.

Ananiah turns to me and calmly advises, "Arena, just wait a minute—"

"No, it begs to be said. To find my brother, the real reason I'm here. And unless you and your men are willing to help me, I'm not going to stay here another minute while my brother rots in a prison in Cairo."

"Well, then you definitely don't want to go wandering off there alone."

"I'm not afraid."

"And that's what's going to get you killed. Cairo isn't a pleasant journey, I assure you."

"I'll take my chances."

"You'll die before you even reach it."

"Then I'll die trying!"

"And if you do, then what hope does your brother truly have? You step with no caution in a storm, not a care in the world. Is this the way we've all come to expect from you?" Sadiq questions.

My eyes wander around the group until they are met by Jacob's stare. I realize in this moment that I may have truly lost my way, but deep inside there is truth waiting to purge.

I stand a little straighter, feeling defiant. "You have a destiny just like everyone else. Before you were born, God knew exactly what was to come of you. Some may accept it, few embrace it, but then there are those who are willing to live it no matter the cost. Most people couldn't care less how their life will play out in the end, but the fact is, every little thing we do or say affects something or someone. So it's not a question of whether I care or not; it's a question if I know it. Well, I know my fate, and I know my brother is supposed to be a part of it."

"Do you want my help?" Sadiq asks sincerely. Before this thing metastasizes out of control, I lower my knife and tuck it back into its sheath. The anger trembling throughout my body has taken me captive, but I'm able to tame it . . . for now. Sadiq opens his hands out to his side as a sign of trust and peers deep into my eyes. "Then you have to trust me."

I'm not sure if I can trust anyone anymore, but in this brief and quiet exchange, my heart listens. "Fine, tomorrow, but not another day can I stay here. I will leave with or without you."

CHAPTER 14

The next morning, I awake from a deep sleep, feeling more rested than I thought. And happy. Jacob was lying in the bed next to me, and I almost cried from joy. Then Father Joseph barged in and I've never felt so embarrassed in my life. I was fully clothed and nothing happened, but I felt like I had just been caught by my father in a compromising position, and I almost mourn the idea of these awkward father-daughter moments. Still, it was embarrassing.

The lobby is practically empty except for a couple of kids playing in the corner with a tin-foil ball. I have no idea where everyone else has gone. Outside, the dark gray sky puts a damper on my mood.

"She's up," Father Joseph announces mysteriously as he enters the lobby, and my cheeks burn with embarrassment.

Carrying my swords, Sadiq enters the lobby from the hall, his face expressionless. "I believe these belong to you," he says.

"Thanks."

"Decided to wake up, I see," he says.

"Why is everyone saying that? How long have I been out?" I ask in annoyance.

"About eighteen hours, dear," Father Joseph gently admits.

"What?" I'm slightly disoriented and not sure how to respond. Either that or my anger has been displaced from the long rest.

"We're ready," Sadiq addresses Jacob.

"Ready for what?" I ask. The surprise in Father Joseph's eyes leads me to believe that I've been excluded from a discussion that's apparently already happened.

"I haven't told her yet," Jacob answers.

"Tell me what?"

"It's time to go get your brother," Father Joseph earnestly replies.

"Well, thanks for informing me of my own plan. Next time I'll just stay awake. Apparently, I'm not important enough—"

"You needed the rest, Arena."

Admittedly, the sleep felt nice, but I'm irritated that they let me sleep for that long.

"Ever since we left the port, you've been consistently justifying your reasons for leaving, and no one close to you has questioned your decisions," Father Joseph says. "But you have to understand, there's a heavy responsibility placed on you for that. That's why we trust you, because you have no fear of it. That is a divine insight we don't have the ability to understand. You've made these choices, not because we asked you to, but because we believe in you."

"The lack of sleep has not made me weak, if that's what you're implying," I huff.

"Your strength is not the issue, Arena," Father Joseph almost shouts, and everyone seems shocked by his sudden outburst. He continues, "It's clarity we need from you. The mind is a curious thing when it's distracted, and you are no different. No one here is trying to keep anything from you. You, of all people, should know that by now. We're all here to protect you."

That sharp sting that pierces through me is a blemished ego. I'm disappointed in myself for not recognizing indifference from sympathy, my reprehensible arrogance notwithstanding of course. Father Joseph, my trusted companion, is right.

"I know I can be a bit moody at times," I say. Sadiq's brows arch, Father Joseph's eyes roll, and Jacob looks away. "Okay, a lot moody. Let's not get carried away now. Look, the fact of the matter is that I sometimes forget who I am among company. It's not intentional, I assure you, just imperfection. But I want you to know that I would never sell your loyalty to gain an affordable advance. We're all in this together now, and we're in too deep. I may have brought you here, but it doesn't mean I'm going to leave you. I just want my brother back."

Sadiq loads a fresh mag into his gun, hands me my dagger, and artlessly asserts, "Then let's go get him."

Part II

The Rescue

CHAPTER 15

Just outside the lobby doors, about a half-dozen of Sadiq's men stand with guns raised. As the doors open, Juliana, Kale, Nadia, and Ananiah surface from outside, each holding a firearm. Seeing Juliana with a gun isn't comforting, but my instinctive reaction to question her motives is kept quiet. She pulls back the slide to chamber a round before placing the gun into her holster. I know I could never talk her out of going with us, and I don't mean to. Her devoted sacrifice to find Gabe is inexorable whether she dies or not, and that I painfully understand.

Henry ambles in from the dark hallway toting two assault rifles that are dangling from each shoulder. His stony face glares with heated urgency as he walks over to Father Joseph. He has the expression of a warrior planning for battle. What happens next takes me by surprise: Henry hands one of the rifles to Father Joseph, who eagerly accepts it. Father Joseph has a disturbing look on his face—one of enthusiasm for holding a deadly weapon—and he embraces the stock of the gun, caresses the barrel jacket, and slides the chamber back like a professional.

"Uh . . . Father?" I stammer.

"Yes?" he says nonchalantly.

"What are you doing?"

"You really think for one moment I'm going to leave your sight again?"

"Well . . . no, but—"

"But what?" He looks up at me and I'm taken aback by the fire in his eyes. The sudden transformation from a holy man to a killer is baffling.

"You . . . have a gun in your hands."

"Well, aren't you perceptive," he concedes sarcastically.

"But—"

"Well, I wasn't always a priest, my dear." He winks. Words trip over my tongue, trying to engage an audible sentence, but I'm speechless.

Father Joseph chuckles. "What? Surely Finnegan shared a story or two about my past."

I'm shocked by this unfolded layer from his earlier life, and I attempt to untangle my mumbling mouth. "I think we need to talk . . ."

"I'm coming too," Caspar chimes in. His smug grin grates on my nerves. "You know you want me to come, sweetheart," he crows arrogantly. If he wasn't here to offer his life, I would punch him in the gut.

"Fine, but I suggest you wipe that damn smirk off your face. I'm in no mood to tolerate any of your advances."

"Calm down, honey, don't flatter yourself."

"Don't push it," I coolly advise.

Just behind the corner of the front desk counter Niki is staring at me, but it's not her face that grieves me. Luke is clinging to her leg, smiling bashfully, innocently unaware of my impending departure. Allison stands next to him softly crying. The time has come for us to sever our friendship for now, and I can only hope that they will understand my decision later.

"Arena," Allison whimpers. I walk over to the children, desperately seeking for courage to walk away from this parting unchanged, but my heart just won't allow it. I'm eternally a part of them no matter where I go.

I bury my emotions deep inside as I avoid making eye contact with Allison. It's a struggle to swallow pride that would otherwise make me break in front of the entire group, but I know who I really am: an ordinary girl with extraordinary feelings. No matter how this ends, pain will not escape me.

Allison hides her face into my chest, soaking up the endless tears, while Luke grabs Allison's arm and tries to comforts her. I peer forlornly into Niki's eyes, and, strangely, a part of Myra stares back.

"Well, sister, once again we part our ways," Niki laments.

"I don't mean to leave you like this," I say, choking back tears.

"Arena, I understand," she acknowledges gracefully. "It was meant to be this way."

"I wouldn't just leave these children alone with anyone. You know I trust you to take care of them for me."

"And what of me, am I not trustworthy?" Harold interrupts cheerfully.

"And I trust you to take care of this beautiful woman." I smile at him.

"I offer you my allegiance, you know that. I would leave—"

"I know you would, Harold, but your fate has drawn you here to be with Niki and the kids." Harold's eyes glow with loyalty. His place is here, but deep inside he knows I would want him by my side if it weren't for Niki. That is a devotion he, Gabe, and I share that will not sever, even if we are apart. Special bonds that come from unexpected friendships last forever.

With Allison's head still tucked into my jacket, I can't help but notice Juliana sitting all alone and gazing at our exchange. Her face is still, but I recognize a striking determination hidden beneath. It's almost catatonic, struggling to resurface to reality. Either she's scared beyond what lies ahead, or her conscience has preemptively left her in disarray. It has become more than just concern to see her in this light. I worry for her emotional state on this journey now.

I give the children and Niki one last hug. "I'll see you all in Jerusalem soon." I keep my eyes fixed on Juliana and nod in her direction, but she barely acknowledges me.

"Father?" I quietly ask as I carefully pull him aside. "I want you to keep an eye on Juliana for me, no matter what."

"She doesn't seem herself anymore, that's for sure," he confesses.

"With this drastic change in her demeanor, I'm afraid she might do something foolish. Her vacant stare speaks volumes."

"I'll try and keep her safe. And what of you?"

"I'm not asking you to risk your life for me. My fate has already been written."

"Be it that, lass. I made a promise to protect you."

"I know I can't stop you from looking after me, but promise me you'll stay with Juliana should it worry you to protect us both when the time comes."

"When the time comes I won't have to. That's in God's hands now, but I will guard you both regardless."

"You really think you can keep two stubborn women under your wings?" I retort playfully.

Father Joseph's brows may arch with pondering reflection, but his answer is as sharp as my blade. "A fool's task admittedly, but I'll do my best nonetheless." He smiles.

I look at the group standing before me with unease. What I should come to expect from this newly formed fellowship is hope, but the reality saddens me to know that this group will probably shrink before we even reach Cairo.

My eyes blur, but I'm not crying, and a sudden sinking feeling fills my gut. I close my eyes and see an image of Nadia holding a child wrapped in a shroud of blankets. I hear her faint voice lament, but I do not know what she says. The distortion around her body keeps me from seeing where she is. A blur subtly moves past her, an apparition perhaps. Her voice grows louder, but her image immediately vanishes and she's now standing in front of me.

"Hey, Arena, are you okay?" she asks, shaking my shoulder.

"What?" I ask a bit addled.

"Are you okay? You look like you've just seen a ghost."

"No," I say, still struck in a daze. "I mean . . . yes, I'm fine." I snap back to reality. I look back at the children briefly.

"I wouldn't worry, Niki is a strong woman. The children will be safer here anyhow, which is far more than I can say for ourselves," Nadia says.

"Do you think what I'm doing is right? I mean, do you think this is right for everyone?"

"I can't speak for everyone, but if it were my brother, I would do the same."

"And I would have gone with you."

"I know, that's why I'm here." Nadia smiles.

"And the rest?"

"They're free to make their own choices."

"All right, everyone, listen up," Sadiq calls out, and the group quiets down. "It's important we stay together when we leave here. We've got a four-and-a-half-mile jaunt on foot, and I expect it to be anything but easy. I suggest you double-check your packs, because once we leave the perimeter, we're not coming back."

"So what's this plan of yours?" I ask.

"I was beginning to think you've lost your sense of curiosity." Sadiq holds up a small metal ring with two keys dangling from it.

"What's that?"

"The keys to our escape, my dear. About three weeks ago, when things began to settle down, I had a company of men scout the city in the hopes that they would find an alternative means out of here."

"Alternative?" I curiously inquire.

"Since the EMP strikes, every vehicle has been disabled. Fully fueled, mind you, but no working electronics to start the damn things. We found ourselves wondering if we would ever leave this place, except on foot."

"I guess we created our own downfall."

"Well, aside from being cursed by technology, yes, but there's always an alternative to even the most problematic situation," Sadiq says.

"And you have one?" I ask.

"Two to be exact." Sadiq pauses and throws the keys to one of his men. "Just across the city near the airport sit two fully fueled Russian armored vehicles ready to deploy."

"How did you manage that?" I ask, shocked.

"Oh, it wasn't easy, lass, but with a little Israeli ingenuity, some copper wire, and a few working fuel-cell batteries, we were able to breathe a bit of life back into them. The Russians may be advanced in technology, but even they realize simplicity wins survival. The little electronics used on these vehicles are so minimal, not much effected them."

"So why did you leave them stranded?" Jacob asks.

Sadiq's brief silence hardens before he answers. "We were being attacked before we could finish attaching the battery on the second truck. A few Russian soldiers came barreling through the fence in full assault on one side while civilians were strangely attacking from the other. To be quite honest, I don't know if the civilians knew who we were. They ran like madmen, crazed with a raging desire to kill."

"Stringers?" Jacob asks. Sadiq doesn't answer, but it's obvious that Jacob's assumptions are correct.

"Whatever they've become, they're not the same anymore, and I don't really think their minds allow them to care either way," Sadiq says.

"Did you kill them?" I cautiously ask.

"I guess they just assumed we were the enemy with our guns firing. They could have thought we were Russian soldiers, but I don't think it would have mattered. We fired, yet they kept storming, so we were forced to retreat into the city with the keys in hand waiting to recoup. After a few weeks, we vacillated around the idea of returning to the trucks. That's when you showed up unexpectedly, and for a purpose I see now. Those keys are our ticket out of here and the fastest way to get you to Cairo."

"And what about the others? How are they to reach the Israeli border, much less out of this city alive?" I ask.

"Ananiah," Sadiq addresses.

Ananiah nods his head. "We've discussed a few options should you reach Cairo—"

"We'll reach it," I assert.

"*When* you reach Cairo," Ananiah corrects himself, "you'll find a man named Darwishi Mubarak. He's the artifacts directorate for the Museum of Egyptian Antiquities."

"And how's that supposed to help us?"

"He's also our inside man for the *Mukhabarat el-Khabeya*," Ananiah says.

"Egypt's military intelligence service," Sadiq explains.

"Israel has been preparing for such a war that's taking place, even the launch of Project X9. Our Israeli military research division spent two years designing a survival vehicle that would sustain an EMP burst, and they succeeded. We built a fleet of armored buses for transporting our people if we ever needed to flee. They have been inactively waiting in an underground bunker for the past two years, about fifteen miles just south of Cairo. You find Mubarak, and he will find a way to get these people across the border unscathed, I assure you."

"Can we trust him?" I ask.

"He's a valuable ally. Besides, he's my brother-in-law. But if you suspect any problems with him, which I don't foresee, just let him know that you will tell my sister he's been cheating on her. He's scared to death of her, trust me, I am too." Ananiah smiles.

"Well, it's good you've thought this through . . . I think. But why don't you just tell him yourself? You act is if you're not going with us."

"I'm not."

"What?"

"I've been with this group through thick and thin, and with Jacob leaving, I figure I need to be here to shepherd these people." I glance over to Luke, Allison, and Niki.

"Don't worry, I'll look after them and make sure they get on the busses safely," Ananiah assures.

I look at Ananiah as I did with Finnegan—like a father. I want to believe everything is going to be okay, but sadness disperses when I turn from him. Could this be the last time I ever see him?

"Okay, everyone, get your gear ready and keep your eyes peeled. Once we leave the perimeter past the northern tower, we'll be entering the outer zone," Sadiq says.

"And what's out there?" Jacob wonders.

"An unpleasant view," Caspar remarks.

"This is not to be taken lightly, my friend," Sadiq warns.

"What should we expect?" asks Father Joseph.

"Let's just say you don't want to go wandering off without backup," Sadiq suggests.

Sadiq pulls out an old yellowed map of the city and lays it over one of the tall tables in the front lobby.

"We're here." Sadiq draws a half-circle in red marker around our current location and divides the rest of the map into three sections. "The outer zone is made up into three separate zones. From what we can tell, the northeastern section has been our safest route. Much of our supplies came from there, but there's really nothing left to scavenge. Most, if not all, has been stripped. It's a long travel on foot and it won't get us any closer to where we need to go. The east or middle section was where the Russian's set camp before the lights were turned out. This is where most of the turmoil occurred — the heart of the war that killed most of my men. The Russians fled after the second ground attack. That's when the last of the EMPs were launched."

"How do we know if all of the Russians left?" I ask.

"We don't," Sadiq simply states.

"And the third section?" Henry probes, but Sadiq dithers to answer. His face looks worn and troubled.

"Stringers?" I offer, and Sadiq nods. My insides feel numb. Not that I would let anything stop me from getting to my brother, but to see a soldier of Sadiq's caliber disquietly shudder frightens me just a little.

"Stringers have been seen around the entire border, but we believe most of them concentrate along this section," Sadiq says, pointing on the map.

"So where is our destination?" Caspar nervously asks.

Sadiq carefully draws a red dot near the middle of the third section.

"You've got to be shitting me!" Caspar yells. "You're telling me that we gotta go through there with all those . . . those *cannibals*?"

"They were people just like you and me," I shrewdly correct.

"Honey, 'cannibals' may be objectionable, but they sure as hell aren't like you and me," Caspar states.

"I'll gladly take my chances with them than spend another winking moment beside you."

"Hey, it comes with the territory, sweetheart, so get used to it," Caspar scoffs.

Unamused, Jacob quickly springs between our stroppy exchange before it escalates. "We gonna have problem here?"

"Keep your girl on a leash and we'll be just fine," Caspar snaps nastily.

I draw my knife and lunge forward in a raging fit, but Jacob and Henry hold me back.

"Jesus, Arena!" Caspar barks.

"Say one more belligerent comment and I'll cut your tongue from your mouth," I seethe.

"Arena, don't," Father Joseph urges. I withdraw my anger temporarily, but not without a tempered eye planted staidly on Caspar's distressed face.

"I'm risking my own neck to help you find your brother. Threatening me like this isn't going to help your case," Caspar says.

"I agree. Aside from Caspar's stupidity, animosity will tear this group apart," advises Sadiq wisely.

"Fine. You just watch yourself," I warn Caspar.

"All right, let's gear up before the shadows become our enemy."

I sheath my swords, string my bow, and peek outside the lobby door, feeling nearly discouraged to move on. If not for two little warm hands grabbing my arm, I would feel almost empty leaving here.

"Here, take this with you . . . for good luck," Allison offers. It's Grace's bracelet.

"Thanks, I'll be sure to return it when I see you again."

"You promise?"

"I promise. Cross my heart and hope to—" Allison gives me one last hug. My heart shrivels, but her love is enough to give me some hope that I will find my brother.

CHAPTER 16

We stay close together in a two-by-two formation within the perimeter before we cross into the outer zone. Just in front of us, nearly in ruin, there's a battered building with two brass bells still hanging from the top of its perch, exactly as Sadiq described. While the northern tower stands in derelict, the streets around us lay in waste, peppered with abandoned cars and a few rotting bodies, but none that can be identified. They've been mutilated beyond recognition, some with limbs completely missing. The odor is relentless. You would think I would be used to this by now.

Nadia silently walks next to me, while I keep a patrolling eye on Caspar who paces five yards ahead of us. "You scared?" Nadia whispers.

"Well, my heart isn't exactly calm."

"I'm not sure it's a good idea we have Caspar taking point."

"Oh, don't worry, I've got my eye on him."

"You sure about that?" Nadia presses. I look up and suddenly Caspar is nearly out of my sight, running like a madman.

"What the hell is he doing?" I shout. Nadia and I run after him, but when we clear the next street, he's gone.

"Just perfect, now we have another idiot on the loose . . . with a gun."

Suddenly, a short burst of shots fire, loud and rapid. It's hard to determine where it's coming from. The shots echo against the empty buildings. I frantically scan the west side street until I see a muzzle flash from within a darkened alley to our right. It's Caspar flailing the gun all over, shooting at the air like a deranged man.

"Caspar!" I shout. He calmly walks out of the alley, eyes widened. "What the hell are you shooting at?" My hands are shaking with anger at his stupidity.

"I don't know . . . I thought I saw something. Something startled me."

"Something or someone?" I demand. I feel close to losing it.

"I'm not sure, but I think it's gone."

"You think?" I take a deep breath and count to ten.

Okay, I'm trying desperately to calm myself, but this idiot is really making it difficult right now. If not for Father Joseph, I'd yank the gun from Caspar's hands before he gets us all killed.

"There's no need to fire your weapon if you don't know what you're shooting at, especially as erratic as you were," I lightly but sharply advise. "What kind of gun are you toting anyway?"

"One of Sadiq's men nabbed it off a dead Russian major." Caspar holds it up proudly. "Why, you like it?"

"Not especially," I say, disinterested.

"Best gun ever made," he says with a smile. "It's a military-issued Russian AK-30. Gas-operated long-stroke piston set up with a sixty-round quad-stack magazine, fully automatic with a one-thousand-round per-minute short burst. Light-weight counter-balance stock recoil for better control," he brags.

"Control must be an anomaly for you then."

"It's the most accurate assault rifle ever designed. The Russians know what they're doing."

"Yeah, well Russians aside, its accuracy is not what troubles me; it's the man operating it that scares me." I glare at him. Dumbfounded by my obvious insult, he searches around as if I'm talking about someone else. This man is an egotistical piece of work.

"I know how to handle my weapon," he sneers.

"Then take it off burst or you're going to get us all killed."

Jacob walks over and breaks up another potentially threatening escalation. "Everybody okay?"

"What's going on here? Who's doing all the shooting?" Sadiq rushes over.

"We got us a grown man with baby hands trying to steer a tractor," I snap. Insulted, Caspar springs at me, but Sadiq and Jacob hold him back.

"Stop it! This fighting isn't going to get us anywhere. Caspar, take the gun off burst and don't fire another round until you're told. This isn't exactly territory we want to freely expose ourselves in."

"Fine, but I'll still take point—"

"The hell you will. You can take your grizzly ass back to the rear," I say.

"I didn't tag along to take orders from you." Caspar gets all up in my face.

His face is inches from mine and I stand a little straighter. "You'll take 'em or I'll shove that barrel straight up your ass."

"Arena!" Sadiq shouts. "That's enough. Caspar, you'll be better suited watching our back while Jacob and I scour up ahead, okay?"

Caspar's blistering eyes waver with discontent before he decides to heed Sadiq's advice. "Fine," he agrees with slight dejection. His face shifts with a haughty derision as he walks away dragging a bit of humiliation with him. I almost feel bad for the guy . . . almost.

"You must really despise this man to enjoy undermining him like this," says Sadiq.

"I assure you, there is no joy in any of it. If he wants to survive, then he needs to learn to live with the reality around him. I'm not here to babysit his insecurities."

"Then I suggest to manage your own," Sadiq warns, and I'm slightly shocked by his response.

"Really?" I cross my arms, trying to suppress my hot anger. "Look, I didn't ask for you to come. And I sure in the hell didn't opt for that bumbling idiot to tag along. Call it what you want, but I'm here to do one thing: keep us alive. If he should die a prideful man, then so be it, but I have no allusions of what I've become."

"And you can live with that?" Sadiq asks.

"I'll have to die with it."

"Fine, but next time try learning to be a bit more diplomatic. You may find that it will ease us all just a little," Sadiq sternly suggests.

"Diplomacy isn't in my nature anymore."

"Well, you better start making it, because we're going to need it when it counts."

"Look around you," I sweep my arm, "this is the result of your precious diplomacy when it counted the most. But if it should exist, I'll be sure to exercise it for you." I glance over to Jacob's disapproving expression before I storm away feeling a bit belittled.

The last hour is an arduous walk around barricades, a wreckage of vehicles, and lonely streets, all the while trying to discreetly keep ourselves from being exposed to whatever the hell awaits for us in the shadows.

My feet hurt, my back aches, and my ego is beginning to bruise a little from Sadiq's comments. I wish I wouldn't have let my temper get the best of me, but men like Caspar—their defiance, their machismo—always set me off. Jacob paces closely behind me, and I can feel his eyes watching my every step. His chivalrous charge is amorous, but it's really more than I deserve from him. He nudges next to me and smiles.

"My lips miss you," he whispers.

"I hardly think this is the time," I utter musingly.

"They miss you nonetheless." If it weren't so dark out here, he would see me blushing, which is much less than I can say for Nadia's mirthless eye roll.

The silence grows eerier and night quickly falls upon us, but Jacob's playful affection keeps me from worrying. Though my fondness rests deep within him, I've grown far beyond just affection. I'm bound to him in a way I can never undo until my last days, which sadly doesn't seem so far away.

The moon rises behind the dark clouds when suddenly I feel a small tremble below my feet. I immediately stop.

"What's wrong?" Nadia worries.

"Did you feel that?"

"Feel what?" asks Jacob.

Again the ground trembles around us. The subtle vibration bends a small reflection of light shimmering from the glass window on the building just to the right of us.

"Okay, I felt it that time," admits Jacob. Both he and Nadia draw their guns, aiming into the shadows. I've never felt so defenseless. It feels like we're being hunted. The rest of the group catches up to us, but they don't look too eager to move on.

"What's going on?" Sadiq worriedly asks.

"Shhhh . . . listen," I caution. "Something is out here with us."

"All I hear is silence," pipes Caspar.

"Yeah, well, it may sound quiet, but I promise you nothing is as it seems around here," Sadiq assures.

Suddenly, a hellish beastly roar fills the air and the buildings to the left of us begin to shake. My bones shudder and my palms sweat. "Now what the hell was that?" I manage to choke out.

"I hate to retort with ambiguity, but that is not a familiar sound," Sadiq says.

The deathly silence after the horrible roar is nerve-racking if not for the call of the wild hiding in the dark waiting to take our heads.

"We're not alone anymore," I whisper.

Like statues, our feet are frozen to the street, waiting to spree safely from the likes of this mysterious and hungry growl. Suddenly, a dark image moves past my eyes, then vanishes between the buildings.

"Did you see that?" I fret.

"See what?" Jacob asks.

I stare toward the alley to my left. "There it goes again."

Something moves stealthily across the ragged back-street, but it does not show itself. Whatever it is, it coolly cowers in the shadow.

"I don't like this." Juliana frightfully shakes.

Henry cautiously steps forward and pierces into the darkened alley before he abruptly stops. A deep, shivering bass gurgles closely in the shade, and it doesn't sound like a friendly invite. "We're being watched," he observes.

"More like hunted," I object.

"I think right now would be good time to slowly move away from the street," advises Sadiq.

Subtlety isn't exactly in Caspar's personality. He clamors obtrusively before running like a deranged lunatic and ducking into one of the cars parked along the sidewalk. The rest of us scatter more discreetly to the other side of the street.

Just a few blocks ahead, shadows dance erratically against the broken buildings. A sudden tremble shakes the bulb loose from a lamppost. Glass shatters and the paved streets madly pound like the sound of a hundred soldiers scampering. I quickly draw my guns, adrenaline pumping, and wait anxiously by a trashcan ready to attack. When the light of the moon peeks from the waning clouds and reveals

the mysterious shadows, I slowly withdraw my guns, cowardly step back, and nearly piss myself.

"What . . . is . . . that?" Juliana fearfully mutters.

"Oh . . . shit. Run!" I shout.

From out of the dark, three rhinos charge with a vengeance down the barricaded street.

CHAPTER 17

Terrified beyond my control, I stumble and hastily sprint to the nearest building. Juliana clings next to me while everyone else scatters. Jacob races from across the street shouting, "Arena!"

My heart races and lungs burn as I quickly scurry the streets for an open door. Debris flies, the earth rumbles, and suddenly Jacob is nowhere in sight.

I scream his name, but there's no answer. I'm completely discombobulated. *Where did he go?*

I yank on the doors, desperate to flee inside, but they won't budge. All the doors are locked or boarded up. I try breaking through the glass, but it's too thick and too late. The charging beasts gain ground, leaving us stranded and picked to be gored. But that's the least of our worries now. An angry lion leaps out from behind the alley on the other side of the street to greet us with jaws wide open.

I grab Juliana, and we quickly retreat to the far side of the building into the next alley. The lion's growl deepens as I shoot aimlessly in the dark behind me. I don't look back, hoping I've at least wounded the hungry beast, as we run straight ahead for cover. But the roar vengefully continues, pacing breathlessly on our heels. Not a limp from the frenzied cat as its paws pound wildly on the concrete and inches closer.

I race side by side with Juliana through the backstreets. Nadia calls in the distance behind me, but I'm too afraid to look back. I can almost feel the lion's breath on the back of my neck. Then the shadows lift between the buildings. My heart sinks as our improbable escape is about to end. A fence blocks our path up ahead. I quickly shove Juliana into the alleyway where the street begins to narrow.

The large hungry cat swipes at my ankles as I turn into the alley, and I lose my balance. I reach for the side of the building, my hand sliding against the gritty wall like sandpaper, as I nearly slip face-first. Juliana screams, the lion roars, and out of nowhere we are tackled from the side.

I struggle to reach my knife, not waiting to be eaten alive, but instead find myself entangled with a man who is sitting on top of me ready to gouge me with a jagged piece of metal. His scar-covered face crinkles, revealing his gnarled teeth. He angrily draws the metal to my face, and I try to kick him off, but the haggard man is too heavy.

"Juliana!" I scream. She's too dazed from the fall to answer. I free my hand and reach for my gun, but I'm too late. The hungry lion lunges at the man's neck, sinks his teeth in, and nearly rips his head off with one bite. Within seconds, the lion chomps in a raging fit, cracking bones and tearing flesh. His incisors rip chunks of meat from the man's shoulders and back until his spine protrudes from his skin.

I draw my guns toward the beast, but he's too enthralled with his dinner to even care. I cautiously back away, pick up Juliana by the arm, and quietly leave the lion to his eating frenzy.

We make our way safely around the edge of the building when two shadows dance across us. Grunts and groans accompany the flickering silhouettes. I rush around the corner, knife in hand, where I find Jacob struggling with a crazed man. I quickly lunge forward and thrust the blade deep into the madman. He falls, twitching on the ground into a feverish seizure.

"Where are the others?" Juliana worries.

Panting with exhaustion, Jacob answers, "I don't know. I turned around and everybody had vanished." Frozen with fear, I hover over the grisly man, startled and numb. "He jumped on me from out of nowhere," Jacob continues out of breath. So these were the stringers Sadiq told us about.

I feel temporarily poised to move until the sudden familiar growl echoes behind me and sprints from the alley toward us. I'm not sure what more I'm afraid of: two-legged raging stringers, or a four-legged hungry lion ready to tear me into bloody pieces.

Through the side streets we race without stopping. The stinging cramp in my side pends me to slow, but I'm much too afraid to stop. Building after building passes in a blur of escaping desperation until the alley ends back into the main street. Breath burning and heart pounding, I draw my guns and prepare for another stringer ambush, but instead we are harmlessly greeted by a woman who's holding a baby in the middle of the street.

Startled by her presence, I hold still in a sedated suspense and slowly put my guns away. Jacob and Juliana run to the nearest building with its front door unhinged. Caspar comes running up the street shouting my name hysterically. I can't seem to move, as I'm almost transfixed on this poor woman.

"Arena, come on!" Jacob shouts. I'm too dismayed to leave the woman like this, all alone and with a baby no less. Her grime-covered face is riddled with a sadness that doesn't compare to the suffering that covers the rest of her scarred body. With sunken cheeks and sallow eyes, she stares at me almost possessed. I approach her with caution.

"Arena, what are you doing? They're coming!" Jacob yells from the sidewalk. The ground suddenly trembles, but I can't leave this woman or her baby.

"Come with us and you'll be safe," I quickly offer. The sudden return of a trampling rhino charges down the street, but she doesn't budge. "We don't have much time, come on!" I say assertively.

A strange surly smile develops on her face, but not without the unexpected hostility that follows. She reaches behind her back and draws a nine-inch blade. She pulls the baby away from her pallid skin, and an immediate sickness casts over me. A decomposed infant is wrapped in a bloody blanket. I've been deceived by her trickery.

She growls at me like a savage and swings the knife across my face. I quickly step back, draw my sword, and decapitate her.

"Arena, to your left!" Juliana screams.

Not one, but two ferocious lions pace violently on top of a car about twenty yards away ready to pounce. With the rhinos now close enough to gore me, I'm left with no choice but to run like hell.

No surprise, the lions quickly chase after me. My heart pumps in unison with my sprinting feet. Jacob rushes out to meet me with guns drawn, when out of nowhere a gorilla jumps from the roof and shoves him to the ground.

Juliana screams and now two more stringers storm from the alley in a raging fit. I shoot relentlessly in a blaze of fury. The two men crash to the street where I leave the chasing lions to feast on their bodies. The gunfire immediately scares off the gorilla, but it doesn't startle the lions from finishing their meal. Juliana shoots near the charging rhinos, but they stay their course thrusting ahead. Frightened, she scampers back into the building with Caspar following. Slightly disoriented, Jacob dizzily stands to his feet. I rush and pull him into the open building, giving us a small window to retreat unscathed.

The rhinos flank to the right side of the adjoining building, where their pounding feet stomp safely away down the street. We quickly push a small table against the unhinged door, barricading the entrance from our not-so-friendly felines.

There we sit leaning on one another in the quiet dusty room filled with nothing but darkness—an old restaurant that not too long ago was filled with liveliness is now bleak and lonely. It smells musty and sour, but it gives us time to catch our breath before we find the others. Without a crass comment, Caspar sits quietly next to Juliana. Fear has consumed him, as it has for all of us.

The eerie silence wastes away, but it soon opens up to an uninviting sound I'm all too familiar with—the painful hunger stirring in my gut. I've been too troubled to eat anything in the last day.

"You hungry too?" Jacob playfully asks. Juliana and Caspar smile.

"I could go for some roast and potatoes right about now," I truthfully admit. The growl in the pit of my stomach has humorously given us a rare moment of peace. Wherever the others may be, I can only hope they have found a place of refuge like us. It's so quiet, I can hear my heart beating against my chest. The deep hungering moan rattles again, but this time it's not coming from me.

"Please tell me that was your stomach," I whisper nervously to Jacob.

"No." He shrugs.

"Well, it's not mine," Caspar says.

"Don't look at me, I ate before we left," Juliana assures.

Suddenly, the purring growl extends louder and deeper and it's not the mingling of our gut rousing with starvation. We're not alone. A new predator has joined our living nightmare. I hold my gun in one hand and my dagger in the other.

"Don't . . . move . . . a muscle," I quietly advise. A glass shatters on the floor behind us. I would shoot whatever is watching us, but it's too damn dark in here to see anything. A chair scrapes the floor to our left, then again to our right. Whatever the hell is in here, it knows we are too.

A soft rustling pans stealthily from side to side, like a rabbit brushing against tall grass. Its subtleties give me no clear direction from where this thing is coming from. I feel lost in the dark waiting to be devoured. I need some light.

The rustling briefly stops, but my anxiety unfortunately has not. The air is stale and still until a chair falls to the floor near the back of the room. Shadows move across my face. Then another. *What in holy God is in here with us?*

"Jacob," I softly whisper.

"What?"

"Give me your flashlight."

"I don't think it works."

He hands me the flashlight and I twist the nob on the end, but nothing happens. Like anything that doesn't work properly, I shake the hell out of it. I bang the head of the light against my palm again and again until it flickers with life. The light finally dims, but it stays lit long enough for me to raise it against the back of the room. My heart suddenly stops and gives way to a cold shiver.

"Oh . . . shit," Jacob gasps.

The room is filled with every kind of wildcat imaginable, a makeshift den for species that wouldn't normally commune together. Tigers, jaguars, leopards, and whatever other glowing eyes that stare at us prowl and pace from one end of the restaurant to the other. The big cats stalk our next move, while others lie lazily atop the tables.

I slowly back up to the front door waiting to make my exit. I'll gladly take my chances with two lions than this horde of pissed-off creatures. After all, we are the ones who came in uninvited.

"Move the table from the door," I softly order.

"Are you crazy, or did you forget about the lions out there?" Caspar recalls.

I glance through a slit in the boarded window. "They're gone, but you're welcome to stay in here with the rest of these guys if you wish," I whisper.

"No, I'm okay."

"Then I suggest we make ourselves scarce."

We slowly walk out of the restaurant and keep the door jarred from opening. The lions have vanished, leaving the streets quiet again momentarily. A ruckus behind the restaurant suddenly breaks out. Metal gashes, voices yell, and a slew of gunshots echo.

"Henry," I say, recognizing his voice among the skirmish.

We creep nimbly between the buildings toward the back. Hellish screams fill the air. I expect to be waylaid by a rhino or greeted by some other carnivore creature, but instead we are met by something much worse.

The dark alley fades and the moonlight draws light on a frightening scene. Two stringers scuffle with Henry, while a third tangles with one of Sadiq's men, but it's the carnage next to them that puts a crawl up my spine. One soldier has been cut up beyond recognition—ears, nose, and appendages have been ripped from his body. Another man dangles from a steel-girded awning. His macerated arm is wrapped with a piece of barbed wire that's tearing the skin from his limb.

"Henry!" I scream.

I fire angrily without ceasing until the stringers lie purged on the ground. I catch my breath, but then two more pop out, leaping from the roof, one of which tackles Caspar. Jacob fires, the stringer plunges, and Caspar rolls out from underneath him. Outnumbered, the other stringer scampers, but I gun him down before he retreats behind the building. Juliana lies still on the ground in shock. Henry kneels, exhausted, and everyone else bathes in terrifying silence. Not a word is uttered over the butchery except for an anguishing moan muttering from the mangled soldier. I race over and push the weight of his legs upward, but he's too heavy. Blood runs freely from his arm..

"Help!" I shout in desperation. Jacob quickly wraps his arms around the soldier's lower body and lifts. I draw my sword, push myself up on the battered foundation, and swing down as hard as I can. The barbed wire snaps and releases the soldier from an impending event.

Jacob untangles the wire from the man's maimed arm and presses his hand against the blood-gushing wound. Most of the skin is torn off, but he'll survive. I cut a piece of the man's pant leg off and tie it tightly around his arm. It's a shoddy tourniquet, but it'll have to do. He can hardly hold it up. Nerve and muscle tissue have been severely damaged and the shoulder has been pulled from its socket. His arm may have to be amputated later, but for now, this will have to do.

I cut some more fabric from his pant leg and craft a sling to rest his arm. The pain on his face is excruciating to watch. At least he still has his legs to sprint, which is what we should be doing right now to escape this hellhole.

"Where are the others?" I ask Henry.

"We got split up. Stringers came upon us from the south side of the bank. Father Joseph and Nadia fled up the street," he pants.

"And Sadiq?"

"I don't know."

"Arena, we need to move, now," Jacob swiftly suggests. Suddenly, not far behind us, a beastly roar sounds out followed by a wretched scream.

"That's enough for me!" Juliana agrees.

We make haste behind the string of abandoned buildings, exhausting our weary legs until we reach an opening that stretches vastly into a surprisingly different terrain. It's a beautifully displaced garden in the middle of a city in ruins — a paradise greenery of tropical infusion painted with tall royal palms and stone pines. Classical Greek and Roman concrete statues pepper the center while a massive villa made for a king blankets one side. It stands stately erect to a once-wealthy owner, a place now with memories that's as empty as its future. But I'll take this desolated green belt over what's behind us.

I feel a small sense of peace buried within the others as we cautiously move forward, but my stomach is anything but peaceful. I wonder what Father Joseph or Nadia would do in this situation.

"Wait," I urge them. They all look exhausted. "We can't just leave them."

"I'm not going back there," Caspar cowardly assures.

"I wouldn't expect anything else from you," I snap.

"Look, I agree with you, but we need to rest," Jacob offers.

"He's right, Arena, we can't go on like this," Henry adds.

"It'll be too late if we don't go now. We must go back," I plead.

"No," Jacob objects. "You do this now and it will be all for nothing. You're willing to risk everyone's lives here?"

I'm shocked he would say such a thing after knowing some stranger had risked his own life for him once. I briefly consider his argument before disappointment grows inside me.

"The only life being risked here is my own. I'm going back by myself," I say.

"Arena, wait, I didn't mean it like that." Jacob's eyes are tired. I ignore him and load a new magazine in my gun, but he stops me. "Arena, what is wrong with you?"

"They have risked their lives for me! I owe them."

His eyes stonily meet mine. "I'm not questioning your motives."

"Jacob, I love you."

"Then why are you doing this?"

"Would you not do the same if it were me out there?"

"That's not fair."

"Isn't it?"

"I have no intentions of leaving anybody behind. You should know that, Arena, but I'm not going to compromise these guys any more. Look at them, they can barely walk for Christ's sake."

"Then leave them to rest and come with me," I shout. He wearily searches my face, contemplating his options, but I can tell by his cold, ominous gaze that it's a feeling of regret.

He turns to the others and cocks his gun. "We'll be right back."

"What? Are you crazy?" Caspar protests.

"Apparently, one of us is. I guess it's contagious. Oh, and I wouldn't plan on leaving this area unless you are forced to. It may be our only hope to find you later."

He's right about one thing: sanity has left this place. Whether our chances are slim or not, I don't plan on leaving anyone here behind either, but if I'm going to die, at least I want it to be next to the man I love.

CHAPTER 18

We make our way back to the main road, but I can't remember which street we found Henry. It's dark and all the stone structures meld together. Our only saving grace is the tall bank building Henry spoke of. Its protruding roof peak and high-arch awnings stands noticeably in the forefront from the rest of the structures beneath it.

Aside from the flesh-tearing maniacs popping out of nowhere, my eyes are searching for the cunning four-legged creatures creeping in the shadows. Wherever they may be hiding, I ready myself this time, sword drawn and poise abiding. I can handle the darkness; the silence is what frightens me. I only hope this discomforting quiet is the result of lions lounging lazily elsewhere, stomachs bulging from gorging on dead stringers.

I'd rather not think of my friends being digested in the carnivorous bellies of those roaming beasts, though the disturbing thought has crossed my mind. This search is both wearing and discouraging, but I refuse to believe they are dead until I see their bodies.

The street is littered with piles of broken glass and immobile vehicles, none of which I see anyone hiding behind, unfortunately. The bank building to our left hovers majestically over the adjacent street and creates a dark path I'm not sure I'm willing to travel down. Instead, we trek cautiously to the backside where suddenly the roads are buckled and broken.

The curious sight of crinkled pavement is far less distressing than the immediate stench we're greeted with. Like a punch in the face, the scent of raw sewage flees into my nostrils and I'm forced to breathe in this malevolent odor through my mouth. I want to gag. Just around the corner, the sunken pavement has collapsed into the underground sewer tunnels. Blood is smeared on a concrete pillar next to the bank. We step cautiously along the recessed street, escaping to the edge of the sidewalk, and hoping not to fall in. Fending off this pungent stench is hard enough.

Jacob suddenly stops, bends down in front of a broken window, and dips his finger into a small puddle of blood on the sidewalk.

"Still warm," he confirms.

"They're close, maybe hiding in one of these buildings," I suggest.

"Don't get your hopes up. This may not even be their blood."

"We'll find them."

"And if we don't? What then?"

"Why do you give up on things so easily?" I ask.

He takes a step back, insulted. "I didn't give up on you." The reality in those words strike hard. I stand there briefly charmed, but my heart is disappointed in his lack of faith.

"Then you should know better." Of course he could be right. I'm just not as easily convinced.

"Okay, fine. We'll find them, and if we somehow make it out of here alive—"

"Somehow? Jacob, we're going to make it, trust me. Besides, I refuse to die here in this cesspool. It smells like the inside of a rhinoceros's ass."

"You see, that's why I love you."

"Because I smell like ass?"

"No, because I trust you. I always have. You can't just trust anyone in this world, and you're not just anyone," he says. My disappointment in him has just shriveled along with my will to resist such a beautiful moment at a time like this. Jacob continues, "Everything you have done up to this point has been about someone else. You sacrifice yourself for others when you don't have to. I admire that. Aside from your beauty, I can't think of better reason why I've fallen in love with you."

His valiant attempt of affection has just won me over and I don't give a damn what's trying to hunt us out here. The smell of sewer is an afterthought. I grab his waist and pull him close.

"I never thought being among refuse could be so romantic." Even now standing here above a flow of noxious gasses, I'm besotted with his words. My heart could warm over for him even on the dreariest of days. Whether this is the time to engage in playful affection or not, I couldn't care less.

"Our days are numbered here, Arena."

"They don't have to be."

"But you know it, don't you?"

I sigh in defeat. The truth harasses me. "So we make the best of what we have then," I say encouragingly.

"Have we really made the best for each other?"

"What are you getting at?" I take a step back.

"I've been thinking about this ever since we left the ship, and I'm not quite sure how to say it."

I cross my arms. "Then maybe you shouldn't." Nervous by his expression, I'm not sure I want to know.

"When we make it to Cairo, I think some changes are in order for us."

"What do you mean?" I ask, worried that I'm about to get my heart broken.

"Love can only hold so much if you're not willing to sacrifice for it."

"I think we've both had our share of sacrificing."

"Then why do I feel secluded from you?"

"Jacob, I never left you—"

"Then let's join together, for whatever days are left. If you truly love me, then let us at least enjoy what little time we have left in union. Take me."

"I have, I always have," I say, not understanding where this is going.

Jacob caresses the side of my face. "As your husband," he says more precisely.

My jaw unhinges, and suddenly the shadows clinging to me fade. Even the reeking stale air has vanished. I'm completely beside myself swimming in a vat of joy.

"Why, Jacob Edward Stokes, is that a proposal coming from your own lips?"

Jacob bashfully smiles. "I do believe it is, Miss Arena Danielle Power."

"Well, this is one to remember." I stroke the back of his hair and glue my lips to his.

After our embrace, Jacob says, "Well, is that a yes or no, or do you really enjoy seeing me suffer?"

Suddenly, a voice shouts from the adjacent street, fizzling my moment with Jacob. It's Nadia. Gunfire scatters, just grazing Jacob and me. The window beside me shatters, spraying shards of glass in the air.

I quickly plant myself behind a column and fire into the moving shadows. Two men race from the west side, assault rifles in hand, firing back. They're definitely not Sadiq's men, and I'm pretty sure they're not stringers either.

Nadia clings to the side of the building across the street. Our eyes meet briefly before she vanishes into the dark, screaming. The two soldiers split and flank to either side of us. In the still they wait before a mad rush of bullets fling down from the roof across the street. It's Sadiq. He gestures for us to run, but several stringers dash madly toward us. I peel off a couple of rounds into the raging mob before I plunge into the broken window, pulling Jacob with me. A shower of gunfire pelts the façade.

Without a caution, we sprint, stumbling over piles of rubble to the back of the darkened building. Suddenly, part of the left wall crumbles. Jacob brushes ahead of me, fires into the shadows, and kicks in the back door. I quickly evade to the right where my legs are greeted unmercifully to a broken chair tipped on its side. My gun slips from my grasp, and I trip face-first onto the dust-covered floor. I fight my way to get up when something violently pulls my leg. I look back in horror; a stringer is clawing at my ankles.

"Jacob!" I scream. I stretch for my gun, but the stringer drags me across the jagged floor. I struggle to reach my knife as I kick my boots in a frenzy toward his face, but the stringer doggedly fights back in a raging fit. I finally grab my blade, ready to throw, but it's too late. His grisly face catches a chasing bullet from Jacob's gun before his body falls limp to the floor.

I jump to my feet, grab my guns, and quickly leave this ragged place behind. We make haste behind the stony wall until we reach the next alley. It's barricaded. The gunfire ceases, but the quiet is shortly eclipsed as an egregious scream fills the air. "Nadia," I gasp.

I should have seen this coming. I hate myself for not acting when I saw her vanish in the alley. We rush down to the next side street. It's dark, but there's a small light at the end that makes me less nervous. The smell of animal waste and whatever else is rotting between these tall buildings makes my stomach churn.

We exit the slender alley, guns drawn and heart thumping. I aim my guns in opposite directions, firing prematurely into what I expected to be a mob of vicious maniacs, but instead we are met by a gruesome carnage of men lying feebly on the pavement, some still twitching, others struggling to move, sliding belly-down through their own blood like wounded dogs. We call them "stringers," but they are no more than just fragile men dying in a broken world.

We cross the street and find two more men lying dead near the sidewalk, but they are Russian soldiers, and hopefully the last two we'll see before we leave this wicked place. The corner of the building where Nadia was standing is empty, but her torment can be felt. Drops of blood speckle the sidewalk. Our feet shuffle softly across the ground in the alley. Gun raised, I step cautiously, one foot in front of the other, through the passage. Suddenly, a hollow clatter echoes between the stony walls, and a glass bottle rolls out from the darkness. I pend myself to the wall and raise my gun.

The quiet haunting step from behind the shaded street draws closer. My muscles stiffen, but my eyes cling sharply to the emerging shadow. I curl my finger tightly around the trigger while Jacob hugs the opposite side of the wall ready to charge. Then, out of the dark, the barrel of a rifle aims at my face.

"Arena?" a familiar voice mutters. I quickly release my finger from the trigger.

"Father Joseph," I sigh with relief. "Did you see Nadia?"

"No, Sadiq and I split up. He left just north of here looking for her."

Nadia's shrill cry echoes in the distance.

"Let's go!"

We rush through the alley, weaving and dogging around broken barricades until we exit onto a broader street. It's empty except for a pillar of smoke rising behind a corner drugstore. I swivel my head from one street to the other, searching for Nadia, but it's lonely and still.

We comb the sidewalks, leering into broken windows and vacant alleys, until the quiet abruptly ends. Nadia's voice cries out near the wafting smoke. Her hellish scream continues, leading us around the next block to a small tower of apartments set ablaze. Suddenly, a gun fires and the screaming ceases. My heart sinks.

A beastly growl roars as two figures whisk swiftly behind the apartments—one splitting to the left and the other bolting to the right. Jacob chases after one of the fleeing suspects while Father Joseph and I sprint in pursuit after the other.

Fleeing into the dark, my heart pounds in unison with every anxious step. My mind wonders what cruelty awaits us. Has Nadia's life come to a tragic end? I falter, trying to breathe as smoke and ash fill the sky. *Just run and don't stop,* I tell myself.

While the smoldering rooftop burns, so do my thoughts. I fight gruesome images of Nadia's body strung on the side of the building or left lying in the gutter waiting to be mauled. I can't wait any longer. My mind is fueled with harboring rage. Faster and faster my legs churn without ceasing. My breath shortens as the burning sting rises in my sides.

The brick façade brushes closely against my shoulder as the street begins to narrow, tunneling deep into a darkened avenue. Pitch-black, I stumble on the cobbled curb and lose my momentum. I clutch the side of the wall to regain my balance, but it has caused us to lose ground. Our assailant has now disappeared.

Nevertheless, I race side by side with Father Joseph, lurking blindly on this endless trail to nowhere. A rare breeze blows cool past my face and pushes the smoke upward from our eyes. The upper apartment floor creaks and flames lift from the corner of the building. A small glimpse into the end of this apartment building is in sight.

Gunshots echo and a horror of pain bellows, but it's not Nadia's cry this time. The familiar holler sinks deep into my crushing heart as I race to the edge, praying for another voice. But like a slow, dying pain, it feels like an eternity before I can reach the corner.

Suddenly, a flash of bursting heat explodes from the side of the building. Its fiery breath blazes out of control revealing two silhouettes in a fighting struggle and another hunched on the ground.

I round the corner, gunshots fire, and a man falls to the ground. Sadiq rushes from around the corner with his gun drawn. Nadia lies disquietly in front of the man's limp body. Her clothes are tattered and her lip bloodied from a struggle, but more gut-wrenching is what lies next to her.

Hopeless and abandoned, I feel my future slipping. My legs are immobile, my body shakes, and my heart spills onto the street. I hover over his body, which is face-down in a pool of red, before I'm brought down to my knees crying. I tremble with agony and defeat as I force myself not to believe.

This cannot be, this cannot be . . .

"Jacob!"

His jacket is riddled with bullet holes, and his skin is charred from the fire. I cannot turn him over to look upon his face. I ball my hands into fists and pound on his back, screaming.

"Arena!" Sadiq shouts.

Father Joseph reaches for my shoulder, but I angrily push him away, crying with an uncontrollable temper. I don't know what to do anymore. I'm completely lost. I pull out my gun and stare at the end of the barrel.

"Arena, wait!" Sadiq yells.

I reset the chamber.

"Arena, put the gun down," Father Joseph calmly begs.

For a brief moment, I tune out the chaos around me. I think of Gabe. I see his face. I hear his voice. But then lost hope consumes me and I'm convinced he's dead. My ears

close and the quiet ring of silence fills my head. It's almost .
. . *peaceful*. I just want to end this torment forever.

I shove the gun beneath my chin and for once, I am in complete control of my own life, suspended in shame and void of purpose. Nadia lunges to stop me, but I caress the trigger and squeeze . . .

CHAPTER 19

Silence is as agonizing as the pain that causes it. I must truly be dead to feel nothing. What dark realm have I escaped to? Without warning, my ears pop. Sound slowly creeps through the folds until a rumble both sharp and deep vibrates through my head. I'm not sure what's worse: being suspended in the discomforting quiet or tortured by this vibrating roar, which suddenly has made me nauseous. Either way, I've made a terrible mistake.

The noise grows louder, but it's not alone. Rising above the pulsating rattle, an unintelligible chatter mingles with it. Whatever evil lurks in here with me, I'm bound to its whispers now floating inside my head. I can almost feel the presence of something next to me, but I cannot see what haunts me on the other side of this darkness. I've lost my way, and to a deeper and greater tragedy — my faith. I've escaped one nightmare for another. *My God, what have I done?*

Whatever paralysis I'm under, it's wearing off. I feel my eyes move over the dark, but I struggle to open them, or I'm just too frightened to. Slowly the shadows of my lids lift. My eyes squint and though them a blur of faint light enters.

After a few seconds, they finally adjust, but I do not trust what I see. I've awoken to my own personal hell.

"Arena, Arena . . ."

What in the holy hell is happening to me? A fixture of my subconscious has finally snapped. Reaching out to me is Jacob's hand. His sweet, tender face neither bloody nor burned. I'm afraid this cruel nightmare will never leave me now. Even his delightful smile haunts me, and to further this

148

sick, twisted nightmare, he's dressed in a Russian military uniform.

Jacob reaches to touch my face, but I'm no fool. This is not real and I won't be tricked into believing it again. I push him back, just as I did with Myra's deceitful illusion, but my wrists are bound.

"Arena, it's me, Jacob."

My eyes widen and suddenly everything around me appears. I must be hallucinating. To my right sits Juliana, Caspar, and Nadia, their faces disheveled and worn. Father Joseph looks discouragingly at me, while Henry and Sadiq stare intently at me. My friends will never leave me now, even in my nightmares. My lips tremble and my mind breaks while tears run down my face. I've completely lost it.

"We made it, like you said," Jacob says.

"No!" I scream.

Nadia reaches out to me with shaky hands. "Honey, what you thought you saw isn't the—"

"Stop! Go away, go away! This isn't real. None of you . . . none of you are real. No, no, no!"

"Arena!" Father Joseph shouts.

I have no interests in listening anymore. It's all just a farce and all I can do now is suffer. Blood boiling and tears raining, I scream hysterically over their lies. An uncontrollable fire-breathing rage consumes me. I squirm relentlessly, kicking and twisting, but my body will not move from its anchored position. My head is dizzy. I try to free my wrists, writhing from the constricted ropes, but I can't. Like a fish out of water, I gasp for oxygen before all around me vanishes and I pass out.

It feels like an eternity that I have left my body, but only moments have passed before I hear the same voices speak over me as if I'm not there. I'm stuck in a hellish cycle, but this time I'm floating in the middle of a disagreeing conversation.

"Jacob, she's lost it. How are we supposed to trust her now?" Caspar says.

"She's in shock, not lost," Jacob says.

"Jesus, she thinks you're dead!"

"What, so you're just suddenly going to rid of her after what she's just been through?" Jacob shouts.

"No," Father Joseph says, "but her sanity is in question now, and that affects us all. Not just her." What he says stings, even if this is just a dream. I crack my eyes open, but he does not see me or recognize that I'm listening. In fact, no one is looking at me. Maybe I'm still unconscious, but does it really matter anymore?

My stomach churns uneasily when suddenly everything around me becomes clear. It's as if I had a veil pulled from my face. The tempering debate about me goes on, but my focus is now on the two men I didn't notice before. Rifles in hand, they sit stationed at the back of what now appears to be the inside of a military truck. Either I'm conjuring up a subconscious perception of a broken memory or this is real. I don't know anymore. Clearly, something is not right. My head pounds.

Sadiq rises from his metal seat. "She's an emotional wreck. We can't leave her alone again, not with a weapon anyway."

"And I don't mean to!" Jacob barks. "Hell, you all treat her like she's the enemy."

"To herself, she is," Sadiq says. Jacob's expression is dumbfounded. His slumping posture leaves him dejected. Nightmare or not, I feel completely sad for him.

"How is she supposed to defend herself then?"

"She's a ticking time bomb, Jacob. I was there—"

"So was I!"

"Then you understand it wasn't an act. She pulled the fucking trigger for Christ's sake," Sadiq barks.

"She's alive, isn't she?" Jacob says.

"Yes, and if wasn't for Nadia, you'd be scraping bits of her brain from the wall."

"She's not a detriment to us."

"She's a liability!"

"You go on like she has no purpose now. She's the reason all of us are still alive."

"I understand, but until we know for sure that she's stable, she does not go anywhere."

"I'm not going to leave her tied up like she's some kind of animal!" Jacob shouts.

"Stop it!" Nadia yells. "I can't believe what I'm hearing. Arena had a traumatic experience, that is all."

"That is everything," Sadiq responds.

"And what would you have done? You think you could have just walked away from that, knowing you've just lost everything you've loved?" Nadia shouts. Sadiq suddenly looks a little crestfallen.

"You know, I try to look at my life with purpose even though it hasn't always been so bright. Some days I'm not sure why I'm here, or if I really want to be. But I make the best of what I have even if it's not much." Sadiq eyes cast shadows of pain so deep even I can feel it in my own skin.

Sadiq grips the seat until his knuckles turn white. "It's been nearly twenty years now that I lost my wife and son to the virus. I can't sleep a wink at night without remembering some part of that misery. I loved my wife dearly and she always trusted in me no matter what. You see, I was supposed to be the warrior in the family, the one to stick it out no matter the pain. She knew I was a survivor. But it was her suffering that made me realize that a warrior's courage can only manifest from accepting the truth even if it's defeat. She experienced that for the both of us." Sadiq's lips tremble. "But my three-year-old son . . . . an innocence torn from me. And why? Because it's just the world we live in? He hadn't a clue of the cruelty he suffered. No one should have to experience that. So, you tell me, could you have just walked away from that? I had no intention to, but somehow I did."

"I'm not saying what she did was right," Nadia says.

"So what are you saying?"

"The world is cruel enough. Extend her a little grace. None of us here are perfect, and we all could use it."

Sadiq's solemn expression wears on me. Whether or not this is a nightmare, I feel indebted to extend him that same grace.

"I'm sorry for your loss," I softly offer. Faces immediately turn to me now, some weary laden, others slightly delighted. "No child deserves such torment, but I assure you he's in safe hands now. Your son doesn't have to suffer ever again."

Sadiq smiles. "Calev . . . his name was Calev," he says proudly. "It's good to have you back, Arena." Behind those masked eyes is a man worn from courage we don't see. He's suffered enough for us all. This man's fight has put loyalty into a different light, and sadly it's more than I could ever offer.

If this isn't a dream, then what I have done has scarred this entire group. I feel sick. I'm not sure I can gain back their trust now.

Jacob bends down and offers his hand, but I'm almost too afraid to touch him, an anxious delay I suppose. I just can't make myself look into his eyes. What I witnessed was excruciating: Jacob lying in his own blood, scarred and burned. My memories cannot deny that. That is something that does not leave you.

"Arena, it's really me," he whispers. "I'm not dead, and neither are you." If his touch is as soothing as his face, then I cannot resist this tormenting nightmare anymore. I'll stay hidden in this dream for as long as I can. He moves closer to my lips.

"This cannot be," I cry. In a moment of weakness, I let my hands, still bound, drift to him for comfort. He slides his fingers in my hair and gently tucks a lock behind my ear. I cringe in pain.

"Sorry, meds must be wearing off," he says.

Pain like this has no feeling in a dream. I gently prod the side of my head until I feel a bandage loosely wrapped around the top part of my ear. Nadia approaches less attentively. She cuts the rope from my wrists with her knife. I quickly grab her hand before she pulls away.

"Thank you," I graciously respond. Her icy azure eyes warm over me, but she says nothing. And she doesn't have to. Those two words, common to most, are anything but between Nadia and me. She has given me a second chance and a newly fortified bond that can never be broken between us. She squeezes my hand and smiles.

It's my ties with Jacob that worries me now. I try to press toward him, but the side of my upper cheek abruptly stings. "Ow!"

"The bullet grazed the side of your cheek and tore the tip of your ear off. Could have been worse, Arena," he softly admits. Now I know this is real.

"Jacob . . . what's happened to me? How are you here? I . . . I saw you—"

He shushes me calmly. "It was a decoy. I switched clothes with the man you saw dead. Sadiq and I used him to flush out the other soldiers where Nadia was taken. The distraction worked. They filled him full of holes while we weeded the others out. That's when the fire exploded from the side of the apartments. The pressure was so great, it knocked me on my ass. I couldn't see through all the smoke until it was too late. The gun had gone off and there you were, lying on the ground."

"Jacob, I . . . I don't know what to say. What I did was. . ." *Cowardly*, is what I want to say, but my lips shamefully quiver instead and guilt consumes me. There's really nothing I can say to change what's happened. I can only offer sympathetic regret. "I'm sorry," I painfully admit.

"I'm just glad you're alive. I really thought I had lost you," he says, easing the sting.

Temporarily, but it has led to an awakening. I don't know if I can overcome what I had done, but I know I will never stray from this second chance again. "Yes," I whisper, "I will marry you."

CHAPTER 20

The long rugged drive through the night leaves me appended to the small comfort against Jacob's chest. While everyone lies quietly tucked away, I struggle to fall asleep. I shiver from the cool desert air with my eyes wide open, much too frightened to shut them. Whatever is on the other side haunting me, it knows my deepest darkest secrets. I feel almost powerless to its deceit.

Alexandria may be in the distance now, but I've brought with me its painful memory. The misery, shame, and guilt I left spilled on that street is a stain that will haunt this fellowship forever. But I must press on now. I can never leave my brother from my thoughts again. I won't. And aside from the demons persuading me otherwise, I know he's still alive. I can feel it. I have everything to live for and yet I have nothing to gain from it. My world is a wasteland of deception, but I pray to see a brighter horizon. This is my hope, my plea, my sacrifice.

Hours have passed quietly through the night, but my thoughts have not. A rumbling chaos digs deep into my conscious displaying the same graphic image of a child lying dead on the floor with a half-eaten apple still clutched in his hands—a message perhaps, or a warning. It's disturbing nonetheless, and it won't leave me.

The truck's low-roaring engine quiets as we creep slowly to a stop. A surly voice approaches the vehicle, but it's neither English nor Russian. It's the native language of Cairo steeped in a Middle Eastern dialect. It's foreign to me. Egyptian Arabic is not familiar territory to my tongue or ears. I only know a few phrases that would not serve us here unless I were a prostitute.

A voice answers back in the same language. It's one of Sadiq's men sitting up in the front cab. Soon another voice joins in, but strangely it's French, something I'm very familiar with. He's asking the driver what the cargo is and where he's taking it. The Arabic voice chimes in again, but I have no idea what he's saying. His voice soon elevates and now an argument ensues.

"*Kafin! Kafin!*" the man shouts. He angrily yells something before the truck door creeks open. The shouting stops.

"What's going on? What are they saying?" Juliana asks.

"They want to search the truck," Sadiq answers nervously. I quickly rise to my feet and reach for my guns, but they are missing.

"Arena, wait. This is not the time," Sadiq advises.

"Give me my guns now."

"No, sit down and do as they ask. We don't know how many more are out there waiting, and I'm not going to risk everyone here to find out. Besides, we may be able to get out of this without causing too much trouble." Sadiq's stony eyes gesture me to be silent. Jacob tugs on the back of my arm, urging me to quietly sit back down, but I refuse. I'm no fool to what's about to happen to us and I will not be taken into some pre-executional jail, not after getting this far and closer to Gabe.

I quietly sit next to Nadia and press my hand firmly against her thigh. Her eyes close tight, but she understands our predicament. She opens her eyes and stares at me; the bond we share now is as close to the instincts we both possess.

She carefully pulls my knife from her side and secretly places it in my hand. Suddenly, boots scuffle toward the back of the truck. Nadia quickly tucks her gun in the back of her pants while I try to distract Jacob to get his. I nestle up against his chest and stroke his hair, but he seems too inundated by the soldiers outside that my intimacy has gone unnoticed. Even a kiss on the lips isn't enough, but my hand gently caressing his crotch delivers the diversion I was looking for. I carefully sneak his gun from his belt and return next to Nadia.

The cloth flap at the rear of the truck abruptly flies open. Two soldiers appear, rifle in hands, aiming with intent to fire. They shout inside the truck in their foreign tongue, pointing and prodding with the end of their barrels. Sadiq raises his hands and converses back. After a small shouting match, he exits the truck slowly and unarmed without resistance. One after the other, everyone files out with their hands locked behind their heads as ordered. Nadia and I are the last to exit.

Hiding behind my neck, I secretly hold my dagger dangling downward between my fingers. Jacob's gun hugs loosely against the back of my pants, but it's in jeopardy of falling out as I jump down off the truck. Looks like we've driven right into the aftermath of a small warzone. The area, paved with concrete, is vast yet quiet. Despite the thousands of dilapidated buildings peppered along the abandoned roads, this place is a barren wasteland.

"*Kaf ha-laka!*" the soldier shouts. He gestures for us to move with the tip of his rifle, an AK-30 to be exact. He walks just slightly in front of Nadia and me toward the front of the truck. Another soldier points his gun to one of Sadiq's men who is stretched face-down on his stomach. The cab door is open, but no one else in inside.

Just in front of us, and blocking our path, is a small booth with a gate arm attached—it's a bridge checkpoint to cross the Nile. Two other men less ominous stand guard next to it. With no weapons in hand except for a clipboard and a radio, this threat seems reasonably extinguishable. Regardless of what Sadiq may believe, it's obvious these soldiers have no intention to let us go. If I don't do anything now, this is sure to escalate into something much worse.

I wrap my fingers tightly around my knife. Nadia turns to me, her eyes wide as my gun suddenly falls to the ground. I stop. The soldier immediately shifts, thrashes his gun in my face, and barks at me to move. Nadia's face pales. I gasp for a split second as everyone watches me. Jacob shakes his head to deter me from what I'm about to do.

The soldier stops shouting and quickly notices the gun. Nadia and I exchange an unspoken agreement, and for the next three seconds oblivion occurs.

I swing the dagger behind my head and hold it tightly against the soldier's neck. He drops his gun and buckles to the ground. Nadia draws her gun to the soldier near the truck.

"Put it down!" she shouts.

The man lowers his weapon and tosses it to the side.

Without warning, the two soldiers in front of us take off running into the booth. I pick up Jacob's gun and drill two bullets into their knees.

"Arena, stop!" shouts Sadiq. He quickly runs over to the two men who are screaming on the ground. One rolls to his side grimacing, while the other shouts God knows what. Sadiq tries conversing with them, but they stubbornly ignore him. Instead, they answer with sounds of anguish.

Jacob grabs my arm angrily. "What the hell, Arena?

"Somebody had to do something." I defend.

"You know not every situation has to be resolved by shooting someone."

I gaze into his eyes. "I'm sorry, I just—"

"Look, I get it. You're just trying protect us, but do you think it's wise to be holding a gun?"

"That's not fair, Jacob."

"I think it's more than fair. I love you, but how am I supposed to trust you?"

I step away from Jacob momentarily, disappointed. Mainly in myself.

"We all have a lot of trusting to do with each other," Father Joseph chimes in. "But right now isn't the time for a counseling session. Here, take this."

Father Joseph hands Jacob a small piece of rope.

"What's this for?" Jacob asks.

"Tie up the soldier and put him over there with the others. No need for any more bloodshed."

Jacob restrains the soldier's hands behind his back and leads him near the booth. He squirms and struggles from Jacob's grasp, cursing.

The man by the truck babbles something in return and reaches for the gun on the ground. He raises it, but Nadia quickly shoots him dead.

The other soldier slips from Jacob's grasp and falls to the ground. I draw my gun toward him.

"Wait!" Father Joseph shouts. He grabs my hand before I fire.

The soldier stumbles to his feet and runs toward the empty desert.

"Let him go. He's as good as dead," Father Joseph insists.

He's right. The man's life will shrivel if escapes into this wasteland. These soldiers are ruthless and would rather die than be held captive.

Voices abruptly argue in Arabic near the booth. I watch impatiently as Sadiq interrogates the wounded men. His methods are far more endurable than I would use, but he knows the language. I approach hesitantly; one of the men shouts at me, while the other turns away.

"I don't think he's grown too fond of you," Sadiq says.

"No shit." While it may be lost in translation, I know when someone isn't fond of me.

"Guys, I don't think we need to be standing around here much longer," Juliana suggests.

"Believe me, I don't want to be here either, but we need these men to get across the bridge," Sadiq says.

"Why?"

"There's at least two more checkpoints just on the other side before we reach the heart of the city, and they may be our only ticket in."

"So what's the problem?" I ask.

"They're not budging."

"Maybe you're not pushing hard enough,"

"Their loyalty is far greater than their own lives. They will die here if they have to."

"*Ayreh Feek!*" One of the men shouts.

I quickly draw my gun and threaten him. The man glowers at me, while the other man turns away.

"Wait!" Sadiq shouts. "You're really going to shoot a wounded unarmed man?"

It's objectionable, but we're in a position where we have no choice. This man is defiant and a threat to us. Strangely, I struggle to pull the trigger. I briefly reconsider, but the venom spewing from this man's mouth pisses me off.

"*Kus Emek!*" he angrily jeers. Now that I understood—an insult among insults in the Arabic culture, and one I will not take lightly. Cursing my mother will not give him any favor. I move closer and stick my gun directly to his head. He spits at me.

I turn to Sadiq with an unconscionable glare, "Would you have me arm him?"

"Killing him isn't going to change a thing," Sadiq says.

"Yeah, well, it makes me feel better." His stony glare is confronting. "What, you think they are going to suddenly forget what happened here?"

"I don't expect them too, no—"

"Then they're better off dead."

"You don't have to do this," Father Joseph persuades.

"Will anyone of you have the guts to? I retort.

"Arena, please, I'm begging you. Withdraw."

I stare into Father Joseph's eyes and wither just a bit. *What am I doing?* I loosen my grip from the gun and lower my arm, but the man pulls the gun from my grasp. I fall back. Boom! A bullet drills his head. Juliana Stands behind me with a smoking Glock, aimed at the dead sol- dier. She's shaking. Not the person I expected to be hold- ing a gun. I may be reckless at times, but even this is a surprise for me.

"Arena is right. We have no reason to trust anyone," Juliana speaks.

Henry gently grabs Juliana's arm and places it back to her side. Her eyes draw blank, but her determination is true. Maybe I'm not the only one this group should be worrying about.

I pry my gun from the dead soldier and draw it to the other man's head. He shivers with fright and buries his head.

"Arena, that's enough," Father Joseph implores.

"Why should we let him live?" I ask.

"Is this how you decide a man's fate?"

"No, it's how he decides. Our choices live and die with us. Life is too precious to change them."

"Is that how you determined yours?" Sadiq snaps. Ouch, that stings deep. Okay, I admit I'm in no position to address such a thing. This is hypocrisy at its finest hour.

"My decisions may not be in your favor," I say, "but I know what I have to do. I'm not capable of deciding inno- cence any more, not since departing that damn ship."

"You really believe that?"

"I don't have the luxury to know —"

"Oh, but you do."

"Look, I'm sorry you don't approve of my interrogation ethics. I'm not here to play a round of moral debate. Getting us across the border is my charge."

"Then you'll understand why we need him," Sadiq says. Sadly, he's right, even if the soldier is the enemy.

Strangely, I feel somewhat sympathetic for this poor man and I don't know why. Either his head is buried in desperate prayer or he's too afraid to see his life come to a tragic end. I bend down and lift his chin up with the end of my gun. He trembles. I speak to him in Hebrew, the only language I'm slightly familiar with that's close to his native tongue. Whether he understands or not, I feel beholden to address him before we depart.

"If you're my enemy, then why shouldn't I kill you?"

He gazes through me as if I'm not even there, and the blood in my veins turns cold. "Because when you pull that trigger, you'll be no different than me," he says.

I sit there for a moment entranced by his words and find myself conflicted by his honesty. I gently release the trigger and withdraw my gun before anything is able to flow from my mouth.

"What's your name?" I ask.

He says nothing for a moment, then struggles to sit up. "Khair," he answers weakly.

"Your fate is out of my hands, Khair," I say. Everyone is watching me closely as if I'm about to do something irrational, but instead I disengage the gun's slide and hand it back to Jacob. "I believe this belongs to you." He grabs the gun, brushes the back of my hair, and wraps his arms around me. I don't want to let go.

Sadiq carefully aids the man to his feet and walks over with a new sense of clarity. "He'll help us," he affirms.

Jacob helps Khair into the truck while the others pitch the bodies over the ravine. No need to attract any more attention than we already have. I pull Sadiq to the side. "This doesn't mean I trust him."

"Honey, we don't live in a world of trust anymore. It's clout I'm looking for."

"Well, now that you have your leverage. What is it you want from me?"

Sadiq searches my face for a moment. "I want the Arena whom her uncle Finnegan praised about. You remember her, don't you? Well, you let me know when she's back." With the cold squint of his eyes, he gently lays his hand upon my shoulder. His words pierce deep. I feel abandoned as he walks away to the front of the cab.

Father Joseph pulls me up inside the back of the truck. I can tell he wants to tell me something, but he leaves me alone. My eagerness to be angry is stretched thin. As much as I despise Sadiq's comments, he's right. What has become of me that I would turn my back on my own convictions? If this is the path I've chosen, then how long must I go before I'm free of it?

CHAPTER 21

The El Tahrir corridor extending across the Nile is an excruciating drive. I curl up next to Jacob and wait like everyone else. Faces are long and bodies are worn. It's distressing not knowing what lies ahead or what other threats we may be subject to. We have no choice but to press on. Anxiety has become my enemy.

The truck slowly creeps to a stop. My heart pounds like the beat of a rabbit's foot. We have reached our first marker. Nadia reaches inside her pack, grabs two guns, and hands them to me.

"I believe these would be better suited with you," she says. She hands me two extra fully loaded magazines. "I feel much safer when you're armed."

Sadiq's men stare uneasily at me. I caress the guns' rubber handles like a child's indulgence before I marry them to my jacket.

"I'll second that," Caspar unexpectedly adds. I furrow my brow at this unexpected endearment. "What?" He shrugs his shoulders. "Well, don't looked so shocked. I want to survive just as much as you."

A smile fills my face. Maybe he isn't so bad after all . . . maybe. I'll reserve judgment until we've safely reached Jerusalem.

Suddenly, voices elevate outside the truck. I aim my guns toward the back and wait anxiously for the canvas flap to open. Realizing this is a do-or-die situation, everyone follows my lead. My heart is practically humming from its fluttering beats. Tiny beads of sweat dot my forehead.

The chatter quickly stops and leaves us with a torment-ing silence. I stand firm. My grip tightens around the gun handles. I count to ten, then, surprisingly, the truck slowly pulls away.

I rest there for a moment before I'm sure we have left the marker. There's a knock on the back of the truck cab and a voice shouts through the reverberating metal plate, "We're clear!" The flutter in my heart desists and returns to its nor-mal spastic groove. Faces sweat and sighs release as fear is momentarily lifted. We have escaped our first obstacle, but it's hardly our last as we head directly into the mouth of an ominous city.

The rest of our drive across the bridge is tense, but I'll choose the nerve-racking anticipation over the alternative. Khair has proven to be a great asset as we pass the next two checkpoints without any trouble.

I sit impatiently next to Jacob inside this ragged box. My ass is numb from the vibrating bed-floor, but Jacob's shoulder makes a nice pillow to lean against. It's a small comfort, but I'll take it.

We've been driving for the better part of fifteen minutes now, and I haven't a clue as to where we are going. Our bodies shift back and forth, as the truck turns and twists down street after street. The nauseating ride makes everyone irritable.

Fortunately, our drive comes to an end. The truck slowly creeps forward and the deep hum of the engine echoes inside my head. It grows louder and louder as if we are driving inside a cave. The light creeping through the back flaps gradually seeps into shadow.

The engine stops and the cab door opens. Sadiq pokes his head through the rear of the truck and carefully pushes Khair up and inside. He crawls on the floor and struggles to lean against the wall. By the grimace on his face, his leg is still badly wounded.

"Keep an eye on him," Sadiq orders.

"Where are we?" I ask.

"Somewhere safe, I assure you. Just stay put, all of you. We'll be right back."

"Wait, where are you going? You can't just leave us here," I say.

"I can, and I will. You're just gonna have to trust me on this, okay? Now sit tight until we get back from the market."

"What if someone comes?"

"No one will be combing this area."

"How can you be so sure?"

"Because we're on the outer edge of the Dead Zone."

A hellish shiver of discomfort fills me. The very mention of this place has everyone aflutter. Many people believe it's the birthplace of the 2035 virus.

"We shouldn't be here," I say.

"The only thing wandering these streets are the rats inhabiting them. I don't expect you'll find anything else. It's the best I can do until we get back. Regardless of what you've heard, this is the safest place to be," Sadiq says.

The first deaths from the 2035 flu strain occurred in the eastern part of Cairo, an unlikely coincidence considering the ICDC used to be stationed here. The death toll rose so quickly, the far eastern part of the city was used as a dumping ground for burning corpses.

Rumor or not, the Dead Zone has become an underground story that people don't like to talk about. It's a conversation that's better kept in secret. Not that there's a contagion left lurking around these streets, but it's still creepy nonetheless.

It's only been thirty minutes since Sadiq left and already I'm getting antsy. I can't take this anymore. It's as claustrophobic in here as it was on those damn ship containers. I need to get out of here or I'm going to go crazy, which wouldn't be good for anyone. I grab my knife, recheck my guns, and walk to the rear of the truck.

"Where do you think you're going?" asks Sami, one of Sadiq's most loyal soldiers.

"To stretch my legs. Got a problem with that?"

"We're to stay put."

"You can stay here as long as you want, but my sanity needs some air."

"Wait, I'm coming with you," Jacob says.

"Disobeying a direct order is not a wise move," advises Sami.

"Wouldn't be the first time," Father Joseph chimes in with a smile. "Besides, I think it would do us all a bit a good to get some fresh air."

"Fine, just don't wander off too far. This is a forbidden area."

The air is warm and arid, but it beats the stale, musty sweat I've had to endure the last hour. The two stone buildings that the truck is nestled between tower four stories. They're in severe ruin and are in danger of collapsing, but they keep us well hidden. Their tattered awnings shade us from the baring sun.

The cobbled streets are empty and the sand left from a windstorm still lies adrift at the feet of every stone building. With the exception of our uninvited presence, the rest of this forgotten village appears to be deserted. Nothing but the memories of desolation remain here now.

Jacob and I roam the adjacent street where a string of worn clothing dangle peculiarly across the end of the alleyway. My spine tingles just thinking about who must have lived here before all the mayhem. The chilling stories of this place really gives me the creeps.

Just to the left of us opens to a nest of smaller buildings, homes perhaps. Each one is attached to the other with a covered walkway. The only other note of interest are the strange Arabic markings painted on the stony bungalows. Below each marking, a large red "X" decorates the walls. It's intrusive, but to the point. Whatever resides in there is not to be disturbed. You'll get no complaints from me.

Our curiosity takes us further just across the next street where the structures are in worse condition. Abandoned for some time now, much of the mortar crumbles away from the stones like chalk.

The building in front of us begs for an invitation, with its doors and windows completely missing. As a rarity, the clouded skies have parted, and the sun's rays peer through the half-eroded roof giving the dimly lit façade a reason to explore it.

I take Jacob's hand and carefully walk through the charred doorway. The buckled floor cracks beneath my feet as I step carefully toward the light. A rat scurries across my boots and back into the shadow behind me. *Nasty rodents.* Half the room brightens under the sun's rays and exposes a room damaged by fire. Despite the insides scorched black from burning ash, the building still stands.

I can't imagine the misery that tried to escape this place. I can almost hear the screams burning in my thoughts as the sick were set ablaze in this room—an atrocity no one should ever have to witness.

I wrap my arms tightly around Jacob's waist. I just want some alone time with him right now, even if it's for just a few minutes. I rest my head on his shoulder while he gently brushes my hair with his fingers. I don't want to think of anything else but this moment. It's the only thing I want to remember from this place.

As I look up into his eyes, my body freezes.

"What?" Jacob asks, startled.

"Behind you!"

A despairingly bleak woman, draped in ragged linens, stands a few feet from Jacob's right shoulder. I tug on his arm and pull him away. Hiding in the shadow, she sways from side to side and moans in agony. She reaches her hand out and steps forward into the sun's rays. The wall shadows half her face, which is covered in bright red blisters.

We quickly jump back, clinging to each other. "You think she's contagious?" I ask.

"I'm not gonna find out."

We maneuver out the side opening, keeping our distance from the diseased woman. She follows us outside where Father Joseph and the others stare in horror. When she exits into the full light, it's apparent she's much sicker than I thought. Her arms creep out from frayed sleeves and expose the pus-filled boils covering them.

"Everybody stay back," Father Joseph advises. She limps toward us, eyes strained and face disheveled.

Suddenly, Sadiq's voice groans behind us, "I thought I told everyone to stay in the truck." The woman stops as Sadiq approaches. "I'm gone for forty-five minutes and you—" And just like that, Sadiq is stark silent. He walks next to me with disbelief. "Tell me I'm not seeing this."

"Believe me, I wish I could tell you differently," I say.

The woman takes a few steps forward before falling to her knees with exhaustion. She gasps for a moment before uttering the word "water." I cringe. I can't watch this torment any longer.

"Give me your water," I say to Sadiq.

"Arena, you can't help her."

"I'm not asking. Give me your water now."

"I suggest you stay clear from her. She's not going to survive, you know that."

"Maybe not, but I'm not watching her suffer either." I swipe the flask from Sadiq's hands and slowly approach the woman.

"Arena, no!" Jacob shouts. "She could be contagious."

"I'll take my chances." I toss the water flask at her. She quickly grabs it and soaks her parched, blistered lips. I leave the flask with her and slowly back away. To my surprise, eight more people covered with the same blisters emerge from the back of the building, one of which is a small boy.

"All right, everybody back to the truck now!" Sadiq shouts.

We quickly leave the virus-infected people and head back to the covered alley. One of Sadiq's men rummages frantically though the cab before tossing a bag to the back of the truck. With everyone waiting inside, Sadiq meticulously draws a packaged needle from the bag, then another.

"What are you doing?" I ask.

"Just a precaution." He opens the package and breaks off the cap. "You first, Henry."

"What are you drugging him with?" I demand.

"ZiademineDiclycoid—ZDC."

"Where did you get your hands on that? There hasn't been any supply of that for years," Father Joseph asks. ZDC was the first virus-combatant drug to prevent viral DNA from forming during the 2035 outbreak. Without it, no one would have survived.

"The Israeli government stockpiled what they could before it was too late. It was dispersed during the second wave a year after the virus struck. What was left was given to the military. Every soldier is required to carry it. In the event of another virus outbreak, we needed to be prepared."

"So there's more? Then we can help these people?" I ask.

Sadiq grows silent for a moment, then says, "Sorry, lass, but what's in this bag is it."

My face wears thin with grief as I think about that sickly boy covered in boils. One by one, Sadiq delivers the rest of the drug-filled syringes into everyone's arm while I watch with sadness. The Egyptian soldier, Nadia, and I are the last to receive the shot. Worry suddenly covers Sadiq's face as he searches thoroughly inside the bag.

"What is it?" I ask.

Sadiq pulls out one packaged needle. "It's the last one. I'm sorry, but only one of you can take it, and I'm not going to make that decision."

A dead calm suddenly fills the inside of the truck. One uneasy stare after another follow me as I grab the needle from Sadiq's hands.

"You won't have to." I open the package, inspect the needle, and contemplate the decision I have to make.

"Arena, what are you doing?" Jacob warily asks.

"Making the choice that's been given to me."

Nadia raises her eyes. "Arena, it was meant for you . . . take it. You need to survive," she says.

I stare at the tip of the needle, weighing my options. I turn to Jacob. He knows me well enough to know that my intentions are sometimes against his will. I can feel the strain about to erupt behind his restless eyes.

"Take the shot, Arena," he says calmly.

"Take it," agrees Nadia. "I assure you, this is the way it has to be."

I sit down next to Nadia as tears escape her eyes. "Are you sure?" I ask.

"You're my only friend. I wouldn't have it any other way." Her loyalty is far greater than any person I've met. I'm indebted to her. I strain from bursting into tears as I wrap my arms around her.

"Thank you. You saved my life. Now I save yours." I jab the needle into Nadia's arm and quickly squeeze the syringe.

Voices erupt. Jacob falls to his knees. "What have you done?" he laments.

"I made the choice no one else would."

"Do you want to die? Is that it? And what about us? What about our future?"

"I believe she's already decided that fate," Father Joseph replies for me.

"Look around you, Jacob. Does our future really look that bright?" I say.

"So when you get sick, I'm just supposed to watch you die?" He's crying now.

"If Arena has contracted the virus, we may have enough time to supply her with the antivirus when we reach Jerusalem," Sadiq exclaims.

"You have more?" I ask.

"We have a small reserve left, but it will do you no good if you don't inject the serum before the virus spreads."

"Then let's go, now!" Jacob shouts.

"I didn't come all this way just to leave my brother to die in a prison," I say.

"Did you not see what happened to those people outside? They didn't have a choice, but you do."

"Yes, I know and I choose to rescue my brother. If death should intercede, then so be it."

"I don't mean to interpose, but we're wasting time," Nadia chimes in.

"Nadia's right, we need to move now," Sadiq agrees. Everyone finds a comfortable position to settle in before another restless drive. I grab Sadiq before he exits the truck.

"How long can I really go without taking the antivirus?" I ask.

"It's going to take more than a strong immune system to delay the inevitable. Our bodies are a complicated machine. We may be strong on the outside, but we are far too delicate on the inside to fight such a strain. Two . . . three days tops."

"And if I don't show any symptoms after three days?"

"You may never show a single symptom. This is a wicked virus that stays invisible until it's too late."

"What about those people outside? They have survived this long."

"If this was somehow caused by the virus, it has reached too far in their blood to save them. They are past the point of curing."

The ride deep into the city of Cairo feels lonely. Jacob, who is less animate over my decision, leans despondently against the back wall of the truck. I nestle against his body and lay my head on his chest during the quiet drive. He doesn't say anything. No more than the delicate stroke of his hand wandering up and down my arm is plenty to fill the void.

CHAPTER 22

At last, we have stopped, but I'm no more overjoyed as we sit idle and wait for uncertainty. The flap to the rear of the truck swings open and standing behind it is Sadiq. He pushes over the gate and tosses an article of clothing to Juliana, Nadia, and myself.

"If you plan on mingling with the culture, you'll have a better chance blending in with these," Sadiq advises.

A means of modesty will serve us well with these hijabs. Cairo's dress code may be less strict than many of her Muslim counterparts, but it's still respectful for women to hide discreetly behind a traditional form of clothing, even if it's under Russian rule. Juliana's darker skin marries perfectly with the head covering, as she will find very little effort blending into the environment. Nadia and I are less convincing, but it will have to do. Father Joseph, Henry, and Sadiq robe with a traditional jellabiya while the others stay rested in their more comfortable attire.

We leave our weapons behind, tucked beneath a shroud of blankets, and exit the truck. I sneak a small knife between my cleavage just in case. Khair, still badly wounded, is left with one of Sadiq's men guarding him. Although he's in no condition to move, it's still a risk to let him go.

The skies have parted from darkness replacing it with the scorching sun beating down on Cairo's dry desert air. Our truck sits secluded between two high-rise buildings, but not too far away from the city's inner dwellings. The sounds from the streets are a far cry from the hustle and bustle of

New York or Chicago. Although those cities don't resemble what they were thirty years ago.

A once-populous city of over twenty million people has suffered the same tragedy as the rest of the world. The virus hit here harder than any other place on Earth, leaving the enormity of Cairo destitute. While Egypt is still mysteriously prosperous, its cities resemble otherwise.

People stand closely to one another along the congested streets. Two soldiers, armed with assault rifles, occupy each block. Some are dressed in Russian uniforms, others in Egyptian militant garments—both are appalling. Planted stately just above one of the domed buildings flies a blood-red flag marked with seven black stripes and the infamous hammer and cycle emblem from the old Russia of years past.

We walk the streets just as everyone else, blending in effortlessly. America is far from our reaches now, which is just as well. The familiarity of my face back home is completely foreign to these people. I want to keep it that way.

Just west of us on the banks of the Nile sits the Egyptian Museum of Antiquities, tracing five thousand years of human history. Its arching entrance rises majestically behind a Sphinx statue guarding it. The open area surrounding the museum leaves me feeling a bit vulnerable. A few soldiers stationed on the far ends of the building scan the adjacent streets. Surprisingly, no one stands near the entrance.

The doors open up to architectural brilliance that is both royal and vast. The front gallery houses granite sculptures of kings, queens, and gods lining the side of the wide hall, but hovering nearly thirty feet high on a throne sits colossal figures of Pharaoh and his queen overlooking the gallery's historical treasures.

People freely wander the museum without a watchful eye from military impediment. This city is quite different than most, though it's still under harsh rule. Sadiq and I search for Darwishi, the artifacts directorate for the museum. He's our only contact who can be trusted, according to Ananiah. We leave the others to roam the halls and take in a bit of Egyptian culture before it vanishes.

There's no administrative official available who resembles Darwishi—just a clerk stationed at the information center, and he's much too young to be an operative envoy for Egyptian's military intelligence service.

"Excuse me," Sadiq politely says in his Arabic tongue, "could you please help us find Darwishi Mubarak?"

"Mr. Mubarak is a very busy man. He's availability is minimal," the clerk says.

"We really need to speak to him."

"May I ask what this is concerning?"

"Tell him an old friend is here to see him."

"One moment." The clerk picks up a phone behind him and converses quietly.

"What is your name, sir?" asks the clerk.

Sadiq, surprised by the question stumbles a bit before picking a random name on the cuff. "Sherif," he finally answers. Sadiq looks at me and shrugs. Not sure why he just didn't say Ananiah.

"He says he knows no one by that name."

"Tell him—"

"Sir, I'm going to have to ask you to leave the premise immediately," the clerk says.

"Tell him it is of urgent importance and I will not leave until I speak with him."

Again, the clerk relays the message, but it's much longer before he replies. "He says urgency is the lack of diplomacy and that nothing will interest him to leave his work. You will need to make an official appointment."

"You tell him I have naked pictures of his wife that might be of interest."

"Uh . . . excuse me."

"Just tell him."

The clerk converses uncomfortably on the phone before he hangs up. "He'll be right up."

I bashfully grin at Sadiq, trying to make a concerted effort not to laugh. I'm enamored by his negotiating tactics, which show to be quite effective.

"Let me do the talking," Sadiq instructs.

Ten minutes later, Darwishi walks briskly around the corner with an eager skip in his step. He's a tall man, medium physique with a receding hairline, but he wears it with confidence. He's dressed in a dark blue suit that is neatly tailored to his build and is made from nothing less than the best quality material. He's a rather good-looking man with strong masculine features that go well with his clean shave and well-maintained hair. He's a meticulous man, or at least one who practices thoroughness.

The clerk quickly directs Darwishi in our direction, but I can see has no interest in listening. His thin lips are pursed with aggravation, but it's nothing compared to the scowled face that's looming.

"Okay, you got my attention," Darwishi says abruptly.

"May we speak privately please?" Sadiq asks. Darwishi motions us to a back room that's privately tucked away from the main gallery. He closes the door and walks over to a wet bar to pour a drink.

"Now what does this hasty matter pertain to?" Darwishi asks impatiently.

"Ananiah sent us," Sadiq addresses.

"And what does my brother-in-law have anything to do with this?"

"Oh . . . the naked pictures? There are none. Just a ploy to get your attention."

"And so you have, but spare me with any political rants, as I have enough on my plate."

"We're not here on diplomatic matters."

"Yes, well, I kind of assumed that when you brought this young woman with you."

"Excuse me," I say, stepping forward.

"Arena," Sadiq calmly advises as he holds me back. Darwishi's eyes widen with surprise, and silence ushers over his blank expression. He searches my face as if I'm one of the museum's sculptures.

"Ananiah sent you, huh?"

"That's correct."

"Come with me . . . now," Darwishi asserts with a sense of caution. He takes us into another room that's less decorated and quickly locks the door behind him. He gazes upon me briefly before moving to a desk in the corner and grabbing a manila envelope from the drawer. He opens it, pulls out a thick document, and tosses it before me on the desk.

"You know what that is?" he asks.

"Not the slightest clue," I answer.

"Within the text of this fifty-page document lies a grim future for us all."

"And?" I shrug, still oblivious to what he's talking about.

"It's an official treaty signed by ten sovereign nations to uphold international diplomacy, Egypt being the last to sign. The Middle Eastern states have no choice but to adhere. Most of them have been plagued by disease or famine. Europe has been dissolved into one conglomerate republic that Germany still holds firm. They serve as a financial asset to the new world order."

"And what of America? How does my nation fit into all of this?" I say.

"Whatever remains there is no cause for concern. She's been torn apart like a ravaged animal. There's nothing your nation has to offer that would benefit the new world. Earthquakes, famine, and turmoil have left her scarred beyond the reaches of saving. America breeds misery, a land purged of its people into slavery or left to rot from existence. I'm afraid that insolvent wasteland is left to wither. Of course, Israel refuses to be a part to any of this. I support her cause, but like America, she will die in this war. This isn't some simple, mindless decree that countries will ignore. It's the beginning of a genocide and you just walked into the heart of it."

"We came here to—"

"I know why you're here, but I assure you nothing will change no matter what Ananiah has told you," he says.

"I came here for help," I say.

"Well, then you are looking in the wrong place! My life is on the line every day, working for these Russian gorillas, and I'm pretty damn sure they aren't going to find favor in me harboring their enemy. You're a fugitive in hostile territory, so you might want to rethink your plans."

"So your loyalty rests with your enemy?" I ask.

"No, but I'm a fool to think Russia is just going to lie down and let Israel dictate their own global campaign. If you don't play by their rules, you are expendable."

"I don't know what Ananiah saw in you, but I see a coward before me," I huff.

"Coward? For the last six years, I've secretly had to maneuver my loyalties between a sour allegiance with my enemy and the most hated nation in the world. And for what? Information that may or may not be pertinent. I'm loyal to Israel, but there's no recompense great enough for such a job. Seems like a small price to pay for a country, but I see things quite differently. I chose to risk mine and my family's lives to help the Israeli government. I'm no coward. I'm on your side."

"Then please help us," I plead.

"I really wish I could, I just—"

"You've done more than enough for Israel. I don't question your allegiance or your efforts and sacrifices. But sooner or later even the enemy will see through you, and I don't imagine mercy will apply to you when that time comes. Help us if you truly want to make a difference in this war. This may be your only chance. Ananiah spoke of great things about you and your devotion. Don't prove him wrong."

Darwishi stares at a picture of an attractive woman— I'm assuming it's his wife—sitting on the corner of the desk and says nothing. The silence is telling. His face is drawn with confliction, but probably not as much as the thoughts swimming inside his head.

"I can't guarantee your safety," he says doubtfully.

"You won't need to."

He struggles to make a decision before turning to me apprehensively. "Okay," he mumbles.

Darwishi glues his eyes upon Sadiq and me as we delineate our agenda for coming to Cairo. He's adherent to the idea of bussing the others back in Alexandria across the border, but sighs with resounding and uncomfortable doubt about the prison break. I can't blame him either.

"I'll have to admit you do have courage coming to Cairo, but breaking into a prison? You got bigger balls than I do," Darwishi confesses.

"What do the grounds look like . . . numbers?" asks Sadiq.

"Tora Farms has been abandoned for quite some time now, but the Russians have put it to good use. The yards are fully open, but the south bank of the building is your best shot in. Since the grid went down, security cameras are nonexistent. The only eye in the sky will be your spotters on the roof. Generators typically run at night, so I'd avoid any escape in the evening. And numbers . . . well, let's just say it isn't quite maximum security. Fifty, sixty guards, tops. Remember, these prisoners aren't criminals. They're for slave trade only."

"How many prisoners are we talking about?"

"The prison consists of seven blocks each holding approximately three hundred and fifty prisoners. It doesn't sound like many, but you have to remember these prisoners are sold. It's a revolving complex, so they continually move in and out like a shipping yard."

"So my brother may not even be there?" I ask solemnly.

"I can't promise that, but if he is, I assure you he's still alive. Consider these prisoners as products or assets. They have to be accounted for like any other commodity. I know it sounds heartless seeing it like that, but this is the world we have become."

"How far is this prison?" Sadiq asks.

"South Cairo is about nine miles from here. I suspect you'll need some men to go with you."

"It wouldn't hurt."

"How many are with you?"

"Including us, ten."

"All right, first thing we need to do is get your group somewhere safe. There's a Roman Catholic seminary not too far from the prison. You can seek shelter there for the night. It has everything you'll need. It's one of the few places secluded from Russian military."

"Is it active?" I ask.

"No, it's no longer in use. It's been empty for years, but it's still intact. It will serve nicely for refuge away from thecity."

"How do you know it's safe?"

"I often use the facility for making exchanges with Israeli intelligence. Not many troops roam the city anymore. Every day there are less and less securing the streets. From what my sources have been telling me, troops from other nations are being deployed to Saudi Arabia."

"Why there?" I ask.

"That's where the Russian Federation Embassy resides. It's also the center point and birth of the Ten, if that's what they still call it. Something is brewing for sure. There'll be a private summit there next week detailing the future of Israel. Ten delegates from ten nations will decide her fate, and President Gorshkov will not return to the Kremlin Senate without resolve, I assure you. He has his best interests for Russia and he will bleed her dry before giving in to the rest of the world."

"What do you know about Gennadi Gorshkov?" I ask.

"He's incorrigible as he is ruthless, but I suspect you already know that. He's revived a nation that was once in exile, but he certainly has the attention of the world in his grasp now. He will stop at nothing, pressing for a global economic policy. A one-world government is too close in his sight and he will destroy anyone who gets in the way of that. Stalin was just a small-time bully compared to Gorshkov. He has backing from China, which doesn't bode well for Israel in this political war."

"Israel will not back down," Sadiq says.

"That's what scares me, and here you are trying to enter a nation that's under a global fire."

"Then we have very little time left," Sadiq says.

"Even if you do somehow break in the prison, rescue her brother, and walk out unscathed, it's the least of your worries."

"How so?" I ask.

"Crossing into Israel isn't a simple task. Between here and its border as far as the crow flies lies a vast wasteland of barren desert. You'll die before you even reach the outskirts. There's only one way in and it's a seventeen-hundred-mile trip around the outer border through some uninviting territory."

"We'll take our chances," I say.

"If you have any left to take."

"We appreciate your help," Sadiq says.

"Let's just hope you didn't come across the ocean for nothing. I can get you to the seminary, but that's as far as I'll take you. After that, you're on your own."

CHAPTER 23

Evening creeps in, yet I feel less inclined to sleep. My brother is all I can think about less the bleak future of Israel. Though nations continue to build immunity for one another, I know the truth behind the Ten will become more frightening as each day passes. War seems inevitable at this point and I'm afraid I have no choice but to be a part of it.

The seminary Darwishi has led us to lies two miles north of Tora Farms Prison. Parts of the facility have been well maintained even though the institute has since been barred from existing. The courtyard flows with evasive greenery hovering over the gated entrance. The paths, paved with cobblestone, connect two other buildings, one of which has been boarded up, while the other is standing derelict.

The streets around us are deserted without a hint of hostility. It's quiet, which is far less than I can say for my growling stomach. I can't remember the last time I've eaten. Surprisingly, the uninhibited inside of the seminary remains undamaged, but it's the abandoned remnants that are a haunting reminder of religious persecution.

The first floor opens to countless cobwebs hanging from its rafters and a handful of paintings dressing the walls. Bookshelves line one side of the room while the other leads to several doors and a darkened hallway. The back wall is empty except for a goliath clock leaning to one side. The gothic nineteenth-century timepiece no longer tells time, as its pendulum lies still against the glass.

"You'll be safe here," Darwishi assures. "No soldiers outside the inner city step foot in these parts. It's much too close to the Dead Zone. You'll find the administration quarters in the back of the building with some beds. I'm afraid I must leave you now. My absence from the museum may lead to suspicion."

"Thank you for this," I say.

"Remember to take the south entrance into the prison. Good luck to you. I hope you find your brother."

"What about the others in Alexandria? Are you sure you can bus them into Israel without compromise?"

"Nothing is guaranteed, but I'll do everything in my power to see them safely across the border. They should be well on their way before you take to the prison. We'll disguise them as prisoners if we have to."

Darwishi leaves me with no choice but to trust him. I'm too close to getting my brother back, though Allison and Luke are still much on my mind. I cannot doubt my decisions now.

The administrator's quarters are dark and bleak, but the beds are quite soft. I help the wounded Egyptian soldier as he limps to one of the beds. Khair's pant leg is soaked with blood, but he is still alive. While Juliana redresses his wound, I lift the flashlight to his face and find it flushed. His eyes wander to one side as Juliana presses the gauze against his bloody skin. He grimaces. Aside from his allegiance, I suddenly feel a bit of sympathy. Sadly, I would pity him less if he were dead.

I leave the others to claim a bed to rest on, as sleep is the last thing on my mind. Instead, I help Sadiq and Jacob forge a barrier against the entrance just in case Darwishi was wrong about soldiers roaming the area.

The afternoon leaves us with the desert sun hiding behind the darkened clouds. Darwishi's men, spaced evenly inside the front of seminary, stand guard near the stained-glass windows. I watch closely over the protection from these volunteered soldiers while I'm left to myself in the lobby. It's peacefully still until a rat the size of a soda can scurries across the wooden floors. It stops, sniffs the stale air, and stares at me for a minute before shuffling off between a large crevice in the wall. This ghostly building is beginning to give me the creeps.

As hours pass into the evening, I stare out the window, hoping I'll see a bus pass by with Allison and Luke on it. I know it's delusional to think so, but it keeps me hidden from the thought that they may never make it to Israel.

There's not much to plan for on this rescue, as Darwishi stated before. It's an in-and-out-as-quick-as-possible kind of plan. With communications conceded and fewer than fifty guards establishing prison posts, this seems too good to be true, which it may very well be.

Even if Gabe is in there somewhere, getting him out isn't the problem. It's the other twenty-five hundred prisoners I'm not sure what to do with. I really never thought that far ahead to consider the possibility of freeing all these people. I just wanted my brother back.

"Hey," Jacob whispers lightly in my ear.

"What is it?"

"I want to show you something."

I smile shyly at his mysterious offer and follow him down the hall. He caresses my hand ever so gently and leads me into a room that feels as claustrophobic as a closet. He shines his flashlight in the corner where a kneeling bench sits slightly askew. Nestled tightly behind it hangs a tattered curtain, eaten by moths. A latticed woven partition, threadbare, encloses the back half of the room. If I didn't know any better, I'd say we were in a confessions' chamber.

A small lantern hangs in another doorway and standing behind its fluorescent glow is Father Joseph. "Are you two ready?" he says in a serious tone.

"Give us a minute," Jacob answers.

"What the hell are you up to?" I ask, slightly beaming.

"I can't think of a better moment than now to confess what we both want."

"What are you getting at?" I ask.

The grin stretched across his face is as lively as his dancing eyes. He reaches in his pocket and pulls out a sapphire ring. The tarnished metal is worn, but the jewel that rests atop glimmers. "I told you when we reached Cairo that I would marry you. Well, here we are."

"Really, Jacob? At this hour?" I tease. His smile falls off his face. I'm not the slightest bit concerned with what hour it is, nor do I wish to reject such a romantic proposal from the man I love, but I should at least keep him on his toes if I'm to be wooed.

"Do you really think we'll have another chance at this?" His tone abruptly changes.

I suddenly feel nauseated at the idea that one of us may not make it out of the prison alive. I'm less sure about every day we live now.

"Look, I'm not trying to convince you because I see things differently. I've loved you for far too long not to waste the opportunity, and you and I both know they have become few and far in-between now. Please, let's enjoy what time we have left. Will you at least consider —"

"Yes! I had no intentions to do otherwise. I will marry you, Jacob."

"I'm pretty sure this is usually something couples discuss months prior to the ceremony," Father Joseph snickers. I glower unamused. "But under the circumstances, this will have to do," he continues.

In the dimly lit room, I stand in the shadows, waiting anxiously beside the man I was destined to be with and before another who has made that possible. I stare upon the weightiness painted on Father Joseph's face and feel forlorn of my parents' presence. If only they could see their daughter now, planting a seed into womanhood.

Jacob and I exchange simple but meaningful vows to each other before our hands are bound with a piece of cloth, torn from the moth-eaten curtain. Through a traditional Irish hand-fasting and a few reverently spoken words from Father Joseph, the five-minute ceremony is all but a memory now. Even if this lasts as long as the rising sun, I will not regret it. I shall savor every second given to me. Outside these doors, our lives may be vulnerable, but in the secrecy of this darkened chamber, Jacob and I are now bound to one another . . . for as long as the will of God allows.

CHAPTER 24

It feels all too surreal that I'm a married woman. I'm just a few months away from my seventeenth birthday and I can now call upon Jacob as my husband. While the tragedy of my world quickly whisks by, I'm suddenly living in another without a care. This is a moment I wish not leave.

I'm too caught up in the idea of a sensual private moment with Jacob that I completely forget about the others. I can already taste his kiss. I'm not sure I have enough sustainable discipline to keep from holding back any lustful desires. In fact I don't mean too, nor should I. I just want to feel his warm skin mingle with mine.

Dusk passes, but the night with my husband is still much alive. While exhaustion has seduced everyone else to fall asleep, intimacy with Jacob draws me further from it. He pulls me close and touches me ever so gently. My body nearly erupts into flames.

The room may be dark, but I easily find my way to Jacob's lips, and I simply melt. There's absolutely nothing keeping me from leaving his side tonight. I'm forever glued to his intimate touch.

He releases his lips and strokes the side of my cheek.

"This is no place for a lady," he says, grabbing my hand and pulling me toward the door. I smile with innocence and follow him out of the room and down the opposite end of the hall. Near the end of the corridor and through a set of double doors opens to a room filled with bookshelves. There isn't a blank spot on the shelves.

"And where exactly are you taking me?" I inquire curiously.

"You'll see."

"Reading is the last thing on my mind, Jacob."

Hand in hand, I follow him to the back of the library where the corner illuminates. Behind a table lies a pallet of blankets surrounded by a row of melting candles, some granola bars from the ship's galley, and a dusty bottle of wine to which I have no idea where it came from. I can see Jacob has been quite busy, and eager.

"Well, aren't you a confident gentleman," I tease. Truth is, I'm besot by his romantic gesture even if it was a premature invite. He smiles, but his tongue stays silent. The only thing emitting from his mouth are his soft kisses wandering around my neck.

He presses against me, seducing every ounce of my will to let go. I simply melt in his arms. One article of clothing after another eventually vanishes and leaves us both as natural as we came into this world. I dig my nails into his back and completely let go. Lying beneath him on the pile of blankets, he ravishes me with his sensual kisses running up and down my body. I savor the gentle touch of his skin against mine as our bodies entangle. My mind is completely numb, but my entire body is anything but. There's not one inch of my skin that doesn't tingle with delight or erupt into a blaze of pleasure. Together we lie intertwined deep into the night in a beautiful moment of passion beyond my wildest dreams.

*　*　*

Night has slipped away and so have my eyes into an unlikely vacancy. My sleep-deprived body gives in to the passing time without a single terror infiltrating my thoughts. For hours, I lie restful next to my husband without worry . . . until I wake. I reach over to pet Jacob, but I find an empty bed of crumpled blankets. Instead, my eyes awaken to an unsightly haunting I'm all too familiar with.

Perched on a melted candle squawks that pernicious crow that has followed me since the start. It hovers over me like a pendulant branch with its beak agape. Tucked between its bloody talons hangs a piece of mysterious cloth.

For once, I'm not afraid of this bird anymore. I grab a granola bar left sitting on the table and pinch a piece off. I carefully reach for the cloth with one hand and offer the granola in the other. The crow flaps its wings and squelches. I jump back. It releases the tattered material, hops to the side, and buries its beak into the granola. I quickly grab the bloody cloth and examine it. I'm not sure what to think, as I now recognize it belonging to Gabe. It's a piece torn from his jacket. Is this a message that he's alive or dead?

I quickly put on my clothes and hide the piece of cloth in my jacket. No one else needs to know about this, especially Juliana. The crow bores his eyes into me every step I take.

"What do you want from me?" I shout.

He just stares back with those black lifeless eyes. I try to leave him, but he follows me out the door just a few feet behind me. If I didn't know any better I'd think he's just trying to help me. If not for this bird, I swear I'm alone. It's too quiet in here. I have yet to hear a voice from the others.

I reach the end of the hall near the sleeping quarters, but no one is present. I'm beginning to think I'm trapped in a nightmare, and this beastly fowl following me isn't helping.

"*Caw, caw*," the crow utters huskily.

I slowly turn around and find him nearly on my heels. He stares almost through me, eyes fixed with malaise. I refuse to look away this time. I will not let this shadow control my fear anymore. Minutes pass, but to no accord this stalemate is unending, as neither one of us is willing to turn away.

And then it happens. I do the most unpredictable thing. I slowly reach out my hand toward the crow and surrender. If I can't rid of him, I might as well befriend him.

He inches closer, but I'm not sure he trusts me. He dips his head from side to side beneath my hand. Suddenly, he flaps his wings and hovers near my side before perching atop my shoulder. I'm not sure who's scared of who. I'm as still as a statue.

"Uh, okay . . . let's not do anything hasty, Mr. Crow. I'll let you stay as long as you don't claw my eyes out."

"*Caw*," he answers.

"I'm gonna take that as a yes," I say as if I understand this ridiculous exchange. "Oh, and while we're at it, please don't shit on me."

I carefully walk to the end of the hall and into the main entrance where I find everyone mysteriously crowded around the windows. Whatever they're gawking at, it must be intriguing. No one seems to notice me standing behind them, let alone a strange crow perched proudly on my shoulder.

"What's everyone looking at?" I curiously ask. Apparently, I don't exist, because no one says anything. Their faces are pressed against the windows and far too absorbed to answer.

A throaty caw creeps from the crow's beak. All heads quickly turn. Three men swiftly raise their guns. I think I've got their attention now. A note of surprise maybe? No, terrified is more like it.

"Arena, don't move!" Jacob shouts worriedly.

"Lower your guns," I caution to Darwishi's men.

"Did it hurt you? Are you all right?" Nadia frantically clamors.

"Of course, I'm fine. I let him perch up here."

"Are you crazy?" Juliana blurts.

I pinch off a piece of the granola bar and carefully feed it to the crow. "You see, he means no harm."

"You mind telling that to his friends," Caspar chimes in.

"What are you talking about?"

"Take a look."

I warily approach the glass and wonder what's got everyone in such a frightened tizzy. A humming of cacophonous chatter grows louder outside the window. I peer through the glass, eyes wide and utterly stunned.

"Sweet Jesus," I whisper.

The outside of the seminary is speckled black. A murder of crows have made it their home. There are thousands of crows staring at me through the window. The ground shimmers an ebony sea of black feathers and glowing eyes. What plague has been brought on us now?

"What the hell is going on?" Nadia asks.

"I don't know," I gasp. I back away from the glass, debating inside my head if these crows have come for me.

"I think it's best that everyone return to their rooms," Father Joseph urges.

"What do you think it means?" Jacob asks.

"Maybe it's a sign," Nadia suggests.

"A sign of what, death?" Caspar says, frightened.

"Calm down!" Sadiq demands.

"I'll calm down when I know I'm safe, and right now I'm not so sure." Caspar looks at me with sullen eyes.

"I suggest you stand down your tone," I say.

"I won't stand here waiting to be threatened by these bloody pigeons."

"They're crows, you gobshite," I correct.

"Whatever ominous force sent those creatures, it's evil," Caspar cautions.

"You know nothing."

"And you've invited one of them in," Caspar accuses. He slowly reaches for his knife.

"Whoa, wait . . . what are you doing?" Jacob asks.

"I'm going to pluck that fucking bird right off her shoulder," Caspar shouts.

"You'll do no such thing. You're not in your right mind," I try to reason.

"Put the knife down, Caspar," Jacob orders.

"That crow is nothing but deceit." Caspar steps forward.

"I'm warning you, if you take one more step, and I'll knock you out!" I shout.

Even with Jacob standing next to me, I feel a bit defenseless without a weapon. Suddenly, the crow expands its wings and emits the most horrendous, hellish scream. Caspar drops the knife, and everyone covers their ears. The piercing squawk stops, but my ears are still ringing. The room turns dark as midnight except for the spot near the window where Father Joseph holds a lantern.

"Oh shit, behind you," Nadia shouts.

The crows outside shadow the glass panes as they peer inside. Caspar jumps back. Everyone is shocked but me. I move in for a closer look.

"Arena, what are you doing? Move back," Jacob pleads.

I can hear Jacob, but I can't seem to move away. I'm possessively drawn to these birds. A voice whispers from the crow, still perched on my shoulder, but its beak is closed shut. Just around its neck, the feathers move about and form a small mouth from which the whispers echo. No one seems to hear it but me as I stand at the window transfixed. It beckons me to move outside.

"Arena?" Jacob calls.

For a moment, I just stand in silence waiting for the voices inside my head to stop. *Am I going mad?*

"Arena, are you okay?" Jacob continues.

"Help me move these tables away from the door," I say.

"You're not seriously thinking about going out there?"

"Are you going to help me or not?"

"Arena, you know I trust you, but we don't know if these birds are carrying some kind of disease. This isn't normal—"

"They're not here to harm us. They're here to help us," I say.

"How do you know that?" Sadiq asks.

I'm reluctant to tell him, because I know he won't believe me, but I have no choice. "He told me," I say, pointing to the crow.

"The crow told you?" he says in disbelief. I nod my head.

"Oh, that's great. Now she's letting a bird talk for her," Caspar jeers.

"Shut up, Caspar," Juliana barks.

"I believe you," Jacob adds as he helps remove the barricade. Juliana, Father Joseph, and Nadia help clear the doorway.

"Have you all gone insane?" Caspar mocks.

I press my hands against the door, but I'm almost hesitant to open it. I take a deep breath and walk outside. I'm completely surrounded by a cloud of black feathers and gaping beaks. The silence from these creatures is as eerie as their gawking eyes following my every step. Everyone watches from the window except Jacob, who is outside with me.

The crow, still perched on my shoulder, abruptly caws in a brash song. Thousands of wings flap in unison. The black birds take flight at once and circle the sky above us. Everyone comes out of the seminary and watches in amazement.

The whispers start again, but this time with explicit instructions. They are repeated over and over inside my head until they are tattooed into my thoughts. The black cloud swarming above us suddenly vanishes. The crow hops off my shoulder and perches on top of a broken fountain in the courtyard. He caws at me as if I'm expected to understand him.

I've been patient enough with this crow to listen, but in no way am I crazy enough to carry on a conversation with it . . . or am I? It's eating me up inside to ask, even in front of the others, who appear speechless. I guess nothing seems crazy anymore. I look straight into its opal eyes and ask, "Who are you?"

Instead of simply whispering his name to me, he garners the attention of everyone and draws symbols into the dirt with his beak. He caws once more and flies away.

Father Joseph gazes down at the letters hypnotized, almost unresponsive. "What is it? What does it say?" I ask. His face is blank and not a word is spoken.

Sadiq walks over and stares at the writing. "They're letters from the Hebrew language," he affirms.

"Well, what does it say?"

"Death is coming," Father Joseph answers.

"You don't seriously believe that damn bird can write," Caspar sneers.

"If you want to question that, go right ahead, but I'm certainly led to accept it, and I would expect you all to do the same," I say.

"Have you gone mad?"

"You think it's a coincidence that this creature has been following Arena?" Father Joseph answers.

"What in bloody hell are you implying, Father?"

"It's been warning us ever since the start," I confess.

"Us? I think maybe you're the one with a death wish."

"Stop!" Jacob shouts. "The very moment we stepped onto the ship, we all took a risk. No one forced you to come."

"Death comes to those who want it most," Caspar suggests.

"I don't remember anyone holding a gun to your head," I retort.

"You're right. You can believe what you want, all of you. But as I recall, wasn't it Arena who stuck a gun to her own head? And now all of the sudden you want to trust her?"

"Enough!" Sadiq barks. "Now I don't give a damn what any of you believe, but I do know we better get our heads out of our asses if we want to rescue Gabe. Midday is approaching, so I suggest we get out gear packed and get ready. This may be our only chance to take the prison."

"About that," I say. "I know Darwishi advised us to go to the prison during the day, but we can't. We must go at nightfall."

"With communications up?"

"I know it sounds crazy —"

"We're past crazy." Sadiq shakes his head.

"The nightshift only employs half the prison guards, most of which are stationed inside the main complex. There'll only be a few snipers dispatched on the roof at night."

"How do you know all of this?" Sadiq questions.

"The whispers inside my head."

"Great, she's lost it," Caspar says.

"What are you talking about, Arena?" Jacob asks.

"I know it sounds crazy, but the crow told me so. Like Father Joseph said, it was warning us."

"You sure about this?" Jacob asks.

"I have no reason not to trust anymore."

"That's debatable," Caspar jests.

"Look, I know it's hard for you to believe, I get that, but I wouldn't be doing this if I thought it was risking any of your lives, including yours. Besides, we'll need the lights inside if we're going to have any chance at finding them. You can stay here if you want. I'm not forcing you to go. But when we leave the prison—and we will—I'm not coming back here to get you. You're on your own."

"Did the crow tell you anything else?" Sadiq asks.

"No," I lie.

"Okay, let's all go back inside. We have enough to think about before we deploy," Sadiq orders.

While everyone leaves the courtyard, I hang back for a moment. I stare at the symbols carved into the dirt with remorse. I've lied. The whispers told me more than what I led everyone to believe.

"Are you okay?" Jacob asks.

"Yeah, I'm . . . I'm fine," I answer with a hint of uncertainty in my voice. The truth is that one of us is not going to make it out of the prison alive. I wasn't told who it would be. It's unconscionable. I don't want anyone to die, especially my friends, but I can't save my brother on my own. It is my fate that guides me, not the misfortunes I'm dealt with.

I take a deep breath and walk back inside. Nadia and Juliana sort through all the flashlights, finding the ones that have power. Father Joseph kneels by the back wall underneath the old clock and prays. Sadiq and his men inspect their guns and reload each magazine. Jacob and I remain quiet, but while he stares out the window, I watch the people I love, knowing one of them will die. I don't know if I can live with that. I want to tell them the truth but instead I swallow some guilt and say nothing. Until we reach Jerusalem, our lives will be in danger no matter what happens.

CHAPTER 25

The night is upon us and it's do or die. I wait impatiently on Juliana's bed while Nadia rummages through a backpack.

"Have you seen my knife?" she asks. I stare at the wall in silence. The only thing on my mind is wondering if Gabe is still alive. "Arena . . . hey," she continues. I'm oblivious to Nadia's voice until a brief moment of clarity breaks through.

"What?"

"My knife, have you seen it?"

"Knife? No, no, I haven't."

"You okay?"

I'll admit that I'm a bit nervous to break into the prison only to find that Gabe isn't there. "I'm fine," I choke out.

"You know, you don't have to pretend around me."

Nadia is right. She's one of the few people I can trust, even in protected secrecy. "I need to show you something, but this doesn't go any further than this room."

"Sure, okay," she agrees.

I reach inside my jacket and pull out the bloody piece of cloth that belongs to Gabe. "This was tucked in the claws of that crow. It belongs to my brother."

Nadia takes the piece of cloth and examines it carefully. "This doesn't necessarily mean that your brother is—"

"But we don't know for sure. Look, I don't know exactly what it means, but no one else needs to know about this, okay? We go in as planned."

"Your secret is safe with me."

Suddenly, the door encases with a shadow. I lift the light up and find Juliana standing with her gun holstered.

"Everyone is waiting out front," she says, face flushed. I follow her out of the room hoping that she didn't overhear our conversation. Darwishi's men and Sadiq hover over a broken table in the main lobby, plotting a course of action. Father Joseph, Henry, and Caspar inventory a pile of weapons lying in the corner, while Jacob stares guardedly out the front window.

I wrap my arms around Jacob's waist. He kisses me on the head and dazzles me with that delightful smile of his. I've finally found someone so contagious, my heart swells with a fever I wish not leave. Jacob's love means everything and only now am I afraid it may be taken from me. I can only hope that after the prison we're both here to live another day.

Out from the shadow limps Khair. Moans echo from his cracked lips as he shuffles across the floor and into the light. Gasps fill the air. His face is red and large sores break the skin beneath his neck.

"Everyone get back toward the entrance!" Sadiq shouts. Darwishi's men flee to the walls with their weapons raised. Khair spouts something before he hunches over and throws up.

"What did he say?" Juliana asks.

"Help me,'" Sadiq answers.

Khair reaches his hand out, but no one acknowledges his request.

"Surely there's an antivirus here in Cairo," Sadiq asks Darwishi's men.

"None," one of them replies, "they've been stockpiled in Saudi Arabia."

"You promise me you'll get me to Israel before I end up like that," I beg Jacob.

Khair walks faster, dragging his wounded leg, but he trips. He stumbles to regain his balance and falls to the floor. Sadiq warily walks over to his body.

"Is he breathing?" Juliana asks.

"Barely," Sadiq answers.

"Leave him be," I say firmly. "We need to leave this place now. We cannot help him. He's as good as dead." It's harsh, but it's the truth, and time isn't on my side either. Though I haven't shown any signs of the virus, I'm at risk with every day that passes. The antivirus is my only hope to survive, but tonight we must save my brother.

Everyone quickly exits the seminary but me. I cannot willfully watch a man suffer like this. I take out my gun and point it toward his head. His eyes glaze over, but I somehow know he's begging me to pull the trigger.

"God, forgive me," I whisper before I pull the trigger.

His stony stare vanishes, but his suffering is relieved. My hands shake and my eyes water. Jacob stands at the door with my bow and swords in hand.

"You had no choice," he offers with a hint of comfort.

I grab my swords and bow and walk away feeling less safe. If I'm not shot, this nasty virus will surely take me. Either way, death is following in my footsteps.

We leave the seminary behind and travel by foot the next mile and a half except for two soldiers; they were volunteered to drive two military trucks a small distance from the prison. They will be better suited for that job in case they get stopped. And let's hope they don't, because it's our only transportation for escape.

Darwishi was right about this area. The streets are empty and the buildings are vacant. The only light emitting a path shines from our flashlights. We're surrounded by darkness except for a few shimmering twinkles just up ahead.

The streets end leaving us stranded in front of an open field of concrete and dirt. Just two hundred yards away stands a stone wall, erected nearly thirty feet high. The barrier wraps around the entire prison, protecting the inner complex. It's a good thing we came at night, otherwise we would have been spotted almost immediately.

Two by two, we watchfully make our way to the south side of the complex as Darwishi had instructed. He was right: this side of the prison is less exposed and the south wall has been breached. A twisted pile of metal resembling a vehicle at one time leans scorched against the wall. A car bomb perhaps, though not recent. Judging by the deteriorated stones and sand drifts covering part of the car, I'd say this happened long ago.

Why the wall was never rebuilt is beyond me. It is, however, a perfect place to sneak into the prison, which scares me. Seems too easy to just walk in unnoticed.

Sadiq eagerly draws his weapon and presses forward around a barricade of wrecked vehicles. Though averse to the idea, I follow cautiously behind. Something is amiss about this section of the prison.

Two spotlights suddenly shine down from the top of the south corner guard post. The generators must have powered up. I hastily grab Jacob's arm and pull him back. About fifteen yards ahead of us, Sadiq, Henry, and three soldiers lie on the ground like opossums. The rest of us hang back out of sight behind a small building in ruin.

Near the top of the guard post, two soldiers survey the perimeter, one holding a rifle, the other operating the spotlights. The bright beams wander about, examining the south grounds. They shine dangerously close to Sadiq and the others, just inches away from exposing them. They are certain to get caught if they don't move right now.

I grab my bow and knock an arrow quickly.

"Arena, don't. You miss and this rescue is all for nothing," Jacob says.

"And if I don't, my friends live to see another day," I retort.

I steady my aim toward the prison tower, but it's too dark to see the guards. Their shadows mingle within the dark. Sadiq inches away on his belly as the lights move closer. Henry and the other soldiers roll to the side. Suddenly, the bright beams stop moving. Loud chatter erupts from atop the turret. *Have we been exposed?*

There's no time. I release the arrow at the first shadow that moves on the tower. *Shit!* It just grazed the concrete wall. I quickly grab another arrow, but this time I have a clearer shot. The misty clouds pass by leaving the moon brightly shining above the tower. The arrow strikes just below the guard's shoulder and pushes him back. He dangles over the railing for a moment before plummeting to the ground.

The other guard hovers over the side staring down at his comrade's mangled body. *Swish!* I fling another arrow. It sticks deep into the guard's chest. His back arches and he stumbles against the wall. He's still alive. I sink another arrow into his skull.

"Go now!" I urge. We sprint across the desert sand and breach the broken wall. Something just doesn't seem right.

"Stop, wait!"

"What is it?" Sadiq asks.

Before I can utter a word, an explosion erupts. Sand and shrapnel scar the side of the prison wall. The debris leaves one of Sadiq's men lying face-down with his legs blown off.

"Stay back!" Sadiq shouts. "We're not getting in here that easily."

"Well, they're certainly gonna know someone's here now," I say.

"What do we do?" Jacob asks.

"Cohen, Peretz, sweep the field," Sadiq orders his men.

The two men carefully guide the end of their guns across the sand and cautiously sweep a path to the prison wall.

The three-story interior structure stretches to the right a good hundred yards. The outer wall runs parallel around the complex where concertina wire sits atop. The prison's derelict exterior hardly seems secure. Broken vehicles and a barricade of debris litter the opening between the interior and exterior walls. Aside from the two prison towers, much of the security must dwell inside this humble-looking penitentiary.

We edge along the prison wall about fifty yards until we reach a recessed undercover. The dark covert leads to a large metal door that is strangely ajar. Sadiq quietly cracks the door. Inside is completely black with an eerie silence. A light flickers in the distance, an aging bulb perhaps, or the struggle of a generator keeping the building lit. Either way, it's not inviting.

"Wait," I say.

"What is it?" Sadiq asks.

"I'm not sure this is the best solution."

"We've accessed the prison; this is our only way in. What other solution could there be?"

"Yes, but tracking down here altogether like this? As a military specialist you should know this isn't the best tactic."

"What are you suggesting?"

"As Finnegan used to say, 'Perhaps there's another way in.'"

Sadiq stares at me as his mind churns. "The roof," he echoes in agreement.

"Splitting up will be our best chance of sifting through these guards," I say.

"And just how do you expect to get up there?"

"I saw a metal ladder attached to the side of the prison at the end of the wall."

"It may be dangerous taking the rooftop with soldiers posted up there."

"It's a risk I'm willing to take. Besides, they won't expect it."

"Fine, but this is on your hands, not mine."

"Has it ever been anything different?" I say with a smile.

"Just be careful."

"Nadia, Juliana, and Jacob will come with me. The rest of you scour the lower levels first and don't leave anything untouched. Hopefully we'll meet in the middle."

"Just remember to be discreet. No need to scatter the ants," Sadiq addresses everyone.

Father Joseph's eyes meet mine. "Don't do anything impetuous," he says.

"Have I ever?" I joke, trying to keep spirits light.

Father Joseph furrows his brow. "We'll revisit that when we're safely out of here." He turns and seeps into the shadow behind the others.

The clouds cover the moonlight and the stony walls bury into the darkness. The steel ladder attached to the side of the prison shimmies side to side as we ascend. Mortar crumbles around the rusted bolts with each step. I'm apprehensive about the climb until I reach the edge of the roof. Not a soul in sight, not even a glimmer of resistance atop the prison.

One by one, we scale over the edge and wait. It's dark and still. The silence is begging for attention. Near the middle of the rooftop sits two small structures about twenty yards apart. A metal door, attached to one of the structures, separates us from what I hope is a successful rescue.

Jacob carefully tools the locked door open with pinning rods. The lock clicks and the handle freely turns. I crack the door open and approach inward. We are met with a staircase descending below to unknown territory.

Lights flicker below us while we are invited by silence. Quietly down the stairs we go, guns drawn. My heart pounds to the beat of uncertainty. I stop. Voices murmur in the distance. They grow louder toward us, but vanish quickly behind the slam of a door.

We reach the bottom of the stairs to a long hallway that extends in both directions. A rusted gate, hinged to the wall, swings freely to the right. A solid metal door lies just on the other side of it, perhaps where the voices exited. The hall to the left stretches quite a distance under flickering lights where it eventually dwindles into shadow.

Nadia grabs my shoulder, and I stop. Boots lumber at the end of the corridor, and small chatter raises from the shadows. I peek ever so slightly around the corner. Two men, half-drunk, struggle down the hall toward us.

I pull my knife, but Jacob stops me. He shakes his head and gestures a neck twist with his arms. Smart thinking. No need for blood to spill here.

Nadia and Juliana peel back against the wall. Our two intoxicated comrades scuffle across the floor past us. I don't think they would have noticed us even if they were sober. Jacob and I sneak up behind each guard. *Snap!* Both soldiers drop to the floor. I don't think I'll ever get used to the sound of someone's neck cracking.

We drag their limp bodies up the steps and into the corner where it's dark. The hall is dark, but quiet.

"It's clear," Nadia whispers.

Silently down the hall we move. The door at the end opens to concrete walls and steel mesh floors. A long corridor stretches to the right into what appears to be a large opening where it's better lit. The metal door to the left stands unguarded. I jiggle the handle, but it's locked.

"Forget it, let's go," Jacob says.

Before we move down the hall, I'm tempted to try once more. I reach out for the handle, but it swivels on its own. My eyes grow big and the door swiftly swings open.

I can't reach my gun in time. A disheveled soldier stands there with an automatic firearm pointed to my head. He barks in Arabic.

"Arena!" Jacob yells.

"Stop, Jacob," I urge. The guard's rifle drifts closer to my head.

I slowly turn my head toward Jacob, Juliana, and Nadia where they can now get a better glimpse of the situation. He shouts more Arabic gibberish, this time toward Jacob.

"Jacob, put the gun down . . . now," Nadia says.

The soldier orders Jacob and the others over by me with the slight gesture of his gun. My eyes have not moved from the end of the barrel. He briefly turns his eyes away from me and glowers at Jacob.

In a swift moment, I do something I probably shouldn't, as Father Joseph said. I push the end of the barrel away from my head and jab my knife into his jugular. The gun goes off, sending several rounds echoing throughout the halls. The guard falls to the floor spewing a river of red from his neck. Not ten seconds pass when a hellish buzzing alarm goes off.

Leaving the dead guard behind, we escape through the door and lock it. The alarm screams. There's no place to hide except behind a small desk in the corner. A steel-barred door connects to another room, but it's locked. No matter how hard Jacob tries to pick it, it won't budge. Soldiers are scrambling down the halls, their boots and shouts heard in the distance. We have nowhere to go now. We're trapped.

CHAPTER 26

The walls feel like they're closing in around me. The alarm blares. Boots are pounding down hallways. We're going to have to fight our way out of this room.

"The guard!" shouts Juliana. "He must have the keys to the other door."

I don't know why I didn't think of that in the first place. I creep up to the door to the hall and slowly crack it open. Jacob stands next to me, rifle pointing toward the knob. He peers through the crack.

"It's clear," Jacob assures.

I push the door open. Jacob slides the soldier across the floor by his feet into the room. Juliana was right; there's a set of keys inside his pocket. I quickly shuffle each key into the lock, but none seem to remotely fit until I get to one that's embossed with the letter *V*. The key effortlessly slips in and the lock clicks. Just then, the squealing alarm stops and the lights go out. Gunshots ring outside in the hall.

"Go, go, go!" Jacob shouts.

We race into the next room and bar the door shut. It's damp, musty, and smells like old sweaty men. I can't see a damn thing in front of me. I struggle to find a flashlight.

"Arena, where are you? I can't see you," Juliana whispers.

"Stretch out your hands," I reply. I feel through the air until I touch her hand, or someone's hand. It doesn't feel like Juliana's at all.

"Jacob, is that you?" I ask. The hand squeezes mine.

"I'm not touching anyone's hand," he answers unsurely.

I quickly let go and fidget once more for my light. An eerie moan courses through the darkness. I take a few steps back and bump against something terribly hard.

"What the hell was that?" asks Nadia.

"Jacob, your torch," I urge.

"I can't find it. It must have fallen," he says.

A beam of light shines down at the ground. It's Juliana. "Sorry, guys," she says. She shines her light around and locates Nadia and Jacob.

"Over here," I say.

She lifts the light into my eyes, and I quickly cover them, blinded for a moment.

"Arena!" Juliana screams.

My head is suddenly pulled back against metal bars. I gasp for air as hands clamp around my neck and I struggle to breathe. Jacob races forward and wrestles the hands. After a short stint, I'm released. I heave for air, trying to filly lungs. Then I aim my gun at whatever monstrous brute tried to kill me.

"Arena, wait!" Jacob yells. "Give me your light, Juliana."

Jacob shines the torch. Hiding beneath layers of grime are four raggedy men in prison cell. Two are badly beaten; one man has a scar slashed across his face, and the other man glares at me with evil intent.

"Go ahead, shoot," the prisoner concedes. I slowly lower my gun and look upon them with despair. "It would greatly be better than this," he says.

A sudden chorus of moans awaken in the dark. Jacob swivels the light to the back of the room. Six more cells occupy this hold and are filled with prisoners.

"Gabe," I call out. No one answers. Just a few grumbles sifting through the dark.

"Give me the light, Jacob," I urge. Juliana clings to me as I thoroughly inspect each cell, but there's no sign of Gabe, just broken men with disheveled faces. Juliana's face saddens.

"These aren't the only cells in this place," Nadia comforts.

"I know he's in here somewhere, Juliana. I can feel it," I add. "We still have the lower levels to search."

"If we're going to do this, we need to move now," Nadia asserts.

"How are we supposed to do that? We can't see shit and the place is swarming with guards," Jacob says.

"Very carefully," I affirm. I shuffle through the ring of keys.

"What are you doing?"

"Look around for some weapons."

"Arena, we need to move now."

"I'm not leaving these men here to rot. At least they have a chance to fight."

I sort through the key ring and find the master key. One by one, I open the cell doors. Fifteen men scuffle out, and they are now free to make their own choice.

"Over here, I found something," Jacob calls.

On the back wall hangs a long metal cupboard with a lock. Jacob tools his pin rig and easily removes the lock. The doors creak open. Nestled on a rack is a row of several fully loaded assault rifles, each equipped with a tactical light.

I hand over the guns to the prisoners. They look at me as if I'm crazy. Maybe that's because I am.

"This is your best chance to get out of here. I'm not forcing you to do anything. It's your choice," I offer.

The man who nearly choked me to death nods with gratitude. "We'll lead you to the lower cells," he says.

"You sure?"

"It's the least I can do. Besides, I know where you need to go."

"Thank you . . ." I search for a name.

"Name is Ari."

"Lock and load, boys," he addresses the other prisoners. "It's time to hunt."

Fifteen prisoners stand together, some with assault rifles, others with no more than a piece of sharp metal as a weapon. All too eager to flee this imprisonment, it's a sacrifice they've chosen. Their fate has been sealed and I will gladly follow.

One by one, the prisoners exit the room and I follow close behind with the others, but I won't hesitate to lead if need be. Ari peers behind the door to the hall with his hand raised. After a few seconds, he gestures us to move.

Orange-colored lights flicker in the halls, emergency lights perhaps. With every flash, I get a glimpse of what's ahead — an unpleasant nightmare. The bleak corridor leads us to a set of rusted metal stairs winding down to the next level.

Bang! Bang! Bang!

The sound of gunshots echoes in my ears. The prisoners sprint ahead where a struggle ensues. Ari wrestles a guard to the ground, while one prisoner jabs him in the side with a piece of jagged metal. Blood pours down the bottom of the stairs.

Ari grabs the guard's radio. Exhausted, he peers around the corner. The hall clears, so we quickly push on to the next floor. The flickering emergency lighting brightens the dim stairwell just enough to see in front of us. The unlocked door at the bottom of the stairs opens to a room where the walls have been fabricated from steel mesh. A broken pool table sits in the middle of the empty room.

"This is the rec area. Just on the other side is where the halls lead to the other cellblocks," Ari explains.

"Is there another way around?" I ask.

"We would have to backtrack and that's just too risky. This is the shortest way."

"How secure is it?" Jacob asks.

"Guards intermittingly patrol the cell block, but most will stand on top of the meshed roof and look down."

"Then won't they see us."

"Not from the second level. The first floor of cells, yes."

"And what if Gabe is in the lower cells?" I ask.

"Let's hope he isn't."

Just across the dingy floor, a broken gate is jarred from its hinges. Behind that are a set of double doors, scarred and decorated with bullet holes. Not sure I want to know what may have caused this.

Just on the other side of the doors, a long hall stretches before us. The lights above flickers. The shadowy prison halls make for a cautious step. Juliana walks in unison next to me. Ari and the other inmates slowly move ahead in front of us. I'm less comfortable dragging behind them, knowing the slightest slip-up will bury us.

Ari stops. A sudden barrage of scuffling boots creep from the right. I pull my gun. After a minute or so, the guards fade into the distance. We slowly inch down the hall to an intersection where one corridor leads to the right and the other leads to a catwalk constructed from steel mesh. This looks all too familiar.

The flickering lights stop, plunging us into darkness. I can't even count the fingers on my hand. *Click.* Ari's torch shines in my face. Suddenly, I feel a bit apprehensive about following this stranger. I fidget with my light until our path brightens. Ari signals us to the catwalk.

"Careful here," he warns. "Stay as close to the inner walls as possible."

Sprawling footbridges interconnect one another to different parts of the prison, but the meshed metal walkway we've taken runs just above a concrete holding facility reminiscent of the den back home — memories I'd like to forget for now. It's empty below except for the massive blood stains on the floor.

We reach the halfway mark and stop. Gunshots fire from a distance, followed by a roaring clash of metal.

"Let's go, let's go!" Ari commands.

We sprint to the end of the catwalk and up a short flight of stairs to another hall. Bullets whiz by, striking just below our feet. One of the prisoners is shot in the head and falls in front of me, blocking the path.

"Let's go!" Ari shouts again.

A rankling of roaring gunshots echo and an all-out raging gunfight erupts. Below, soldiers run and scatter like cockroaches. People scream and metal clangs. Behind us at the end of the hall, several guards sprint toward us, assault rifles in hand.

"Come on!" Ari yells.

We scamper around the corner and through a set of steel doors. I grab a piece of metal from one of the prisoners and shove it tightly inside the door handles. It won't hold for long, but it's better than the alternative. About twenty meters down the hall, the catwalk opens up to the upper cellblocks. Cell after cell, prisoners hang their hands out and shout. The roar of desperation is deafening.

"Watch the doors!" I shout over the rioting crowd.

Ari and his men guard the barred door while I fight to find Gabe. It's much too loud to yell out his name, so I search each cell. Juliana sprints ahead to cover the other end. Her face, cold as ice, examines the cells with determination.

Cell by cell, Jacob and Nadia use the master key to free the prisoners, but it's a madhouse. They escape their concrete holes and flock toward an exit, which is unfortunately on the other side of the barred door. Some quickly grow impatient and descend over the balcony to the first floor. Many make it, but a few attempts are fatal.

Juliana and I search until we meet in the middle, but there is still no sign of my brother. I'm frustrated beyond anger. I don't know how we will find him now, not in this riot we've created.

Clank, clank, clank!

The metal snaps against the handles and the door flies open. The guards have breached the barred doorway and open fire. Ari and his men mow them down one by one as they cross the doorway, but not without a casualty. Two more prisoners are shot dead.

We quickly follow Ari through the door and around the corner. Another passage before us ascends down a flight of stairs. A few guards lie dead, hunched over on the steps. Our only hope is that the rest of the guards have left the lower cells.

We rush to the first floor and down another hall. Shots fire around the corner and Ari falls to the ground. I shoot the guard in the head.

"Ari, you okay, are you okay?" I assert, shaking him. His shoulder is bleeding, but the wound isn't gushing. The bullet passed through and singed the skin.

"I'm fine," he answers as I help him to his feet.

We press on around the next corner and down the long corridor to the lower cells. The cellblock is littered with blood and a few who didn't make it out. Juliana's face hardens as we approach the cells. They're completely empty.

"They're gone . . . they're gone," she mumbles. She's in an almost catatonic state. I reach out to comfort her, but it's cut short by gunfire ringing out behind us.

We sprint past the cells to the other end where the block exits into the next section. I take aim at anything that moves. Footsteps trample the floor in front of us. I lean against the wall as voices chatter closely behind the right corner. I pull my katana and wait while the voices grow louder. Closer and closer they come. I let go of all the anger pent up inside, and without any hesitation, I raise the sword.

Just as I'm about to swing, a familiar voice stops me cold.

"Arena!"

I drop my sword. Father Joseph, shirt bloodied, comes around the corner with his gun drawn. Beside him is Gabe, with Sadiq and his men following behind.

"Gabe!" I shout.

Dirt covers his face and his hair is long and shaggy. He has lost weight; the prison garb—a long-sleeved shirt and matching tan pants—hangs off him. His face is worn and he weakly scuffles as if his body has been battered.

Juliana rushes to Gabe and locks her arms around him—an embrace that's long overdue. Like Juliana, I'm overcome to see my brother again, but our moment of joy is overshadowed by a flinging cry. Out of the dark Caspar lunges in a panic.

"There's more behind us, reinforcements!" he screams. His eyes meet mine, but there's no smug arrogance hiding behind them. He nods his head and says something I would have never expected to exit his mouth. "Go on, I'll hold them off!"

"Don't be foolish," I interject.

Jacob pulls me by the arm. "Come on, Arena, let's go!"

I stare at Caspar wondering why he would sacrifice himself.

"I'll be okay, just go, now!" he assures me.

Hesitantly, I grab my sword and follow behind Jacob and the others. Midway I stop while the others retreat. I turn back, hoping to convince Caspar one last time.

"Caspar, come on!"

He stands his ground armed and ready to fight whatever is soon charging.

"Caspar . . . please," I say calmly. This isn't right. This isn't how this is supposed to happen.

"Go, Arena! Get out of here!"

"Are you trying to die?"

"I'm trying to protect you."

The floor trembles and the doors down the dark hall-way burst open. Soldiers surge through like a pack of wild animals. I fire alongside Caspar until the last soldier collapses dead. Caspar's side is bleeding. He winces and grabs his ribs.

"I'm fine," he grimaces.

"Good, now come on and let's get out of here."

His eyes widen and his face fills with fear. "Arena!" he screams, as he whips his arm around me.

I whip around and together we fire at the lone guard who emerged from the bellows. The guard slumps against the wall holding his stomach. I shoot him in the head.

I turn to Caspar who's as pale as a sheet. Sweat dots his brow. He lets out a groan and collapses in my arms. He's so heavy, it forces me down, and I have to shift his body weight off me with everything I can muster. Panting and shaking, I rest his head in my lap. His face is stone-like, waiting for death to take him. I stroke his cheek waiting for his eyes to move, but there's nothing but the silence of passing.

"Arena, what are you doing? Come on!" Jacob yells, running up to me.

"He's dead," I simply answer. Caspar saved my life. I close my eyes for a moment, harboring a strange feeling of guilt. He truly was a hero.

"Come on!" Jacob shouts, then grabs my arm. I leap to my feet and race down the hall leaving behind a better man than I gave him credit for.

Heavy gunfire rains in the distance and there's no sign of Father Joseph or the others. They have disappeared. Jacob stops and examines our position.

"This doesn't look right. I don't remember the others going this way," he observes.

The hall ends in front of us where it's barricaded with barbed wire and a chained gate. We backtrack down the hall through a steel door to the left. Inside there's a trail of lifeless bodies—prisoners and guards mingle in puddles of red.

Two guards, badly wounded, struggle to get up. Without an ounce of remorse, I shoot them both as we pass. We exit the room to one of the main corridors that stretch in both directions. No matter what path I choose, I feel something bad forthcoming. A shot fires where lights glimmer to the right followed by a chorus of shouting.

Adrenalin flows, bursting into a roaring engine as my legs thrust like pistons down the hall. Bullets chase past, buzzing and scraping the floor between Jacob and me. The end feels so far away, but in an instant, the broken door swings open and we exit the front of the prison.

Outside we are met with a barrage of soldiers surrounding us. Juliana and Gabe are on their knees with their hands locked behind their head, while the others lie helpless on the ground. About a dozen prisoners follow suit and surrender. How can it end like this?

"Popast' na zemlyu!" a Russian soldier shouts.

"Get down on the ground, Jacob," I carefully explain as I kneel.

Arabic chatter ensues among the guards. One moves in closer, his gun pointed at my head.

"Ant!" he yells in his Aramaic tongue. I don't understand what he says, so I stay put. He jabs his gun into my shoulder and shouts, *"Inhath, inhath!"*

I meet his watchful eyes and slowly stand to my feet. There's nothing I can do but comply. We are outnumbered. Jacob stands up, but the soldier eagerly slams him back to the ground.

A large military truck pulls up and a dozen soldiers exit the back, fully geared. A strange, eerie calm hovers over us followed by a surprising bellow of thunder. A warm breeze blows in and with it comes a hellish scream from the sky. The clouds move over the moon and darken the earth below. The guard grows restless and shoves the gun in my side to move, but he freezes. The unusual squelching distracts him. I try to plant my eyes on his gun, but I divert my attention to the strange noise as well.

The clouds pass and leave the moon to illuminate a terrifying sight. Like smoke from a fire, a billow of darkness falls. A wretched, foul odor fills the air. The smoky shadow ascends toward us, and I'm afraid it's something more menacing. A squall of cawing crows parade down out of the sky. Tens of thousands of flapping feathers move swiftly like an angry storm.

A crow with eyes as red as blood swoops down toward me, mouth agape. I fall to the ground and cover my head. The guard behind me screams as a half dozen leather fowls torture him relentlessly. Over and over, they drill their sharp pointed beaks into his skin until he's dead.

I rise to my feet and run. Every inch of the sky is now draped in black feathers flapping a fierce wind strong enough to nearly push me over. The wind blows like a roaring freight train, screeching into the night.

I stumble through the raging squall toward Jacob, who's lying on the ground in front of me. He covers his head while the black birds dip down and attack the soldiers around him. One by one, they drop. The devilish birds fly past me as if I don't exist. I can't see anything in front of me from the hurricane of crows dashing by. The noisy crows grow louder and louder to the point my ears begin to hurt.

Jacob's face flashes past, but quickly vanishes. A soldier nips my heels and I crash to the ground with him. He crawls on his belly and pulls on my ankle. I raise my other foot and try to kick him off, but the crows descend upon him, pecking and clawing at his body, then dragging him across the ground and out of sight. I scramble to my feet and frantically search for my friends, but there's nothing but a black sea of chaos sifting through a battalion of soldiers to my left. Gunfire sprays the sky, but it's too late. The crows diminish toward the prison leaving the remaining soldiers ravished.

The sky clears and the screeching stops. The grounds are stained red. Not one soldier or guard among us lives. The rest of us, prisoners included, have been spared from what I can only conclude to be divine. The dead lie unmercifully, eyes plucked and throats gouged.

The breeze calmly ceases while I gaze in horror, almost frightened to move. The sea of black birds perch atop the carnage, waiting silently. The prisoners kneel and plead mercy beneath their breath. Out of the shadows swoops a lone crow. It flies directly at me, but I do not move. Instead, I holster my gun and invite its presence.

The same crow slows and rests on my left shoulder. Gabe cautiously walks over, bewildered.

"I've seen this bird before," he exclaims. He gazes mysteriously at the crow. "There's something in its mouth."

Gabe stretches out his hand. A peach pit falls from the crow's beak and drops into Gabe's palm. Just then a voice whispers from its feathers, and like before, I'm the only one who can hear it.

"Gather as much water as you can, enough to sustain for seven days."

Seconds later, my black-feathered friend flies away. And like the sound of a roaring twister, the rest of the murder ascends quickly behind.

"What the hell is this supposed to mean?" Gabe queries over the peach pit.

"Symbolic maybe, I don't know. Maybe it was just hungry. I guess it thought you were a trashcan."

"There was a reason I missed you, but this, not so much." Gabe smiles and wraps his arms around me. I hold him tightly, realizing how thin he's gotten, but I don't want to let go.

"We better go while we have a chance," Sadiq suggests.

"What about the prisoners?" I ask.

"We don't have time. I'm sorry, but right now we need to get you and your brother to safety."

"How can you forget about these people?"

"It's basic combat triage," advises Sadiq.

"What exactly are you suggesting?"

"We don't know what kind of army is on its way to relieve the situation. We don't have the room anyway."

"This is cruel, even for you, whether you want to admit it or not."

"Call it what you want."

"You really want to leave on that account?"

"Let the laws of nature risk resurfacing. It's out of our hands now, and you know it. We have to leave now." My heart suddenly empties.

"It's the only way now," Sadiq says less aplomb. While his voice strains for confidence, I know deep down he wants no more part of this plan than I do, but he's right. He's made his choice and so have I.

"Fine," I say.

The prisoners scatter like cockroaches, except for Ari. "I'm indebted to you. Wherever you go, I go," he says.

"Welcome to the family," I say as I gaze coldly at Sadiq.

The trek back feels much better than it was coming here. I find a small departure from the normal gloom and embrace the little joy we've been given, even if it's short-lived. My brother is back and I'm at peace.

Not long after we reach the seminary, we pack up our gear, ready to leave. Sadiq and Ari converse over the truck's problematic engine, but I'm more concerned about the crow's warning to gather water. How am I supposed to explain this to the group?

I wander inside the building to find anything resembling a jug to hold water, but there's nothing remotely usable. Near the back of the building, I find two five-gallon buckets, tipped on their sides.

"Hey, you're not gonna die on me, are ya?" Gabe jokes as he sneaks up behind me.

"What?"

"Nadia told me what happened. Why didn't you just take the antivirus shot, Arena?"

I sigh in relief that Nadia didn't tell him about the other *shot*, the one where I pulled the trigger. I feel overwhelmed at the thought . . . "Would it have mattered? I take the shot, Nadia is exposed, and we are all still susceptible of getting the virus."

"Yes, but—"

"We'll make it to the Israeli border and I will take it then."

"And if it's too late?"

"I guess we have to let fate decide."

"What are you doing with those buckets?"

"Here, take them to the kitchen area and fill them up with water. There's a hose underneath the sink. We don't have much water left in our packs."

Gabe and Jacob take the full buckets and put them inside the truck.

"Good thinking," says Father Joseph, "I'm just about out of water."

Black smoke blows from the truck's exhaust and the engine struggles to turn over. After a few seconds, the roar is back. Sadiq closes the hood and secures the gate. The truck is packed. I lean against Jacob with Gabe next to me. Our group has lost a good man in Caspar, but we've gained two more because of his sacrifice. He will be forever remembered.

We leave Cairo behind, and what sets before us is unknown, but I'm not weary. I have my husband, my brother, and my friends. It's all I need right now.

Part III

The Cost

CHAPTER 27

The car drives lazily over a dirt road. My eyelids feel heavy and I allow myself to rest, even if it's for a moment . . .

I can't stop thinking about what Gabe said earlier. Maybe he's right. Maybe the virus has spread inside me and I won't know it until it's too late.

A deep rattle hums from the truck bed and suddenly our vehicle slows to a crawl. The truck stops and the cab door opens. Sadiq pops his head inside the back. "Bad news, I'm afraid," he grumbles. "Looks like we're going to be here for a while."

I eagerly jump out the back and stretch my limbs. Steam spews from underneath the hood. We've stopped in the middle of nowhere near what looks like a landfill. A road stretches in front of us surrounded by an empty desert.

"Where are we?" I ask.

"Agrod, Ataqah, or what's left of it. Used to be a small city, but looks like it's been leveled," Sadiq explains.

"By what, an atomic bomb?"

Sadiq, Ari, and Jacob promptly examine the overheated engine. Being out here isn't safe. I sit on the bumper next to Nadia and wait impatiently. My brother and Juliana embrace one another, enjoying their sweet reunion as long as they can. My mouth, parched from the arid desert, draws for some water. I cough and can't stop.

"You okay?" Nadia asks as she hands me her water. I gulp the bottle clean. Father Joseph walks over and looks upon me, concerned, but doesn't say a word. I know what he and Nadia are thinking — the infection.

"It's just the dry air," I reassure them.

"Good thing you fetched some water, because we aren't leaving anytime soon," Sadiq addresses.

"So we're stuck here until someone comes by?" Juliana asks jadedly.

"That all depends on if this sand-riddled engine wants to cooperate. We don't have any other choice right now."

"Home sweet home," I jest.

"I wouldn't get too comfortable just yet. Finding a place to dwell in here could be dangerous. We don't know what's out there," Ari cautions.

He's right. If this ever imitated a city, you wouldn't know it. It's a bombing site now. We abandoned the truck and sift through the forgotten town. The streets mingle perfectly with the ramshackle façades. The only sound structure left standing lies at the center—the three-pointed artistic statue hovers erect amid the refuse that covers the city. Desert sand has engulfed most of what is left.

"Over here," Sadiq says. Just off the main road, a tiny but livable bungalow hides beneath a pile of rubble. It's in derelict, but it's all we have.

The front door actually opens without falling off its hinges. The walls are cracked and the ceiling bows, but the main room remains unscathed. The kitchen in the back reeks of rat droppings, but it's the only room not buried in debris. Sadiq and Henry clear the rubble from the hall where two large rooms hide. They're in bad shape, but livable.

Some broken furniture piles up in one of the corners next to a working bathroom. The tiled floor buckles and the tub is filled with broken ceiling tile. I remove some debris from the bathroom sink and turn the faucet knob. It hisses with air for a minute before water struggles to pour out. I wipe away the dust from the cracked mirror and sadly stare at my reflection. My hair, greasy strands and all, has grown past my shoulders. My face is worn and my eyes resemble a raccoon. Lack of sleep has not been kind to my appearance.

The sun beats down and warms the structure like a preheating oven. Nadia and I take shade outside among a slight but fetid breeze. It beats slowly cooking in that hot box.

"You feeling okay?" Nadia asks.

"Yeah, yeah, I feel fine," I mutter unconvincingly.

"I know you better than that."

"I don't know. Something just feels wrong."

"Wrong?"

"The others, back in Alexandria. I just have a bad feeling, that's all."

"They had less resistance than us. I'm sure they made it to Jerusalem just fine."

"Maybe."

Evening approaches, as does the cool desert air. The night sky grows black without a twinkle, and the waning moon glows with malevolence. The sky rumbles like a growling lion.

"Haven't heard thunder like that in a long while," Ari says excitedly.

"Yeah, we should probably go back in," I warn.

"Looks like we're about to be blessed with rain."

"Or cursed by a storm."

I take refuge in the bungalow and lie against Jacob on the floor. I can't seem to get any rest without everyone watching over me and asking if I'm feeling okay. I understand their concern. It's been days since I was exposed to the deadly virus, but nothing has changed about me.

This exhausting journey has taken a toll on us all. My brother's eyes, fatigued and distant, turn to me. I can tell he senses my uneasy concern, but Juliana's warm kiss on his cheek squashes that feeling. I smile. Maybe someday he'll share his experience in the prison with me, but this isn't the place nor the time to prod. I leave my brother to enjoy the glowing smile on Juliana's face.

Night approaches and so does the eerie storm. The thunder hasn't stopped growling since it parked over us an hour ago. The wind falls silent, but the angry sky remains active. And then it comes, like tiny fingers tapping a drum, the pelting rain dances on the roof.

We reserve our batteries and keep the flashlights off. Darkness covers the room, as we all lie peaceful on the dusty floor. There's a mystery behind the beautiful sound of a storm you can't see, but this one feels different.

Ari jumps to his feet and paces.

"You okay?" I ask.

"I just need some air. It's too stuffy in here."

"Like a prison."

"Exactly, reminds me too much of one. Besides, I haven't felt rain in over a year."

Ari opens the door and steps out into the rain. A punch of foul air enters. My bones chill and pushes the hairs on my neck to stand. Ari, arms extended, embraces the cool shower.

"Ari, get in now!" I shout.

"Arena, what is it?" Father Joseph asks curiously.

"Ari!" I shout.

Ari turns and smiles. "Come on, it feels good." He walks through the door dripping wet. "What has got you all in a bunch?"

"Jacob, give me your flashlight," I eagerly assert. I shine the flashlight upon Ari's face.

"Oh my God!" Juliana screams.

"What?" Ari asks worriedly.

"You're bleeding," Jacob answers.

Ari, drenched in blood, hysterically wipes his face and arms. Jacob hands him a small rag. Ari wipes his lips and spits out blood as if he's been contaminated. I'm not so sure he isn't. Not a wound on his body shows where the blood came from. I reach out my hand and catch the rain in my palm, but it's not rain. The sky bleeds instead.

"Close the door," Father Joseph advises.

"What the hell is going on?" Ari asks, alarmed.

"I believe God is stirring things up," I say.

"God? Are you completely out of your mind?"

"You've seen anything like this before, my friend?"

"Look, let's just all calm down," Sadiq diffuses. "No one goes outside until the storm blows over."

Ari strips his clothes and sits worriedly by himself in the corner. The rest of us lie uneasy and wait for the storm to die down, but it doesn't. The blood falls from the clouds hours into the night and the thunder doesn't cease.

I curl up next to Jacob and lay my head on his chest. Though the blood-riddled sky continues to fall, my eyes struggle to stay open. For now, I'm safe in my husband's arms and nod off into the night.

*   *   *

My mouth is parched and my neck hurts. For a moment, I forget where we are. Gabe and Juliana sit quietly next to me while a debate ensues. I grab my flask and fill it with water from one of the buckets.

"How long can we wait this storm out when those buckets run dry?" Sadiq argues.

"We drink sparingly, only what we need," Henry answers. "Besides, how much longer do you think this storm is going to last?"

"Six more days," I interrupt.

"Excuse me?" Ari pipes.

"I'm afraid we'll have to stay inside for a while."

"What? You're telling us—"

"Wait," Father Joseph interjects. "What do mean, 'six more days,' Arena? How do you know this?"

"That's what I was told."

"And who told you this?" Ari asks curiously.

I'm not sure what I say will satisfy him. I'm disinclined to mention anything at all, but I must. "The crow," I state plainly.

"Well, of course. A crow. Why not?" Ari huffs. Facetious or not, he can't deny the strange phenomenon falling from the sky.

"We have enough water to get us through this."

"If this blood shower lasts six more days, I'll streak buck naked through the streets of Jerusalem," Ari teases.

"I'm sure no one wants to see that, but I'll take that bet."

"Let's all just settle down," Sadiq calmly pleads. "If we're here that long, I suggest we conserve our food as well. Everyone empty your packs."

We pile up the food and divide it up accordingly. Not much to make a meal, but enough to survive on. I've eaten less than this when Gabe and I were stuck in the woods.

*   *   *

Day two is anything but pleasant. The house reeks of sweat and the rotting air outside seeps in. Old stories from Father Joseph and Sadiq make the restless evenings pass by. The time we spend together makes this fellowship tighter.

On day five we are down to a half-bucket of semi-clean water. Impatience sets in and the group grows agitated. Whether from heat and stuffy air or simply being closed up in tight quarters, I'm hallucinating.

The walls bleed and the floor moves in a circular motion. Maybe it's just lack of prokein, but whatever it is, it's making me nauseous. I take a few gulps of water and eat a small piece of granola. Soon after I fall unconscious to the floor.

*   *   *

I wake from a nightmare that has ended with Juliana screaming and blood running from her chest. Jacob presses against me and holds my face gently with his brawny hand.

"Hi, love," I say with a smile.

"Didn't think you were going to wake up, Arena," he says. "You've been asleep for a long time."

"How long?"

"It's day seven."

The storm has not ceased, but soon it will all be over. The house has not flooded and the roof has not leaked once.

Midday passes while everyone anxiously waits. Ari tips the bucket of water up to his lips and a few drops trickle into his mouth. Silence slowly creeps above us and eyes widen with optimism. Ari gazes over at me as if I've done something wrong. He walks to the door and carefully opens it. The thunder vanishes and the blood stops pouring from the sky.

I step past Ari and walk outside to a cool breeze. The house, painted red, glistens. The parched desert earth has absorbed the red rain. It now seeps into fertile ground and poisons any vegetation left standing.

The scarlet street drains into bloody puddles on either side. Steam rises from the ground like morning fog. The smell of burnt blood lingers and I almost throw up.

"Now that's peculiar," Sadiq remarks.

Jacob follows Ari and examines the main road while Sadiq stands befuddled. Our truck has mysteriously vanished. I hardly doubt the storm moved the truck, but it really doesn't matter. We have no transportation and our water supply is gone.

The pile of wreckage and blood-gumming streets makes it difficult to explore the grounds for transportation. I'm afraid we're stuck here for a while. Trekking by foot in this heat is suicidal, especially when water is scarce. I feel like I'm in control of nothing. Why would God lead us to this forsaken place to whither?

"What are we gonna do, Arena?" Juliana asks.

I'm desperate for an answer, but I have not one. This is completely out of my hands now. All I have to offer is a discouraging face.

"I don't know," I simply answer.

"Well, we better come up with something quick or this whole rescue mission was meaningless," Sadiq adds.

We're all alone, deserted in the middle of nowhere, and surrounded by toxic warm-congealed blood. Only an idiot would ask if this could get any worse. I bind my lips.

"This is going to get real ugly soon," Sadiq warns.

"I second that," Jacob adds.

As if our incessant grumbling struck a chord, a rumbling crash breaks the sky and rain falls on my face. Clean, clear water drips into my mouth as the cool rainwater soothes my aching neck. I smile with pleasant delight and remove my shirt. I let my body soak and bathe the sweat from my skin.

Henry and Gabe quickly fill the empty buckets with rainwater while the others dance like children in the rain. The bloody streets wash clear and the ground softens. The dark cloud camps over us and the cool shower continues for several hours.

Nightfall approaches, but my restless mind cannot sleep. The less I know, the more irritable I become. How are we supposed to reach the Israeli border without a vehicle? How much longer will we have to stay here before we start turning on one another? I have more questions than answers, but I must keep my faith. This group depends on me to a certain extent.

Unlike the previous storm, this one is more inviting. Ari braces the door open and watches the rain fall outside.

Jacob, Henry, Father Joseph, and Sadiq converse over our options. I sit next to Nadia and muse over what might have happened to the others back in Alexandria. I'm suddenly struck by the absence of Allison and Luke. *How are they coping right now?* I wonder.

"Do you ever wish sometimes you never left the States?" Nadia asks.

"Occasionally," I reply.

"I wish sometimes I could just leave this place behind. A quick death is better than living this nightmare."

"I know the feeling, but without you by my side, I couldn't have gotten this far. To see my brother again was worth it. Even if this is short-lived, I owe you everything."

Nadia places her arm around me as we sit together wondering to ourselves how this nightmare will end.

CHAPTER 28

Day eleven and our food rations have all but diminished. I've shown no signs of the virus, but I keep my hopes hidden. While most get sick in two or three days after contraction, there's a small fraction of a chance that the virus could stay dormant for a while in some. Because the rarity of such possibilities, I see no raise for concern. But Jacob and Sadiq feel very differently about it. I'm constantly monitored and given special treatment. I try to ignore the possibility of dying, but whenever Jacob kisses me, I'm scared deep down inside.

Three times rain has fallen, and three times we've taken advantage by filling our buckets to quench our thirst. The struggle to find transportation keeps us from departing this hellhole, but we've survived somehow. Our group grows with discouragement after scouring nearly every inch of this desolate town for the past three days. If we don't find food soon, we won't have the strength to move on.

It's midday, but you wouldn't know it from the gray skies. Nadia and I explore the west side once more while the others attempt to pillage what looks like a military facility.

After hours of wandering and drifting from the others, we stumbled across a sign of hope. A concrete block with a metal door attached protrudes three quarters through the earth. The door is unlocked, but the sand barricades it from opening. Nadia and I dig anxiously, sweeping the sand drift from the bottom of the door. We pull the door with all our strength until the latch breaks free from the rusted strike plate.

The door opens and a breath of stale air releases. I shine my light inside the dark hole where steps lead down into a small twenty-by-twenty chamber. We have found a bunker buried beneath the sand.

Inside the dormant walls there's a stockpile of food, medical supplies, and a small arsenal. This day has gone from a hot, steamy pile of shit to, "Oh my, is that a can of pork and beans?" I'm completely beside myself with joy.

While Nadia takes inventory, I race to tell the others. Sad faces are replaced with smiles. One behind the other, like a trail of ants, we empty the bunker's supplies and organize our rations.

Gazing wide-eyed at this much food, I waste no time and cut the top of the lid from a can of pears. I indulge in an uncivilized moment and scrape the can clean with my dirty paws. If that's not enough, I drain the can and sip every drop of juice left. It's the little things in life that make me smile.

Another night comes, but this one manages to arouse a joy we haven't had in quite some time. After consuming a meal for three, I secure my arms around Jacob, close my eyes, and let my satisfied tummy rest through the night.

*　　*　　*

It's been nearly a month since we first took refuge in this barren town. I hate to think we've settled here, but it's safe. We have enough food to survive a few more months if we have to, but I don't intend to exercise the idea. I want to leave.

I sit on the same rock with Jacob as I've done every night and wait for something miraculous to happen. The main road is deserted and hopeless. Not a single vehicle has traveled it since we first came. The wind blows and shifts the mysterious sand beneath us into wavy patterns. Drifts can strangely creep up against the house by morning, and dunes can move in a day. The desert is the epitome of loneliness.

I kiss Jacob before going back into the house to sleep. I open the door and stop. The side of the house shines faintly of orange hues, and it's not the moon. Jacob takes my hand and cautions me to go inside, but I don't. I grab my gun and watch curiously as the faded lights move toward us. After a month of waiting, good fortune finds us — one of Darwishi's busses, riddled with bullet holes, pulls up next to the house. Steam spews from the engine cover and black smoke hovers behind the rear like a cloud.

Ananiah steps off the bus, disheveled and fatigued. No one else departs. My heart sinks. Sadiq's face brightens with subtle joy while I bury mine into Jacob's chest. Seconds later, about sixty people exit the bus and wander like cattle. Hardly the number I was expecting. This can't be all of them, surely. Some carry a few wounded and help them inside the house. Sadiq explains our predicament to Ananiah, but I'm not so sure our situation will improve. This bus is on its last leg.

I open my arms to Ananiah and greet him with adoration. "I'm so glad to see you, my friend," I lament.

"The feelings are mutual, but why so sad?" he prods.

"I was hoping to see . . ." I stop midsentence, and suddenly, my sadness leaves me. Allison, Luke, and Niki bring up the rear behind the pack. I hug Ananiah tightly once more and assure him of my joy. "I'd kiss you if I weren't married," I joke.

"Married?"

I wave my arms high and race over to Allison. Her eyes light up and a smile follows. Luke tugs on my leg and holds onto me like a baby capuchin clings to its mother.

"Hi, sis," Niki bubbles joyfully as she hugs me. "I'm so glad you're safe."

"Safe? Depends on what your definition of 'safe' is," Harold chimes in as he steps off the bus.

"Ah, Harold, what would I do without your sarcasm?" I banter at his cynical expense.

He extends his arms and begrudgingly hugs me. He won't admit it, but he loves me. Standing around, lackadaisical, fifty of the bussed refugees wait for instruction. Many I remember from the ship, but some faces I don't recognize. A few sport irritated expressions.

Jacob, Henry, and some of Sadiq's men empty the bus of supplies—water, rations, and medical are a few among them. I just hope this isn't a permanent stop. I'm not sure we can survive that long with this many people.

Juliana, Niki, and a few others tend to the wounded. Gabe and I stay clear and survey our supplies instead. We have plenty of water for a few days and the food supply is ample if we conserve properly. We have enough medical supplies to open a small hospital. Not sure where half this stuff came from.

"Hi, I'm Roland," says a tall man with an English accent. I greet him. His hair, half-gray, sweeps over to the side. The permanent crease on his face bends with his gentle smile.

"I'm Arena," I reply.

"Yes, I know. I've heard all about you."

"Good things I hope." His smile disappears and is quickly replaced by a stoic gaze. I'm briefly paralyzed and somewhat embarrassed of what he may have been told. Gabe chuckles at my humiliated expense.

"Of course. I'm just teasing with you." Roland laughs. I'm not sure if I should grin or walk away. "I see that you have taken an interest in our medical supplies," he continues.

"Never seen this much before. You have everything here—scalpels, clamps, needles, morphine. You plan on doing surgery?"

"If need be," he answers plainly.

"What are you, a doctor?"

"As a matter of fact, I am. Did my studies at Oxford before moving to Cairo."

Gabe rummages through the rest of the supplies while I converse with Roland. "You have just about every pain reliever in here," he marvels. "Antibiotics, that's good to have. EpiPen, Iodin, Modrin. What the hell is this for?" Gabe holds up a package of pregnancy tests.

"Gabe, seriously, we're trying to have a conversation here."

"It's okay," Roland chuckles.

"So how did you come by this group?" I ask.

"We met in Cairo under unfortunate circumstances, but that may be better told by your friend, Ananiah."

I nod my head. "Gabe, why don't you take the supplies and the good doctor inside so he can tend to the wounded."

"It was a pleasure to meet you." Roland smiles and walks away.

I chase down Jacob, but I can't find him among the crowd. Sadiq gestures for me from the right corner of the house. I'm greeted by a few disgruntled stares as I walk past. In particular, a large grizzly man with a gnarly cut across his cheek.

Hiding near the side of the house, Sadiq, Jacob, Ananiah, and Father Joseph wait.

"You all are probably wondering what's happened the past few weeks," Ananiah quietly explains.

"It goes without saying," I reply.

"A few days after you left Alexandria, we were attacked by a small band of Saudi militants. We held them off, but not without some casualties of our own. We were able to capture one of the radicals and interrogated him, but he had nothing to spill. Didn't claim any ties to Russia or China, but he was donning a band resembling an old Soviet emblem with black stripes."

"It's the same, like Cairo," I say.

"Same?"

"I saw a flag like the band you speak of planted on one of the government buildings. Red flag, black Soviet Union emblem, and black stripes."

"Interesting," Ananiah says.

"You don't suppose this is just Russia posturing?" Sadiq questions.

"It may be just a simple threat," Father Joseph suggests.

"And it could be a way to force protocol on other countries," Ananiah offers. "The Ten have been residing under this constricted and lawless organization for a while now. I don't see it changing. Maybe those stripes represent a Russian agreement among the ten nations brought together."

"There were only seven stripes on the flag," I explain.

"I don't know what it means, but I'm sure it's not good."

"So where are the rest? Were they ahead of your group when you left?" I ask.

"This is where it gets interesting," Ananiah says. "Before the busses arrived a couple of weeks later, a caravan of military trucks invaded the streets of Alexandria, but no soldiers were present. Just people like you and me, except well fed, groomed, and without an ounce of dirt blemishing their face. I never noticed one being armed. And then he came."

"Who came?" Jacob curiously asks.

"He called himself Mikhail—well spoken, English accent, and carried himself with confidence. He was never a threat. In fact, he was extremely generous. He and his followers brought us food by the masses, fed and dined with us. In these times, you can trust no one, so I questioned his motives. He claimed he wasn't associated with the new world order and that he and his organization would protect us from villainous autocracy and provide us with a safe haven even Russia could not touch."

"You believe his claims?" I ask.

"Not for one second, but he carried on like some right-eous nut job, and people began to feed on his bullshit. What-ever he was selling, they were buying. I'm not going to lie, he was convincing and was never at any point a threat to us. He was sharp, well-mannered, and compassionate. He warned us of some new virus the Chinese were perfecting for depopulating and assured us he had a vaccine that would keep people from contracting it. There was some-thing strange about him, but I just couldn't put my finger on it." Ananiah takes a sip of water.

"What did this Mikhail look like?" I ask.

"Tall, slender, blond hair, mid-fifties, wore a solid black suit that was noticeably tailored."

This seems all too familiar now. It's the same descrip-tion Matthew described when his group split up. Matthew traveled with a larger group before I first met him. Nearly two thousand people parted ways when Mikhail offered them a place of safety. The few who stayed with Matthew felt a lack of trust for Mikhail and his followers, so they trav-eled south instead where they made a permanent camp — the same camp where I met Luke, and the same camp the Rus-sians invaded before we escaped.

"So what happened?" I ask.

"Mikhail stayed with us for two days, offered a sanc-tion-free environment with livable conditions, and protec-tion from the Ten. It was an offer people couldn't refuse, and before you knew it, there were all but a few hundred of us left. Those who went with Mikhail lined up in single-file, had their wrists braised with a laser for the vaccine, and loaded up in the trucks."

"Braised?"

"Looks like a tattoo. You can get a closer look at Augus-tine's. He was the only one who changed his mind before he got on the truck. Two weeks later, the busses came, and we left. I haven't seen or spoken to anyone else except for the passengers on our bus. I haven't a clue what happened to the others. I just hope they had an easier time dealing with that freakish blood storm. After witnessing that, everyone was afraid to move on. The arduous trip to Cairo was filled with pestilence. Bodies are draped alongside the road and cattle lie dead in the fields. If the rain wasn't poisoned, then something else took their lives. We didn't move any further until it was over. After reaching Cairo, our caravan was separated for good. We were stopped, boarded, and detained for ten days in some fenced village in the southern part of the city," Ananiah says.

"On what grounds?" Father Joseph asks.

"Trivial reasons, I suppose. The Egyptian police warned that the city was on high alert. I'm sure you had nothing to do with that," he says, looking at me.

"How did you manage escaping that?"

"You can thank Roland for that. Don't know what strings he pulled, but he knew we were in there. He claimed to know Darwishi and said he was our eyes when we reached Cairo, but I don't ever remember a Roland."

"You trust him?" I ask.

"I do. We were released, but it wasn't easy. The strings Roland pulled were cut short. Soldiers began to occupy the outside gates. Not sure what was going on, but it was unusual. More and more soldiers came and Roland urged us to move faster. The bus pulled around as if it was planned. Suddenly there was gunfire, and before I could figure out where it was coming from, one of the men standing next to me fell to the ground, bleeding." Ananiah pauses a moment, then continues. "We left with scars, but we made it this far. I couldn't tell you if we were being chased or not, but with the engine overheating, this was the only place to stop. I don't know what kind of damage we have. We'll have to wait until the morning to see."

"I think right now we need to get everyone fed," Sadiq suggests.

Hungry people line up patiently to get their portion of food. Only a few, slightly cross, grumble in line. The air cools significantly and chills the desert sand. Gabe and I forge a fire outside the house and watch over the restless flock.

Many find comfort on the sand while others hover around and inside the house. I search over the group inconspicuously for a tattoo-covered wrist. I want a better idea of what we are dealing with.

A young man, maybe in his twenties, sits alone in the corner in one of the empty bedrooms. He's completely ignored as others mingle beside him. I get a small glimpse of black ink peeking from his crossed arms.

If he's shy, I'm not going to make it any easier for him. I plop down next to him and introduce myself. He fidgets with the hair on his arms like a nervous tick. I skip the small talk and dig in right away.

"I know you probably get tired of people asking, but do you think I could get a look at your tattoo?" I ask gently.

He shyly lifts his head and turns his wrist over. I examine the raised markings and find something most peculiar. Burned into his skin are three solid black six-pointed stars that resemble the Star of David.

"Does it hurt?"

"A little," he shyly answers.

"What made you change your mind?"

"I don't know. Something just overcame me and I decided not to go. It was almost like I couldn't control myself when I got in line."

"Well, I'm Arena, and you're here with us now. I will do everything I can to keep you safe, okay?"

"Thanks, Arena. I'm Augustine."

"Why don't you go get some food? I'm about to get myself some."

I head to the kitchen and fill my plate full of canned stew. It's not exactly cuisine, but it's better than nothing, and we are only allotted one helping each. I'm starving.

I join Jacob outside where a heated discussion erupts. A few men dance around a conversation about not leaving with Mikhail. I move closer and listen in on the argument, but apparently my presence silences their tongues. The brawny man with a scar decorating his face cuts me with a stony stare.

"You," he addresses me hotly.

"You have a problem with me?" I ask, irritated by his tone.

"You're the very reason why we're here, wasting away in this godforsaken desert."

"Excuse me!" Jacob puts his hand on my shoulder, but I swipe it way. Now I'm just aggravated.

"I could be relaxing in my cabin back in Texas, but instead I sit here and struggle to find a reason to live," the portly man crows.

"How is this on me? Why am I to blame for your choices?"

"Look, I'm not here to blame you for everything, but you certainly didn't help things back home. You buried a nation. I just wish I was buried with it."

I stand up. "Are you seriously suggesting I planned Russia's advance?"

"I'm implying you made some horrible mistakes that may have cost us a sustainable life. I admit my mistake for not going with Mikhail and the others, but it should have never gotten to that point in the first place."

"I never forced you to leave America."

"Not from my perspective." He looks forlorn. "Look, I know you're not a bad person, Arena, and maybe it wasn't your intention, but I'm tired, weary, and I just see no semblance of hope from this. Yes, I'm angry, and I probably overstepped my bounds, but you really can't blame me for that with what we've been through," he says.

"I've been to hell and back and have suffered just as much as you. I've lost more than I can handle and I'm not sure how much more I can take. We live, we survive, but you're not willing to make a sacrifice, are you? You'd rather blame everyone else for your hardships."

"You act like you're the only person who's lost someone."

"I've lost enough." I clench my fists and walk away.

"So have I!" he shouts.

I storm over to him, defiant. I grit my teeth and strain my jaw from cursing this man.

"We've all lost someone we love," he says, never breaking his gaze. "I remember every detail about her. My wife was a beautiful woman who was ravaged by sadness. She was an emotionless splendor trapped within a flower. I loved her so much. I would have happily given my life for hers if she hadn't taken her own in front of her own son. What a waste, and for what? To escape from one nightmare to another?"

"I'm . . . so sorry. I . . . didn't know . . ." I say, feeling ashamed.

"Would it have made a difference?"

I'm completely numb as I stand before a broken man. All I can offer him in this surreal moment of humility is my plate of food, but he vehemently rejects my feeble gesture of condolence.

"Don't sell me your goddamn pity."

I stand there feeling berated by this cruel man, but I've done nothing to help heal this moment. I've just made it worse. I tuck my head and return to the kitchen, saddened by the display. Two women comfort me on the way.

"I see you've met Garrett," Roland says.

"You mean the belligerent asshole?"

"So that's his middle name," he chuckles. "I wouldn't worry too much about it. He'll get over it. He'll have to."

"Yeah, well, he isn't helping this group any." I abruptly grab my side and grimace. A sharp pain runs up my chest.

"You okay?"

"Yeah, I'll be fine. Probably just heartburn."

"How long has this been going on?"

"I don't know, a few days," I say. "It's fine, really."

My stomach churns like a brewing volcano and my neck tingles. I discard my plate of food on the table and find Jacob. I walk outside a little lightheaded and grab Sadiq's arm. I nearly faint. I'm nauseous to the point that I'm about to lose more than my pride. Jacob rushes over and secures my lack of balance.

"Arena, what's wrong?" Jacob worries.

"Jacob, her nose," Sadiq gestures. My nose drips blood and my vision blurs.

"You don't think . . ." Jacob's voice fades, and everyone watches me stumble to my knees. Nadia's arm wraps around my shoulders. I weakly stand, and then it hits me. I turn my head and vomit.

"What's wrong with her?" Garett asks. I'm surprised by his sudden concern.

"Roland!" Jacob shouts.

The earth stops spinning and my vision comes back. Roland wipes the blood from my nose and examines my eyes. I feel less tingle in my neck now.

"Surly she doesn't—"

"Can't be," Nadia expresses. "Khair didn't last two days after exposure."

"Exposure to what?" Garett demands.

"It's nothing and doesn't concern you."

"Oh, I beg to differ. We have a right to know." Unfortunately, he's right. We can't trust one another if we keep secrets. We need to lay it all out on the table right now.

"Jacob, it's okay, go ahead," I beg.

Reluctantly, Jacob discloses everything. "When we reached Cairo, we settled not far outside the city to a remote village, not fully knowing we had reached the Dead Zone. There, among the barren town, we discovered a small group with possible degrading flu symptoms."

"Symptoms?" Garett queries.

"Bloody nose, blisters, boils. Typical symptoms of the later stages of the 2035 flu strain."

The crowd gasps.

"Sadiq was lucky enough to give those who were exposed an antivirus shot. There wasn't enough to go around, and Arena, by her own free will, gave her antivirus shot to someone else. We weren't sure if it was indeed the same virus until one of our unfortunate comrades, who was also exposed, died within two days."

"And you're just now telling us while we've all been in contact with this sick girl?"

"She had been fine up until today."

"Yeah, but you and I both know it can stay dormant for weeks. Now we're all exposed. This shit just keeps getting better," Garett shouts.

"We don't know anything for sure," Sadiq interrupts. "I've seen this nasty plague up close and her symptoms don't fit this strain. Besides, it's been too long for it to stay dormant."

"But you're no an expert," Garett gravels.

"I've certainly had my share of cases to deal with in my platoon during the epidemic. So it's in my expert opinion that she's not infected," Sadiq retorts.

"Then what's wrong with her?"

"Why don't we just all calm down and let Roland do his job."

The dizziness fades completely, but my stomach still stirs. I follow Roland inside one of the bedrooms and sit on a tattered mattress. He examines my vitals and gives me a complete check-up. My stomach stops churning, but my bladder feels tender. He pushes on my stomach and below my belly button and feels for internal abnormalities.

"Have you had any headaches recently, maybe a migraine?" he asks.

"No, not until last night."

"Feeling fatigued, shortness of breath?"

"Yes, especially lately."

"I'm going to be candid with you," he says, and I don't like where this is going. "I'm pretty sure you're not infected with any flu strain." Finally, a brief respite.

"But I would like for you to take this." He hands me a pregnancy test.

"You can't be serious?"

"We need to rule out everything. Take your time and let me know when you're done. I'll be right outside the door."

I take a flask of water and shut the bathroom door behind me. My hands begin to tremor. *Pregnant?* I'm too nervous to take the test, so I sit on the toilet and stare at the tattered wall. My foot nervously taps against the floor. Why am I so afraid to take this test? Screw it! I open the package and urinate on the stick as the instructions say and wait for the results.

These two minutes feel like two hours. The suspense is killing me. I grab my flask of water and relieve my dry throat. I hold the stick between my fingers, but I'm too afraid to look at it. Having a child should be a blessing, but not in this world, not now. I can't imagine being a mother to an infant in these horrible conditions. I'm nearly seventeen. What do I know about being a mom—how am I supposed to carry on now?

I take a deep breath and swallow hard. I stand and shuffle weakly to the sink. I'm still too afraid to look at the results. My heart races. I shut my eyes for a moment, breathing deeper and faster now. *This is it.* I open my eyes and look down at the stick. I stare into the broken mirror and cry.

CHAPTER 29

My eyes burn as the tears streak my cheeks. What have I done? I sit on the edge of the tub and try not to hyperventilate. My hands prickle with pins and needles. Anxiety consumes me. I wipe away the tears with my shirt and stare into the mirror. My face reddens. I wait soberly for the color to fade before I leave the bathroom.

I'm not ready to be a mother.

Roland sits on the bed patiently. My tears dry up, but my face is painted with anything but joy. He doesn't say a word. I sit beside him, lean my head against his shoulder, and weep.

He places his arm around me and whispers, "You'll get through this just like everything else."

"How?"

"The same way you approach everything else . . . with courage."

He softly smiles, quietly reaches into a bag of supplies, and hands me a bottle of prenatal vitamins. "I guess a congratulations is in order," he says brightly.

Emotions mingle inside of me. I hardly think this is a moment for celebrating. Sharing the news with my husband should be a joyous occasion, but I just can't see past the hardships that are ahead. I have cursed this child. How can I bring such innocence into a world like this?

I start to panic. How can this work logistically? With all the traveling and the fighting? A horrible thought races through my frazzled mind: what if I don't have this child?

What if I miscarry? What if I terminate the pregnancy? I want to scream.

"You have to promise me, you won't say a word about this," I beg.

"Sure, but—"

"You can't tell anyone, even Jacob."

"You know you can't keep this a secret forever."

"I know, but right now isn't a good time. Let me deal with that on my own."

"It's your choice."

"You promise?"

Roland hesitates to answer before finally saying, "I promise."

I hide the bottle of vitamins, wipe my eyes dry, and shuffle out of the room to find a place to rest. I just need to be alone right now.

*   *   *

The scent of burnt beans drift past my nostrils and agitate my already stirring stomach. I open my eyes and find myself lying on a dingy mattress.

"How are you feeling this morning?" Roland asks.

"Like I'm about to puke. What's that smell? Beans?"

"Breakfast I suppose."

"I need some air or I'm going to lose it."

I rush past the kitchen and escape outside to an aroma of charred beans dangling over the fire. Without anyone noticing, I exit behind the house and vomit. I will never eat beans again.

Suddenly, the engine roars from the bus. I rinse my mouth and spy around the corner. Several men gather behind the bus with the engine cover open. Sadiq and Ari are among them. Some of the people in the group enter the bus, belongings in hand. The others circulate outside the house, waiting. I meet Sadiq and Ari as they mingle toward the front of the bus.

"Arena, go fetch your things and get on the bus," Sadiq says.

"Where are we headed?"

"Suez for now."

"What's in Suez?"

"Food, water, supplies, and shelter. It's a small city, but I'm sure we can find better transportation there. This bus isn't reliable. We'll be lucky to make it there."

I find Jacob, grab my pack and weapons, and privately take my vitamins. Gabe and Juliana stand next to me unnoticed and wait.

"What are the pills for?" Gabe asks.

"Nothing, just for my headache," I answer. I quickly bury the bottle in my pack before Jacob returns to the room. Everyone exits the house and promptly boards the bus. Some of the men have already stored our food and water supplies in the storage compartments beneath the bus. Sadiq and Ananiah urge everyone to take a seat. The low-idling engine struggles to sustain a constant purr.

"How far can we make it?" I ask Sadiq privately.

"We should be able to make it to Suez. We can regroup and replenish our supplies there at the market."

"If it's still there?"

"I know this is out of the way, but it's the safest route for now."

I stash my pack beneath my seat and secure my weapons to the seat in front of me. These buses can hold up to three hundred passengers, but with only sixty-eight of us on board, it will make the drive a bit more comfortable.

Eyes closed and mouths open, Allison and Luke snooze in the seat behind me. Jacob stays near the front with Ananiah, Father Joseph, and Sadiq and monitors our surroundings. I take advantage of the down time and stretch out my legs to the adjacent seat. Unfortunately, the choking engine and intermittent bumps on the road makes sleep almost impossible. I peer out the window and try to ignore my queasy stomach.

After an hour or so, the bus violently shakes and we swerve over to the side of the road. *Do we have a flat?* I think, as the bus comes to a stop. I pop my head up from the seat and peer out the window. I gasp. A large plume of dust, maybe ten miles to our north, explodes into the atmosphere. The ground rattles as the wall of dust climbs into the sky.

Allison and Luke watch in fear. After ten minutes, the earth quiets and the dust dissipates. It's unknown what just occurred, but I can't imagine it's anything good.

I keep my eyes planted on the explosion site while we continue down the road. I feel uneasy about this. The sun hides behind the clouds and gives shade to the earth below. Some people creep up toward the front of the bus to watch the landscape from the windshield. .

Sounds of tiny whispers flutter in and out. Sadiq stops the bus. I pull down the window and listen. High-pitched buzzing covers the air like the sound of a fan blowing against a piece of paper caught in its propellers. Patches of black move swiftly across the sky in intricate patterns. They dip and rise in large clusters like a swarm of bees. At first glance they resemble the murder of crows that flocked over Cairo at the prison, but when they fly closer, I realize that is not the case. One slams against the bus window. It's a locust the size of my fist. The insects dip down from the sky with a shrieking hiss.

"Close all the windows!" Ananiah yells, as he steps on the gas.

The dark swarm moves quickly to the south east, but a few veer from the pack and fly full speed into us. The large insects kamikaze into the bus and pelt the windows like rain. One insect successfully breaches a cracked window in the back and terrorizes everyone. It swoops down and attacks over and over until it stings a woman in the neck. She falls to the floor in pain.

I grab my jacket and swing at the bastard, but he skillfully maneuvers from every swat.

"Move back!" I shout.

I jump over and swipe my jacket across the seats. The insect flings against the side of the wall and falls dead. Ananiah picks up the creepy bug with his knife and examines it. Its head and body resemble a common locust, but its head bears the features of a mutated human—sharp teeth, large eyes, and swollen lips. Beneath its wings curls a scorpion-like tail with a stinger attached to the end. It's truly frightening.

Augustine lifts the young woman's head and helps her to her feet. She clutches his shoulder and sits breathless on the seat. The locust-like creature left a bulging red sore on her neck. Roland gives her a shot of Benadryl and tends to the stung area.

After using our bus as target practice, the rest of the swarm moves on. First the blood and now the locust. This is beginning to feel like hell already. I sit between Allison and Luke and wait out the rest of the arduous drive with my eyes open. After seeing that, I'm not sure I want to close them again.

The bus chugs at a measly forty miles per hour. According to Sadiq, it's about as fast as we can go without putting a dangerous strain on the engine. It has been over an hour and the landscape hasn't changed. Mountainous terrain and desert sand surrounds us. No man could survive out in this barren wasteland alone—a land not fit to traverse without water.

Billows of smoke rise ahead just above the outskirts of a city across the horizon. Another city in peril, or just another act of war? Midday approaches and the dark sky vanishes. The scorching sun shines with unforgiving hate. The air conditioning stopped working thirty miles ago.

Father Joseph gestures for me to join Sadiq, Ananiah, and Jacob in a private conversation at the front of the bus.

"We are about to come up on Suez. This might be a good time discuss our options from here," Sadiq explains.

"Is it safe here?" I ask.

"Safe is relative amid these conditions, but it will be our only stopping point for a while."

"By the sound of this struggling beast, this may be a good opportunity to rethink transportation. It's about three hours until we reach the southern border of Israel. Once we get across, we can regroup at Fort Eliat, but it's a long stretch of nothing from here to there," Ananiah adds.

"Just seems like extra miles out of our way. Why south when we have a shorter distance to the northern territory. It would be a much shorter distance to Camp Anatot near Jerusalem," Jacob pipes in.

"The northern territory of Egypt has been dangerous for years now. Russian and Palestinian adversaries have taken that area captive. Besides, it would be suicide traveling near the Gaza Strip. The Russians own that territory now. Be it a longer journey, south is the safest route for us," Sadiq says.

"So what's Suez like?" I ask.

"It's a port town with a lot of bad history. It's since been rebuilt following a nasty uprising that left it destroyed by Egypt and Israel. Most of the city is pretty modern with the exception of the industrial district near the canal. It has a huge marketplace and plenty of places to retreat. It's one of the last places the Russians haven't taken over. We should find exactly what we need."

"If it hasn't already been destroyed," Father Joseph says.

The smoke we saw earlier rises above the northern part of the city and spreads across the sky. This doesn't look inviting, but we have no other choice. We must stop and repair our bus or find some other reliable transportation.

Our only hope to thrive and move forward dwells within this city, but the closer we approach, the smaller our chances become. Warm, rotting bodies flood the outskirts of the northern district—a mixture of military and civilians.

Empty streets and boarded windows decorate the market entrance. A few people scatter across the abandoned strip mall and exit into the alleys. The bus, barely drivable and begging to stop, drags down the street. Sadiq parks it in a deserted lot as the suffering beast chugs on its last breath of fuel.

A child stands on the corner adjacent to us and grabs a sack left on a bench. He flees as soon as I step off the bus. I cry inside a little, knowing I may give birth in these conditions. The people who occupy this town have either died or abandoned it. With the exception of a few citizens wandering out of a grocery store, the market district lies uninhabited.

I don't care how safe Sadiq or Ananiah suggests this place is, my guns are locked and loaded. After what we've been through in Cairo, I suggest everyone else do the same.

Buildings on top of buildings, mostly old and some new, mingle tightly together, forming a claustrophobic area. This is, according to Sadiq, the most populous district in Suez, yet it's almost completely deserted. The streets narrow between structures, but the center of town opens to a circular intersection.

Dotted in the middle, all alone, sits a metal trashcan followed by a path of blood. At a closer glance, something familiar decorates the top of it and it's not trash. A human head, badly severed, rests on the lid. The rest of its body lies slumped over against a storefront on the other side of the street.

The only oddity here is the military uniform that clothes the decapitated body. This could be the result of a rebellious fight or the start of an endless plague. Either way,

I don't find comfort from this display. It's time to find some transportation and get the hell out of here.

"Okay, so what's the plan now?" I ask Ananiah.

"We need grab what food we can and find some shelter."

"You think it's safe to leave the bus and wander around?" Juliana asks.

"We have no choice. We need to find sufficient shelter before dark," Ananiah reaffirms.

"I don't want to stay in this city another minute," I argue.

"I feel your concern, but unless you can summon some reliable transportation, I'm afraid we will have to stay."

Everyone exits the bus and grabs what they can carry. I keep Allison and Luke under a protective eye. Scouting for shelter with the children may not be the best idea, but I'd rather have them by my side instead of leaving them behind on the bus.

Suddenly, gunfire echoes behind us and a black cloud of locusts buzz the sky. Everyone drops what they have and rushes for cover. Some scatter, but most follow behind Jacob and me. Allison, Luke, and Nadia race beside us to the nearest storefront, but it's locked and the windows are boarded. Allison gasps for air.

"You okay?" I ask her.

"Yeah, I'm fine."

"You stay close to Luke, okay."

The buzzing grows louder. I look back and see no sign of Gabe or Juliana.

"Wait, where's Gabe?" I panic.

"There!" Nadia shouts.

Juliana, Gabe, and Father Joseph are on the opposite side of the street.

"Take Nadia's hand," I tell Allison.

I grab Luke, pick him up, and race across as fast as I can. A diving cloud of the menacing insects swoop down at us. I protect Luke's face while I dodge the stinging kamikazes, but many of the people in our group aren't so lucky. A few lie in the street comatose. Most scatter under the bombarding locusts and flee in every direction.

Father Joseph turns and whacks a locust diving toward Juliana. It falls unconscious for a few seconds and flies off. The weight of Luke puts a burden on my back.

"Can you run?" I ask him. He grabs Nadia's hand and nods.

We push forward down the next two blocks and head south. Most of our group have fallen astray, but some still chase behind us.

Door after door we search, but nothing opens. We have no time to stop and fidget with the locks. The locusts swarm above us. Closer and closer the sky fills with a fluttering hiss.

Two men pop out of nowhere in front us and we nearly collide. I catch my breath as they rush past and flee across the street like madmen. One trips and slides face-down into the pavement. The shadowy swarm swoops down and pelts him unmercifully. He flounders on the ground, sting after sting, before getting up and stumbling behind a building.

"Come on, this way!" Ananiah yells from around the corner. Luke leans exhausted on Nadia's leg.

"He's too tired to go on," Allison pants.

Jacob kneels down to Luke. "Come on, I'll carry you," he offers. Luke wraps his frail arms around Jacob's neck and secures himself like a baby Koala.

"We need to go now!" Ananiah insists.

Another swarm builds loudly in the sky about a hundred yards to the north. Exhausted or not, we run nearly a quarter of a mile before our legs give out. The locusts vanish behind the city buildings — some that look significantly more lavish than where we just came from.

Nestled within the city's most populous area, government buildings stand tall in front of us. A young woman stands next to an open door to one of these structures. We scurry up the steps to a majestic front of broad windows and arched columns. The woman dashes inside before we reach the top.

I pull my gun, as does Sadiq and Jacob. We're not sure what to expect anymore. This place reeks of danger as much as Cairo. I creep up to the top and meet the young woman hiding behind the glass door. She slowly swings it open. A dozen people huddle together behind her.

Sadiq and Jacob follow me inside, but I stop and lower my weapon. A man sitting in the middle of the group threatens us with a Russian-issued ADS assault rifle. Sadiq calmly lowers his gun and speaks to the man in his native tongue. Whatever he says, it diffuses the threat. The man lowers his weapon. We cautiously leave the building and continue down the street.

"What did he say?" I ask.

"Doesn't matter. We'll find shelter elsewhere," Sadiq answers.

"Seriously?"

"What do you want hear?"

"The truth."

"We are the enemy to him. He believes we brought a pestilence with us, and we're not welcome here. Satisfied?"

"That's all you had to say." I smile.

Block by block, we travel until we reach a safe distance from the man. We've covered a lot of ground in an hour. We cross the district border where scenery drastically changes from the old world to modern architecture. It's almost like we've crossed over into a different dimension.

A surprising number of people walk the streets, but their faces are as fatigued as ours. Many dress their mouths with masks made from handkerchiefs, while others tote assault rifles.

The farther we travel, the more I see why these people have armed themselves. Dead Russian and Egyptian soldiers are scattered across the city. A revolt lingers here. I turn one of the soldiers over with my boot and notice a bluish tint surrounding his mouth and a peculiar rotting along the side of his face. It looks like he suffocated or choked to death. No bullet wounds or knife scars have taken his life. This man died from something more sinister; perhaps that's why people are wearing masks.

We examine a few more of the soldiers and uncover the same mysterious death. The likelihood that all of these men died from the same thing is frightening. A few streets over doesn't get any better. Corpses are rotting in the sun. I'm not so sure we'll survive if we stay here any longer.

The scorching sun passes over and we're almost out of water. My stomach growls for food and my feet undoubtedly are unhappy. I feel a blister on my toe sliding against the inside of my boot.

Suddenly, just to our right, a man dashes out of a small domed building carrying a bulging knapsack. Not sure what he's toting, but it could be useful. Sadiq carefully opens the door and gestures us over.

The inside is gorgeous. Lively paintings decorate the walls and intricate detailed moldings and columns flourish the entryway. A spread of food — water, wine, breads, and cheeses — fill the two long dining tables. Another dining section displays a smorgasbord of sweets and meats in the nextroom.

Very little of the spoils have been taken or eaten, and plenty still remains for all of us to enjoy. Allison and Luke drool over the untouched feast. They run their dirty hands over the end of the table and try to snatch some bread.

"All right, you two little monsters, why don't you both stand over by the wall before you get a mouthful of dysentery," I say.

"But I'm so hungry," Allison grumbles.

"Don't worry, there's still another room over there filled with sweets you can indulge in later."

My mouth waters and my tummy rolls, but something doesn't seem right about this. Why is there so much food still sitting here? Where have the people gone to leave such riches?

"Wait!" Ananiah shouts before everyone starts digging in. "Let's not get too hasty just yet."

"What is it?" Augustine asks as he grabs a bread roll.

"Ananiah is right. You have to be just a little curious as to why this food hasn't been touched," I reply.

I walk alongside the table and examine the spread of food while Jacob inspects the opposite side. There's no mold or signs of decay, but there's really no way of telling how long this food has been sitting out. With all the growling stomachs, I'm not sure that even matters anymore. Not even a common cockroach scurrying on the table would stop me from eating such good food.

Garrett crumbles off a piece of cheese sitting on a small platter and smells it. A centipede slithers out from underneath it and hides behind a loaf of bread.

"I wouldn't put that in your mouth if I were you," I caution.

"I don't care. I'm hungry," Garrett disobeys.

"Stop. Don't eat it!" Jacob shouts.

Jacob walks to the end of the buffet and pushes a chair back away from the table. A man, hunched over, falls to the floor. His bluish mouth was rotting in a bowl of soup. He displays the very same condition as the dead soldiers outside.

Garrett immediately drops a piece of cheese and Augustine tosses his roll to the floor. Roland inspects the corpse and confirms that the man has died from poisoning. Our hungry stomachs grow disappointed, but at least we're alive. I turn around and notice Allison and Luke are no longer standing against the wall.

"Where's Allison and Luke?" I call with extreme alarm.

"They were just over there," Nadia frets.

"Allison!" I scream. No answer. The door to the adjacent dining area is open. "Oh shit, no!"

Jacob, Nadia, Henry, and I all race into the next room. Allison holds a piece of chicken to her mouth while Luke is stuffing his mouth with a cupcake.

"Allison, no!" I shout.

Jacob knocks the chicken from Allison's hand and pulls her away from the table. Luke swallows the cupcake. Henry holds Luke forward and I force my finger down his throat. He gags a few times before he expels the cake. He cries, not knowing what's going on. I hold him tight and cry with him. I feel so sick inside.

"It's okay, sweetie. You didn't do anything wrong. We're not trying to hurt you. This food is bad. It will make you very sick," I say. "Was this cupcake the only thing you've eaten?" He nods his head; his eyes are watery. I ask Allison to make sure and she confirms.

We leave the dining hall better informed and less trusting. Cramping and dehydration sets in after an hour of wandering for a place to camp. Water is at our mercy. No one will last another block.

I've exhausted my legs far enough. I plant my ass down on some steps and rest. Gabe sits down next to me.

"Don't you miss those good ole days in the forest, resting in a soft meadow and waiting for that perfect hunt?" he reminisces.

"You have no idea," I muse.

"Seems so long ago, doesn't it?"

"We did the right thing, didn't we, leaving the den?"

"You can question every single decision you've made, but it won't change anything now."

"But it could have if I just—"

"The friends we've lost is not your fault. It's just a part of the world we live in. This was our path from the beginning."

I reach my arm around my brother and squeeze him close to me. I never want to lose him again. If this is the path we've chosen, then so be it. I'd rather die next to my brother than live a moment without him.

My body has adjusted to the steps and I'm too tired to get up, but we've rested enough. Evening sneaks upon us. Our water supply, now completely gone, gives us reason to move. Finding shelter has become an afterthought. Our parched lips and dry mouths are in need of quenching.

The streets grow dark and lonely, but not all hope is gone. Our group may have diminished, but it hasn't broken yet. Our weary legs drag across the pavement. I'm afraid the child I carry will not survive if I don't find water. Just when I feel depleted and forsaken, something unexpected happens.

Just beyond a deserted high-rise, lights flicker and voices ring with laughter. We reach the other side where the streets are lively. This city has been a deception and it's anything but silent in this area.

Fires burn in the middle of the streets, people run amuck, singing and dancing as if the world hasn't stopped. Dim lights fill the inside of several buildings along the street, one of which resembles a pub. Two hotels, parallel to one another, divide the street with drunkenness. One sparkles brightly, as people walk casually in and out, while the other hotel hovers gloomily over a sidewalk filled with women and men passed out on top of one another. It's a far cry from the invitation we received in the market district.

A strange voice rings out in the distance, but it's hard to understand over the rowdiness. Again, the voice calls, but this time I hear my name. Behind the shadows of a less active street, a man waves his hands in the air. Nadia's face brightens as she moves closer to this stranger.

"Kale!" she shouts excitedly.

I never thought I would be this happy to see Kale, but oddly his eyes look at me quite differently. He's just the good fortune we need to keep this group from falling apart. He ushers us inside an office building where a dozen of our friends from Alexandria wait.

"What happened to you guys?" Nadia asks her brother.

"I'll tell you later. You all look like you're in need of some water and food. Please help yourself. Just follow Ariel and she'll take care of you," he kindly offers.

Like the others, I soak my parched lips and dry mouth with clean, drinkable water. I fill my starved gut with rations of bread, canned soup, and fruit. I'm even offered slices of cooked knackwurst. I'm so hungry, I reject the slices and shamefully grab the entire link instead. I can't afford to be malnourished with this baby.

I finish my gluttonous feeding and return to the lobby with the others. Our group has expanded, but certainly not in the numbers we originally expected. Thousands have since departed, but I will lead and protect those who remain as far as they allow me.

Several people watch the main lobby door while others lie comfortably in a few leather chairs and on the soft carpeted rugs.

"All right, Kale, explain to me why you're here," Nadia urges.

"I'm sure Ananiah already told you what happened in Alexandria. Most of our delay happened when we reached Cairo. We stopped to refuel and rest. I made sure to keep our group close and secluded. Thirty minutes later, we left to get on the bus and out of nowhere soldiers stormed the streets. People were screaming and running. Then some crazy rebellion across the way began shooting. Not halfway to the bus, the group split and we were left there caught in the middle of crossfire. At this point one of the other busses had already left.

"We loaded up, left the scene, and headed south of the city. We stayed hidden for a few hours before we were able to get back on the road. We stopped here to replenish our supplies but got stormed by some other militant group heading deeper into Suez. The bus driver was shot and our bus crashed into the side of building about a quarter mile from here."

Kale takes a sip of his drink and continues. "Shots were firing in every direction. We couldn't hold 'em off, so we fled. That's how we ended up here. So what you see is what's left of some three hundred people. We set camp in this beautiful building, and then two days later, a menacing reminder showed us just how evil this world had become. I've never believed in God most of my life. Hell, even as a kid when our mom took us to church, I had no interest in wanting to believe that some deity holds power over me. I don't know what any of this means or why we're even here, but I realize I have been naïve. When the sky wept with blood, I knew then that I was truly afraid. I'm convinced we weren't meant to survive this. Humanity has never been in control, just out of control. This is completely out of our hands, isn't it?" He looks at me.

"For the most part . . . yes. But we must continue," I reply.

"How did you come by this food and fresh water?" Jacob asks.

"Before the storm hit, we pillaged most of the water coolers from the surrounding buildings. Emptied bottled water and snacks from the vending machines. We were able to survive comfortably before the place was invaded."

"Invaded?"

"Soldiers were sweeping the streets and searching for civilians."

"Russians?"

"Not entirely, but it didn't matter. The people fought back in greater numbers and squashed them. They've taken on a resistance of their own, and it's been that way ever since. We just stay clear until we have to go into town for food. They're a bit rowdy, but they leave us alone."

"Is there no other transportation around here?" I ask.

"Yeah, as you can see, most who were here before this city fell apart deserted this place quickly. Some of the townspeople believe you might find something near the port. We just haven't tried yet. Look, these people have no intention of leaving. They're just glad to have food and water . . . and libations. There're no rules here, no laws to govern this city. It's feast or famine, and I'd like to keep us closer to the feast side."

"We'll wait until morning before we search for transportation. Right now my people need some much needed rest," I say.

"Morning? You can't seriously think there's a way out of here, do you?"

"I don't intend to stay here any longer than I have to. I know I don't speak for you, so if you want to stay here, that's your choice. But I'm leaving and I'll take anyone else who wants to join me. My home is Jerusalem," I say.

"That's a long way from here through no-man's-land, but I can respect that," he says.

Shouting and screaming echo behind the glass window. I'm not used to hearing jubilance and merriment.

"Do these people party like this often?" Sadiq asks, peeking out the window.

"Most of the time, yes. They sleep during most of the day."

"I'm not so sure I trust who the enemy is or not," I say.

"I can sympathize with you on that. Come with me." Kale leads Sadiq, Father Joseph, Ananiah, Jacob, and I down a long hall. "Trust is a luxury these days. I don't think any of us can afford it."

"What do you mean?" I curiously ask.

"Just when you think you know your friends well, that's when you get blindsided."

He opens a door and ushers us in a small dark room. Something wails in the corner. The light comes on and reveals a man with his legs and hands bound to a chair. He moans uncomfortably behind a gagged mouth. His dirty, sweaty hair drips down across his face. What the hell did this guy do that Kale would torture him like this?

"This is the result of deceit. Like you said, Sadiq, how can we ever trust anyone? Well, this sly bastard slipped through the cracks and fooled us all. There's no telling how long he's been working for the Russians."

"How do you know?" I ask, aghast.

"I noticed something very strange about him when we left Cairo. I didn't remember him being part of the original group, but I didn't fret it; I just thought he was trying to escape during the mayhem in Cairo. But when the soldiers invaded down the street here, I noticed right away that he wasn't among us in the building. And that's when I began to worry. Before the radicals dispersed from across the street, I spotted this son of a bitch conversing with a Russian officer. He was using the officer's radio and handing a package to him. I don't know how he knew the Russians were going to show up, but he was well aware of it . . . piece of shit!"

"Why is he still in here?" I ask.

"Because I know he's hiding something, and I'm going to get it out of him sooner or later. Come on, leave him." Kale closes the door behind us and wedges a piece of wood under the bottom of the door.

"Maybe we should take a different approach with this interrogation," Sadiq suggests.

"Perhaps I can persuade him," I offer.

"Yeah, I don't think that's such a good idea," Father Joseph objects with a slight grin.

Most of the exhausted group empties the lobby and leaves to their sleeping quarters. A few of us who can't sleep stay back and relax against the wall. Augustine and Gabe plop down on the carpet next to me while two men I have yet to formally meet wander the lobby. One pulls up a chair and sits across from us, while the other, less friendlier, stares out the window.

My eyes glaze over as Gabe and Augustine share stories with one another. The older man staring out the window looks less enthused over Gabe's embellished tales. I attempt to needle a little life in the mind-numbing conversation and brave a thought-provoking question.

"If you could experience anything you've never done before, what would it be?"

"Jump out of a plane," Gabe quickly responds.

"Catch a shark," the old man blurts. "Always wanted to hook me one of those."

"I want to at least feel something," Augustine shyly answers. "Even if it's a feeling of loss."

"Watch what you wish for, boy," says the crotchety old man.

"I want to know what it's like to at least love once. To hold someone who wants to hold you back. Even if I have to lose someone to feel loved, I would," Augustine says.

The man looks at Augustine in anger. "Don't you ever say anything like that again," he scoffs.

"He was just being honest," I calmly remark.

"He should feel lucky not to experience that, especially now. I often regret it myself."

"I'm sorry if you lost someone, but I meant no harm, honest," Augustine apologizes.

"I know you didn't, son. It's just hard for someone to truly understand the responsibility and consequences of love until it's taken from them. I've watched my share of friends walk the tightrope of life and tempt death, but nothing comes close to the reality of loss." Tears fill his eyes.

"I think it's time we all get some sleep," Augustine suggests.

"I agree," Gabe adds. "You coming, Arena?"

"I think I'm going to stay up just a bit longer. You go ahead."

While everyone retires for the night, I stay downstairs with Kale, who unexpectedly joins me. I stare out the window at the obnoxiously loud and somewhat dangerous exhibition and wonder why Kale would ever consider staying here.

"You know, it's not as bad as you think it is here." He peers out the window next to me.

"Depends on your perspective," I retort.

"Look, I know we differ on this, but you have your agenda and I have mine."

"Since when, Kale?"

"The day you led us on that ship."

I turn to him. "What do you mean by that?"

"We all make mistakes. You haven't exactly made the best choices so far. We trusted you and I'm wondering to myself why we should continue to."

"Really? I've done nothing but try to protect you. I've been through a shit storm of problems making sure this group stays alive and now you just want to abandon it all?"

"Abandoning death? Yes."

"You owe this group more than this."

"And you owe them more than what you have given them."

"Follow me to Jerusalem, and I promise you won't have to ever worry about who to trust—"

"Oh, Christ, Arena, don't sell me your bullshit."

I squint my eyes in anger. "You really can't see beyond your own desires, can you?"

"You're reckless! You don't make the decisions that are needed for the safety of us all. It's whatever you please. Do you make decisions based on our best interests or your own?"

"I can't believe what I'm hearing. I'm your friend, not your enemy, Kale."

"I don't know who you are anymore."

"You're right, Kale," I say in a huff. "As long as you stay, there will be no hope for you. You are truly gone."

"No, we have found a semblance of peace here; it is you who's lost."

Kale storms out of the lobby and retreats upstairs. I don't think there's anything I can say to change his mind. I'll have to leave it up to Nadia to convince him.

My eyes glaze over, but my mind is anything but calm. Kale's unsettling remarks linger and makes me now wonder if he's capable of keeping anyone safe. He leaves a prisoner tied up in a room unguarded, yet questions my decisions.

I remove all my weapons except for my large knife that I sheath behind my back. I grab a cup of water, a plate of food, and head down the hall to the prisoner. It's my turn to take a crack at Kale's failed interrogation.

The light brightens and he squints his eyes. I set the food and water on a table and remove his gag. I wipe his sweaty face off with a rag, and push his chair up to the table. He peers at me with curiosity.

"I don't know what they told you, or how they've treated you, but I suspect some courtesy is due."

I grab the cup of water and bring it to his lips. He gulps a few sips then snickers behind a cynical smirk. I'm not in any way fascinated by his expression, and I can only assume he's any bit interested in indulging me with my less than riveting approach.

"It must be important that this would result in such pedestrian methods of deception," he mocks.

"Don't get too cocky. I haven't offered you a deal yet."

"Oh, I see. So this is just another interrogation then. Butter me up and threaten me for information I don't have." He pushes his face to the plate and gobbles the food like an animal.

"No, that would be cliché. I'm just offering you a last meal. Consider it a kind gesture." I pull my knife and place it in the middle of the table. He stops chewing and his eyes widen slightly.

"Your false kindness is a far stretch that you would have me eat like a dog. Untie me so I can eat like a civilized man."

"Don't make me a fool."

"You're so callous that you would kill a man after offering him a plate of generosity?"

"I used to have a conscience, but I'm afraid it's buried too deep to find."

"And if I tell you what you want to know?"

"I'll let you walk free."

He contemplates my offer before spilling his guts.

"Russian intelligence is looking for a group who attacked the Toro Prison in Cairo. They believe the rebels responsible for the attack are connected to a string of attacks that began in the United States. They are hell-bent on impeding this revolution. But as you already know, the soldiers who are deployed here have all been killed, so there's no need for your group to worry anymore."

"Is that all?"

"I promise that's all I know. Anything else you've heard is just fraudulent claims."

This sounds all too familiar. Nic, a member of the Northern Resistance and a member of our fellowship in America, turned out to be a Russian spy. The tracking device buried deep inside his gut put our fellowship in jeopardy. His deceit forced me to kill him.

"Strange, because we had a deceiver in our group once, and he said the same thing, but he lied."

"So where is he now?"

"Rotting against a tree." I jab the tip of the knife on the table and spin it playfully. "You sure you're not missing anything that I should probably know?"

"Honest, that's it. I'm no threat to your group."

I pick up my knife, grab the man's hair, and slide the sharp blade beneath his scruffy neck. He briefly squirms until I dig the sharp edge into his skin.

"I told you everything! You said you would let me walk free!" he shouts.

"Don't worry, I'm not going to stick this knife in a place that will kill you."

"Shall I ask why?" He shakes feverishly.

"Because you'll be spending the rest of your short life wishing I had." I spin the knife from his neck and push it firmly against his crotch. If he's anything like Nic, then anything he says is suspect. I wouldn't be surprised if he's wearing a tracking device as well.

"Wait!"

"Where is it?"

"I don't know what you're talking about." I push harder and tear through his tattered pants.

"The tracker!"

"Okay, okay! It's on my wrist!"

"Don't lie to me!"

"I'm not."

I pull back his sleeve behind the chair and rub my fingers over a protruding knot buried beneath the skin.

"Open your mouth," I say.

"What are you doing?" He panics.

"I'm doing you a favor." I shove the wadded gag between his teeth. He screams and squirms.

"Hold still. This will be quick." I instruct. I grab his arm and jab the knife into his wrist. He wails and fights me. I twist the blade beneath the skin and pull out the device. A tiny red light blinks on the back of the tracker so I set it on the table and smash it with my knife. I remove his gag.

"You bitch!" He wrestles out of the chair and falls to the floor. I cut the binding from his shoes and grab the back of his shirt. He struggles to his feet as the tip of my knife sticks into his back. I take him through the lobby and outside.

"Where are we going? I thought you were going to let me walk free," he stammers.

"I will, just be patient."

A small crowd of people, half-drunk, gather as we walk toward the unruly chaos booming in the streets.

"What are you doing?" he says, frightened.

"Giving you a taste of uncouth culture."

I stop in the middle of the street among perverted bedlam and unbind his bloody hands. An Arab man walks up to me and shouts God knows what. The crowd immediately calms and we are now at the center of attention. I'm forced to speak Hebrew, so I can only hope at least one person will understand what I'm about to say.

"M'ragel Rusiy!"

The Arab man spits on the ground and shouts back to the crowd in his native tongue, "Russian spy!"

The crowd erupts.

"What have you done?" the prisoner asks. He shakes within my grasp.

"I've kept my promise. I'm setting you free." I remove the knife and push him forward.

Two men jump down off a concrete pillar and grab the prisoner. A crowd of others join them and carry him away. What I've done is of my own accord and I refuse to let it summon any guilt.

A man with coffee-stained fingernails and whose teeth are as black as coal motions to me by the corner. He looks me up and down like a piece of meat and smiles. A young woman, half-naked, sits on her knees beside him like a dog and cries.

"You are American, no?" he says in English.

"What does it matter?"

"Your generosity is welcome to stay here for rest."

"Spare me your false courtesies; I have no intentions of staying."

"If you change your mind, just ask for Nasir. I can give you whatever you desire."

I walk away disgusted by his perverted offers. I'm just angry enough to jab his wrinkly throat. This city may still stand, but it's lawlessness keeps it in ruin. While there's a smell of revolution in the air, a presence of darkness hovers like a cloud. I suspect a certain sense of impression when I walk the street, but what I haven't expected is the depravity flooding this broken town. From one side of the street to the other, dignity and morality has fallen.

While others starve and fear to the north part of the city, orgies linger and debauchery runs rampant in the heart of this district. Is this the kind of world I want my child to grow up in? I suddenly feel sick.

Jacob stands waiting at the glass door. "Where have you been?"

"Just peeking in on the local culture."

He smiles and hands me my guns. "Lose these?"

"Thanks. You tired?"

"Not really."

"Then come help me take watch."

"Let me check on Allison and Luke first."

For my own security, I climb up a ladder and take post atop an awning with my guns firmly resting in my hands. I lean against the building and stretch out my legs. My mind races with anxiety of the thought of being pregnant. I still can't accept it and I just want to cry. I'm truly scared.

The clouds flutter past and leave a nearly full moon to display. A few of Kale's men drift out of from the dark and enter the building below. Soon after, Jacob climbs up and joins me on the awning. Together we protect and watch over our friends while they rest through the night amid a clashing of drunkenness.

CHAPTER 30

Smoke rises from the pile of smoldering ash left in the street after a night filled with inebriation and perversion. It's hard to believe silence exists in the middle of this raucous district after last night. Most are either hung-over in a pile of piss or still asleep from wherever they last lost consciousness.

I wake Jacob and jump down from the awning. Nadia stands outside the door with a cigarette dangling between her fingers. I've never seen Nadia smoke, but right now she appears to be distraught.

"Everything okay?" I ask.

"These things will kill ya, you know," she playfully jests. "I quit smoking four years ago, but I figure what the hell, what does it matter now?"

"Whatever gets you through the moment."

"Well, you might want to seize a moment with my brother in there," she says, pointing through the window.

I open the door to a noisy dispute between Ari and Kale. Father Joseph looks on with disapproval while Henry and Harold try to calm Kale down.

"What's going on here?" I demand.

"Seems we have another rat among us," Kale gestures toward Ari.

"What are you talking about? Ari has done nothing to impede our group or help the enemy, I assure you."

"Then explain to me why I saw him walking out of our prisoner's room, who has conveniently escaped?"

"I was checking in on the prisoner," Ari clarifies.

"Were you?"

"Listen here, you little shit—"

"I let the prisoner go!" I admit. The room silences.

"What? Why in the hell would you do that?" Kale questions heatedly.

"I thought I'd take a shot at questioning him."

"You went behind our backs and interrogated my prisoner?"

"Your prisoner?" I step crossly toward Kale. "Seems to me grilling isn't a skill you possess."

"Arena!" Sadiq shouts, as he and Ananiah enter the room. "Arguing isn't going to pull this group together."

"Neither is letting the enemy escape," Kale retorts.

"I did what I had to do to keep us safe," I say.

"Letting him go keeps us safe?"

"Where's the prisoner, Arena?" Ananiah asks.

"Not in a good place, I can assure you."

"Please explain."

I reach into my pocket, pull out the tracker that was buried in the prisoner's arm, and toss it to Sadiq.

"What is that?" Kale asks.

"That's the shadow that's been following you. I dug it out of your prisoner's wrist last night before I handed him over to your rowdy friends. Like I said, you won't need to worry about him anymore, but staying here isn't a wise option either. The Russians will be back."

Kale's dejected face moves over to Nadia, but she doesn't look up or say a word.

"We need to put our petty differences aside and find a way to get the hell out of here," Sadiq orders.

Everyone leaves the room and packs enough gear for a day's worth of exploring the city for transportation. I gather my weapons and grab Jacob. We retreat outside and leave Kale and Nadia to talk alone.

Since rescuing Gabe, I've had very little time to spend with my brother, but I respect his time with Juliana. I just hope Kale and Nadia can work things out before it becomes too late. I don't know what kind of bond they share, but if it's anything like Gabe and me, then I mustn't worry.

Nadia walks outside a few minutes later and loads a mag into her firearm. Not sure what has transpired, but an urgency is painted on her face. Whatever pain cages behind the intensity of her eyes, I leave her alone.

Gabe and Juliana are followed by Sadiq, Father Joseph, Henry, and Harold soon after.

"Are we ready?" I ask.

"Waiting on one more," Sadiq answers.

I assume Ananiah will follow, but instead Kale walks out the door with gun in hand. He glares at me before he walks in front of the group.

"I can take you to the port side near the canal, but I cannot guarantee we won't find trouble on the way. Most of the east side is clear, but you can never be for sure, right, Arena?" Kale boldly explains. "Why don't you take point with me?" he continues. "I could use another set of experienced eyes to watch over us."

Not sure where this is going, but I would feel more easy in the front anyway. I meet his uncomfortable command and walk next to him. He tilts his head to the side and whispers privately, "This doesn't change anything about my decision. I will help you and your friends find some transportation and you can be on your way."

He's as stubborn as he is prideful, but I can't force anything against his will. He'll have to live with that decision.

After hours of walking, the sun rises midafternoon and beats down through the clouds. Rows of tan stoned structures, most of which are apartment housing, litter the east side. Between government monuments, a residential area of small bungalows flood our surroundings. The crumbled stone houses nestle tightly together in a community where your neighbor can physically touch your house outside their window.

The sprawling compacted village opens to a section of businesses, wider streets, and a mammoth medical facility. Several abandoned cars park alongside the main thorough-fare next to the hospital, but none will start. Starved of fuel, they sit here wasting away like the rest of this city.

The farther we walk south, the more industrial the scene becomes. Small factories and distribution buildings pepper the streets along the port side, but a government complex sits just to the west of us. Roads flow to and from the canal to this small exporting harbor.

Like Kale had mentioned earlier, several trucks are parked along the street. Some line up behind one another near an unrestricted military outpost or a customs facility. The trucks are military grade, but the small compound opens to the free-roaming public.

Sadiq, Henry, and Jacob try to start one of the trucks, but it fails to turn over. The next truck in line chokes a few times before it successfully cranks. The fuel gauge shows to be nearly full and roars like a diesel truck should. Out of the seven trucks, only two start up, but it's more than I had expected.

We're more than lucky to have near-full fuel tanks for both trucks, but it's still not enough transportation for our entire group. We need at least two more trucks to haul these people across the desert. Sadiq, Jacob, and Henry stay to find fuel for the remaining trucks while the rest of us head back.

The short drive gives me little time for my feet to relax. We arrive minutes later and are greeted by a horrific sight just outside our building. A half-dozen people lie comatose in the middle of the street. I nudge a woman lying face-down on the pavement. She moves slowly and rolls onto her back. Red boils and sores cover her face, neck, and arms.

A few dead locusts are under her feet. Three men roll on the ground in agony from the throbbing pain of the stings. Over a dozen stings cover the men's bodies.

Out of nowhere, a small boy sprints across the street and into one of the adjacent buildings. I run after and shout for him to stop, but he doesn't listen. I open the door and find another woman covered in multiple sores. She sits up against the wall inside the building.

The young boy dashes behind a pillar and hides. I try to lure him out with a soothing voice, but he won't come. He just cries over and over, *"Ajealh yatawaqqaf."*

Father Joseph opens the door behind me and kneels beside the moaning woman. He speaks a few words in Arabic and suddenly the boy moves from behind the pillar. He has a gun in his hands and sores dot up and down his arms. He shakes as tears fall from his eyes. He looks no more than ten years old, but he holds the gun like a veteran.

He points the gun at me and cries the same words over and over, *"Ajealh yatawaqqaf."* I bend down and hold my hands up high as non-threatening as I can. His small hands tremor with his finger planted on the trigger.

"What is he saying?" I whisper to Father Joseph.

"He says, 'Make it stop.'"

"Make what stop?"

"I suspect the burning pain from the sores."

"Tell him we can help him."

Father Joseph speaks comforting words to the young boy, but he refuses to put the gun down. He's too afraid to listen. The door opens and Kale walks in. The boy screams, looks at the woman, and puts the gun to his mouth.

"No!" I scream.

Bang!

His body falls to the floor and leaves the wall behind him painted red. I clutch the boy's leg and stare motionless at the floor. Hope has escaped these people and I'm afraid nothing can save them. My heart is numb. I look down at my belly and cry. *What just happened?* I've cursed my own child. Is this what he or she will expect—hopelessness? I can't bear this much longer. Right now I'm sure I would be sad if I miscarry.

The woman refuses to move for Father Joseph and hugs the floor instead. I get up, wipe my eyes, and walk past Kale's blank face.

Harold, Nadia, and Ananiah stand outside with guns drawn while a small caravan of vehicles drive slowly down the street. They stop near the stung victims that are lying in the middle of the street and wait.

Father Joseph and Kale, unarmed, walk closely toward the caravan. I hold my gun and watch from a distance. Two men exit a truck and converse with Kale and Father Joseph. Minutes later, a third man approaches with a small silver case in hand and kneels down to one of the victims. He pulls out a syringe and sticks him in the neck. Feeling a bit more curious, I walk closer and watch this man inject God knows what into the remaining people.

Suddenly, one of the bodies convulse. I run over to help.

"Wait!" the man says as he holds the convulsing woman. I carefully kneel down beside her and watch as her eyes roll back. After a few seconds, she stops trembling and her eyes relax. With deep breaths, she dizzily sits up. The other victims move about, dragging themselves across the street.

"Help me get her up," the man says to me.

I put her arm around my shoulder and help raise her to her feet. She gingerly shuffles across the street. Another man relieves me and takes the woman to the back of the caravan. Others exit the truck and help the remaining wounded to their feet. I'm awestruck by the extraordinary reaction to whatever they were injected with.

A blond-haired older man dressed in all black speaks fleetingly with Father Joseph and Kale before he walks to our building. Harold, Nadia, and Ananiah immediately lower their weapons and escort the gentleman inside.

"Are you going to tell what this is all about?" I ask Father Joseph.

"I'm not quite sure yet, but they don't seem to be a threat."

"They never do at first."

"He's come a long way to help these poor people. Let's hear what he has to say," Kale adds.

I don't trust this man no matter how much Kale convinces me. Sure, they helped these people, but at what cost?

The man pulls up a chair and sits at the lobby table as if he's in control of this assembly. Everyone follows suit and sits around the table, but I choose to stand next to Gabe. Juliana and Nadia watch carefully out the window while I plant my eyes on this man.

"I remember you from Alexandria, but I never got your name," Ananiah says.

"Pardon my disrespect for the lack of introductions. My name is Mikhail Blatov," he address in a peculiar Russian accent. I'm already uncomfortable with this.

"My name is Ananiah."

"What are your intentions here in Suez, Mr. Blatov?" Sadiq boldly asks.

"I'm merely on a mission to help others in need."

"How so?"

"The world is crumbling before us, and there seems to be no real direction for humanity to continue, but I have a solution."

"So does Russia," I blurt.

Mikhail turns to me. "Yes, but Russian political ideals are set up to fail."

"Tell your president that."

"Arena, please," Ananiah asserts.

"No, it's okay. I can sympathize with the distaste in her voice," Mikhail says. "Yes, I may be from Russia, but I can assure you that our political ideals differ quite a bit. What I'm after is an economy that will help all people, and the Ten Nation Accord has made it possible. There's been an agreement among the ten nations that has showed a tremendous interest in bringing a new world order into play. The Ten Nation Accord, as the delegates have branded it, will accommodate safety and the well-being for each nation that's willing to sacrifice independent government for economic growth."

"This Accord doesn't benefit everyone," I respond.

"Aside from an economic reform, what makes you think Russia's ploy for injunction will change?" Sadiq asks.

"Because it already has. I've found a way around it."

"So what's your solution?" Father Joseph asks.

"Regain an independently governed nation while still benefiting under the economic ideals of the Ten. We've already made plans to rebuild America under this idea, and Russian delegates have issued a strong support for this move. We can have a nation of our own where all are safe again and where all are treated equally."

"I've heard that same drivel before. Those are just words," I chide.

"The past is the past. It's time to start building a new future."

"Without Israel? Because I'm pretty damn sure they tried to govern themselves before Russia and her allies dumped on them. Russian leaders want nothing more but to control its people, and now they have declared the Jewish state as its enemy. Why, because they wouldn't conform? You spat with words, but I have not seen any change," I say.

"I seek to change lives for those who need it most, not to destroy it on the battlefield. I have no quarrel with Israel, but they aren't exactly helping themselves by standing alone. That is a nation that will destroy itself and I won't be a part of it," Mikhail says.

"All I hear is false assurances. I saw what happened to America. I lived it," I sneer.

"And I was there to save it. I granted safety to your people who wanted it and now they have it. And I'm offering you all the same comfort."

I laugh. "What? A comfort in knowing that nations will collide and bicker over money and political gain?"

Mikhail interlaces his fingers and takes on a more serious tone. "China had taken drastic measures over the years to partner with Russia in this dangerous political move, but they knew, just as the rest of the world did, that in order to have a sustainable economy, nations will have to merge with this idea."

I can't help but scoff. "Russia destroyed America, why should we trust you?"

"America was doomed before Russia got involved," Mikhail says flatly.

"I beg to differ. Your plan may sound enticing to the foolish, but I know deep down Russia would never give up its political ideals to this ridiculous proposal."

"I assure you, Russia isn't the enemy—"

"Maybe you are then," I declare harshly.

Mikhail stands up and walks over to me with a sinister smirk planted on his face. Everyone straightens and is on guard. I stand my ground as he towers next to me.

"These people here, your friends, look up to you. Instead of talking for them, why don't you extend the courtesy and let them decide for themselves. Why would you keep them from wanting a better life?" Mikhail says.

"Because I don't trust you. Together we stand and divided we fall is a complete farce. I'll gladly stand alone with my convictions rather than follow the other sheep. You and your followers can stand together for something I will not take part in."

"I'm with her," Gabe agrees.

"So you choose to run from one city to the next, struggling to survive with little food and water, and not knowing what tragedy you may run into next?" Mikhail chuckles.

"I've led these people from being enslaved—"

"You're leading them down a dark path!" Mikhail shouts. His beady eyes pierce through mine. "And that prideful ego of yours will be the death of them."

I grit my teeth and pull out my dagger.

Sadiq quickly grabs my arm. "Wait! There's no need to let this escalate out of control," he diffuses. "I don't know what your ploy is, but if you're negotiating with Russia under these terms, what's to say they won't change? You claim to be savior to the very people who Russia enslaved, and now you're working with them? I'm sorry, but I have to agree with Arena on this. This seems far from ideal."

Mikhail takes a deep breath. "There's far less reasons to follow a dream than following a fool. But with this young woman at the helm of your fate, I only ask you this: Who's more foolish? The fool or the people who follow?"

Sadiq holds me back from smacking this man in the jaw. I ball my fists and lunge forward. Ananiah quickly moves in between Mikhail and me.

"You might want to put a leash on this one," Mikhail provokes. He walks to the door and addresses us before he leaves. "Look, I came here with the best intentions to help you. My offer still stands for any of you who want to come. You can either wander around waiting to be killed or receive shelter, safety, and never-ending food supplies. You have until the morning to decide."

There's an expressive rage glowing behind Kale's eyes. "Insult the man anymore and he may not have extended the offer," Kale barks at me.

While the others debate over Mikhail's proposal, I go outside to cool off with Gabe and wait for Jacob, Henry, and Sadiq to return. I stew over Mikhail's words. I convince myself that he's no different from the current new world order regime. I can't deny his compassion for helping people, but his sympathizers will eventually turn on him once they see through his political rhetoric. Earning a man's trust based on words is never a good idea.

"What do you think about all of this?" I ask Gabe.

"There's nothing to think about. The guy is a fraud."

"It's going to be hard to convince the entire group."

"All he's done is sugarcoat the conflict. He sounded genuine at first, I admit, but there's something in his plan that just doesn't add up."

"What's that?"

Gabe picks up a rock and throws it. "Remember when Ananiah told us about the people in Alexandria who lined up to get their shots because of some kind of virus it was rumored that China created?"

"Yeah."

"If China is Russia's ally, then why would it be necessary to give shots if Mikhail is dealing directly with Russian leadership?"

"I'm not following."

"Russia would never allow China to do something like this, and even if they did, this virus would have to be a controlled. So, did Mikhail know about this virus, and how could he have an antidote so quickly? Think about it, you plant fear in people, then provide a cure. It becomes an instant following."

"It's just a ploy to persuade people?"

"Precisely."

The sun departs and night falls upon us. There's still no sign of Jacob and the others. I'm nearly pressed to go looking for them until a low-rattling engine bellows deep down the street. A less than desirable box van in moderate condition pulls up next to the building.

Jacob, Harold, and Sadiq exit the truck, but what I'm not expecting is a man holding them at gunpoint. All I have is my knife and I'm in no position to diffuse this. Gabe and I back up inside the building.

The man levies the gun to Harold's head and releases Jacob and Sadiq. Kale and the others draw their weapons, but they are quickly ordered to drop them. I'm just close enough to knife the man, but Harold's life is in jeopardy.

He shuffles Harold closer to me, pushes him away, and grabs me instead. He smells of body odor and sweat. The barrel of this gun jabs into my head, causing pain.

"What do you want?" Ananiah asks.

"I want some food and water, now."

"We have plenty of food and water for you, but you need to let her go. We're not going to hurt you. We're just trying to survive like you. Put your gun down and you are welcome to join us."

He grabs the back of my hair and digs the barrel to my skull. It feels like he's ripping the hair from my scalp and I wince in pain. Without hesitation, I elbow him in the gut, toss his gun, and bury my knife beneath his chin. The tables have turned quickly and now I'm in control.

"Arena, hold up!" Sadiq orders.

"I don't trust him."

"Put the knife down," Kale argues.

"He's not armed, Arena. You can let him go now," Sadiq urges.

I release his hair and lower my knife, but I'm not convinced. I turn over his arm and rub my fingers over his wrist. The same knot our other prisoner had, but this one blinks an orange glow. I raise my knife again and slit his throat. An alarming chatter booms as I pluck the tracking device from his wrist. I raise it to the others to affirm my gratuitous actions.

"Trust no one," I simply say.

I drop the tracker on the floor and stomp it with the heel of my boot. I wipe his blood off my hands in the sand. The body is removed and so are the doubts about staying here any longer. Only pride would keep Kale here now.

"We could have questioned him," Kale badgers.

"Priorities have changed. Your safe haven has been compromised."

I leave Kale standing there to ponder his foolish decision to stay here. My intentions aren't to humiliate him, but only to convince him to come with us to Israel.

The sleep-deprived retire to their sleeping quarters except Nadia and myself. I pull up a chair next to Nadia and guard the door. Sleep has abandoned me over the last two days, but I feel its return coming quickly.

"Kale won't listen to me, Arena. I've tried and tried, but he's too stubborn to admit the truth. With this Mikhail guy in the picture, I'm not sure there's a way to persuade him to go with us now," Nadia discloses.

There's really nothing I can say to make her feel any better. Kale has already made his choice. I can only hope the rest of the group will follow us. I lean my head against her shoulder . . . it's the only thing I can do.

*　*　*

I wake up next to an empty chair with a major crick in my neck. It must be early morning because no one is in sight except Kale. He apologizes about yesterday, something I didn't expect. He may be sincere, but convincing him to go with us seems hopeless.

"I know we differ on things, but I can't see passing on this opportunity to start a new life. Mikhail has given us the best chance to survive," he says.

"If you tie your allegiance with Mikhail, you'll never be free."

"It's loyalty to this man that will keep us safe now."

"Wrestling with political bullshit to garner trust is not my idea of loyalty."

"Neither is killing a man in cold blood," he snaps assertively.

I pause for a moment and brew over his provoking retort. I know he will never understand my stance in this war.

"I could have just as easily left you back in San Jacinto to defend your words. Would it have mattered to you then? Can't you see what's in front of you? Your sister is broken. Does she not matter to you anymore?"

"That's not fair, Arena. My sister means everything to me."

"Then why do you ignore her?"

"Can you not see that this man is offering us a second chance at life?"

"Seeing what is at hand isn't difficult. Not knowing what you are looking at is what makes you blind."

"These men have given—"

"These men do nothing but squabble and deceive. They are what they are, politicians. And what has come of it but corruption and death?"

He peers to me with a surly gaze. "Yes, but at least they have given us hope. What have you done? You've only brought us closer to death. How many more loved ones are going to die before you realize that?"

He storms off. I was hungry, but now I don't feel like eating. Maybe he's right. *Am I leading my friends to their death?*

*   *   *

The clouds pass over and morning has come and gone. The streets are empty with the exception of Mikhail's convoy of trucks. Either the unruly district has surrendered to a plague of locusts or fallen victim to Mikhail's false ideals.

Kale walks proudly from the back of the lobby and leads a massive group of followers with him. He stops before he exits the door. "This is your last chance for freedom," he offers.

I can hardly look him in the eye. He's made his own choice even though I believe it's foolish. I cannot goad any further. He leaves the building somewhat reluctant as he watches Nadia cry from a distance.

"Best of luck. Don't let your guard down around this man," I warn before he exits. Those in the group I've managed to keep safe follow out the door. Many won't look at me as they pass by. Augustine stands alone in the back next to Ari. He's the last from a group that once filled three ships. The lobby now holds the only survivors left I must keep safe: Allison, Luke, Niki, Harold, Roland, Juliana, Gabe, Nadia, Sadiq, Ananiah, Henry, Father Joseph, and Jacob. Our fellowship begins a new chapter.

CHAPTER 31

Kale and the others leave us, but not without a few emotional scars. It's hard to tell if Nadia can move on without her brother. She wipes her eyes and tucks a water flask into her pack. As harsh as it may sound, she must bury those feelings if she wants to survive. Though I could never tell her that, I reach down and take her hand instead.

"I can't do this without you," I say. "My trust in you is invaluable. You are my eyes, my ears, and my friend. I need you by my side."

"Thank you," she whispers.

She hugs me and heads out the door behind the others. With a lighter load now, we split our group up into two trucks. If one decides to stop running, we'll have another truck as backup.

Our destination lies in Eilat, a southern Israeli port and resort town on the Red Sea near Jordan. An old naval base resides just off the harbor where Israeli defense forces are stationed. There we can rest and refuel.

We load up our gear and leave another deserted city in ruin. The road behind us fades and the sandy stretch of land broadens. We spend the next several hours traveling across a barren desert and winding around a canvas of rugged mountains. The drive makes me nauseous.

Allison lies peacefully in Nadia's lap while Luke leans against her on the other side. She has made quite an impression on these kids. I'm not sure Allison and Luke have a better person to look up to. Is that the kind of mother I'm going to be? I'm much too sad to think about it. I badly want to cry right now, but I mustn't. I hold back my tears and let them fester deep inside. My gut twitches, but joy is the last thing on my mind. The delight of a tiny being moving across by belly only worries me further.

Gabe snuggles with Juliana in the corner of the truck while everyone else remains silent through the long ride. I have no idea what to expect when we reach Eilat, but I'm going to know soon enough because the truck stops. Ari sweeps the canvas covering to the side and peeks his head out.

"Doesn't look any different than where we came from," he observes.

I grab my gun and join Ari near the back.

"Caution, Arena," Father Joseph warns.

"I just want to see where we are," I assure him.

Southerly winds swirl desert sand around us, a dreadfully oppressive occurrence here. All seems to be normal until a spark of chatter erupts outside the truck. I quickly pop my head back in and draw my gun. Everyone takes notice and arms themselves.

"What is it?" Jacob asks.

"I don't know yet, but there's a lot of discussion going on out there."

The conversation falls silent leaving just the wind to howl. The truck slightly rocks and the cab door shuts. Footsteps brush against the sandy ground toward the back of the truck. I step away and kneel to the side of the truck wall next to Father Joseph. The canvas flap draws back and Sadiq stands behind it with a look of discontent.

"A slight change of plans," he sighs.

"How slight?" I ask.

"That all depends. Are you an optimist?"

"Yeah, I don't like where this is going."

"Just sit back and relax. We'll be stopping soon to camp."

The truck growls before taking off to who knows where. After ten minutes of wondering what the hell Sadiq is planning, we slowly come to a crawl. I open the back flap as we drive inside a fenced compound right outside the harbor.

The engine stops and several Israeli troops order us out of the truck. They lead us inside a large metal building filled with shipping crates and a row of cots. I undress my gear and weapons on one of the small beds and examine the facility.

A metal staircase ascends to a catwalk above where a few rooms look over us. The airplane hangar-like building stretches long and wide and extends upward maybe three stories. I can feel the soldiers' eyes stare at me as I wander the building.

"All right, listen up," Sadiq addresses. "Make yourselves comfortable because we might be here awhile."

"Why?" I question.

"We've run into bit of a snag."

"Just get on with it, will ya?"

"Eilat has been taken over by a small band of Chinese troops—the marina, airport, and most of the downtown area. I would take a different route, but Private Ehrlich here says that Highway 12 has been buried beneath the desert sand. It's too much of a risk to circumvent without getting stuck in the middle of nowhere."

"So what are our options?"

"Option one: we wait 'em out and proceed north."

"And option two?"

Sadiq pauses, then says, "See option one."

"This is bullshit, "Ari barks.

"No, it's much worse. Trust me, I've smelled it," Sadiq sarcastically retorts.

"I think I'd rather take my chances in the desert."

"Look, I understand, but their troops are starting to

dwindle," Ehrlich encourages. "It's possible we could wait it out. I think they're realizing how unforgiving the sandstorms out here are going to be."

"I hardly believe that. They're probably drunk off their asses right now in some pool at one of the resorts," I say.

"How long have you and your comrades been hiding out here?" Henry asks.

"About a month now. Most of our troops stationed here deployed north to guard the western wall two months ago. Only a few of us stayed per executive orders. We lost communication a couple of week after, and that's when the Chinese came in, gained ground, and overran us. There were fifty-seven of us trying to defend this port. Only eight of us made it out alive."

"How many troops are we looking at?" I ask.

"I don't know, maybe three or four hundred."

"Well, shit," Ari grunts.

"I second that motion."

"How many citizens in the city?" I ask.

"As of recent, ten or eleven thousand."

"Well, now we have something to work with," I say, wringing my hands.

"How so? What are you getting at, Arena?" Sadiq asks.

"A lot easier for us to blend in."

"You're not suggesting—"

"Oh, I am."

"Let's just wait it out first before we get to that point. Right now, I suggest those who need rest better take advantage of it now. Harold, Jacob, Ehrlich, and I will figure out a way to refuel these trucks. It would be wise for some of you to watch the perimeter while we're gone. And I want no one leaving this compound under any circumstances. Got that, Arena?" Sadiq says with a heavy sigh.

"Affirmative . . . Dad," I say with a chuckle.

CHAPTER 32

The moon rises once again on a chilly evening while lights glow over the port town. We've made peace with this place longer than I have wanted. After a month and a half of strategic planning, I haven't the tolerance to wait any longer. Chinese troops have moved in and out across the Red Sea, yet we're still stuck here. My patience is wearing thin.

I station myself outside the small barracks as I have done every three days. My time to watch comes on a night that's surprisingly frigid. I holster my guns and lean back against the brick façade. Nothing changes—the same night sky, same waterfowls flying over, and on occasion, I'll hear a Nubian Nightjar flattering its mate with a song in the brush. Ananiah taught me about the echoing birds and the rarity of their kind. Sometimes I imagine I'm deep in the woods back home, enjoying the serenading sounds of night. It's simple, yes, but peaceful.

The cool desert breeze forces me to wrap my shivering body with a blanket. It's not much, but it does warm my numb hands and covers my ever-growing tummy.

My body is forever changing, as I fear my belly has swelled beyond the delights of just good food. I'm nearing four months of pregnancy now, and no one has noticed except for Nadia. Her eyes move frequently at my belly whenever I remove my jacket. I don't know how much longer I can keep this a secret from the others. I'm afraid I have brought nothing but pain and misery upon the innocence that will soon deliver from my womb. I'm beginning to think we're not leaving here anytime soon, and I'll be damned if I'm stuck here nine months pregnant.

Gabe rambles around the corner with a can of beans and sits next to me. "I figured you're tired of being alone out here," he hints.

He's right, but I'm a bit surprised that my brother would offer to keep me company. I haven't been able to really talk to Gabe without him being attached to Juliana, but I don't blame him.

"Dinner?" I ask as he dips a spoonful of beans into his mouth.

"You know, I never thought I would say this after being starved in a cell for months, but I'm really getting tired of eating the same thing out of a can. I really miss your hunting."

"We've been here way too long."

Gabe takes the last scoop of beans and tosses the empty can at a mountainous pile of other cans, a further reminder that we've been here too long.

"Seriously, I think it's time to make our move."

"What are you suggesting? We haven't seen any changes in the number of troops since we got here."

"What are we talking about . . . three, four hundred soldiers at most? We've taken on those numbers with much less back home."

"Yes, but we also had some badass weaponry to help us. Look, I'm not saying this can't be done. Hell, I want to leave here too, but trying to convince the others is going to be almost impossible."

"I can't stay here any longer, Gabe. We need to reach Jerusalem."

"I understand, but—"

"I'm pregnant."

He drops the spoon into the can. Shock covers his face. I didn't want to say anything, but he's given me no choice. I can't be here, not like this.

"You're what?"

"I didn't want to tell anyone . . . not yet anyway."

"Does Jacob know?"

"No, I wish to keep it that way, for now."

"You need to tell him—"

"No! And I expect you to keep silent on the subject."

"Sure, okay. Just tell me why."

"I wouldn't be able to lead if they knew I was pregnant. I'd be treated differently and you know it. Do you honestly think Jacob or Sadiq would leave me with a gun? No, they'd have me sitting on some fluffy pillow. We would have never made it here if they knew, and I'm damn sure they wouldn't leave here either. I'm going to need real medical aid, and Jerusalem can supply that. It's safe, heavily guarded, and one of the few functioning cities left I trust."

"I understand, but I don't know if Jacob will."

"So you agree then? You'll follow me?"

"Of course, sis. We've been in this together since the beginning. I trust you."

"Then the impossible just became possible."

"What are you getting at?"

"Just come with me."

Darkness hovers inside the hangar with the exception of a couple of dimming lanterns casting shadows on the wall. Sadiq, Anaiah, Father Joseph, and Ehrlich gather around a table where the lanterns sit. Everyone sleeps peacefully with their arms and legs dangling from the cots.

If these men want to take me seriously then I must be firm with my decision. I can only lead those who put their full trust and faith in me. Whatever discussion they are having I aim to interrupt it.

"Anything the matter?" Sadiq asks as I approach. "You need me to take watch for a while?"

"No one needs to take watch anymore. There's nothing out there to see. It's the same every night. I've spent enough wasted time watching nothing while you all wait for some-thing to happen. I hate to break the news to you, but nothing is going to change unless we strike first."

"We've been waiting for a reason—"

"I haven't heard a good one yet."

"Look, I understand your passion and frustration, but we can't just waltz into town and ask for a pass," Sadiq says, frustrated.

"Who said anything about asking?"

"I think you just need some rest—"

"I'm done resting."

"Why are you so anxious?"

"Why are you not?" I raise my voice.

A few people rustle from their cots over our heated dis-cussion. Jacob and Ari wake up and leave their beds.

"What's going on?" Jacob asks as he rubs his eyes.

"Maybe you can talk some sense into her," Sadiq pleads.

"Arena? You clearly don't know this woman. So what's this about?"

"I'm tired of waiting here. Nothing has changed and I think it's time we move on," I state.

"You can't expect to just drive through without some hostility. Our opposition outnumbers us. You're willing to risk the lives of your friends just because you're tired of being here?" Sadiq argues.

"I've been risking my life for these people far before I met you."

"You think this is wise, Arena?" Ananiah asks. "You can second-guess every choice you've ever made, but in the end, our decisions have already been made. So you are either with me or against me. Because tomorrow I'm leaving with or without you."

"I'm with her," Gabe adds.

"You too, huh? Should have known," Sadiq says.

"Me too," Ari chimes in. "If there's anyone in this group I had to trust, it's Arena."

"She's irrational you know."

"Always listen to the woman," Jacob gibes. "And never under any circumstances call them irrational unless you aim to have your nuts twisted off."

"Count us in too," Harold says as he and Niki join the discussion.

"Well, I guess democracy does exists after all," Sadiq submits. "I hope you have a good plan then."

"Yeah, I hope you do too," Gabe whispers.

"They won't know what hit them," I answer with confidence.

To be quite honest, I don't really have a plan per se, but they don't need to know that. My hope was just to convince them.

"I think we all should get a good night's sleep before we discuss this plan of yours," Sadiq suggests.

Everyone returns to their beds except Gabe and I. Sadiq gives me a cold stare before he turns the lanterns off. I leave the building more uncomfortable than when I entered, but this is all on me now.

"You don't have a plan, do you?" Gabe utters.

"Nope."

"Yeah, I figured."

My restless mind keeps me from sleeping. If I want Sadiq's trust and assurance for the others, Gabe and I better conceive a plan by morning. It doesn't have to be complicated. With Allison and Luke in our group now, simplicity must be our goal. It should be quick and effective.

"Okay, we're talking no more than four troops who are unlikely assembled in one area. We already know from Ehrlich's team that many have taken over the downtown resort area, right?"

"Yeah."

"Good, because our focus here is on the main road traveling along the port. Route 90 is the only way in and the only way out, and I'm pretty damn sure most of the troops will be stationed alongside that busy stretch, especially near the airport. With as many as ten thousand citizens still roaming the city, troops will be spread out, which might be to our advantage," I say.

"This is just speculation though."

"Sure, but my point is that you and I will be able to blend in better."

"Whoa, what do you mean you and me?" Gabe says, holding up his hands. "What about the rest?"

"The less we have to worry about the better. I want our group in those trucks and ready to move. So if we want to clear that road, we're going to need a massive distraction."

"And how are we going to pull that off?"

"You and I will be the distraction."

"Do I dare ask?"

"My dear brother, this is where you come in."

"Yeah, I'm not liking this plan so far." Fear fills his eyes.

"Did prison make you lose your nerve?"

"No, but now that I have Juliana back, I really don't want to lose her. And you . . . you have a husband and now a baby to worry about. You're willing to risk that?"

"Remember the time Dad took us to the lake and you got stuck up in that old, gnarly oak tree in the park?"

"Yeah."

"You were too afraid to climb down, so Dad told you he would catch you if you'd jump, but you refused over and over."

Gabe's cheeks turn red. "I was scared. I thought I was going to hit the ground and break my head or something."

"So what made you jump?"

"I don't know," he says. "But for a split second I felt everything was going to be okay. And when Dad said, 'trust me,' I knew right then that was my one chance to believe him."

"So what happened?"

"I fell and broke my face, shoulder, leg, and wrist." He grins.

"Stop it, you jerk." I playfully nudge him.

"Yeah, yeah, he caught me."

"Look, I'm not Dad, and this isn't a tree, but I'm asking you to trust me on this. I won't let them lay a scratch on you."

"It's not me you have to worry about. Convincing Juliana to go for this is your problem."

"Well, I figure you can use that charm to persuade her."

"Seriously, that's what you got?"

"She'll listen to you way before she would consider my thoughts on it."

"Okay, but I can't guarantee she'll go for it."

"How confident are you at making a bomb?"

"Hmm, I think I know where you are going with this. I change my mind after all. I very much like this plan. I don't have much to work with, but I think I can create something to get their attention."

I haven't seen Gabe smile like this in a long time. I nestle back into my warm spot against the wall and wait for morning with a bit more confidence. Gabe leaves me and does what Gabe does best. He tinkers through the night in the ammunition bunker while everyone sleeps.

CHAPTER 33

The morning sun rises over the city and parks behind a couple of dark clouds. Father Joseph waits around the corner and watches Jacob and Ari work on one of the trucks. I would stop and chat, but I'm too anxious to see what Gabe has come up with.

The ammunition bunker is exactly what you would think. The concrete square building houses firearms for troops and other heavy artillery supplies that haven't been used for quite some time. The roof rises about four feet above the ground while the lower half rests ten or so feet beneath the sand.

The stairs descend into a dark hole where I find Gabe slumped over on a table. A small bulb, glowing orange, dangles above him. A smell of hard work hovers as sweat seeps into the musty air.

Open grenade pods and pieces of removed bomb casings scatter the floor. A small square contraption surrounded by a spaghetti of wires sits next to a two-way radio that has been completely dissembled.

"Hey." I nudge Gabe's arm.

His eyes, a little bloodshot, open unpleasantly as I run my fingers over his creation. "Can you please not touch that?" He slaps my hand. "You want to get us both killed?"

"So this is it then?"

"I'm fairly certain we're gonna leave this place with a boom."

"So how does this thing work?"

"Uh, it goes *boom*."

"Aren't you the sarcastic little shit this morning."

"Shouldn't have woken me up so early."

"Yeah, well you can get your beauty sleep later. Let's go present our plan before they change their minds."

Gabe carefully places the bomb in his pack and tucks the dangling wires securely inside. I leave the bunker feeling confident except for that devise hanging on Gabe's shoulder.

"That thing can't go off accidentally, can it?"

"Of course not, silly. I mean I'm pretty sure. Stranger things have happened."

"Yeah, when I'm speaking in there . . . please don't mention that."

We walk into the hangar among anxious faces waiting for my proposal. Despite Gabe's aforementioned comments, I feel we have a solid plan of action. Ananiah gathers the group by the table, with the exception of Sadiq and Ehrlich who aren't in attendance.

"Has anyone seen Sadiq?" I ask.

"Not since late last night," Ananiah answers.

This isn't like Sadiq to be absent for something that's important. The whole purpose for this meeting was for him, but I make my pitch nonetheless.

"As you all know, some of us have decided to take our chances to move on from here. Now I'm not saying this won't be dangerous, but I feel confident enough that it'll work. There's only one way out of here and that's through town along Route 90. Our goal is to force the troops along that route to relinquish their posts so we can have a clear passage without any resistance. We'll have our trucks positioned just out of sight and ready to go. Henry and Jacob will take point and make sure we aren't exposed. I want everyone else in the trucks, no exceptions. The less we have running around, the smoother we can get everyone across safely."

Nadia raises her hand. "Question: how are you going to force their soldiers to leave their posts?"

"With this." I point to Gabe's pack.

"What is that?" Juliana asks.

"Our distraction," Gabe answers.

"Can you be a little more specific?"

"The pack is filled with explosives and I assure you it will get their attention."

"How are you going to detonate it?" Ananiah asks.

"With this." Gabe holds up a small two-way radio. "I've set the frequencies on the transmitter to the same on the receiver that's wired to the charge. We can use the PPT to activate the signal, thus creating the charge from the nine-volt battery and boom . . . detonation."

"Cleaver concept, but who's going to plant the explosives?"

"That would be me," I answer.

"I'll need her to activate the receiver once the pack is planted," Gabe says.

"So you're going alone while we're in the trucks?" Jacob asks.

"Actually, I'm going with her," Gabe clarifies.

"What?" Juliana exclaims.

"The distance from the transmitter to receiver can be no more than hundred yards. I have to be close by. Plus, if something goes wrong with the charge, I am the only one who can fix it."

"I'm not letting you go alone," Juliana says.

"Yeah, I'll let you deal with that," I whisper to Gabe.

"Okay, so let's say you plant the explosives, boom, and troops flee. How are we supposed to come get you?" Ananiah asks.

"The first chance you get, move. Meet us on the other side of the airport and Gabe and I will be there. If there's a threat keeping you from stopping, just go. We'll catch up down the road where it's clear. And don't worry about us. We're used to traveling on foot."

"I must say, Arena, you really thought this through. I'm in. I'm sure Sadiq will approve as well, if only he was here," Ananiah says.

The door swings open and Ehrlich rushes in, panting. Dirt and dried blood covers the side of his face. He clutches his ribs, grabs Juliana's water, and sits at the table completely exhausted.

"Where the hell have you been? Where's Sadiq?" I ask, troubled by his appearance.

"They took Sadiq," he explains.

"Who?"

"The Chinese. We were doing some reconnaissance early this morning, just trying to get ahead of things. Most of the portside was guarded, but Sadiq insisted we get a closer look. He just wanted to get a better make of the numbers we might face. Downtown looked considerably empty. We only saw a few citizens wandering around, but they were soon detained and were led to some trucks. They didn't seem to resist either. Everything was going fine, and then something just triggered Sadiq. He saw some man in a black suit get out of a car like he knew the person. He was sure he looked just like the man that you all described back in Suez."

"Mikhail?"

"Yes, that's the name Sadiq spoke of. I insisted we return, but Sadiq didn't want to leave. He was hell-bent on shadowing this man. Well, we stayed our visit too long and got too close. A few soldiers on the bridge spotted us and took fire. I got a bullet to the ear, but Sadiq wasn't as lucky. They shot him in the leg."

Ehrlich takes another sip of water, then continues. "I tried to help him up and escape, but it was too late. Sadiq pushed me away and told me to hide, so I did. I didn't want to leave him, but he didn't want to risk both of us being captured or killed. He was very adamant that I leave. I hid in one of the parked cars in the lot and watched through the tinted windows. They threw him to the ground and kicked him a few times before that Mikhail fellow approached. I don't know what was said, but they picked him up and took him inside the Dan Panorama Hotel."

"And he said I was irrational? Now he went and got himself captured," I say, frustrated and worried.

"He did because of you. He was trying to help you out."

"Yeah, well now our plan is shit!"

"Are they going to kill him?" Harold asks.

"Unlikely," Henry says. "Of course, he may prefer death instead of the brutal interrogation he's about to receive. Chinese probing can be unmerciful."

"He wouldn't tell them about us, would he?" I ask.

"Don't worry, Sadiq is nails. He won't budge. They may beat the hell out of him, but he isn't going to spill anything," Ananiah affirms.

"Change of plans," I say. "Henry, Father, you're coming with Gabe and me. The rest of you stick to the original plan. No matter what, when you see an opportunity to go, take it. We're going to get Sadiq back and blow that fucking hotel and anyone who's in it back to hell. Anyone object?" The room stays silent, not even a whisper. "Good. We leave tonight, so have your gear packed and ready to go."

"Where do you want me and my men?" Ehrlich asks.

"I want you driving point with Jacob and Ari. Split your men up between the two trucks and I suggest you have them well armed."

"Nadia," I say, "I want you to protect the kids with your life." She agrees.

I return to my own discomforts. My bladder rages with sharp pains. From anxiety perhaps or the fact I'm carrying a small person inside me. It feels like someone is stepping on my ovaries. My jeans have stretched its last stitch. I'm forced to unbutton them and fashion a belt from a piece of my blanket. My swollen gut breaches the top of my pants and rests comfortably. I don't know how many times I've woken up and wished I wasn't pregnant. I slide my hand over my belly and cry every time. How am I going to tell Jacob?

With everyone resting up in the hangar, I join Niki, Augustine, and Harold outside. Niki packs the last of our gear in one of the trucks and Harold sorts through a box of weapons. Augustine leans against the front bumper and stares toward the harbor.

"Everything okay?"

"Yeah. I just keep thinking about all those people who left with Mikhail back in Alexandria. I could have been one of them." He rubs his hand over the black stars tattooed on his wrist. "Kind of an ugly reminder of a potential bad choice, isn't it?"

"Yeah, but you traded it in for a better one," I say.

"Why do suppose they'd mark us like this? Seems like a strange way to inject a virus vaccine."

"May I?"

"Sure."

I grab his wrist and gently glide my fingers across the ink. It's smooth, just like the first time I examined it. Still, no detection of a tracker that I was expecting."

"I'm not sure. Does it hurt?"

"No, but occasionally it itches."

"Really? Will you humor me for just a second? I want to check something."

"Sure."

I search around for a magnet, but come up empty. Then I remember the box of weapons Harold went through has a magnetic gun case holding the assault rifles.

"Come over here, Augustine. Let me see your wrist?"

I slowly wave his tattoo over the strong magnet until I notice a slight pull in his skin. I move it back and then over the magnet again. Same result.

"See that?"

"See what?"

Harold kneels down and watches Augustin's skin pull toward the magnet.

"Oh shit. You need to take care of that now!" Harold warns.

"Take care of what?" Augustine's face pales with fright.

"It appears you have some kind of device stuck in your skin and I'm pretty sure it isn't drugs," I answer him.

"Tracker?"

"Maybe."

"Get it out then!"

"Go get Roland and tell him to bring his scalpel and bag," I order Harold.

Roland returns slightly confused with his medical bag. "What do we have?" he asks curiously.

"Augustine's marking may have a tracking device in it. His skin pulled back when we moved it over the magnet. It's got to be some kind of nano-circuit just below the top layer of skin right here," I explain.

"Here, bite onto this. I don't have any local anesthesia."

Augustine's face cringes with some forthcoming pain. He grabs my left arm and squeezes while Roland cuts away at his skin. Agony screams through the piece of chewed leather and Augustine nearly claws my arm off with his tight clutch. Roland peels the flap of flesh back and trims it off. I hover the piece of skin over the magnet once more just to be sure we got it.

"We're good," I confirm.

Roland patches up the wound and gives Augustine a strong dose of painkillers to fight off the initial discomfort.

Tracker or not, I'm taking no chances, so I burn the piece of skin. It makes sense now that Mikhail and his adversaries would want to keep tabs on their assets. He's just another wolf in sheep's clothing. These are no longer people he's catering to; they have become the sheep, and now his flock grows larger by the day. Humanity has fallen into deceit, but it's our own fault. We've been pandering to our own ignorance for far too long.

Roland, Niki, and Harold take Augustine back inside to rest with the others. I wait outside in front of the truck and watch the day pass by. The sun almost sets and the time to leave creeps up on us. The scarlet sky wanes into darkness.

"You ready for this?" Ananiah approaches me.

"I'm never ready, but I'm always willing."

"I'll wrangle the rest of the group."

Ananiah leaves me with reservation swimming in my mind. I caress my bulging womb and wonder if I should have told Jacob. The assurance I once had fades. With the added burden of finding Sadiq, I have to convince myself of this new plan. I recheck the magazines in my guns over and over like a nervous tick.

"Arena, we're ready," Gabe mutters from behind like a sneaky cat.

I turn around and find Father Joseph standing proudly with an Ironman five-hundred-round ammo pack strapped to his back and a M240 bravo attached to it. He looks like he's ready to cut down a small forest with that ridiculous indiscreet contraption.

"Really?" I questioned.

"Yup." He smiles like a child on Christmas morning.

"Why?"

He cocks back the firing sling and removes that shit-eating grin. "Because reloading is stupid."

I sit there for a moment, but I fail to object. Sounds like solid logic to me.

Henry joins shortly after with an IMI Micro Tavor sub-machine gun. He wears a black vest that sports two Jericho 941s, a couple of M26 grenades, and a smoke canister.

"When I asked for backup, I was thinking a little more discretely, but I can see your point now, so to speak."

They both smile and hop into the back of the truck. Gabe shrugs his shoulders and joins them minus the usual sarcastic remark.

Jacob's staid expression carries some unwanted weight as he exits the hangar behind Ari. I want to tell him I'm pregnant, but now would be completely unwise. It was hard enough for him to accept my plan to begin with. Henry and Father Joseph joining me may have softened his initial tone, but I know beneath that detached façade is a worried man.

Jacob struggles to smile and hugs me like he's never hugged me before. I want to cry, but I don't. I suck it up and carry on plainly as I watch the others load up. A leader must reassure her followers.

The last of the group tucks away inside except Juliana. Tears fills her eyes as she gives Gabe one last embrace.

Gabe and I hang off the back bumper as we pull away from camp. We slowly drive alongside the port for a quarter-mile before we're dropped off. The rest of our trek must be on foot.

The trucks pull off the main road and head west amid sandy dunes and rocky ground. Our hike, on the other hand, will be a bit more arduous. In order to keep hidden, Ananiah must drive cautiously around the desert banks and park near a residential area just off Route 90. The unpopulated suburban streets should serve well for concealment.

The sandy road stretches far, but the open field of vision forces us to creep closer to the edge of the banks. The moon's absence leaves us in shadow and gives us a slight advantage, but a few lights still glow off the harbor.

For thirty minutes we trek across a beautiful landscape of beachfront views, green gardens, and fancy hotels. This resort town is an oasis not like any other. The skyscraping pomposities blanket the northern bay as they illuminate above the waters. You don't have to be close to enjoy the luxury getaways.

Just ahead there's a small bridge that crosses a narrow waterway. Two soldiers to the west of the bridge stand guard. Perhaps the same soldier who shot Ehrlich and Sadiq is there. We reroute to the foot of the bridge and camp underneath the eroded pillars for a few minutes.

The guards rotate posts every five minutes, which leaves us a small window to pass over to a small parking lot. Palms and other greenery mask one side like a wall. We wait.

"Get ready," I whisper. Like clockwork, two men leave momentarily. "Now."

We rush up the grassy hill and over a small concrete barrier that fences the parking lot. Father Joseph covers us while we crawl behind a couple of abandoned cars. Footsteps approach and it isn't Father Joseph. I crouch lower to the ground.

I peer under the rear of the car and find a pair of soldier's boots grazing the pavement near the front. They stop. I clutch my knife and position myself at the edge of the bumper. I have no clue where Father Joseph is. The soldier moves hastily down the side of the car and just past us. He turns, shouts, and raises his gun. I slice his ankle and he falls. *Bang!* His gun goes off. He moans and reaches for his gun. I jab his throat and rip through the vocal chords. There's nothing but silence as blood pours from his neck.

"Shit," Gabe grumbles.

I wipe his blood off my hands onto the ground. "Don't move. Just stay here for a moment," I say calmly. We wait and hope that the dark, secluded area shields us from a terrible mistake.

Father Joseph sidles from the corner and silently gestures toward the lot entrance. I guess I was wrong. Three soldiers rush toward the car.

"Go!"

Henry and Gabe scatter behind me. I tug on the soldier's radio, but it's stuck between his belt and the holster. Like dancing shadows, the three men creep closer out of the light. The belt rips and the radio pulls free.

There's nowhere to go without being noticed, so I slink toward the front of the car and out of sight. They stop, examine the body, and chatter heatedly back and forth. I could just shoot them, but I'm afraid our covert plan will be curbed.

My sword dangles next to the car, but I pull it from its sheath anyway. Slowly and carefully, I slide the tip of the blade from my back. I stop as it scrapes the front bumper ever so slightly. The prattle immediately ceases. *Crap!* I can feel their steps inching closer to my left as boots scuffle across the pavement.

I roll around the corner and duck beneath the car frame. The soldiers now stand near the corner of the front bumper. Like a nimble cat, I tiptoe behind the car and glance around the corner. All three men face the front with guns slung from their shoulders.

My steps soften, closer and closer, before I raise my sword and swing. Still as the air, I strike down and dismember all three heads. Silence falls except for a muffling voice behind me. I turn around and find a soldier, neck cracked, lying at Henry's feet. I sign a gesture of gratitude. Gabe pops out of the shadows and hovers over the mangled bodies.

"Well, I didn't expect that," Gabe gawks.

Father Joseph crouches behind a leaning palm and scopes the corner near a private fence. "Let's go," he orders.

The fence wraps around a large pool just outside one of the towering hotels. Well-mannered hedges block the west side where we kneel behind. Two soldiers stand on either end of the pool. One comfortably smokes a cigarette ten feet away while the other observes the landscape through a pair of binoculars.

Henry stoops near the steps right below the shrubbery. The soldier flicks his cigarette over Henry and moves closer to the edge. Henry turns to me and nods his head. I pull my dagger and steady myself behind Henry.

The soldier walks halfway down the steps and stops. With his gun hanging to his side, the man reaches to tie his boot. Henry swings around the corner, pulls him down to the ground, and cracks his neck.

I peer through the hedge and watch closely over the soldier still viewing through the binoculars. He's completely oblivious to the absence of his comrade who lies dead. Father Joseph signals from the corner of the hotel that it's clear.

"Nǐ zhǔnbèi hǎole ma?" the soldier curtly asserts. He lowers the binoculars and peers back perplexed.

"Donghai?" the soldier says, but no one answers. He slowly grabs his gun and moves to the other end of the pool. "Donghai?" he says, apparently calling out to his mate. Henry taps on my dagger and points to the hedge.

The soldier raises his gun and slowly sidles closer to the steps. Sweat drips down my forehead as I watch. Suddenly, he stops and shouts. Henry signals. I grip the side of the blade and throw. The dagger slides effortlessly from my fingertips and sticks into the man's chest. His gun drops to the ground as he grabs the knife.

I rush forward and twist the dagger deeper. His eyes roll white and he stumbles backward into the pool.

A storm of troops gather across the hotel and our opportunity quickly vanishes. Father Joseph pushes back from the corner and runs. "Go!" he yells.

Several tactical vehicles drive by and light up the road. There's more activity than expected, but it won't impede us from moving forward. We dart across the lawn and scale a small fence that borders another parking lot.

Two hotels stand tall on the other side. Several troops evacuate one of them and board an eight-wheeled Israeli

Eitan AFV. Something is surely brewing to bring in this kind of armored vehicle. They're escorted by a AIL Storm Four, an Israeli combat jeep.

"Which hotel is Sadiq being held up in?" Gabe asks.

"The Dan Panorama just over there," Father Joseph answers.

"That's right in the center of a shit storm," I interject.

"Were you expecting to skip to the front doors?" Gabe asks.

"Funny guy."

"I wish this was a joke. We have to cross that street."

We maneuver through a covered parking lot and backtrack one block to the north. A less active street gives us a better chance to circumvent the chaos brewing near the front of the hotel. Maybe a couple hundred troops parade proudly in methodical rows just outside the front doors of the lobby rotunda. A note of arrogance extends from these soldiers.

This hotel can hold its own among the others that surround it. The esthetically pleasing view from atop the stair-stacked floors gives this architectural layout originality. I'm sure the frills of this luxurious resort have catered nicely to the small Chinese brigade. It's almost a shame we have to blow it up. *Almost.*

The back, less illuminated, fades into the dark except for the glimmering luxury pool. An indoor spa sits adjacent and connects to the bottom floor. We take advantage of the unguarded poolside and break into the spa rooms. The doors easily open to a long room filled with exercise equipment and a Jacuzzi next to a small cabana.

We sneak down the hall into the laundry area and find a cart with a bloody towel hanging from it. Chatter from the next room erupts. Henry leans his ear against the wall and listens. The thick insulated barrier distorts the conversation inaudible. The mumbling voices raise to a frenzy and then it stops. A thud hits the side of the wall and rattles. A few minutes later the door slams and footsteps fade down the hall.

"Wait," Henry whispers before I peek outside the hall. The room quiets, and for a moment, I know something has gone awry. Henry gives me a nod to proceed. I quietly step out into the hall and open the door to the next room. It's empty. Nothing but a chair, some chains, and drops of blood stain the stark-white floor.

"You sure this was him?" Father Joseph asks.

"I'm positive," I say.

"How can you be sure?" Gabe doubts.

I reach down and grab a bloody piece of metal. "Know anyone else missing a Jewish dog tag with Sadiq's name?"

"Good point."

"They're taking him somewhere else. We need to follow now," I say.

We press down to the end of the hall into the maintenance section. Electrical wires encased in steel tubing run along the ceiling and stop at a junction. An electrical room station is up ahead, but two guards are posted at the end of the hall near the elevator.

"They've taken him on the elevator," I whisper.

"What do we do now?" Gabe asks.

"We get the guards' attention."

Henry pulls his gun and aims to the edge of the corner.

"Save your bullets." I hand him my dagger and quietly secure my sword in hand. "Get ready."

I take one last peek and call out for help. My voice rings down hallway and summons the two soldiers. With a skip in their step, they abandon their post and ramble toward my voice. I raise my sword to the thundering clap of boots trampling closer and closer. Henry kneels in combat stance, knife in hand and ready to strike.

The closer they reach, the tighter I grip the sword handle. *Thud, thud, thud,* the soldiers breach the corner and I swing. Blood splatters and bodies fall. The soldiers are ravished: a dagger struck in the jugular and a gashing crevice carved from the throat to the crotch.

Henry and Gabe slide the bodies out of the way. The six above the elevator doors lights up. Unsure of awaits us when the elevator doors open, we take the stairs instead.

There's an eerie echo in the stairwell as we ascend to the top floor. On the other side of the walls, a ruckus flares up on the first floor as we pass. We reach the fourth floor when all of a sudden voices shout from below. Several soldiers spot us from the ground floor of the stairwell and shoot.

"Henry, grenade!" I shout.

Henry pulls the pin and drops one over the side of the railing. The aerial strike sinks to the bottom stairs and clears whoever is left standing. The gunfire stops and the shouting ceases, which forces us to hastily climb before any more soldiers arrive.

Step by step, we reach the top where the stairs end to the last door. I can only pray that Sadiq is on this floor.

I catch my breath for a second and push in the handle. Father Joseph and Henry rush in and cover an empty hall. A set of double doors open to an empty balcony. The elevator is to the left of the hall while the right leads around a corner to an enormous room filled with extravagance.

Greek white pillars stand erect around the perimeter of the marbled floor. A fictional depiction of Greek gods decorate the curved walls. A display of dazzling murals hover like clouds on the ceiling rotunda. Heavy blue curtains bunch to the sides of each pillar. Alone in the middle of the large room sits a long conference table pending an invite.

The room is silent except for the chatty shadows that dance passed a set of frosted glass doors in the back.

"Father, you and Gabe stay close to the stairwell and cover the elevator," I order.

"What do you intend on doing?"

"Open those doors, kill everyone inside, and get Sadiq back."

"Just like that?"

"Yup."

"Just clarifying."

"Henry, give me your smoke canister. Hide behind the pillar over there and wait for my signal."

"You're going to lure them out, huh?"

"Like snakes from a den."

Whatever is taking place behind those doors, the conversation elevates. A thud bumps against the wall and shouting erupts. Without warning, I open the door, pull the pin, and toss the canister inside. A cloud of green permeates the room followed by a trail of coughing and confusion.

Like ants from a disturbed mound, soldiers pour out from the room and scatter. Henry attacks from the right while I slice and dice my way from the left. I cut through the drifting smoke with my sword and strike viciously; one by one as bodies pile up on the floor.

Within minutes, the shouting and chaos stops. The smoke clears and leaves the nice marbled floor stained with a bloody mess of tangled limbs—three decorated officers and a half-dozen minced troops. I wipe the sprinkled blood from my face and arms with the curtains.

Inside the smoke-faded room, Sadiq lies on the floor, hands and feet bound. Blood and bruises cover his face, but he's still alive. Henry quickly releases his bound limbs and aids him through the doors.

"My God, what happened?" he gasps.

"We don't have time, let's go!" I demand. "This place is going to be crawling with troops shortly."

"Arena," Gabe shouts as we exit around the corner. "The stairs are covered. There's no way down."

"We'll have to take the elevator," Henry suggests.

"Are you kidding me?"

"It's our only chance."

"Come on!" Father Joseph shouts.

Guns raised and expecting to fire, we wait impatiently for the elevator doors to open. It's empty.

"Let's go, let's go!" Henry shouts.

Just as the stairwell breaches with troops, the doors close and the elevator descends to the floors below. It seems to take forever, especially with the Muzak piping from the small speakers in the ceiling.

I pull both guns and ready for a firefight. The doors open; three soldiers stand there shell-shocked. Two are unarmed and the other holsters a pistol to his side.

"Going down?" Gabe mocks.

He's without a doubt the most unconventional person I know, but give him credit, sarcasm wins out in this situation. The two soldiers in the back act confused, but the one in front inches his hand closer to his holster. I smile and shoot them all dead before he reaches for his pistol. They all fall in unison and the elevator door closes.

"Guess not."

Each floor lights up above the doors as slowly as possible. "Come on, come on, two more floors," I anxiously plea to the elevator gods.

"You mean one more," Gabe corrects.

"You pushed B right?"

"Oops."

"Oh shit," Henry huffs.

Ding! The doors open on the first floor. About two dozen troops, a few suits, and one pissed-off looking major parade around rather confused. There's an awkward pause before Father Joseph goes all ape and lays into the entire floor with his meaty five-hundred-round ammo pack. He clears the floor and everything standing outside the lobby doors.

"To the right!" Henry yells.

"Gabe, come on! What are you doing?" I shout.

"Just give me a second," he says.

He quickly removes his backpack and sets the charge detonation on the bomb.

"Okay, let's go!"

We make a break down to the side entrance and around the pool. Gunshots shower the side of the building. Sadiq limps painfully with Henry and me, but pushes on despite the agony.

Bullets graze past as Father Joseph returns fire. We've more than stirred up a mound; we've pissed off a colony. Troops from the west side of the harbor filter in and engage. Bullets whiz next to my cheek like fluttering bees.

"Over here!" Gabe shouts.

The street ends and dips into a small drainage ditch that hides us momentarily. Our only opening lies between the parking lot across the street and a large shopping strip nearly two blocks away.

The firing ceases and so does our will to move from exhaustion. Gabe tinkers with the transmitter and fails to get the signal to ignite. Suddenly, the sky lights up orange and fire bellows from the hotel behind us. The tremendous energy shakes the ground and sends debris soaring through the night sky.

No rest for the weary as the quick breather ends. We dash across the street toward Route 90 just a block away from the small airport runway. No sign of our trucks, but it's much too early for them to reach the marker.

A small hangar sitting just outside the partially fenced airport provides enough protection while we wait. Sadiq lies back and grimaces. His grabs his wounded calf and pulls back the pant leg. A nasty lesion about six inches hinders him mobile. I tear a piece of material from his pant leg and wrap it tightly around the cut to stop it from bleeding.

"You okay?" I ask.

"Do I look okay?" he playfully responds and smiles.

"Well, that all depends. You're always quite grumpy," I grin.

"Here I was trampling your plan and doubting your intentions, and I'm the one who got you into this mess."

"Irony is the song of a bird that has come to love its cage, as they say."

"Is it impossible for you to not be a smart ass?"

He smiles. "Thank you for getting me."

"You would have done the same."

"Would I?" His grin overshadows the pain beneath it.

"Your face has enough bruises. I'll let you have that one."

"I owe you my life," he says.

"Save that sentiment until we're on the road."

Smoke fills the sky and drifts across the resort, keeping us well hidden. The hotel burns out of control and makes a dominative statement to the Chinese before it collapses to the ground.

"I can see the trucks!" Gabe says as he looks through his binoculars.

"You ready, old man?" I ask Sadiq.

"Better old than dead," he answers.

Father Joseph takes point while Henry and I help Sadiq across the runway. Just another hundred yards away and we can finally leave this place behind us.

The trucks slow just on the other side of the airport. Jacob and Harold rush over and help Sadiq. Suddenly, from behind one of the grounded planes, gunfire follows. An eruption of fire rains down as we sprint across the paved road. Henry and Father Joseph return fire and slow the attack.

Gabe jumps into the back of the truck followed by Henry. Gunfire erupts again and bullets graze past me and into the side of the truck. I lift myself up on the bumper, but I'm shot. I fall to the ground and reach for my side.

"Arena!' screams Jacob.

All I can see is the dark sky as I lie my back and wince. I knew I was hit, and I didn't feel pain, but now that I've had a moment, I can almost envision the bullet lodged in my gut, and hot pain erupts. Hands reach under me and pick me up. I feel like I'm floating into the truck and suspended on a cloud. The roar of the truck ignites and takes off.

Blood pours from my side and rags are pressed against me. Faces hover above me, but I only notice Jacob.

"Arena, Arena!" Jacob cries.

I'm in a daze for a moment before I recognize Roland tending to my wound. The initial shock wears off and is replaced with a burning pain in my ribs.

"You're going to be okay," he assures.

Jacob sits next to me and brushes my hair back while Roland stitches my bullet wound. Luckily it went through me. I don't think I could bear the pain of having the bullet removed.

Roland's eyes wander over my face with worry seeping from them. I try to sit up, but the pain knocks me down. *My baby.* I have no choice but to tell them.

Roland grabs his stethoscope. I can't hold back the tears knowing my baby may be dead. He lifts back my shirt and places the diaphragm on my womb.

"What are you doing?" Jacob asks, perplexed.

"Is it okay?" I nervously ask Roland.

He focuses intently and listens for a heartbeat. Juliana and Nadia look at each other knowingly. It's not as easy for a man to understand these things, as Jacob still appears to be dumbfounded. Roland lifts his head and removes the stethoscope from his ears. He smiles.

I wipe the tear from my cheek and a sigh of relief overcomes me. I turn to Jacob and smile. "I'm pregnant."

CHAPTER 34

I never thought I would enjoy the sound of a diesel truck roaring across the long desert stretch. If not from the humming engine, it's the endless delight of Jacob's grin that's comforts me. He hasn't let go of me since. I've never quite seen him this excited before. I probably should have told him from the beginning, but what's done is done. He's happy. From here on out, nothing will stop him from allowing me to go on my own. I give him no reason to do so. I've risked enough.

We've come so close to reaching our destination amid deadly pestilence and unwanted sacrifices. And now for the first time I step on soil I can call home, a place of historic pilgrimage for over five-thousand years and a mingling of antiquity and modern culture.

We've made it to Jerusalem.

Morning rides upon us, but the sun has yet to rise. The eastern horizon is as dark as midnight. The streets are full, but there's a nervous urgency among the people. Almost a sense of knowing bad things are to come, and I can't blame them. Being under harsh scrutiny from the rest of the world, Israel prepares for the worst. Its history stands proud here, but is on the brink of crumbling in the hands of a political nightmare.

The cities we've drifted through the past two years brought more death than hope, but this place certainly changes my perspective.

We wait outside the botanical gardens near the Rabin Hotel, a grand structure that sits atop a mound with two sets of sprawling steps descending below. They bring such a grandeur to the ambience of this majestic hotel exterior.

Across the way is the Israel Museum of Jerusalem and the garden landscaping that surrounds it springs with beauty. I feel like I'm in an oasis after what we've been through. Though we establish refuge here, I still keep a level head and a close guard.

Ananiah and Sadiq exit the hotel lobby with an older gentleman. Everyone waits by the truck except for me and Gabe. Instead, we move closer to meet this mystery man at bottom of the steps. He wears a beige *kippah* and dresses in his traditional Jewish vestments.

"Arena, Gabriel, this is my good friend Ovadia," Ananiah introduces.

"Nice to meet you, sir," Gabe replies. The slender man shakes his hand but holds mine gently. Solemnity crosses his eyes.

"And you must be Finnegan's niece," he addresses. "I'm deeply sorry for your loss. He was my friend." I nod and accept his condolence.

Ananiah briefly explains where we will be staying while Ovadia, pale and stoic, stands quietly next to him. I dare not ask any questions of Ovadia just yet. I leave the serious expression drawn on his face at peace.

Sadiq and Gabe help the others unload our gear and retreat to the luxury hotel. I stay back with Roland and Jacob waiting as a car pulls up to the steps. Ovadia opens the door and invites us in.

"Where are we going?" I ask.

"Hadassah Medical Center. We need to properly treat those wounds and give you a full checkup. We need to keep that baby healthy," Roland replies.

We leave central Jerusalem and cross over to the other side of the western wall. The sacred concrete stronghold has since been extended and wraps around most of the city. Its height soars unimaginable, towering at least two hundred feet.

After the Dome on the Rock was destroyed, another temple was erected in its place but had since been occupied by Muslim leadership. The ongoing war hasn't ceased, but has now escalated.

The conclusion of the wall expansion and a nine-day bloody battle led the Muslim quarter to broaden farther west, which has currently left the temple mount in control with the Jewish state. Unless Russian headship accepts Israel's stance, I'm afraid their plight will continue to harden. Battles have been fought, but a war is about to begin. I refuse to let this nation fall in the hands of political mongrels.

Years of fighting has left this side of Jerusalem desolated and in a state of decay. With the exception of Hadassah and the temple, much has been laid in waste and abandonment.

Hundreds if not a thousand Israeli troops line the outer wall behind mammoth artillery. Military trucks drive in and out through the wall's thick metal gates. It's unlike anything I have ever seen.

Two Israeli jeeps escort us down the road and into a complex that resembles a small city. The hospital campus, while heavily guarded, opens to territory that has been occupied my threatening enemies. Not sure I'm liking this idea.

"Why all the way out here for treatment?" I question.

"This is the only remaining hospital that's fully staffed and offers the best equipment," Ovadia explains. "Over the last couple of decades, most of our hospitals were shut down due to an economical cataclysm. Yes, it seems unimaginable that hospitals would be on the list, but we've survived because of Hadassah. Due to the massive number of transfer patients, in-home care was established. Unfortunately, the '35 flu epidemic took care of the rest."

"It's safe here?"

"Where we are taking you . . . very."

The two jeeps check in at the front gates and lead us around the back. The curvy road twists and dips down toward the entrance to an enormous tunnel. Two large doors slide back as we enter. We take the tunnel beneath the belly of this colossal hospital and park inside a secluded garage.

Upon arrival, a nurse waits outside and converses with Ovadia before we are led down a stark-white hall. She opens a set of double doors and invites Roland and myself into a small room. Jacob and Ovadia are left standing outside.

I lie back on the cold paper-covered table while my wound is cleaned and redressed. Roland rolls up my sleeve and jabs six inch needle into my skin.

"Damn, what was that for?"

"Anti-virus," he says. My face pales.

"What?"

"Don't worry, it's just a precaution. Your baby will be fine. I'm quite certain the virus would have taken you by now anyway, but just to be very sure, you're safe."

After thirty minutes of poking and prodding, Roland sits by my bedside and grins.

"Everything seems to be normal," he assures.

"So, no problems then?"

"Nope. Would you like to know the sex of your baby?"

"I think I'd rather not know."

"It's your choice. I'll go get your husband."

After the long worry over my child the past months, I finally have a reason to smile. My baby rests comfortably in my womb, as I'm now four-and-a-half-months pregnant. Roland invites Jacob in, explains my condition, and leaves the two of us alone. Jacob kisses me and wraps his arms around my pudgy belly.

"So, we're really going to have a baby, huh?" Jacob grins.

"No, I'm going to have this baby. You're going to watch," I joke.

"Thought of a name?"

"Joshua if it's a boy, and Lily if it's a girl."

"I like that."

I struggle to smile and embrace Jacob's joy, but deep down inside, I'm broken.

"What's wrong?" he asks.

"Nothing, why?"

"Seriously, Arena. You're a terrible liar, you know that."

"I can't help it, but I just feel . . . guilty."

"About what?"

"About bringing a child into this cruel world."

"You said yourself that 'perspective is everything.' So change it."

"How? Every time I look down, I'm reminded by this lump sticking out of me."

"And a beautiful lump it is."

I grab his face and press my lips against his, letting the warmth of his kiss linger. The scent of my husband takes me to a place I want to stay forever.

*   *   *

I'm not sure I'll ever get used to the dark sky hovering over us like a blanket. The sun has ceased to exist for the last seven days. The people of Jerusalem worry it's a warning sign for punishment, but I succeed to the notion. These people have served more than enough retribution. Though I admit it's quite creepy, I stand by God's power to see beyond the sinister clouds. A few stars still cling above and remind me that not all is lost.

Israel feels like a first-world country hiding in a broken world. The people have come to know what to expect during times like these. It's no surprise they will be persecuted no matter the outcome. While a quarter have established themselves as messianic Jews, most still cling to their Orthodox beliefs.

Many places in central Jerusalem continue to be sacred, especially the old city. We've made efforts to respect each other's cultural differences. The state of this nation is in peril, but I pray it can overcome its adversaries. She is my home and I will not abandoned her.

After an incredible meal at the hotel, Ananiah takes Gabe and me to meet with some respected leaders. I really have no care in the world right now; I just want to enjoy some peace for once. I'm sure it won't last.

Gabe and I stand in a holding room no bigger than the metal containers on the ship and wait for Ananiah and Sadiq. They, with a few others, meet outside the doors under a secret summit. Among those include Egyptian leadership, Israeli dignitaries, and the General Defense Council headed by General Alexander Eizenkot.

The only surprise in attendance are the few Egyptian supporters that have considered rebuilding an alliance. Not since Russia's global immersion have they positioned themselves to do so. Something just feels wrong about it. They've been in there for quite some time now, and I'm not sure why Gabe and I were brought here for this political conference.

A debate heats up and arguing arises behind the closed doors. After five minutes of what seems like childish banter, it grows quiet. The doors open and Ananiah invites us inside. A round conference table stands in the center of the room and sixteen cantankerous men sit stately around it. They all stand in unison while Ananiah introduces each one. The only man who is not standing sits quietly in a highly decorated military uniform with his hands folded on the table. It's General Alexander Eizenkot as Sadiq had described earlier.

The men return to their seats and Ananiah introduces

the general. Eizenkot stands and shakes our hands. If there's an indication of a smile hiding on his face, he makes a great effort to reserve it behind his stoic expression. The wrinkles on his forehead scrunch like an accordion and fade back to his bald head. The little gray hair he has is thin on each side of his head. Behind the meaty frame hides a man that probably resembled a body builder in his youth. His arm muscles stretch the shirt that appears to be a size smaller than what he should be wearing. Aside from the potbelly, this man stands strong and tall.

"So, you're the twins," he says plainly. He's as emotionless as a head of lettuce.

"You seem disappointed," I reply. The men around the table chuckle.

"On the contrary. Go ahead and have a seat."

"I still don't understand why we are here."

"You're here because you've started something unfathomable. There's nothing ordinary about you two or we wouldn't be having this conversation right now," Eizenkot says.

"So what do you want from me?"

"You've created a global revolution of war and that pilgrimage has led you here. I want to know why."

"I don't know who you think I am or what you've heard. I only came here to save my brother from those Russian pigs."

"Arena!" Sadiq blurts.

"Then why have you led your fellowship here to Jerusalem?"

"Why are you so interested for a reason?"

"The history of this nation is going to change because of you."

"What are you talking about?"

"Rabi," Eizenkot calls across the room.

Father Joseph, sitting in the corner of the room, stands

and moves toward the table with troubled eyes. "Have you lost your faith?" Father Joseph asks me.

I wrinkle my brow in confusion. "I've lost my loved ones. Isn't that enough?"

"You've started a revolution not because you wanted to but because you were meant to. Your destiny lies beyond Israel, Arena, and I will help see it through."

"Maybe it's time for you to move on. I'm done fighting," I say.

"Are you? Beyond these borders is a future. A future for your baby. Is your child's life not worth fighting for?"

I feel frantic. I don't know what Father Joseph wants of me. I've led everyone to safety. What more can I do? "That's not fair—"

"Life's never fair."

I grip the edge of the table in frustration. "This is the last place Russian repression hasn't put their boots on. My family and friends are dead because of the Russian's ruthless regime. Sue me for wanting to find a place to settle and call home."

"If Russia breaches the border, there won't be a home."

"I've lost so much."

"We've all lost something," Eizenkot interrupts.

"Yeah, well, we nearly lost our entire group back in Eilat because you left the border unprotected. You pulled your troops out and now China has taken control of the Red Sea."

"Mistakes were made," he says without offering an apology or a hint of culpability.

I chuckle with resentment. "Make more mistakes like that and you're going to lose this country quickly."

Eizenkot's brows furrow. "That's why we need you."

"What could you possibly need me for?"

"An iron will."

"You don't need a seventeen year old girl fighting your battles."

"No, but we need her desire to overcome the odds. You didn't start a revolution, Arena. You are the revolution. I want the girl who's faith goes unyielding, the girl who God seeks favor with, the one girl who took on an army, and the one who is going to lead mine."

"My killing days are over."

"I'm not asking you to fight on the battlefield. I need someone strong-willed and cunning to lead."

"You got the wrong person."

"What happened to the Arena that everyone looked up to for confidence . . . the killing machine that made her an icon for hope, or the fear she planted inside enemy minds?"

"That Arena is dead."

"Is she now?"

"I'm going to be a mother soon. That's who I am now."

"Has the desert sun scrambled your brain?" Father Joseph asks me.

"I've changed."

"No, I don't believe that for one second. Only time has."

"I just want this all to end."

"Which is why we are in talks with Russian envoys," Eizenkot concedes.

I stand up and shout, "What?"

"You're bloody kidding, right?" Gabe adds.

"The Ten has offered a substantial amount of support for border trade," Eizenkot responds.

"I can't believe I'm hearing this. You're out of your mind!" I scream.

"If we can't negotiate a deal, bad things are going to happen."

"Bad things are going to happen either way, trust me."

"Under the Ten Nation agreement, seven nations have reached a diplomatic decision to begin developing and building up their armed forces. These armies will be under

Russian control, which makes these negotiations necessary. Don't get me wrong, our defense forces are strong, but we cannot sustain the magnitude of this seven-nation army Russia has declared," Eizenkot says.

"You do this and you're going to lose everything this country has stood for. Thousands of years of history will vanish under Russian and Chinese authorities. You're making a huge mistake," I say.

"I understand your stance, but I'm only trying to protect your future. It's in my experience that even the powerful must make sacrifices for the greater good," Eizenkot says.

"Experience doesn't necessary lead to wisdom."

"I've held my position for twenty-five years and—"

"And you've been fighting for thousands, so what's your point?" I slam my hands on the table. "I will not sit here and let some bullheaded egomaniac ruin this nation because he's too chicken shit to protect a cause that's much greater than his own ambitions. I'll take my bloody swords and do itmyself!"

"You've just illustrated my point as I'd hoped." Eizenkot grins, as does Father Joseph, Sadiq, and Ananiah.

I'm confused. "What is going on?"

"That's the Arena I've been hearing about. That's the girl I want on my side when it counts. I'm the supreme command of this military outfit, the general chief of staff of the Israeli Defense Forces. Do you honestly believe I would do something as . . . how did you say, 'chicken shit,' as giving up my stance? I will not lead you to your death. I will follow you to mine."

I'm at a total loss for words, unsure whether I should feel flattered or annoyed. I'm mostly annoyed. "Next time, just lead with that. It'll make this a whole lot less awkward," I snap.

"I knew what you were doing the whole time," Gabe boasts. I'd like to slap that sarcastic grin right off his face.

I cordially leave the meeting. Gabe trails behind like a puppy dog. "You can be a real jerk sometimes," I joke as I pass Sadiq.

"Get rested up. We'll get you both briefed at oh-sixteen-hundred tomorrow," Eizenkot reminds.

"Fifteen, sixteen, whatever." The door closes behind me. I really have no interest in Eizenkot's politics, but I will do anything to keep my friends alive. If I'm to lead, then so be it, but my child comes first.

The sky has been scorched with darkness, but it grows even darker as night approaches. I sit unnerved on the edge of the bed next to Jacob.

"You okay? You seem a bit anxious about something," Jacob observes.

"I just need to get some air, that's all."

"Is it the baby?"

"If it is, this is going to be a long and painful pregnancy . . . for you." He smiles. "I'll be back."

I leave Jacob alone and grab Gabe in the next room over. He's not too thrilled about my presence, but he obliges to walk with me outside.

It's been awhile since Gabe and I were alone. It doesn't seem too long ago that we were hiking in a thicket of barbed trees. But here we are in a foreign land walking the city streets of one of the most historical places on Earth.

Lights from afar dim above the cityscape, but many illuminate brightly down the next block. The curfew that was once issued here has been lifted. It was just a temporary precaution when threats were received from the western border. It was no more than just political posturing from the Palestinian government. Nothing new.

Modest housing lies on both sides of the street with a few commercial buildings peppered throughout, but one in particular catches my eye. An armored jeep sits outside of a building that's under heavy construction. I gaze at the vehicle with joy.

"Really, you're stopping to look at a stupid jeep?" Gabe rolls his eyes. I can't help it. I'm enamored by it. I didn't know they made jeeps like this anymore. "Can we go now? I really don't like leaving Juliana waiting—"

I shush Gabe and feel my defenses kick in. "You hear that?"

"So, it's people talking . . . like us."

"No, they're arguing. Come on, it's coming from over there by that building."

Gabe huffs. "Seriously? This is borderline stalking, even for you."

We sneak alongside the unfinished stone construction as the voices grow louder.

"You're going to get us in trouble," Gabe whispers.

I stop near a busted window and peer inside. Two men stand in a room filled with boxes, but their faces allude me from the shadow casting on the other side. They're in the middle of some argument.

"Your nation is vulnerable and your leadership is weak. Your allies are but a simple cold, and Israel is the contagion," the man on the right says.

"You know, I can remember not too long ago when your government came to us with besieging favor, or have you conveniently forgotten?" the other man says.

They move from the shadow and into the light. I recognizes them both from the conference—an Egyptian delegate and an Israeli representative, but why are they debating each other over the state of Israel?

"The only thing I remember is a country under mercy." The Israeli pulls a red patch from his coat pocket and raises it to the other man's face. A black Russian insignia and seven black stripes decorate it, just like the flag flying atop one of the buildings in Cairo. We have a spy among us. His eyes briefly stray from the conversation before they slope with convincing dejection. "And for all its glorious past, we see a new covenant being shadowed. It's quite ironic, don't you think?"

"We still have a fight in us yet, and I'm no fool to believe otherwise. No, I believe we've come too far in this war to lay down now."

"I will not come to negotiate with your country again. This is my last offer. You join and help us thwart this political stalemate with Israel and the Ten will see that your country receives great endeavors."

"And if we refuse?"

"Consider our next meeting to be quite hostile."

"Okay, but I hope your promises are better than your negotiating tactics."

The Russian spy glowers during the heated exchange. He walks closer until he's face to face with the Egyptian delegate. With the violent grit of his teeth he sneers with an asserted promise. "You lead me astray, and I will break you and your country."

If I had a weapon on me, I'd kill both of them right now. As it is, we must warn the others and hope these men don't leave. We sprint back to the hotel and find Sadiq standing in the lobby.

His smile leaves him and is replaced with a frown after we explain what we overheard. He dashes behind the lobby counter and contacts Eizenkot. Within minutes the streets are swarming with military vehicles and troops.

"Go back upstairs, we'll take care of this," Sadiq orders.

We leave the lobby and wait with our significant others, but I'm too anxious to know what they intend to do with these two traders. It's been hours since we last spoke to Sadiq and no one has told us a thing.

The door knocks and Ananiah stands outside. "They want you and Gabe to come down to the holding facility as witnesses only. All they want to do is ask you a few questions, then you can leave," he explains.

I grab one of my guns and hide it underneath my shirt.

"What part of 'witnesses only' did you not understand?" he says.

"I have a right to carry my gun just as anyone else."

"Well, keep it in your pants and let the military handle the interrogation."

"Of course."

Rather than taking us to Ofer Prison, the closest confinement base, Ananiah drives us to the Underground Prisoners Museum in the Old City—an appropriate place for an interrogation.

Two military police take us to down a long hall and past the courtyard. We are escorted inside a small room where we wait.

The door opens and Eizenkot enters. He pulls back the curtains that hides a two-way mirror. The two men we saw earlier in the building sit behind a metal table with their hands bound.

"Are these the two men you saw?" he asks simply.

"Yes," I reply. "And the one on the right is your Russian spy."

"That man on the right is Yoseph Segen Rishon, lieutenant first class, company executive officer. He's served in the IDF of this brigade for many years. You're telling me this man is a Russian spy?"

"Yup."

"I don't doubt your accusations, but I really need some serious understanding why this highly decorated soldier has been practicing espionage under our noses this whole time. Are you positive?"

"Yes, she is!" Gabe interjects.

"He claims you made this up."

"And what do you think?" I say.

"I value your trust."

"Then act like it."

"I'm the chief of general staff of the IDF—"

"I'm not questioning your leadership; it's your interrogating tactics that concern me."

"Be my guest."

He opens the door to the interrogating room and escorts me in along with an armed officer. "Someone would like to have a word with you," Eizenkot relays to the prisoners.

The door closes behind me and the two men just grin.

"Something funny?" I ask.

"This ridiculous debriefing," Yoseph spats.

"It's about to get a whole lot funnier." I pull out my gun and shoot point blank into his skull. Blood sprays the back of his chair and his body drops to the side.

"Next!"

The door opens and Eizenkot rushes into the room. "Stop!" he shouts.

Ananiah and Sadiq struggle to hold him back while the Egyptian delegate shivers with fear.

I turn my gun on Eizenkot. He abruptly stands still.

"Arena, put the gun down," Ananiah pleads calmly.

"Let me finish what I started, then you can have this dirtbag," I say.

Eizenkot backs off and leaves the room. I press my gun into the delegate's temple. He mumbles nonsense beneath his trembling lips.

"I didn't get your name. What was it?" I ask.

"Haahaahadwwin . . ."

"Your name sounds like you're about to sneeze."

"It's Hadwin," he corrects. I press the gun harder into his head. "Wait! Wait! I'll tell you everything, I swear. Please don't shoot! I'll tell you whatever you want to know."

"I know you will."

I turn to the two-way mirror and wink. The officer in the back of the room panics and draws his gun to me.

"Put that away before you kill someone," I tell him.

The door swings open and Eizenkot relieves the somewhat terrified officer. He stares at me, but can't muster any words.

"You want to take over?" I ask him.

"Why don't you go back to the hotel and get some rest. I think some sleep will do you some good. We'll take it from here."

"You sure? Because I'm feeling awfully trigger-happy tonight."

"I'm positive." Eizenkot grits his teeth.

"We've learned a very valuable lesson today, haven't we, Hadwin?" I mock. He nods nervously. "Lying will get you nowhere."

Although this little episode illustrated an unpleasant outcome for some, it has made us more aware of our surroundings. Trust cannot be overstated enough. Disagreeable or not, it's a part of this world we have to expect now.

CHAPTER 35

Four months have passed and the luxury of this fine hotel has lost its luster. The wonderful amenities we once embraced have faded, but it has been our home and we are extremely grateful. The south side crumbles a little more each day from the heavy mortar damage.

I'm a little over eight-and-a-half-months pregnant, and it's all I can do not to pee every five minutes. It's been nearly two months since the first attack. Russian and Saudi troops invaded from the south and wreaked havoc on the city. The battalion pushed through the first line but was halted by the Etzioni Brigade. Prisoners were detained, but most died in battle. Although their attempt to infiltrate was staunched, it did substantiate the weakness this city could be under.

We've since been removed from the hotel and sent to more protective quarters—an underground dwelling just below the Jerusalem Museum. The small concrete rooms suffice, but they are far from comforting. Normally I wouldn't care, as I'm used to these conditions, but when you're carrying a tiny person who presses on your bladder, things just aren't the same.

We have everything we need to survive, but it's far from what we were used to when we first arrived to Jerusalem. Food is becoming scarce and our water supplies have been detracted from bacterial leaching that had breached the wells. The blood-pouring rain nearly eight months ago has left behind remnants of poisonous bacteria in the grounds. The time it will take to dig new wells and replenish our supplies is futile. We've survived on alternative resources from rain-water silos and a few reserve tanks. The water has been plentiful, but it's unclear how long it will last.

Central Jerusalem has sustained damage, but it still stands to provide safety. Mingling crowds no longer exist. Fear fills the empty streets now. Many stay indoors, while others have long dispersed to other regions.

I sit up against my pillow and watch tiny feet dance inside my belly. The first four months of pregnancy have been mentally dreadful. I've neglected the idea that I've been given a blessing inside my womb. I've blamed myself for the misery this child may endure when he or she is born. What possible future can my child have? But now, things are different. I accept this child as a precious gift from God and will do everything in my power to protect him or her. It's the only joy I can hold onto while Jacob and the others are gone.

Two days have passed since I last kissed Jacob. He and the other men have left to protect west Jerusalem. Israeli defenses have grown in mass numbers but are still out-matched by Russia and China's military forces. Several attempts to negotiate with Russian leadership have gone unresolved.

Jerusalem has a stronghold on Russian adversaries, but the seven armies will eventually breach the borders and force this nation to fall. And here I sit, swollen like a balloon, not being able to help this insurgency.

But at least I'm not alone. Allison and Luke keep me company and stare at my tummy every ten minutes. It's the small things that put delight in their eyes. Roland rests in the adjacent room waiting patiently for this baby to be deliv-ered, but it's Nadia who has waited on me day and night. She's more than a great friend. Nadia has gone beyond her will to protect and sacrifice for me. I'm truly indebted to her kindness.

The doors slam up above and descending down the stairs comes Nadia, drenched in sweat. She wipes her face with a towel and redresses a small stab wound she received from a Russian Dragoon, a first-class private in the foreign regiment.

"How's it looking?" I ask.

"It's healing better than I thought it would, but I should probably get some more antibiotics from Roland just in case," she speculates. She wraps her arm, tapes it up, and hands me a glass of water.

"I'm not thirsty."

"Too bad, drink it. You don't need to be dehydrated." Her bedside manners have changed since the beginning, but I like it. She's a straightforward, no-bullshitting kind of woman. She hands me a package wrapped in green paper.

"What's this?" I ask.

"It's from Marissa."

Marissa is a genuinely kind woman who assists her husband, Eli, the museum curator. She and her husband have offered us this place for protection. I unwrap the package and brighten with joy at the hand-knitted blanket for the baby. It's perfect.

"I see your little helpers have cleaned up the room," she says, referring to the children.

Allison and Luke play quietly in the corner of the room with a pair of dice. Luke's grin is too adorable for Nadia to resist. "Someone deserves a surprise," she says.

Both Luke and Allison jump from their corner and beam with excitement.

"Hold out your hands."

Nadia reaches into her pocket and drops two pieces of candy into their palms. It's a luxury to receive a gift like this nowadays. Shops have been closed down and people have moved on away from this unnecessary war. Many still endure the hardships of this broken city, but as recluse as they are, central Jerusalem remains lifeless.

Since the borders have been closed, international trade no longer exists and has caused a depletion in goods and food supplies. If Russia can't negotiate a deal with Israeli leaders, then they will starve this nation. Russia and China have blocked all foreign trade in an attempt to force closure.

"If you're good, I just might give you both another piece," Nadia coaxes.

These kids have shown more maturity than most. They've had their share of ornery moments, but they're irreplaceable.

"Still the same?" I ask Nadia, concerning the plight of our recourse.

"Negotiations have stalled, but so far no hostility as of yet."

"And Jacob?"

"He and the others are fine. There's been discussions between Eizenkot and Ananiah about a peace deal, but I don't think there's any resolve. I'm afraid this is going to get worse."

"Why do say that?"

"I didn't want to upset you—you have enough to worry about—but we may have to leave here. Things are mounting quickly from the north, and I can't see that we have an advantage to slow this regime."

"Where are we supposed to go? I can't leave like this."

"I don't know, but unless God Himself reaches down and wipes clean of this war, this city is going to fall."

"Ow!" I grimace.

"What is it?"

"I keep getting these sharp pains down below. Feels like this kid is dancing on my uterus."

"Roland, can you please come here?" Nadia calls.

"What is the pain?" Roland asks while he rubs his eyes and mouth stretches to yawn.

"I keep getting these sharp pains below my belly."

"How often do you get them?"

"Every now and then."

"It's pretty common at this stage. Unless the pain worsens and continues for a long period of time, this is no more than Braxton Hicks contractions. You should get some rest."

I take Roland's advice and lay my head back on my pillow. Worry hovers over me like a dark cloud. What is to come of this city, this nation, and this life now? I rub my tummy gently and resist the discomfort that haunts me. I forget about what takes place above ground and relax my mind. My eyes glaze over and soon I fall asleep.

*   *   *

A small breeze blows past my face. I wake up expecting one of the kids playing around with me, but instead I'm petrified. There's a puddle of blood in the middle of the floor and blood trails up the stairs. The door swings back and forth against the wall. Am I dreaming? I pinch myself and it hurts. Even the contractions go in and out with burning pain. This is very real.

I pull my legs over the bed and reach for my gun out of habit, but of course it isn't there. I slowly get up and glance up the steps. No one is there. The empty room feels cold and smells rancid. An arm lies in the doorway of the adjacent room where Roland sleeps. I'm scared to look inside, but I have to.

Roland lies dead with several gunshots to his chest. Nadia's fear has come true. We've been overpowered by an unstoppable regime and now they have taken the city.

My dizzy head spins and I shuffle unsteady from the room. My knees buckle and my stomach sinks as I struggle to stand. I wobble in shock before I fall to the ground, paralyzed. I feel completely lost and abandoned. What happened to the others? Were they forced to flee and leave me, or have they all been killed? My brother, Jacob, Juliana, Niki . . . I just can't take it anymore. *God, please end this, now.*

The basement door slams. Two shadows emerge as tiny footsteps trample down the stairs. Allison and Luke reach the bottom in tears. A Russian soldier follows behind with a Makarov pistol pointed to their heads.

I try to move, but I'm still bound to the floor from shock. The soldier brings the children closer and shouts, "Where is he?"

"I don't know who you are talking about. Just let the children go," I plead.

"Tell me where your head of state is hiding or I'll be forced to shoot." He grabs Luke by the shoulder and presses the gun to his head.

"Please! I don't know where he is. I beg you, don't do this. Take me instead."

"You leave with no choice, woman."

Luke's eyes clench tight before he falls to the floor dead.

"No! You bastard!"

I scrape myself from the floor and lunge toward the man. His powerful grip stops my momentum and sends my womb on fire. I've been stabbed. I clutch the air and fall back to the floor.

The soldier's stony cold face bores down on me before his head is pierced with a bullet. Jacob rushes in and Allison screams at the top of her lungs. He holds my hand as tears pour down his face. My extremities begin to go numb. Blood runs beneath me as I watch two more soldiers stand behind Jacob ready to shoot. It's in that split second that I realize hope is gone.

Bang!

I wake up, cold sweat on my face, and exit a nightmare I wish never to have again. Allison and Luke are asleep in the bed across the room and Nadia sits at my bedside.

"You okay?" Nadia asks.

"Yeah, just a bad dream."

The basement door slams open and a small shiver runs up my spine. Ananiah, Sadiq, and Jacob rush down the stairs in a panic. Roland emerges from his quarters wide-eyed.

"What's going on?" Nadia asks.

"We need to leave here now!" Ananiah shouts.

"Troops have breached our northern base and are pushing through quickly. We can't hold them until we receive reinforcements from the Fifty-Third and Sixty-Fifth Brigades. Our stronger armor battalions have their own battles to fight and until they get here, this place will be overrun," Sadiq explains.

"Where the hell are we supposed to go? She's pregnant," Nadia argues.

"I was hoping it would never come to this, but it's time," Ananiah says.

"Time for what."

"To the mountain," Ananiah adds. "There's a refuge beneath the mountain that can serve up to fifty thousand. It's well hidden, secured, and in secret. Food and water supplies to last five years. Project Sanctuary was developed for times like these. It's been going on for a hundred years."

"There's only one catch though," Sadiq confesses. "The nearest tunnel into the mountain is on the west side. We're going to have to cross some hostile territory to get there."

"Come on, let's go!" Juliana's voice shouts from above.

I haven't been above ground for four months, so these stairs are kicking my ass. Jacob and Sadiq carefully help me up the steps and into a jeep parked outside the museum. Smoke billows from afar and air-raid sirens scream throughout the city. People scatter like ants and flee into the shadows.

"Where're the kids, are they safe?" I panic.

"They're with Nadia and Gabe in the armored truck behind us," Jacob assures.

"Let's go!" Ananiah shouts.

The jeep drives off like a bat out of hell as fire explodes from the museum. Debris sprays the streets and smoke fills the air. Dust blows against the windows and hinders our vision. *Kerplunk!* The jeep swerves to the right and bounces over the curb. I hold on tight. We diverge to the adjacent street where a firefight erupts in front of us. A mortar blasts. *Boom!* A gash of radiant light bursts into the sky and building stones plummet. We're forced to detour yet again, but this time in the opposite direction. We are driven back from the mountain. No hope moving forward as the vicious assault lingers. We must retreat.

The bumpy ride sends me to side of the jeep, swerving left and right. Jacob holds me close and secures me tight. A loud explosion erupts. The jeep rattles over the curb and screeches into an alley. My heart sinks. I brace myself as we plow through a barricade onto the next street. A truck slams the front side of the jeep. Windows shatter and metal clashes as we skid across the pavement. The truck plunges forward, penning our jeep into the corner of a building.

Steam spews from the truck's engine. I stare helplessly at Jacob and Sadiq speaking to me, but I can't hear a thing. My ears ring behind a wall of silence, drowning out the chaos around me.

Smoke suddenly envelops from the truck and smothers the cab. Jacob struggles to open the back door. It's stuck from the impact. He kicks the door open as flames erupt under the hood of the truck. I step out of the jeep and get a glimpse of a man whose face is buried into the steering wheel of the truck. Blood runs down his dangling arms.

The cab engulfs with flames. I rest my arms around Sadiq and Jacob as we scurry away from the volatile truck. We reach the other side of the street and fall to our knees. *Boom!* The truck explodes, sending a gnashing of metal airborne. Black smoke billows.

"Everyone okay?" Sadiq asks. He coughs from the smoke and cascading dust.

"I think so," I gasp.

"What happened to the others?" Jacob asks.

"They were right behind us," Sadiq coughs.

The armored truck creeps out of the ally and stops. Ari and Roland jump from the cab and sprint over.

"You guys okay? What the hell just happened?" Ari asks.

"That truck came out of nowhere and slammed into us," Jacob explains.

Roland carefully helps me to my feet. "Come on, let's get you out of here."

I struggle for a few steps before a sharp pain blazes across my belly. Suddenly, a thunderous explosion rocks the sky. Clouds quickly darken and gunfire rings in the air. Gabe and Juliana quickly exit the back of the armored truck. Nadia and the others follow swiftly behind. Clinging like a baby, Luke wraps his body around Ananiah while Allison runs beside them.

I stammer with my arm wrapped around Roland, one unsteady step in front of the other. Jacob lifts my right shoulder before I collapse dizzily to the ground. The sky blurs momentarily as I adjust to a glowing fire peeking from behind the clouds.

Augustine surfaces from one of the trucks with a rifle clutched in his hands. "My God!" he exclaims as he looks up into the sky. "What the bloody hell is that?"

Small glowing embers pepper the sky like flaming sparks from a campfire. They glow brighter and move closer by the second. My dizzy spell releases. Several soldiers charge from behind the adjacent building.

"Move!" Gabe shouts.

Shots scream past us and shatter the storefront windows. Glass flings into the air like shrapnel and brazes the back of my neck. Father Joseph and Nadia quickly return fire. The small firefight escalates as more soldiers barrel down the street.

"Come on!" Augustine shouts a few steps ahead of us. He pushes us safely into an alley and fires back into the streets. I retreat with the others and crouch behind a shielding dumpster.

Shots trade back and forth as the gunfight rages in the middle of the street. I peek around the corner of the dumpster. Several soldiers lie dead. Within minutes, the fury fades and the intense exchange abruptly stops. Just then, the cobbled street shatters with a deafening thud and sets a few soldiers ablaze. Screaming with agony, they fall to the ground and burn to their death. The corner of the building right behind us crumbles.

"What in holy hell?" Ari gasps.

"My sentiments exactly," Sadiq echoes. Gabe, Juliana, and the rest of the group join us in the alley.

"Let's go, now!" Gabe yells.

"What about the soldiers?" Ari asks.

"That's the least of our worry."

We leave the alley to an empty street except for the three soldiers who have been charred, their bodies burning. The rest of the small battalion has vanished. It's a short reprieve from one hell only to be welcomed by another. Fiery rocks plummet to the ground, pelting the earth like rain.

Ananiah grabs Luke and carries him. Allison tags closely beside him along with Nadia and Father Joseph.

The pain inside my belly disappears, but fear has not left me. Fire glows from the streets to the top of the buildings. Burning stones crash all around us. Jacob and Ari guide me down the walkway as quickly as possible. Gabe opens the front doors to the Incubator Theater.

"No, not here," Sadiq advises. "These buildings won't protect us. The ceilings are too vulnerable. We need to seek underground. If we can cross Barukh Square, we can find safety in the Synagogue Tiferet. There's a refuge underneath the sanctuary."

Shifting from one street to the other, we maneuver through the falling rocks. A stone the size of a basketball plummets right in front of us. My knees buckle. Jacob and Ari lift me out of the way as the side of a building crashes down. Fire rains from the sky more plentiful now. It's near impossible to predict when the next stone will fall.

We cross the square and are met by another battalion of soldiers, most of which are fleeing like the rest of us. They scatter like ants seeking shelter. One raises his gun at us but is quickly drilled into the ground less his head from a blazing rock. Gunshots fire from our left, then our right.

Flaming stones plunge around us. It's a game of chance now. If the rocks don't kill us, the soldiers will. I gasp for a breath of air. The hindrance of this extra weight may be the death of me.

"Come on! We're almost there," Sadiq urges.

There it is, like a beacon waiting for us. The synagogue is in sight, less than a hundred yards away. Ananiah and the children sprint safely to the temple, while Niki and Harold follow close behind. Unfortunately, my condition keeps me at bay and slows my pace. Roland and Augustine stay close.

Shots echo to our left once again. A couple of soldiers storm from behind a pile of wreckage. Gabe and Juliana race past and fire. The two men fall dead. A slew of fiery rocks slam the earth near Gabe. His gun flings from his hands and he falls on his back.

"Gabe!" I scream.

I push forward to get him, but Jacob holds me back.

"Arena, no," he demands.

"Don't leave him!" I cry.

"Ari, go help him, I'll get her to the synagogue," Jacob orders.

Jacob forces me away, but I cannot turn from my brother. I struggle to move forward and lose my nerve. "No!" I scream.

Several fireballs cascade from the sky and rock the side of a building next to Gabe. The side wall cracks open and shifts downward. Gabe lifts his head and quickly rises to his feet. I exhale a sigh of relief, but it's not over. Juliana and Gabe sprint beside Nadia and Father Joseph. The building side breaks apart. It gives way and crumbles to the street, creating a cloud of dust rolling toward us. As fiery stones continue to fall, a wave of soldiers charge behind us and fire at will.

Jacob and I reach the entrance to the temple and quickly move inside behind Roland and Augustine. Ari follows, panting. I catch my breath and wait. An explosion of fire and wrath pound the streets. Soldiers charge from the east and the west. A wall of dust drapes behind Father Joseph. He clears the entrance and nearly collapses. Jacob guards the door and the gunfire intensifies. The pain in my belly returns.

"Can you see them?" I grimace.

"Yes, they're not far," Jacob confirms.

I peek out the entry as my plucky band of friends wait behind me.

"Arena, get away from the door!" Father Joseph shouts.

"Not until Gabe and Juliana are safe," I refuse.

Both run in tandem as soldiers barrel across the street toward them. Closer and closer they get. Shots zing past and strike the outer building.

"Get back!" Jacob warns.

A truck explodes spewing a rage of fire and metal. Juliana tackles Gabe to the ground as shards of steel graze their heads.

"Come on!" Jacob encourages.

Just twenty more yards. Come on, you can make it, I pray. Suddenly, the wind blows like a hurricane and pushes the wall of dust back. Hell-burning stones smash the street. Soldiers blaze with fire and fall to the ground except for one sole survivor still chasing. Gabe finally crosses the entrance tugging on Juliana's hand behind him. A gunshot breaches the door before Jacob slams it shut. Juliana falls limp to the ground.

CHAPTER 36

Blackness covers us. My heart sinks while my brother's cry overshadows our escape. Sadiq lowers his torch. Juliana's back turns red. A small glow from the entry lights burn faintly and reveals tragedy. Juliana, barely breathing, weakly grasps Gabe's hand. Gabe gently turns her over. Blood flows fluidly from Juliana's chest. Jacob presses his hand against the bullet wound, but it's useless. Blood seeps between his fingers.

Juliana's dry lips turn white. Her ashen face flushes and reveals the inevitable. There's nothing we can do for her now but watch in agony as she fades away. Jacob releases his hand and cries. Gabe hovers over Juliana and showers her with tears.

"No!" he screams. "Do something!"

Father Joseph kneels beside Gabe and holds him. I'm too numb to move and comfort my brother. Juliana struggles to lift her head. From her last stony gaze, she squeezes Gabe's hand and smiles.

"I love you," she gasps.

Her head lowers and her body relaxes. The grasp of her fingers let go as death comes for her. Sorrow blankets the room. Not a word is spoken. Only the cry from my brother breaks through the silence. Gabe rests his head on her chest and loses it. Jacob and Father Joseph try to lift Gabe from Juliana's body, but he refuses to leave her side.

"She's not dead! She's not dead!" Gabe cries.

I fall to my knees, hold my brother tightly, and cry along with him. Denial is a hard thing to accept. I know how it feels.

The walls shake and rumble the floor. A war still tempers outside the door. Sadiq urges us to leave quickly and follow him to the catacombs below the sanctuary. Though completely heart-broken and ravished with grief, Gabe abides. He and Harold carry Juliana's body.

We follow Sadiq down a long hall and through the main sanctuary. Lavish chandeliers, each holding well beyond fifty candles, hang beautifully from a multitude of arched ceiling coves. Stained-glass windows of bunting clover leafs, Jewish symbols, and many Old Testament stories surround the interior.

The short jaunt through the sanctuary leads us behind the Holy Ark of the temple center—a small section where Rabbis and other religious dignitaries of the church sit. We reach the end of the main temple section and follow Sadiq through a small gated room. He and Ari pry open the barred entrance.

"Through here," Sadiq urges.

He opens a set of private doors that lead to a set of rocky stairs descending to a stone floor. We follow Sadiq through a maze of tunnels and into a large stony room. Amber lighting gradually glows from the flick of a switch. The musty underground space is filled with cushioned beds, a working sink with fresh water, and prayer alters that align the stony walls. It's slightly damp and cold, but it's safe.

Gabe and Harold gently place Juliana on one of the beds. My heart can't bear to look upon her pallid face. Gabe disengages from the group and mourns over her lifeless body. Father Joseph urges us to leave the room while Gabe takes rest and grieves.

Jacob holds close to me as we retreat into the bleak halls. Small light fixtures dangle from the rocky ceiling about every thirty feet. They barely illuminate the concealed tunnels. We explore the underground dwelling and find more spacious rooms with prison-like beds. Some are nicer than others. It's apparent this place was built as a shelter from the potential hostility waging on the surface. We're putting it to good use.

I find a bed to rest on, but I'm much too restless for a nap. Jacob and the others take advantage of the little peace given to us. He rolls onto his side next to me and fades into a deep slumber. My mind races and keeps me up. I would much rather cuddle next to my husband, but instead I sit on the edge of the hardened mattress and stare into my bulging belly. So much has taken place in the past few days. I'm not sure I can recover from it.

An hour passes and still I'm too overwhelmed to lay my head down. I exit the room quietly and find Gabe all alone in the room down the hall. I watch helplessly through the door.

He hovers over Juliana's body and weeps into the night. My heart stings. There's nothing I can say to make him feel at ease. It's hard, but I can't look upon his face right now. His anguish burns inside me. Words are just words. Platitudes have no place here. They cannot heal in this moment. Instead, I weep inside and leave him alone with her.

I lean my head against the stone wall and wonder how long we must live like this. While a bloody fight and a hell-fire plague ravishes through Old Jerusalem above, we stay hidden below in the dark and wait.

*　*　*

It's been two days since I last saw the sky. I'm more uncomfortable now than I have ever been. My baby must be stretching his or her legs because my womb has changed its shape. *Ugh! Please get back in your fetal position.*

The room is quiet except for the small sleepy murmur coming from Allison and Luke as they lie peacefully in their beds. Aside from Niki pacing the halls, I'm left alone with

Nadia in this cold dungeon. The rest of the group left an hour ago to examine the surface.

"How are you feeling today?" Nadia asks.

"Not sure if I'm having heartburn or contractions. This kid is bloody hurting me," I grumble.

Nadia grabs a few extra pillows and places them behind my neck. Sitting up is a chore, but it beats lying on my side. Another hour passes and still no sign of Jacob and the others. Surely nothing terrible has happened to them. I should be more concerned, but this pain in my uterus rivals their absence instead. I'll reserve my worry for another time. Right now I just want to get out of this bed and leave this place.

A door slams in the distance and the halls echo with smattering footsteps. Nadia watches outside the door.

"Is it them?" I ask.

"Just three," she replies.

I slide out of bed and peek out into the hall. It's empty. Voices faintly mingle and boots totter just two rooms down. Gabe, Jacob, and Harold trundle into the stony corridor with Juliana's body wrapped in a shroud. My heart, still numb, grows cold.

"Stay with the children," I whisper to Nadia.

"Arena, you're in no condition to leave," she discourages.

"I'm in no condition to do a lot of things, but I must go. I don't want Juliana's lasting memory to be swaddled down here in this tomb."

"Arena, wait—"

I defy her advice and follow behind them instead. I shuffle at a distance as they carry Juliana carefully down the hall and up the stairs. The temple brightens slightly as I emerge from the basement. They carry her to the back of the synagogue and into a small garden that is nestled between the temple and an adjacent building.

Pillars of smoke rise from the east into the near starless sky — the remnants from a wrath not of this earth. The horizon fades into absence among a brooding, coal-black sky. This battle is over, but a war has just begun. I'm afraid darker days lie ahead.

Juliana's body is lowered into a semi-shallow grave that has already been dug. Jacob and Harold step back and leave Gabe to trowel the dirt over the body. Father Joseph enters the garden and begins to bless the ground where Juliana lies.

My eyes meet Jacob's. His brows arch with a slight disapproval, but he gestures me over nonetheless. I lean against him, saddened and numb. Gabe hovers over the grave, hands soiled and trembling. I can't bear this. I lift my head to the clouds and struggle to utter my frustration.

"Why?" I whisper to myself.

I kneel down next to my brother and wrap my arm around him. Tears blur my vision. I stare into the dirt and reminisce the first time we met Juliana. It was the first day of school and she was sitting all alone at lunch. Our friendship fused the moment we sat down with her. I remember the look on her face when she first saw my brother. She was smitten from the start. A rare moment for my brother, but a well-deserved one. It's probably the happiest moment for Gabe, the very antithesis of the one I'm witnessing now.

Gabe shudders under Father Joseph's eulogy. He clutches clods of dirt and balls them in his fists. The cry from his breath turns to anger and his knuckles turn white.

Father Joseph's voice fades into silence and is met with Gabe's hellish scream. I'm strangely afraid. I back away as a deep hum rambles from the side of the building.

An Israeli jeep followed by two military trucks pull around the corner of the temple. Sadiq and Ari exit the jeep and scuttle toward us with an urgency in their step. Ananiah lags behind, toting a rifle with Augustine and Roland standing next to him. A dozen or so Israeli soldiers spring from one of the trucks and position themselves in a two-by-two formation. This doesn't look good.

Sadiq approaches the grave, panting. His face is stricken with worry. "Grab your stuff and let's go," he demands.

"What the hell is going on?" Jacob asks.

"We've found our open window and we better move fast before it closes."

"How long?"

"I can't be for sure, but this is our best chance to leave. Our ground defenses have pushed the Russians back across the borderlands. It's a small victory, so we better take advantage."

My eyes widen despite the solemn circumstances. Though my heart spills onto the grave next to my brother, I'm quite eager to leave this place behind. This is a now-or-never moment—a moment we've been anticipating the past two days. Our food supplies are nearly gone and the water has run dry. This sanctuary is no longer a place of refuge. It will become a tomb if we stay. Sadiq is right: this is our best chance to retreat toward the eastern ridge into the Mount of Olives, a place that has seen plenty of death. The irony of this historical safe haven houses more than one hundred and fifty thousand graves. I'm not sure how I feel living below it. Despite the morbid thought of rooming next to a bunch of dead people, this underground asylum will serve a safer place of refuge, and more importantly, a place where food and water will never run scarce.

"Arena, let me help you to the jeep," Ari offers, lending his hand.

"I'll take her," Jacob offers.

"I'll be fine, Jacob. Just go get the children and bring them to me," I insist.

He and Harold retreat swiftly back into the synagogue. Gabe, standing over Juliana's grave, refuses to move. Sadness has left his face. Anger and rage bitterly grows in its place.

"Gabe!" I shout. "We have to go, now."

He stands there, numb and broken. My words have fallen upon deaf ears. Suddenly, squelching sirens blast into the city. The earth shakes and a bellowing thud explodes in the distance.

"We have to go, now!" Sadiq asserts.

"Gabe!" I shout once more.

He lifts his head and scowls, then reluctantly runs to the church. Sadiq helps me into the back of the jeep where I wait anxiously. A sharp sting rides along the side of my belly; it stretches deep inside, throbbing off and on. My insides twist and turn in an unbearable pain of tug of war. I grimace with excruciating agony. My teeth clench. I try to fight it, but it's nearly intolerable. A tear rolls down my cheek as an indication. Sadiq opens the door and hands me a pillow.

"My God, are you okay?" he cringes.

"Do I look okay?" I sneer.

"Roland, get over here, quick."

Roland's actions are warranted. I feel like I'm being turned inside out.

"What's the matter, Arena?" Roland gently asks.

"Something's not right. I feel like my insides are being pulled apart. The pain is piercing."

He presses his hands on my stomach and searches around. The pain intensifies when he touches the underside of my belly.

"Ouch!" I cry.

"How fast can we get to the mount?" Roland asks.

"Why?" Sadiq stutters.

"Because this little child has decided to turn around," Roland explains of the baby's position.

"What does that mean?" I ask worriedly.

"It means we need to get you to the medical bay inside that mount before your water breaks."

The sky rumbles and for a split second the jeep rattles. Niki barrels around the temple façade with packs in hand. My insides twist harder and my legs begin to numb.

"Argh!" I moan.

Niki rushes over. "What's going on, Arena, you okay?" she distresses.

"Not if we don't leave now," Roland expresses more urgently.

Flashes of light explode in the distance as Jacob's face blurs past the front of the jeep window. Gabe is standing next to Juliana's grave with a rifle dangling from his shoulder. I'm afraid peace won't surface with him for a while. He pulls something from his pocket and lays it on her grave.

"Come on, Gabe, let's get out of here!" Ari shouts.

Gabe races behind Roland and jumps into the back of one of the military trucks along with the Israeli soldiers. The thunderous sky shakes. Clouds bundle overhead and shadow the ground.

Ari jumps in the front seat and starts the jeep. The engine roars, but not before the hellish shrill of sirens ring from the city. I wince once more as the door opens to my left. Luke, face painted with fear, climbs in, quivering. Nadia shuffles in next, but her face is blank, almost detached to what's going on. Allison hastily piles in and sits on Nadia's lap while Luke trembles next to me.

The impending child-bearing pain escalates. I grab onto the jeep's roll bar and squeeze. I'd give anything right now to quell this burning in my uterus.

"You okay?" Nadia asks.

"As good as it gets," I grimace.

I lean my head against the door, but nothing seems to suppress this agony. My insides are being used as a punching bag. My belly stretches from side to side until it swells into a raging fire of pain. I scream through clenched teeth and squeeze Nadia's arm.

"Deep breaths, deep breaths," Nadia comforts.

"My God, please tell me you're not having this baby now," Ari panics.

"What the hell are we waiting on?" I yell.

Jacob slides into the passenger side and slams the door. "Let's go!" he asserts.

Ari stomps on the gas and sends the jeep thrusting one hundred and eighty degrees. We race behind the convoy of trucks and hastily leave the synagogue deserted.

The scarred streets leave an unwanted bumpy ride across the city. Buildings burn and bodies blanket the grounds. Gunfire echoes through the streets under the cruel shriek from the sirens. Chaos lingers abroad. Soldiers spring in and out between buildings and rain fire. We are far from safe.

A car crashes into a building and explodes. The convoy quickly breaks off to the right. Mortar crumbles in front of us as we swerve sharply to the left. The tires squeal around the corner and the side of the jeep scrapes the side of the wall. We exit to the next street where a caravan of vehicles hurriedly parade past.

Our convoy flashes briefly to the right and races toward the east. My insides tear like cutting razorblades. I grab the side of the door and squeeze. I scream.

"Hurry!" Nadia yells.

Ari steps on the gas and cuts through the next street. We exit onto a narrow sandy road inside Jerusalem's old city. Most of the damage has occurred here. Buildings have collapsed, but the eastern wall still stands firm. A raging battle erupts as soldiers from both sides collide around us. Our jeep takes a few hits as we pass through the east side of the wall.

Suddenly, the desert wind blows past a cloud of sand making anything visible quite difficult. The Temple Mount rises above the storm just to the east. The skies darken ever-more.

"Where are they?" Ari asks.

"They're behind us," Jacob confirms as our convoy rejoins.

A blaze of fire streaks across the desert just as we reach the outside of the Temple Mount. *Boosh!* The ground explodes in front of us. The jeep swerves off the road and tumbles over and over across the sand. My head bangs against the ceiling and I'm thrown into the door. We all tumble like ragdolls inside the jeep. The rolling metal scrapes against the earth and tosses upside down.

I can't move or see, but I feel pain throbbing from my side. One voice whimpers while another moans, but it's the gunfire in the background that has my ears at attention. My arm hangs out where the window is missing. Wind blows past the desert sand, but when it clears, my heart shatters into a thousand pieces.

Luke lies limp beside me. I stretch for him, but I'm stuck. Something jabs me in the side and keeps me from moving. I yell his name, but there's no response.

"Arena!" Jacob screams.

"I can't move," I answer.

"Hang on, we'll get you out."

Jacob and Ari pry open the door opposite of me and pull Luke from the wreckage. Just outside the door, Allison cries hysterically next to Nadia. Blood drips from her forehead.

Jacob crawls in and unhinges my bloody shirt from the jarred door. I gingerly slide out the other side and take in a deep breath. Jacob presses a rag over the wound near my ribs to stop the bleeding. Sadiq and father Joseph sprint over from the convoy. Sadiq kneels over Luke's body. I watch impatiently for him to move, but he doesn't respond. And it's not until Sadiq nods to me with despair that Luke is truly dead.

I'm completely numb. I feel nothing but painful sorrow drilling into my heart. Blood runs freely from the wound in my side and I don't care. I'm flushed and dizzy, but I cry out nonetheless.

Jacob lifts me from the ground and removes me from enemy sightlines. Sadiq wraps his arms around Luke's lifeless body and carries him to the back of the truck.

Gunfire pegs the truck as enemy troops gain ground. Two mortar explosions from Israeli defense backup stalls their assault.

"Let's go!" Ananiah shouts.

Jacob lowers the gate on the truck while Nadia and Harold pull me in. I've lost a large amount of blood and I'm woozy. My eyes blur and faces begin to fade. I'm too weak to say anything. Roland and Nadia sit me up against the truck wall.

"Arena," Roland calls.

I hear his voice, but I'm too weak to answer. Instead, I draw myself from everything and stare over at Luke's body resting in Sadiq's arms. I've never seen Sadiq cry until now. Not even a soldier made of steel can overcome this. Allison buries her tears onto Luke's shoulder.

"Arena, Arena, you okay?" Roland calls once more.

"No," I cry.

The ground shakes and Jacob climbs in as gunfire pierces the side of the truck. Niki rolls over and screams.

"Niki!" Harold shouts.

Nadia slams her fists against the cab wall. The truck rumbles away, spinning sand behind us, but the damage has already been inflicted. Harold drags Niki across the truck bed where blood trails behind her. Niki's leg is badly wounded.

Roland tends to her wound while Jacob stops the bleeding in mine. I'm feeling myself fading into a dark place. I clutch onto Nadia's shirt and say nothing. I just want all of this to end now. Luke's life will never be forgotten and mine will never be the same.

The discouraging expression on Sadiq's face stings my heart. If not for the tears running from his eyes, I would feel differently. "I'm sorry," he sobs.

The burning in my belly resurfaces and it's worse than ever. I can feel the blood leaving my face. It's cold. My eyes blur as I slump over.

The last I see of this group before I fade is absolute brokenness.

CHAPTER 37

Voices argue and scream over me in the background. My eyes open to a white ceiling and my back painfully rests on a thin padded bed. Plastic tubes dangle beside me and into my arms. A bucket of bloody-soaked rags sits on a small table to my right. A sudden sting in my uterus propels me to sit up and scream.

"You need to decide now!" Roland shouts at Jacob.

Agony rests on Jacob's face. The pain worsens and forces me to scream even louder. Tears roll down my face, but no one seems to be doing anything but standing around and yelling.

"Get this baby out!" I shout.

"The baby is breech," Roland explains.

"I don't care, get it out now!"

"Arena, we can't. The baby will lose oxygen. It may die."

I flail my arms, screaming, "It hurts! Do something, now dammit!"

"Do the cesarean," Jacob urges Roland.

"You let her know now. It's her choice."

I wail in agony over their chatter. "What's going on?"

"We can do a cesarean, but you've already lost way too much blood and . . . " Roland pauses.

"And?"

"You may die," Roland answers. "It's either the baby or you, but you have to choose, and I suggest you do it now."

Jacob looks at me, but I'm afraid to answer. He kisses me on the forehead and nods his head.

"Save my baby," I answer.

Niki dashes over with a rolling cart of medical utensils, a blanket, and other miscellaneous things. She rummages through a box of vials.

"Sadiq, Jacob, hold her down!" Roland yells.

"What's going on?" I ask.

"All of our local anesthetic is back in the city. We didn't have time to get any when the troops showed up," Roland says.

"Not even a general anesthetic? Are you kidding me?"

Nadia holds down one arm while Sadiq braces the other. Jacob stands over me with tears dripping down his face. No one will face me.

"This is going to hurt, isn't it?"

"Here, open your mouth." Roland places a piece of leather in my mouth and I bite down. "I'm not going to lie: this is going to hurt like shit."

"Wait!" Niki shouts.

"We don't have time," Roland advises.

Tears fall from my eyes and I whimper. This isn't how my child is supposed to enter the world, in such a violent manner. Luke wasn't supposed to die. Juliana wasn't supposed to die. None of this should be happening . . .

A woman, whom I've not seen before, stands close to Roland with rags in hand. Is this the sacrifice I've been expected to give? If so, why like this? I should have died by my own hand back in Alexandria. Hell, I should have been killed long ago. Maybe it was all in God's plan for me to make this choice, right here, right now. I tried to take my own life and now I have a chance to redeem myself for a better one. I'm ready to leave this world. My child deserves better than me.

Roland picks up a sharp scalpel from the cart and presses it against my skin.

Pain floods through my body, and a host of screaming banshees exit my lungs. "Make it stop! It hurts so much!"

"Not much longer."

"I can't, it hurts!"

Niki fills a syringe with one of the vials. She rushes over and jabs the needle into my arm.

"What is that?" Jacob asks.

"Fentanyl, it's the only thing I could find. Should activate quickly," Niki says.

"Not quick enough!" I scream.

The knife slides deep into the tissue and I lose it. The woman next to Roland grabs my legs. I scream until my voice vanishes. The fentanyl kicks in, and my eyes roll back. I see a dancing rabbit and tree made of shoes. A toddler smiles at me while I feed him mushed carrots. Jacob's blue eyes and his smile. I'm in a wonderland of nonsense, but it feels good. The walls around me bend inward and the bright lights fade quickly. Faces blur and I fall into nothingness.

CHAPTER 38

While the will of men limps into another day of darkness, I struggle to wonder if I will remain on this earth with my husband much longer.

Most of the stars buried in the skies above have all but fallen to decay, leaving most of us helpless to the world in shadow below. Evil continues to scour the ends of the earth with unrelenting cruelty. There seems to be no escape from this except through death. The only thing we can abound from is our will to fight it with conviction. The rest have been left to pillage or wither. This is no longer my world anymore—it's an oblivion, and I'm afraid a new hour of darkness has yet to come.

There's an everlasting kingdom that awaits us, but I'm afraid most of us have fallen to the grips of the self-righteous impression that prideful men should be secluded from judgment. The horror is far from over, for a new malevolence is sure to rise from the gates of hell. The pain and agony has just begun.

I may never fully comprehend my existence in this world, but I will hang on as long as I can. I realize that what is to come is for a cause greater than man can completely understand. I have no regrets of my choices nor will I justify to any other that I have done so. Though I'm indebted to my Father's merciful hand placed on my brother and me, I'm still deeply saddened that I was born into such a dark age of history.

* * *

Six long months held captive in these wandering caverns I lie still, waiting desperately for a calm whisper to soothe me. But all I have heard is pain and grief from the holds of this endless nightmare. The loss of Luke has yet to leave me and I'm afraid it never will. What have I done that I cannot finish this? I'm tired of struggling with my conscience, wondering if I have done what has been asked of me. All I can do now is wait restlessly until my time has come to pass in this world. My friends are my comfort, yet I feel lost in their pain.

Day after day, Gabe sits in silence. Mourning has not lifted from him since Juliana's death. He struggles to regain the same kindness I've come to know him for. It is bitterness that stains him now. A man of humility has taken a slight detour toward a dark path that I pray falters.

The horrific death of Juliana has beset him far beyond my control. Though he still remains steadfast to move forward, his face pierced with a gloom suggests otherwise. I believe his efforts have stretched beyond his ability, yet he still continues to comfort others through an agony that will not leave him. There may be a small glimmer of hope left in him, but his pain has not gone unnoticed. It is with a great sadness that my brother is no longer the same.

I've forfeited so much, yet I feel I have gained very little. In the last year, I have failed my fellowship, lost close friends, and found a husband who will soon be torn from me. My bulging womb has recessed, and my scar heals, yet my life still endures an endless secret. I have since conceived a child with Jacob with utter gratefulness, but its unexpected presence draws forth a new mystery I cannot comprehend. Why have I chosen to bring such innocence into this cruel world?

My beautiful son, Joshua, clings to my milky skin. I wrap my arms around his tiny fragile body and press my cold cheek against his. Jacob kneels by the prayer stone with his fist clenched and cries out. I can feel my husband's anguish, but I must leave him alone to his internal dwelling while I tend to my own discomforts. I pray for stillness and peace for my husband as I hope this moment will soon pass. Joshua has fallen asleep in my arms and the shadow from the cave entrance slowly lifts. A shiny crescent unexpectedly glows. I carefully hand Joshua to Niki and walk out to the small lit opening where a bright beacon of light glosses from the heavens onto the ground below. I wrap my body with the woven cloth Marissa had made for me and lean against the side of the stony entrance. Out beyond the burning horizon feels empty. I still smell the scent of my son pressed against me as I stroke the side of my cheek with my calloused hand.

Our losses have been great, and hope is beginning to slip from our grasp. I may be broken, but I will remain committed to my promise amid these tragedies. For even the shadow that follows me cannot chasten my clairvoyance. I have not come this far to understand the existence of my fate just to give in without a fight. I will not entertain the idea.

My faith lies within something greater than these pestilent sacrifices. I can slowly feel it creeping in. Time is sacred now, but I will clamor at the chance when I leave this place. What will free me of this will soon come, but I feel my fate has stretched from the far reaches of heaven, for it's not the prize I seek: it's the intentions behind it.

I look down below the mountainside where people stray into the darkness and I wonder what could have I done to change their fortunes. Plagued by a sinful world, these poor souls are not far from death now.

Israel is all but lost—falling into the hands of Russia, a country that's at its capacity of transcending as much evil now than it has in its grim past. Blood runs deep in its streets, as does the evil that perpetuates it. Murder, rape, and savagery have become rife. Those still alive waiting in darkness have left the cities beyond the borders of Jerusalem plundered. They suffer like primal savages now, feeding on dogs, rats, and anything that scurries the ground.

I don't know how this is going to end and I don't care what tomorrow may bring for me. Whether it's Jacob's life that is taken or my own, I live now for whatever little peace I can take security in. My body is bruised, but sheltered; my heart is broken, but healed. I feel cold inside when I look down below to those who are deceived, yet it's the small peaceful cry from my son that gives me warmth to comfort in. Small things can be great expectations.

This is truly a dark hour, but I know a moment of swift reprieve will approach us soon. Though death has not come to pass us yet, as we stay sheltered deep in the mountainside, I can feel the end nearing. And for all that sleep with the enemy, the truth will soon be revealed. The whole world will know who we are and who we stand with.

It's our choices that separate us now from living among glory or dwelling in exile. I choose to believe in the hope of salvation that I will no more be tempted into the fathomless depths of darkness. I have no answers to this chaos and ruin before me, but one thing is for certain: Humanity will not be forgotten for the savagery it has become.

And now with the lights glowing dimmer from the horizon, the city that was once the birth of history is fading into a distant memory. Jerusalem now lies in ash and cinder. The fires slowly burn until the last of the smoke settles, leaving a fallen city and its past to vanish into the wind.

It has come to this: misery and dread is all we have left to secure. There is no mercy for anyone. Death is standing at our doorsteps. What have we done?

THE END